Praise for Lindsay Lovise

"Lovise writes with a spritely pen, her story bursting with cheek and humor while also remaining unrelenting in its twists and turns. An extremely promising debut, one that blends the best hallmarks of each of its genres...we can't wait to see what's next."

—*Entertainment Weekly*

"Edgy and enticing...Lovise is sure to win fans with this."

—*Publishers Weekly*, starred review

"Deftly combines equal parts romance and mystery. A strong historical romance debut, for fans of Sarah MacLean and Erica Ridley."

—*Kirkus*

"Gripping and fresh...Will have you hooked until the last page!"

—Amalie Howard, *USA Today* bestselling author

"The kind of fast-paced, sexy historical romance I love to lose myself in."

—Manda Collins, bestselling author of *A Governess's Guide to Passion and Peril*

NEVER GAMBLE YOUR HEART

Also by Lindsay Lovise

Never Blow a Kiss

NEVER GAMBLE YOUR HEART

THE SECRET SOCIETY OF GOVERNESS SPIES

LINDSAY LOVISE

FOREVER

New York   Boston

Forever
Hachette Book Group
1290 Avenue of the Americas, New York, NY 10104
read-forever.com
@readforeverpub

First Edition: February 2025

Forever is an imprint of Grand Central Publishing. The Forever name and logo are registered trademarks of Hachette Book Group, Inc.

The publisher is not responsible for websites (or their content) that are not owned by the publisher.

The Hachette Speakers Bureau provides a wide range of authors for speaking events. To find out more, go to hachettespeakersbureau.com or email HachetteSpeakers@hbgusa.com.

Forever books may be purchased in bulk for business, educational, or promotional use. For information, please contact your local bookseller or the Hachette Book Group Special Markets Department at special.markets@hbgusa.com.

Print book interior design by Taylor Navis

Library of Congress Cataloging-in-Publication Data

Names: Lovise, Lindsay, author.
Title: Never gamble your heart / Lindsay Lovise.
Description: First edition. | New York ; Boston : Forever, 2025. |
    Series: The Secret Society of Governess Spies ; book 2
Identifiers: LCCN 2024036045 | ISBN 9781538740552 (trade paperback) |
    ISBN 9781538740576 (ebook)
Subjects: LCSH: Governesses—Fiction. | LCGFT: Spy fiction. | Romance fiction.
Classification: LCC PS3612.O8746 N484 2024 | DDC 813/.6—dc23/eng/20230908
LC record available at https://lccn.loc.gov/2024036045

ISBNs: 978-1-5387-4055-2 (trade paperback), 978-1-5387-4057-6 (ebook)

Printed in the United States of America

LSC-C

Printing 1, 2024

To my dad, for all your support and love.

In the Secret Society of Governess Spies, there are rules one must follow, along with things one must never do.

1. Never blow a kiss.
2. Never gamble your heart.

Chapter 1

August 1838
London, England

Jasper Jones lowered the letter of recommendation from Perdita's and studied the governess who was impertinently scanning the oil paintings in his sitting room. She was a slip of a thing, with wheat-colored hair that curled in wisps around her face and a complexion that spoke of hours indoors. A high-necked gown of serviceable dark green concealed her from wrist to boot. If her oversized spectacles and dull dress were any indication, she was a plain and severe woman.

The governess, Miss Francis Turner, finished her perusal and returned her attention to him. Jasper was struck by surprise when her gaze boldly met his. Having been distracted by the ridiculously large spectacles, he'd almost missed how sea-blue and thickly lashed her eyes were. He had several female acquaintances who would kill for eyes like those.

Miss Turner adjusted her spectacles and gave him a lopsided grin.

Jasper frowned. What was Perdita's Governess Agency about? He'd requested a mature and experienced governess to help his niece deal with her circumstances, and instead they'd sent him a woman who appeared to be about five and twenty.

"How long have you been a governess, Miss Turner?"

"Two months and six days."

"And do you consider your two months and six days enough experience to handle a fifteen-year-old girl who has recently lost her father?" he asked, lifting his brows.

"Yes."

That was it. No explanation, no detailed list of her accomplishments, no attempt to convince him she was the right person for the position.

Jasper waited.

Miss Turner stared back with those guileless blue eyes. Finally she said, "When can I start?"

Jasper was not caught off guard often, but twice now the governess had surprised him. He stood, straightened his cravat, and glanced at his pocket watch. It was already half past eleven, and there were menus that needed his approval at Rockford's.

"I fear your two months will not suffice for the difficult task at hand, Miss Turner."

Miss Turner frowned. "Then why did you ask me if it would?"

"It was sarcasm."

"I have a difficult time comprehending the use of sarcasm. It seems to me a very lazy form of expression."

Jasper's lips quirked involuntarily. He'd always had a perverse soft spot for candor. "Do not consider my concerns a comment on your abilities, Miss Turner. My niece is a handful, and because she lacks a female presence in her life, she requires a governess who can guide her with consistency and firmness. I will write to Perdita's first thing in the morning. Until another governess arrives, you may do your best with Cecelia. However, you must know I require two things of all my servants. First—"

"Oh!" she exclaimed, interrupting him. "You are mistaken, Mr. Jones. I am not a servant. I am a gov-er-ness." She said the word *governess* slowly, as if he were an imbecile.

Jasper's eyes widened. As the son of a fishmonger, he'd been raised rough, and it had taken years of polishing to become the man he was today. He had more money than most of the men who visited his gaming hell, more power than half of Parliament, and a ruthless reputation for punishing cheats. He had climbed to the top with nothing but his rapier-sharp mind, and yet this innocent-eyed governess was acting as if he were as dumb as a bag of bricks.

"Are you well, Mr. Jones? You look"—Miss Turner waved her hand over her face—"frozen. Yes, that is the word. You froze up a bit. Do you need a drink? Perhaps a nice, fortifying brandy?"

"Miss Turner—"

She had already found the bell and rung it. Jasper watched in astonishment as she promptly ordered the maid to bring him a stiff drink.

"Miss Turner!"

"Mr. Jones!" she replied, raising her voice to match his. "There is certainly no need to shout. I assure you my hearing is quite adequate."

Jasper was speechless.

"Oh, I understand your reservations now," she said, her eyes landing on the clock on the mantel. "My apologies. I suppose eleven thirty in the morning is a tad early for liquor. I should have ordered tea. Can I meet Cecelia?"

"I am not sure that would be wise."

"Well, *I* want to meet *her*!" a young voice cried from the door.

Jasper closed his eyes, counted to three, and turned to bare his teeth at his niece. "Cecelia. How long have you been standing there?"

Cecelia was a tall girl with big brown eyes and thin, chestnut hair that looked pasted to her scalp. When Jasper had clawed his way out of poverty, he'd brought his only brother and niece with him. His brother had worked in the kitchen at Rockford's, and Jasper had bought him a quaint house in a quiet district of the city where he could live with Cecelia and Cecelia's great-aunt.

Jasper had seen his niece on special occasions, but he had never spent much time with her, or even noticed her beyond bestowing a generous dowry upon her. Then his brother had died in a carriage accident, and Jasper, Cecelia's only living relative under the age of eighty, had had the sullen, angry girl thrust upon him. And because he could not simply leave the great-aunt to her own devices, he'd taken her in, too.

The great-aunt, Madam Margaret, was fine—she spent most of her day sleeping or gazing out the window, and Jasper quite enjoyed the silence of her company. Cecelia, on the other hand, had only been with him a fortnight, and he already had the distinct feeling that she hated him. If she sensed Miss Turner made him unhappy, she would insist on keeping the odd governess.

"Long enough to hear Miss Turner order you a drink." Cecelia flounced into the room, her gown a bright yellow confection of far too many ribbons and bows, designed for a much younger girl. She took Miss Turner's hand in hers and gave her a dazzling smile. "Are you to be my new governess?"

"No," Jasper said quickly. "She is standing in as your governess until the real one arrives."

Cecelia stuck out her lower lip like a child and crossed her arms over her chest. "Phooey!"

Jasper pinched the bridge of his nose. When had his life come to this? He was a gambler. A rake. The devil of sin. His goals in life were to make money and enjoy himself, and everyone else be damned. But here he was, standing in a far-too-sunny receiving room with a fifteen-year-old who despised him and an awkward governess, both of them staring at him as if he'd sprouted a tail and horns—and not the devil-of-sin type.

"'Tis all right," Miss Turner said, smiling gently at Cecelia. "I am sure we will get along splendidly in the meantime. Mr. Jones has to leave and we are delaying him. I will have the head housekeeper show me my quarters, and then I will meet you in the schoolroom so we can become acquainted. What do you say, Cecelia?"

Jasper's eyes sharpened on Miss Turner. When had he told her he needed to leave?

Cecelia gave Jasper a defiant look and assured Miss Turner it was a wonderful idea before skipping from the room.

"Now if you will ring for the head housekeeper, I shall see my way out," Miss Turner said, bending to pick up her valise.

At that moment the maid returned with a crystal glass of brandy, and damn it all if Jasper didn't drink it. He usually made it a point not to drink until the early hours of the morning; he needed his wits about him on the hell floor. Today, being an exercise in irritation, was the exception.

"Send Mrs. Hollendale to me," he ordered the maid, who giggled and blushed before exiting the room. He frowned into the half-empty crystal glass in his hand. "Why do you assume I am in a hurry to leave, Miss Turner?" Something about her put his senses on alert, and Jasper had learned never to ignore his instincts. They had served him well over the years.

Miss Turner was fingering a doily on a table and jumped when he spoke to her. "Please, call me Frankie. I cannot stand to be called Miss Turner."

"Unfortunately, you will have to grin and bear it, Miss Turner, as I am not in the habit of calling the women in my employ by their given names. And you may continue addressing me as Mr. Jones."

His lips twitched when she barely refrained from rolling her eyes. "*Mr. Jones*, I assume you are eager to leave because you have glanced twice at your pocket watch and you have been edging toward the door since I arrived. I must be keeping you from something terribly important. I shall find the head housekeeper myself."

Miss Turner—or Frankie, as she'd called herself—curtsied, rather mockingly he thought, and went to slide past him. Jasper reached out without thought, grasping her slender arm in his hand. The moment his palm made contact with her skin, the impropriety of the act struck him, but it was too late. She was as soft as satin, and for an insane moment Jasper fought not to rub his thumb over her bare arm.

"You are not going anywhere."

Chapter 2

Frankie stood as still as a child caught with an illicit sweet, stunned by the improper touch. Jasper wasn't wearing gloves, and his hand felt rough and warm on the skin above her own matching green gloves.

He towered over her, so dark and sinfully handsome that she instantly understood how he'd come by his reputation as a collector of lovers. His hair was inky black and cropped short. Heavy brows drew over a pair of insightful eyes that looked as if they could see into a person's soul. His skin had been kissed by the sun, which was surely something a gentleman would not have allowed, but Frankie understood Jasper Jones was no gentleman. It was rumored he carried a blade on his person at all times, and that he had engaged in more than his share of lethal fights on his rise to the top.

"Do not underestimate him," the Dove had cautioned her in the carriage the night before. "I have seen him charm men from their purses and women from their corsets, and he does an excellent job at passing among the gentry. But let me warn you: He is a wolf disguised as a sheep. No man is born a fishmonger's son and becomes the person Jasper Jones is today without extraordinary cunning and ruthlessness."

Frankie did not know the Dove's true name, only that she owned Perdita's Governess Agency, which hosted the most prestigious governess school in all of London, and that she used her governesses to spy on the *ton* to hold them accountable for their crimes. With the information her governesses collected, the Dove tipped off the police, who did not have the contacts or social standing to gather information on the *ton*'s transgressions.

Although Frankie knew very little about the mysterious vigilante who'd sent her to be a governess in Mr. Jasper Jones's house, she *suspected* plenty. She suspected the spymaster was as cunning and ruthless as Jasper Jones, but rather than using her skills to build an empire, she used them to deliver justice for the lower classes. Frankie was almost certain it was the Dove who was responsible for the sharp increase of reporting on upper-class crimes in the papers and the scandal sheets—Frankie had plotted them on a graph. Frankie also suspected her governess friend, Emily, was one of the Dove's spies. It would explain why Emily had been placed in Lord Eastmoreland's house earlier that summer, when the entire city was anxious to unveil the identity of a murderer targeting prostitutes in Bethnal Green.

A murderer who ended up having intimate ties with the Eastmorelands.

Still, even knowing how well-informed the Dove was, Frankie had been stunned when the night before, while she'd been crouching behind a rubbish bin outside Rockford's, spying on every person who entered, the Dove had appeared at her side in the flesh—no longer a rumor or a ghost.

Frankie would not typically risk her reputation, even as a spinster, by spying on a gentleman's club in the middle of the night, but she had been out of options. Rockford's was the most prestigious gambling hell in all of London, and it was the last clue Frankie had that might lead to her missing sister.

Fidelia was eight years Frankie's junior and her only sibling. Fidelia was expected to "come out" next Season and make a suitable match that would save the family from destitution now that their father was deceased, but three weeks ago she'd run away, leaving behind nothing but a one-sentence explanation: *Lady Elizabeth Scarson has been caught up in something dastardly, and I must help.*

Their mother had panicked and sent for Frankie, who had been working her first governess position to help support their family since she had failed to make a marriage match. Their mother had insisted that Frankie find her sister *immediately,* before her reputation was ruined. Their mother was telling everyone that Fidelia was visiting her aunt and "taking the sea air before the Season," but the lie wouldn't last forever. And if it were discovered that Fidelia had run off, unchaperoned, to God knew where...

Well, Frankie couldn't let that happen.

A shiver tripped across Frankie's skin, and she pulled her arm out of Jasper's grasp. He easily released her, but he did not back away. He was so close that Frankie could feel the heat emanating from his body and smell the lingering traces of the shaving cream his valet had used on his face that morning. Frankie suddenly realized he was trying to intimidate her with his proximity. Well, that simply would not do!

Frankie lifted her chin and met his eyes. "If we are to establish an appropriate and successful employer and employee relationship, no matter how temporary, I must ask that you refrain from using your size as a form of intimidation."

Jasper's lips curled into a slow smile, but he took a step back. "I will admit that I have not had occasion to employ a governess before, and yet I am entirely certain you are different from most."

Frankie flushed as she realized that once again, she was missing normal social cues. Her mother had spent a lifetime despairing of Frankie's social blundering and ineptitude, never forgoing a chance to loudly bemoan how Frankie's oddities had made finding a husband impossible. Frankie had accepted who and what she was a long time ago, but now she wished she'd tried a little harder to fit in. She needed to blend into her role so that she might accomplish her mission of spying on Jasper Jones.

Because Jasper Jones was the link to everything. Frankie was sure of it.

Frankie adored mathematics and puzzles, and she made a game out of routinely scanning the papers for patterns that others couldn't see. In fact, a month ago she'd spent time cross-referencing attendance at balls and other events with the Evangelist murders, and had come very close to uncovering the killer's identity.

During her avid consumption of newspapers and gossip rags, Frankie had recently noticed a new pattern emerging: a spate of hasty, high-profile weddings, but she simply had not thought much of it, not until their outspoken family friend, Lady Elizabeth Scarson, had become one of the brides—married off to an ill-suited man thrice her age—and Fidelia had run away.

Then, Frankie had begun looking at the pattern in earnest. While poring over gossip rag reports, she'd discovered that every single one of the grooms involved in the suspicious weddings, including Lady Elizabeth's husband, was a member of the *ton*'s most beloved gaming hell: Rockford's.

Frankie had left the information with her governess friend,

Emily, hoping she would share it with the Dove. If anyone had the power and influence to understand the pattern Frankie had found, it was the mysterious vigilante. But Frankie had never heard back from the Dove, so she'd had to take matters into her own hands.

After leaving her first governess position, Frankie had spent several weeks visiting her sister's friends and subtly inquiring if Fidelia had written from the "seaside," but none of them had heard from her. Lady Elizabeth Scarson was apparently holed up in the countryside with her new husband, not taking visitors, so her sister couldn't be there.

Left with no other leads, Frankie had taken to spying outside Rockford's. If Mr. Jasper Jones had anything to do with the strange weddings, Frankie would discover what it was, and then maybe she'd find her sister.

That was where the Dove had found her last night, materializing at her side like a shadow. A half-mourning veil had hidden the woman's eyes, and she'd been concealed from throat to toe by a dark cloak.

What the Dove had proceeded to share with Frankie over the next half hour had changed everything.

"My deepest apologies, Mr. Jones." Frankie pushed her spectacles up her nose and blinked with what she thought was a dramatic show of timidity. If she wanted to fulfill her end of the bargain she'd made with the Dove, she needed to appease his suspicions. Her mind raced as she imagined how a properly socialized lady would respond to him in such a situation, what her *mother* would say. "I desire only to see to my new duties."

Jasper's eyes flashed with amusement. "That looked as if it nearly choked you."

She'd rather choke him.

"I accept your apology. I have two rules in my home, Miss Turner, whether you are a servant or not," he added, cutting her off before she could protest. "First, entrance to my study is not allowed. No one may go in there; not even the butler."

Frankie's heart sped up and the next words were out of her mouth before she could stop them. "Why not?"

Jasper stared at her. "Are you certain you were sent by Perdita's?"

Too late Frankie realized it was wholly inappropriate to question her employer's decisions. "Oh, pardon me." Frankie pushed at her hair. Holy Queen V! She couldn't seem to stop bungling her role. Her father had always encouraged her natural tendency toward bluntness because he had found it amusing, while her mother had warned her time and again that it would land her in trouble one day. When Frankie had needed to find employ as a governess to support her family, she had not thought it would be so difficult to assimilate. As the genteel granddaughter of a baron, she was not so lowly ranked as a servant, but that did not mean she could speak her mind to her employers. "My apologies. I am indeed from Perdita's, and I assure you that as a Perdita girl I am more than capable of guiding Cecelia's education. I am excellent at mathematics."

Jasper shifted a step back, allowing her more breathing space. "That is well and good, although I do not know what Cecelia will ever need mathematics for."

Frankie was going to faint dead away.

"My second rule is that you must not fall in love with me."

Frankie's mouth popped open. *"Pardon me?"*

Jasper grinned in such a wicked way that despite Frankie's dislike of the man, a tingly sensation worked its way down her nerves. "Both sexes tend to desire me. It is a curse I have learned to live with. However, romantic entanglements create tension I neither care for nor have the time to deal with. It is best if you know straight away that I do not liaise with my staff. No exceptions."

Frankie did not know if she was astonished by his declaration or uproariously amused. "I can assure you, Mr. Jones, that I would *never* fall in love with you. *Ever.*" She should have stopped there, but her tongue was faster than her brain. "You are the last person I would give my heart to, just behind the cat food cart man who has invented a language comprised entirely of belches. Indeed, the chances I would desire your company beyond mundane employer interactions are"—she paused as she rapidly calculated the numbers in her head—"one in six million."

That devilish grin returned to his face and an odd dipping thing happened to Frankie's stomach. "You remember that, Miss Turner. I assure you that whatever you have heard of my reputation has been watered down. I am all the things they say I am, and more. There will never be one woman for me, or marriage, or any of the other fanciful things people tell themselves when they fall in love with me. Consider yourself warned."

The conceit of the man was without compare! Frankie had once imagined herself in love with a boy who'd acted as if he knew the answers to why the stars fell and how heaven looked, but even *his* arrogance paled in comparison to Jasper Jones's.

"Mr. Jones, I do hope it will not wound your ego when I prove to be entirely unaffected by your—" As words failed her, she waved her palm in a circle in front of her to encompass all of him.

Jasper tugged his coat into place and went to step around her. Before he left the room, he bent his mouth to her ear and said in a low, shivery voice, "You already are."

Chapter 3

Frankie marched down the corridor of the Jones house toward the schoolroom, thinking of all the things she wished she could say to that sodding Jasper Jones. Her encounter with the gambling hell owner had been trying to say the least, but she had to remember why she was there.

"You have read about the recent tribulations of Lady Diane Cuthburt?" the Dove asked, rapping the top of the carriage with her cane to signal the driver to move. After catching Frankie spying on Rockford's, she had invited Frankie into her carriage for a more private conversation.

Everything inside the carriage screamed wealth, from the stitching of the black velvet cushions to the thick, luxurious fabric in the windows. Frankie sniffed and caught subtle notes of peony and vanilla, and wondered just how fat the Dove's coffers were.

"I suppose even the French have heard about Lady Diane Cuthburt," Frankie replied, discreetly wiping her forehead with her handkerchief and reminding herself it was scientifically impossible for a person to melt into a puddle. The blasted London heat had been unbearable that

summer. "She has been in the newspapers for weeks. She was caught unchaperoned in an alcove at a musical soirée with Lord Grant Parsons, fourth son of the Marquess of Dembeyshire. She refused to marry him, and now her reputation is destroyed. She has three sisters, and they shall never marry because of the stain on her family. In society's eyes she is ruined."

In the illumination of the swinging carriage lamps, the Dove's lips had pressed together. "Lady Diane's scandal was a harsh reminder of what happens when a woman is compromised and then does not marry. In London, social standing is everything." The Dove interlaced her fingers in her lap. "I am aware of the unusual *ton* weddings that have taken place over the past six months—and based on the note you had Emily deliver, so are you. Desperate men with debts have recently had unconscionable luck marrying women with sizable dowries. And they are not just any women: Lady Anne Bolsey, Lady Clara Florten, Lady Mable Ezra, and Lady Elizabeth Scarson are but a few."

Frankie nodded. Lady Anne Bolsey had been lobbying for her father to introduce a bill that would end the entail, which allowed only men to inherit property. Lady Clara Florten had been causing ripples over the imminent extinction of birds used for hats, and Lady Mable Ezra was an advocate for public schooling. Lady Elizabeth Scarson had been outspoken about cleanliness and disease. "They're troublemakers," Frankie said.

"Troublemakers," the Dove repeated, rolling the word on her tongue and then nodding with satisfaction. "Brilliant women, all of them caught in risqué situations that forced them into marriages with destitute men. Miss Turner, I believe there is a set of men acting as Dowry Thieves, and they're targeting women they wish to silence."

Frankie blinked with horror. "You think someone is engineering compromising situations in order to secure the women's dowries?"

"Yes. Women of the *ton* are almost always closely guarded and chaperoned, meaning it would be no easy feat. That is why I believe there is one mastermind behind the scheme. One man moving the chess pieces in order to orchestrate the fateful meetings."

Frankie's stomach roiled. Women were already treated like cattle, but to be tricked into matrimony so that the lords of London could steal their money and breathe a sigh of relief when the women were silenced—why, it made her blood boil.

"Mr. Jasper Jones has to be the man responsible. All the grooms hold a membership to his club," Frankie accused. Could her sister know about the Dowry Thieves? Was that the "dastardly" thing she had spoken of in her letter? If so, how did she plan to help her childhood friend, Lady Elizabeth Scarson, now that the lady was already married? "Do you know where Fidelia is?"

"No, but I may have a lead. I have been aware of your sister's disappearance these past weeks, and I have recently hired a private detective to look for her. Leave finding Fidelia to me."

Frankie pushed at her spectacles, excitement, relief, and confusion warring for space in her brain. "Why would you do that? Why are you helping me?" She could not afford to pay the Dove whatever fee the detective was charging to find Fidelia. That was part of the reason why her mother had enlisted her to find her sister: Their purse strings were so tight they could barely be prized open, and on top of that, it was imperative that they keep Fidelia's escape quiet.

The Dove's eyes took on a cunning gleam. "Because I need your expertise with numbers. I will help you find your sister, if you help me discover who's behind the Dowry Thieves. I will not stand by while revolutionary women are silenced."

The Dove rapped the top of the carriage again and it came to a standstill. Through the drawn curtains came the sounds of two younger gentlemen clearly in their cups, along with the strike of horseshoes on cobblestones. "I am not convinced Jasper Jones is behind the Dowry Thieves, even though all the grooms hold a membership to his hell. In truth, most of the ton have a membership to Rockford's. Jones would not benefit from silencing the 'troublemakers' as you put it, and Jasper Jones never does anything that does not benefit him.

"That being said, I still need someone with a keen eye to look through Jones's business ledgers. Mr. Jones is suspicious and private by nature, and he keeps his ledgers at his personal residence. I have governesses gathering financials on several of the grooms in question, including the husband of your friend, Lady Elizabeth Scarson, but Jones's household has been difficult to infiltrate because he is a confirmed bachelor without children, and he is very... security conscious."

"Then how do we figure out if he is responsible?" Frankie asked, sweat sliding down her spine.

The Dove withdrew a creased letter from her reticule and handed it to Frankie. It was addressed to Perdita's. The author required an experienced and patient governess for his niece, who had recently come to live with him after the death of her father. The signature at the bottom was from Mr. Jasper Jones.

The Dove's lips curved. "I have a plan."

That plan was for Frankie to become Cecelia's governess and use her position to investigate Jasper Jones's private papers and ledgers in exchange for the Dove finding her sister. The Dove had warned Frankie that Jasper was a notorious rake, but she had *not* warned her that he was also insufferable.

"Arrogant toad!" Frankie hissed under her breath. She was on her way to the schoolroom and there was no one about, giving her license to mutter freely.

After Jasper had left, the head housekeeper had taken Frankie to the guest wing, where she'd been given a medium-sized room next to Madam Margaret, an elderly maiden aunt inherited with Cecelia. Although Frankie's chamber lacked a receiving room, she did not mind. At her last situation she had been put in with the servants, so this was quite a rung up for her, however temporary.

Frankie had left her valise and parasol in a corner of the room, washed her face, re-pinned her hair—for all the good that did—and set out for the schoolroom to meet with Cecelia. She had sensed the girl's animosity toward her uncle, and there was an ancient proverb Frankie had once read: *The enemy of my enemy is my friend.* As a bored adolescent, Cecelia would have explored the lay of the house and, like any young person, gravitated toward that which she was supposed to leave alone. Namely, Jasper Jones's study.

That meant Cecelia was about to become Frankie's friend.

"I have not heard any woman call him a toad before."

Frankie squawked and spun around, chagrined to find Cecelia peering at her from a guest room doorway.

"Most women simper and do this." Cecelia fluttered her hand in front of her face and pretended to drop to the ground.

Frankie laughed. "Your uncle certainly fancies himself a catch."

"He fancies himself a lot of things," Cecelia said solemnly. "Why are you not staying long?"

"Your uncle does not think I am mature enough to take care of you properly."

Cecelia fell into step beside Frankie and made a face. Frankie wondered why she was dressed as an eight-year-old rather than as a young woman of fifteen who would soon be considered ready for her "coming-out."

"He wanted to hire a nanny. A nanny! Can you imagine? I finally convinced him that I only need a governess, and so he said he would write to the best agency in all of London."

"And here I am!" Frankie cried, holding out her arms.

Cecelia eyed her and, having come to some internal conclusion, smiled. Her front teeth were adorably large. "I like you. You are odd, and you did not look as if you wanted to ravish my uncle."

Frankie supposed she should admonish Cecelia for speaking in such a manner, but Jasper had made it clear she wasn't the *official* governess, and she needed Cecelia on her side. Additionally, her role was to teach Cecelia French and Italian and arithmetic, not pounce on frowned-upon vocabulary such as *ravish*. Heavens knew Frankie said enough inappropriate things herself.

They reached the end of the corridor and Cecelia naturally turned into the schoolroom. It was spacious and had clearly been built for a much larger family. It consisted of tables, jars of quills and watercolors, stacks of papers, and a bookshelf that ran the entire length of one wall. A brass globe sat suspended at an angle by the window, and a map of the world was pinned beside the chalkboard on the opposite wall. It smelled of chalk, dust, and that delicious scent of old books that Frankie absolutely adored.

"You seem not to care for your uncle," Frankie said, striding to the bookshelf and scanning for the mathematics section.

"Some people are unlikable."

Frankie turned to her, but Cecelia's face was shuttered, and even Frankie knew a mulish countenance when she saw one. "What is your favorite subject?" she asked. She would circle back to the topic once she and Cecelia were better acquainted.

"Gambling," Cecelia said, looking through her lashes for Frankie's response.

Frankie smothered a smile, which would have offended the young woman who was doing her best to shock her. Frankie imagined Cecelia would have succeeded with most governesses, but

Frankie's sister was Cecelia's age, so she was well versed in how to handle girls who were almost, but not quite yet, women. "Is that so? What game?"

Cecelia's eyes widened. "You...you want to know what game?"

"Whist? Vingt et Un? Hazard? Piquet?"

"Vingt et Un, I suppose."

"Did your uncle teach you?"

"No." Cecelia's gaze dropped to her slippers. "My father did."

Frankie felt a pang of sympathy for her. Cecelia was fortunate that she had an uncle to take her in when so many children did not, but that did not mean the agony of losing her father was any less real. "I am sorry to hear of your loss."

Cecelia tossed her head angrily. "Yes, well, Father would not want me to mourn. He always told me that when his time came, I was not to dress in mourning, that I was too pretty to waste my youth in such a dreadful color."

"He must have loved you very much."

With an unladylike sniff, Cecelia dashed the back of her hand against her eyes and strode to the ladies' writing desk. She lowered the lid and pulled out a fresh pack of cards from within. "Do you play, Miss Turner?"

Frankie did not, but she was already making progress with Cecelia, and she didn't think it would do to turn her down now. "No. Will you teach me?"

A gleam appeared in Cecelia's eye. "I only play for money. That was Father's rule."

"I will not play for money," Frankie said evenly, "but I will play for terms."

Cecelia skipped to the table and sat down, gesturing excitedly for Frankie to join her. "Best six out of ten. If I win, you convince Uncle Jasper to let me attend the Houndsbury house party in three weeks by offering to chaperone."

"Best six out of ten," Frankie agreed, "but first with a practice game. I accept your terms—if another governess has not replaced me by then. If I win, you will owe me one favor, no questions asked, for future redemption on your honor."

Cecelia beamed and stuck out her palm. "Deal."

Frankie shook her hand.

"I cannot wait to attend the house party." Cecelia sighed. "Uncle Jasper says I am too young and half the people there are vultures, but I am sure I will enjoy it immensely."

"All right, enough with that. Teach me how to play."

Cecelia described the game as she expertly shuffled the cards and laid them in a stack. She turned two cards over, one for her and one for Frankie. "It is very simple. Each card is worth the number on the face. Jack, queen, and king are worth ten points. An ace can be worth either one or eleven. You will ask for another card, and depending on what you are dealt, you may ask for another. The goal is to reach a total of twenty-one without going over."

Frankie's mind whizzed as she sorted through a multitude of strategies. She grinned. This was going to be fun.

Thirty minutes later Cecelia stamped her foot and tugged on a strand of hair. "I do not understand it! You did not lose a single game! Are you sure you have never played before?"

"Positive," Frankie said, gathering the cards together.

"I find it suspicious that you should be so lucky."

"You certainly should!" Frankie exclaimed. "It would be very unlikely to win all those games on luck alone."

"Then how did you do it?"

Frankie tapped her temple. "Mathematics."

Cecelia's pacing ceased. "Are you jesting?"

"I am not. Mathematics can tell you more about the world than almost any other discipline. If you can master it, you can master anything."

Cecelia dropped into her chair again, her bright-yellow skirts puffing like a mushroom. She leaned forward eagerly. "Teach me."

Frankie was sure there was an unwritten rule that one did not teach one's charges mathematics with card games, but no one had explicitly taught her this rule, and so she decided it was as solid a method as any. Besides, teaching Cecelia mathematics was the part Jasper Jones paid her for.

"There are a few methods one can use. In the first game I assigned a value to the lower cards..."

Chapter 4

Jasper tamped down a smile as Cecelia paced the corridor outside the sitting room. He conducted his business affairs in his study, but since Cecelia had come to live with him, he had taken to writing his morning correspondence at a desk in the sitting room. Since no one was allowed in his study, he had found this gave Cecelia the opportunity to interact with him on her terms. She rarely chose to do so, but he made himself available all the same.

Today it seemed she had something to say, because she had been pacing the marble tiles outside the room for nearly half an hour. Jasper was hoping she would work up the courage to enter. He was curious to know how yesterday had gone with the odd new governess, Frankie, and if he asked Cecelia outright she would thwart him by purposely avoiding the question. Adolescent girls were a damnable curiosity, but Jasper was experienced in strategizing against his opponents, and he knew instinctively that if he wanted answers from Cecelia, the best course of action was to act as if he did not.

The sun shone brilliantly through the diamond-paned window

over the desk, and Jasper would have liked to open the windows for fresh air, only there was no such thing to be found in London in the dead heat of summer. Lavender and honeysuckle were scattered in crystal vases about the room, but even those fragrant blooms were not enough to mask the pungent odor of sewage.

He finished his letter to Perdita's requesting a new governess and used candle wax to seal it. He had moved on to writing a letter to his solicitor about funds for his wharf project when Cecelia entered the sitting room with a too-bright smile on her lips. She was outfitted in a horrid, shockingly orange gown that was entirely too short and probably hadn't fit her in years. Jasper set aside his letter and wondered why Cecelia insisted on dressing in such a way, when a thought struck him. Did she *have* any other dresses? When was the last time his brother had updated her wardrobe?

"Cecelia," he said before she could speak, "do you require a new wardrobe?"

Cecelia crossed her arms over her chest. "I do not require anything from you, Uncle Jasper."

He bit back a sigh. Replace "Uncle Jasper" with "Brother," and those words could have come straight from his brother's mouth. Jasper had loved his brother and had given to him freely, but his brother had not felt the same toward him. Not wishing to be "indebted" to Jasper, his brother had always been just shy of hostile, and it had not mattered how many times Jasper told him the money was a gift. His brother had always resented him, and that hadn't changed with their rise in society. Jasper couldn't blame him. He'd done plenty in his lifetime to earn that resentment.

"Nevertheless, it is clear your gowns do not fit any longer so you shall have a new wardrobe."

"Thank you," she said stiffly. Her features, which had been

anxious upon entering, hardened with resolve. "I have come to ask you if I can attend the Houndsbury house party in three weeks."

"No." There was no beating around the bush. Cecelia was far too young to attend one of the *ton*'s frivolous and lengthy house parties. At fifteen she was practically still a baby and years away from coming out. Besides, he rubbed shoulders with enough nobility at his club to know exactly how men viewed a young woman with a hefty dowry, and he did not particularly feel like knocking out anyone's teeth in the next month.

"I thought you might say that, so I have come with a proposition."

Jasper lifted a brow. He crossed one booted ankle over his knee and gestured with his hand for her to continue. The black insignia ring he wore on his middle finger caught a ray of sunlight from the window and glinted.

"I will play you for the opportunity. Ten games of Vingt et Un. If I win six out of the ten, you will allow me to attend."

"Cecelia." Jasper said her name as gently as he could. "You cannot win. We both know that."

She lifted her chin. "Then what do you have to lose?"

He shrugged and rummaged in the desk for a pack of playing cards, which he always had on hand. If she wanted to play it would give him time to subtly probe about Miss Turner. "My terms are that if I win, you will not scowl at me for one whole day."

"Oh, Uncle Jasper, I do not think that is possible. Can you choose something else?"

He swallowed his exasperation. "Fine. You will not scowl at dinner."

She wrinkled her nose but nodded. Jasper shuffled the pack and dealt the first round, which he won. He swiped the cards away and dealt again. "What did you think of Miss Turner?"

Cecelia was concentrating so hard her eyes were almost crossed. "She is wonderful," she answered absently. "Deal me a card." He did so, and then dealt himself a card. She had nineteen, he twenty.

"Deal me again."

"Are you sure?"

"Do it."

Jasper flipped the card over. It was a two. Cecelia crowed with delight and Jasper smiled. Everyone deserved to get lucky once in a while.

"Did she teach you your lessons? Did she appear competent?"

"She called you a toad, so she's more intelligent than most."

A toad! Miss Turner was hardly a princess herself. Her hair may have been the color of sun-struck wheat, and her huge eyes were as blue as a summer sky, but she had the spectacles of a ninety-year-old spinster and appeared constantly frazzled. In their one brief meeting he had noticed she'd missed a button on her gown and her hair was falling down her back. She was an unorganized disaster.

"I imagine she would thank you for the compliment," he said dryly. He dealt again.

The third time Cecelia won Jasper scented a scam. He had been gambling from the time he was four. He'd played dice in the street, winning trinkets from other boys, and then had moved on to card games with men. He'd slowly built enough savings to invest in a gaming tavern with Jimmy "Bird Eyes" Parson. Their partnership had dissolved with a bloody fistfight, but Jasper had limped away with even more money to his name. He now owned the most exclusive gaming hell in London, but he still walked the floor every night, smiling and shaking hands, his presence subtly reminding the patrons he was watching.

He could spot a cheat a mile away.

He dealt the cards and watched Cecelia closely. Her lips moved as she tallied a number, and he slammed a fist on the table. She jumped in surprise.

"Cecelia! Are you counting cards?"

She frowned. "What does that mean?"

"Are you using mathematics to figure out what cards should show next?"

"Yes. Are you all right, Uncle Jasper? Your face is turning awfully red."

Jasper took two deep breaths. "Cecelia, if you were in Rockford's right now, I'd throw you out on your ar—ear."

"Is it not allowed?"

"*No.*"

"Do you not do it?"

That was a less clear-cut answer. He had certainly counted cards to work his way up the ladder, but he did not tolerate it in his own club. He ignored the question. "How did you learn to do that?"

"A book," she answered quickly. Too quickly.

Jasper stared her down. Cecelia was a tough nut to crack, but Jasper Jones had earned his reputation as the devil incarnate fairly. He may appear civilized on the outside, but when it came down to it, the only moral code he abided by was personal. When he wanted something, he got it.

And right now he wanted a name.

Cecelia squirmed and looked at the ceiling, then her nails, and finally blurted, "It was Miss Turner! But you musn't be cross. She was only teaching me my mathematics lesson and—"

Jasper's blood began to simmer. "Cecelia, go to your chamber."

"I do not want to."

"Then go to the library or the larder for all I care."

Cecelia stuck her tongue out at him and raced from the room.

The moment she was gone Jasper stomped to the door of the sitting room, and he wouldn't have been surprised if every person in Mayfair heard him roar, "MISS TURNER!"

Chapter 5

Frankie was dining in the morning room with Madam Margaret, who had smiled kindly at her when she'd entered and then promptly fallen asleep, when Jasper bellowed as if he were several houses away rather than several rooms. With Madam Margaret dozing by the window, Frankie dared a sigh and pushed her plate aside. Heavens knew what the man was in a tizzy about now. It was only half past ten, and that was nearly ten, which made her only half an hour late starting Cecelia's lessons. Her mother had once told her she was the least punctual person in all of England, but Frankie knew for a mathematical fact that was impossible.

Yesterday Frankie had sent a missive to the Dove warning her of Jasper's reluctance to employ her. The Dove had replied promptly, the message arriving that morning, and Frankie had read the letter while munching on a plate of toast and rashers. She had anticipated that the Dove would be disappointed over Jasper's desire to dismiss her, but the vigilante had appeared unworried.

I have not received his correspondence, which means you have time yet. Your priority is the business ledgers. If Jones is behind the Dowry Thieves there may be a duplicate ledger recording his transactions with the grooms. I trust that you will be able to tell the difference when you see it.

I must warn you again that Jasper Jones has an unforgiving reputation. Do <u>not</u> allow yourself to be caught.

—*The Dove*

At Jasper's rather rude summons, Frankie folded the letter, tucked it up her sleeve, and stood. She followed the echo of his roar to the sitting room. As she was about to enter, she caught sight of a flash of orange at the end of the corridor; it was Cecelia, peeking from behind a stone bust. She mouthed an apology before quickly disappearing.

Frankie's brow furrowed. Whatever the cause of Jasper's ire, it seemed to involve Cecelia.

Before she crossed the sitting room threshold, her gaze landed on a tightly closed mahogany door just beyond the stone bust. The knob and keyhole gleamed silver in the morning light. *Jasper's study.* Her heart quickened. He had made it strikingly clear that no one was allowed in his study, not even for a cleaning. If he were hiding a duplicate ledger, it would be there.

"I am waiting, Miss Turner." His voice was deadly calm, and it reminded Frankie of the stillness in the air before a winter storm. The hairs on the nape of her neck lifted. The Dove's warning echoed in the back of her mind: *Do not allow yourself to be caught.*

Jasper was standing by the desk at the window, his black hair gilded with morning light. His boots were polished, his navy morning coat brushed smooth, and his dark eyes flashed with barely concealed irritation. He smelled of fresh air and leather, as if he'd taken a ride earlier that morning, and it mingled with the sweet scents of honeysuckle and lavender. For an instant Frankie imagined herself in the countryside, dipping her toes in a pond and letting the sun wash over her face. She quickly banished the fantasy; she ought to be ashamed of thinking about relaxing by a pond. Her sister was heaven knew where, and this man could be responsible for the ruination of a number of women. Whatever he was frothing about, she would have to meekly rectify it if she wanted to complete her investigation during the few days he'd granted her.

Frankie inclined her head. "Mr. Jones."

"Miss Turner." Odd, it sounded as if he were gritting his teeth when he said her name.

Frankie met his eyes and waited patiently.

After several moments of silence, where the air in the room grew increasingly thick, he said, "Cecelia came to see me this morning."

Frankie shoved at her spectacles and wished he would hurry up and say what he had to say.

"She desires to attend the house party at the Houndsbury country estate in Richmond."

Frankie suddenly understood, although she did not think a modest request deserved shouting down the house. "Very well, Mr. Jones. I will have you know it is not generally within my purview to chaperone a pupil at a house party, but this one time I will make an exception, assuming I am still here. I know how much Cecelia wants to attend, and I must admit I think it is very good of you to allow her to go. She is clearly devastated by the loss of her father and terribly lonely. It will do her well to mingle with other young women her age, perhaps even find a companion or two. Goodness knows we could all use a few nights away from this pungent city."

"That is not at all what I—" Jasper's heavy brows drew together. "Why do you think she is lonely?"

"How could she *not* be?" Frankie exclaimed. "She is a fifteen-year-old girl rattling about a behemoth house that is not her own, with no one but Madam Margaret and the servants to keep her company. All the other girls of her social standing are in the country for the summer, and yet she is stuck here with far too much time on her hands to think. It must be universal knowledge that when one suffers a great loss, the best remedy is to keep busy. The party will do her a world of good."

"I haven't yet—"

"You are a very caring uncle," Frankie continued. "Caring, but thoughtless. This is hardly enough time for the modiste to sew Cecelia an entirely new wardrobe. She absolutely cannot attend the Houndsbury function wearing dresses designed for an eight-year-old."

"That we are in agreement on. As for the—"

Frankie snapped her fingers. "Perhaps there is hope! Surely Madame will have a few pre-sewn gowns on hand that will take only a few adjustments to fit Cecelia. The ball gown will be more challenging, but I suspect it can be managed. Have you written to Lady Houndsbury yet to accept her invitation? It would be awfully rude to simply show up."

"No, I have not. And I am—"

Frankie heaved a sigh. "I shall write to her if you would like, and we will send it expressly. Now if we can—"

She squeaked as he closed the distance between them with three long strides and gripped her shoulders. His hands were powerful, the heat of them searing through the thin fabric of her gown. She lifted her eyes and her breath caught at his nearness. His face was closer than anyone's had been since she'd snuck a kiss from the milk delivery boy when she was twelve and fancied herself in love. That was before she'd learned that no man could love a woman as odd as she.

Up close Jasper was even more handsome, and she was sure he knew it. Despite his defined physique, his lips appeared full and soft and...and for a moment Frankie could understand why women threw themselves at him. If he ever looked at her with as much passion as he did conceit, *she* might even feel fluttery, and Frankie Turner did not flutter. It wasn't that she didn't want to flutter, but in her experience very few men were able to look past the fact that she was smarter than they were, which meant she had little practice with flirting and flutters.

"Miss Turner," he said, his voice bordering on desperation, "if you do not let me finish a single bloody sentence, I shall dismiss you on the spot."

Frankie snapped her mouth shut so hard her teeth clicked, but she didn't avert her eyes.

"We are not going to Richmond. I cannot leave the gaming hell that long."

"You do not have a man you trust?"

"I do—"

"Then I don't see why you cannot—"

"Miss Turner!"

She clapped both hands over her mouth. The corners of Jasper's eyes creased in what nearly looked like amusement. He released her and stepped back. "Beyond the gaming hell, there are a number of other issues, not the least of which is that Cecelia is entirely too young, the venue entirely too far, and I am entirely too uninterested in attending a stuffy party that lasts for days on end. And because I suspect you have a hundred solutions to each of those issues, I shall add that I doubt *any* modiste has a ball gown ready on the drop of a hatpin for someone of Cecelia's height."

"Modiste? Did you say *modiste* and *ball gown* in the same sentence? Oh, Uncle!" A blur of bright orange streaked into the room and flung itself onto Jasper. "I just knew you would let me! I knew it! Have you forgiven me for before? I promise I will not do it again. I am so thrilled I cannot even express myself. Did Miss Turner convince you? No matter, I must go pack."

"Cecelia." Jasper caught the girl's wrist before she could dash from the room, his expression resolute. "We are not..."

Cecelia blinked at her uncle with wide, adoring eyes, and Frankie was reminded of the time her sister had brought home a street puppy and begged to keep it. One look at Fidelia's radiant face and her mother hadn't even bothered arguing with her about turning it out. The dog had lived with them ever since.

"We cannot go to the Houndsbury party because"—a barely audible sigh escaped Jasper's lips—"we are having a party here."

Cecelia clapped both her hands over her mouth to muffle her scream of delight. "That is even better, Uncle! I have not seen my friends since...since before. May I invite them? They are not society people."

Jasper frowned. "Why have you not invited them before now?"

Some of Cecelia's excitement dimmed and she gave a small shrug.

Inspiration appeared to strike Jasper. "Why do you not plan the party, Cece? You are the lady of the house. I am sure with Mrs. Hollendale's expert guidance you will do splendidly at putting together a small gathering."

Cecelia beamed at him. "Thank you!" she squealed before skipping from the room.

As soon as she was gone Jasper shot Frankie a smug smile. "Being a guardian is not so hard as everyone makes it out to be."

"I fear you underestimate Cecelia."

"I am not worried," he said, returning to the desk to collect his correspondence. "This is the happiest I have seen her since she came here. Besides, what is a small gathering? I have the means to support her project, and with so many peers in the country for the summer there is little risk of it turning into a stuffy society crush."

"Do you want to bet on it?" Frankie asked impudently.

She caught Jasper's head whip up, but she was already spinning around and sailing toward the door, a single doubt worming its way into her mind. Jasper had been resolute about not letting Cecelia attend the house party, and yet when it had come time to crush her dreams, he had offered an alternative instead. There was taking care of family, and then there was sacrificing for family. Hosting a party at his notoriously private residence would indeed be an enormous inconvenience for a man like Jasper, whose reputation excluded caring about anyone but himself.

So why had he done it?

Chapter 6

Jasper's eyes followed Frankie's disappearing back and his brows drew together. Had her parting comment been a saucy reference to what she had taught Cecelia? And how the hell had he ended up granting Cecelia a party when he'd meant to be chastising the governess?

He flipped open his pocket watch. It was made of cheap tin and was dented and scratched from decades of use. Jasper could have afforded a watch of gold and rubies, but he refused to dispense with the one item he still possessed from his former life. The watch had belonged to his father, but that sure as hell wasn't why Jasper prized it. He had meant less to his father than he had to his mother. On the wharf there had been no love, only hungry bellies to feed. No, Jasper kept the pocket watch because it was a tangible reminder of where he'd started. Whenever he spent the night mingling with a duke or flirting with a fine lady, he'd take out the watch to remind himself that he was not one of them and he never would be. They loved him because he fed them fine food and wine, because he held the deeds to their estates and the betting books to their secrets. Should he ever lose his edge and misstep, nary a one of them would be there to soften his fall. Rather, he thought they would gleefully crush him beneath their heels.

He should have been at Rockford's a half hour ago, but now he needed to conference with Mrs. Hollendale about Cecelia's party. Mrs. Hollendale was wonderfully efficient, and he did not want her taking over, so he would instruct her to give Cecelia full rein. Jasper reached for the letter he'd written to Perdita's and rang for his butler.

"Sir?"

"Send this out," Jasper said, handing him the correspondence. At his butler's silent glance at the address and twitching lips Jasper demanded, "What?"

To his surprise, the butler's eyes *twinkled*. "Miss Turner is a delightful addition to the household, sir."

"How is that?"

"She opened *all* the windows on the second floor to 'try and catch a breeze,' and Mrs. Hollendale was severely put out."

The butler had a long-standing rivalry with the head house-keeper, Mrs. Hollendale. Whatever irritated Mrs. Hollendale was sure to delight the butler.

"I am sure it reeked," Jasper said.

"Indeed it did. Even Madam Margaret commented, and I do believe that is the first I have heard her speak. I will be sorry to see Miss Turner go."

Jasper clapped his butler on the shoulder. "You shall have to find an alternative way to needle Mrs. Hollendale, my friend."

Jasper tucked the watch into his coat and exited the house. Rockford's was less than a mile from his residence; an easy walk no matter the weather or time of day—or night. Jasper had made the trek in the pouring rain, four drinks deep, and once with a nasty knife wound to his thigh. He knew the streets like the inside of his lip and could have made the trip blindfolded and backward.

St. James's Street was easily the liveliest street in London. It had once been a mix of hatters, perfumers, grocers, and tailors but now hosted grand town houses—including his own—on the west side, as well as high-end shops, exclusive offices, and some of the most popular clubs and gaming hells London had to offer. The facades of some of the buildings boasted ornate white stonework, while others, having once belonged to the trades, were structured of simple brick.

The street was always bustling with activity, even in the quieter months of summer. Horses and carriages trundled past, men and women from all social classes patronized the shops, and at night there were the sounds of rolling dice and the convivial laughter of comrades deep in their cups.

Or maybe that was just at Rockford's.

When Jasper reached his gaming hell he paused, as he did every time, and simply soaked in the grand building. *His* grand building. It was a monstrous hall constructed of white stone, gleaming windows, and a balustrade that ran the length of the roof. Imposing Corinthian columns decorated the front facade, and several balconies overlooked the bustling street. A neat row of polished marble steps led to the front door. It had been an added expense that many had turned an austere eye toward, but those steps said everything he'd wanted them to: We are exclusive. We are lavish. We are *riche*. Enter only for pleasure.

The interior was even more opulent.

Jasper had taken a gamble when he'd opened Rockford's; he'd spent every last shilling to his name. He'd known deep down, in that instinctive place that whispered to him when he gambled, that if he wanted to engage the membership of the *ton*, he had to offer the absolute height of glamor and luxury. So when it came time to decide on how many chandeliers, he chose one more than he already thought was outrageous. When it came to employment, he paid an astronomical salary for a premier French chef to serve courses that would make the staid meat-and-potatoes dishes the other hells served looked like dog food. That Persian carpet copy had been nearly identical, and yet Jasper had dismissed it with scorn. He would absorb the exorbitant expense for the real thing. If it wasn't the best, it would not pass through the doors of Rockford's.

It was a gamble that had paid off handsomely.

He knocked at the door and it was opened by Toby, one of the muscular men who monitored admittance. Toby dipped his chin and stepped aside.

"How are you today, Toby?"

"Fine. An' you, sir?"

"I am well. Has your wife had the babe yet?"

Toby's quagmire of a face split into a grin. "Any day, sir. I'll keep ye updated, sir."

Jasper slapped the man on the back and crossed the black-and-white marble tiles, nodding at maids and servants in livery who bustled about, readying the hall for the evening. Railings and silver needed to be polished, windows washed, the velvet curtains brushed, and the wallpaper cleaned with paste to remove smoke stains. The kitchens would be in a roar as the team chopped vegetables and prepped for the mackerel roe baked in clarified butter that Bizet, the chef, served only once a month and to great fanfare.

Jasper greeted most of his staff by name. He made it a point to acknowledge them all, even the delivery boys. He had been a fishmonger's son, and he knew what it was to feel invisible. Loyalty was tied with luxury for Rockford's top priority. Jasper paid well and he cared for his team, and in return, he demanded the highest-quality service and their complete and utter loyalty.

Jasper found his inspector and right-hand man counting decks of cards and jotting the numbers in a small leather book.

"Guy," Jasper said in greeting, leaning against the lacquered counter.

"Jasper," Guy returned. He was a slight man with small, bright eyes and a head of thinning brown hair. His attire was proper and crisp and his manners impeccable, and yet he had the most astounding quality of being almost completely forgettable. Sometimes Jasper struggled to remember what he looked like when he was not standing in front of him.

One of Guy's most important duties was sitting in a tall chair in the corner of the gaming room floor and overseeing the gambling and collecting of Rockford's debts. He handled drunks with the same finesse and firmness as a stable hand with a skittish mount, and he never once lost his temper while doing so. He was invaluable to Jasper, and Jasper trusted him implicitly.

"What would you say if your fifteen-year-old niece challenged you to a game of Vingt et Un, the stakes being the chance to attend a *ton* house party?"

Guy tucked the notebook inside his jacket and gave Jasper his full attention. "Do not tell me you lost."

Jasper twisted the silver-and-black insignia ring on his middle finger. More than one person had commented that it made him look indulgent and rakish, an image Jasper not only encouraged, but also actively cultivated. "Not at first, but by the fourth game I realized the little rabbit was counting cards."

Guy's placid expression cracked into one of merriment. "It must run in the blood."

"Not entirely. It wasn't she who took it upon herself to learn. It was the governess who taught her."

"One would never accuse you of living a dull life. I assume you dismissed the governess?"

"No! When I called her in to speak with her, I somehow ended up agreeing to allow Cecelia to host a small gathering in lieu of attending the house party. I never had a chance to address the matter."

Guy pressed a hand to his heart and said with complete sincerity, "I would be honored to meet this woman. The King of Cards, twisted about by a governess. And one who counts cards!"

Spoken aloud, the words sparked a whisper of warning in the back of Jasper's mind. "Is that not odd?" he asked. "What are the chances a governess like that joins *my* household?"

Guy's finger tapped on the counter. He too wore a ring, but unlike Jasper's, his held a lethal surprise within. "It does seem unlikely. Governesses are not generally known for their gambling prowess. What do you suspect? That she is a plant from another hell?"

Jasper slowly shook his head. "I do not know. She has not even been in my employ twenty-four hours and she has already turned my house upside down. I shall have to make it a point to become better acquainted with her. By the time she leaves I will know more about Miss Francis Turner than she knows about herself."

Chapter 7

Two Days Later

"The soirée will be in four days," Cecelia informed Frankie when she finally deigned to visit the schoolroom where she was to have met Frankie over an hour ago. "I have been terribly busy. It is quite a joy playing mistress of the house."

"Is that not too soon?"

"I think it is enough time for people to gather," Cecelia hedged, but there was a mischievous gleam in her eyes that Frankie did not think boded well for Jasper.

Frankie spent the next hour giving Cecelia increasingly difficult tasks in mathematics, composition, and French so that she might gauge where her pupil's education had ceased. Although she was not to be Cecelia's governess for more than a few days, it was imperative that she play the role. More important, Frankie thought it a shame when a girl's education was lacking and she would not be complicit in the gaps in Cecelia's knowledge.

"Miss Turner, you are too hard," Cecelia complained at last, slumping in the chair in her new gown. Yesterday, Frankie had gone with Cecelia and her lady's maid to the modiste, where they had ordered a scandalously expensive, but well needed, wardrobe. The modiste had found a gown that had been stitched but never paid for, and for a hefty sum had altered it on the spot for Cecelia to wear in the meantime. Cecelia was now dressed in a gorgeous shade of turquoise, the fashionable gown nearly reaching the floor instead of mid-calf as her prior gowns had. With the new dress Cecelia's entire demeanor had changed. She was still impish, but some of her more outright childish defiance had disappeared with the outdated clothes.

It was sweltering in the schoolroom, and Frankie attempted to muscle open the stuck window again. At last admitting defeat, she asked, "Shall we have tea and then continue in the courtyard?"

Cecelia groaned. "I cannot concentrate, Miss Turner. Do you not understand that I am soon to host one of the summer's most important soirées?"

Frankie narrowed her eyes at that, but Cecelia was busy spinning the book of sums on the table and did not notice. "May we take a walk instead?"

Frankie gnawed on her lip. The last time she'd taken a charge to Hyde Park, the boy had thrown both of his shoes into the Serpentine.

"Please? I promise you can teach me all about the geometrical shapes of the buildings, or whatever other boring math facts you would prefer."

Boring! Frankie did not understand how anyone could find math boring when it was a discipline of infinite possibilities. "Fine." Then with sudden inspiration she added, "Let us stroll along St. James's Street."

The Jones house had been in an uproar the past two days as

everyone prepared for the soirée, and the chaos had given Frankie free license to wander into rooms she had no business being in. She'd "accidentally" found herself in the wine cellar, and even the attic. She had "bumbled" into servants' stairways and knocked on walls in case there were secret passages or hidden rooms. All of the house's square footage was accounted for, and she had not found a single secret room where Jasper might store his more illegal papers. The one thing she had not yet been able to accomplish was sneaking into Jasper's study. While Frankie waited impatiently for her chance to search for the ledgers, she thought that perhaps the view of Rockford's might spark conversation with Cecelia that could lead to new information.

Cecelia agreed on the destination, and after the two had donned hats and opened parasols, they strolled leisurely toward Rockford's.

"Who have you invited to your soirée?" Frankie asked, skirting a pile of horse dung covered in a swarm of flies. Perspiration slid down her neck and she vowed that *when* she found her sister, she would never take another governess placement in the city. London was unbearably hot and smelly in the summer and far too damp and windy in the winter. Perhaps someplace on the coast would be nice.

"I have invited two chums from when I lived with my father."

"Is that all?"

"Perhaps a few more. Oh, there is Rockford's!"

Frankie suspected Cecelia was avoiding the question, but before she could say as much to her pupil, the sight of Rockford's in the daylight stole her breath. It was every bit as imposing and exquisite in the harsh sunlight as it was by the more forgiving torchlight. The windows gleamed as if they'd been recently polished, as did the exorbitantly expensive marble steps. The white facade did not show a single smudge. Frankie imagined the coal smoke of London dared not antagonize Jasper, who would surely not tolerate the slightest hint that his club was anything less than pristine.

Cecelia paused outside the marble steps and looked upward, her tight sausage curls falling down her back. If Frankie was not mistaken, there was a glow of pride on the girl's face. Cecelia exhaled noisily and said, "'Tis not fair. My uncle owns the most resplendent golden hell in all of London and I have never been allowed to step foot inside. If I were a boy, I wager he would allow me to visit."

Frankie was not so sure. From what she had observed, Jasper seemed intent on keeping his personal and professional lives entirely separate.

"You have never been inside?" Frankie asked. When Cecelia shook her head Frankie said, "And he does not bring anyone home from the club?"

Cecelia howled with amusement. "If you mean ladies of the night, no! Never! He runs a gaming hell, but you would think he was a monk by the way he acts at home."

That had not been what Frankie was alluding to—she'd merely been trying to make the point that Jasper preferred to keep his private life separate from his public one—but the opening was too good to waste. "Is that because he has conservative thoughts on marriage?"

Cecelia kicked at a pebble with the toe of her slipper. "No. That seems like an odd question, Miss Turner. Why do you ask? Please do not tell me you have designs on Uncle Jasper's affections."

Frankie's expression must have cleared her from Cecelia's suspicion because the girl voluntarily added, "He acts as if he lives an austere life around me, but I have ears, and the servants gossip."

If Frankie were acting solely in the capacity of a governess, she would gently change the topic, but in this placement she was first and foremost a spy. "What do they say?"

Cecelia was happy to have someone to share her gossip with. "All boring things when I am around and all sorts of sordid things when they think I am not listening. Uncle Jasper has a *scandalous* reputation as a rake, and a lot of them think he will take a flyer with anything that has breath, but there are others who say it is exaggerated and he only dallies with widows."

Frankie was a bit shocked by Cecelia's frank recital, as most coddled children of the upper-class *ton* would have died before repeating such gossip, but then Cecelia had grown up in very different circumstances before coming to live with Jasper.

"Er—well, that is interesting," Frankie said.

"You want to know what I think? Everyone makes Uncle Jasper out to be some devilish rake deflowering virgins left and right, and he *encourages* that, but when it comes down to it, no one has ever been able to name a single reputation he's ruined. *I* think it's more gossip than fact."

Frankie knew she was supposed to admonish Cecelia for talking about deflowering virgins, and the girl was looking at her sideways while she waited expectantly. In an attempt to emulate a normal governess, Frankie made a stab at pretending to be offended. "Do not say *virgin*, Cecelia."

Despite her mother's best efforts, Frankie was practical down to the bone, which meant a startling frankness toward the facts of life, including reproduction. She'd read numerous books about the topic. For the life of her she could not fathom what all the fuss about virginity was. Animals did not care about such things, and neither did anyone care about a man's virginity. She suspected she knew why it only applied to women: because they were considered property.

At the thought, her rage over the dastardly life sentence of the women targeted by the Dowry Thieves flared.

"Whyever not?" Cecelia demanded. "Everyone is always talking about it as if it were this wonderful thing, except I only ever hear it in reference to women. Are men supposed to be virgins? If so, Uncle Jasper will never make a good match. He is definitely *not* a virgin."

"There is an unfair double standard when it comes to virginity and the sexes."

Cecelia nodded, as if Frankie had confirmed something she'd always known. "You are easy to talk to, Miss Turner. I love Aunt Margaret and I am so happy she is still with me, but I cannot speak frankly with her. She nods off halfway through our conversations, and she is quite conservative. You are different, though. I do hope a lack of virginity will not affect Uncle Jasper's chances with—" She stopped suddenly and shot Frankie a guilty look.

"Out with it, Cecelia."

"Oh, all right, but you must promise not to tell Uncle Jasper."

"I cannot make that promise if what you tell me is harmful."

Cecelia thought about it. "It is not harmful."

"Then you have my word."

"I may have used my soirée as an opportunity to invite several debutants who did not make a marriage match this past Season. Uncle Jasper almost never goes out in polite society; I cannot ever recall hearing of him attending a ball, and so he has little opportunity to find a suitable wife."

Jasper had made it plain he was not in the market for a wife, and Frankie was certain Cecelia was well aware of that.

"When you say you invited several debutants, exactly how many do you mean?"

Cecelia stuck her tongue in the corner of her mouth as she thought. "All of them."

"All of what?" Frankie asked, alarmed.

"All of the debutants who did not make a match. And just as many men, as I do not want it to appear that Uncle Jasper is desperate."

Frankie stopped and pressed her palms to her cheeks. If Jasper heard about this, he would cancel the soirée in an instant. "Are they not all in the country?"

Cecelia lifted her chin with pride. "Uncle lives with the pretense that he is an unworthy fishmonger's son, but he is rich. Did you know that, Miss Turner? He has so much money that when he sends an invitation, people jump." She snapped her gloved fingers. "We had so many responses the next day that Mrs. Hollendale was quite overwhelmed."

"She knows about this?"

"Yes, but Uncle Jasper told her to give me whatever I want in regard to the soirée. Besides, I think she would like to see Uncle Jasper suitably married."

A carriage clattered by, lifting a plume of dust from the street. They veered farther from the road, where Frankie could smell the roasted chicken and nuts being sold at a cart farther ahead. "Why are you so keen to see your uncle married?"

"Because I have only been with him a fortnight and he has meddled in my life more than my father ever did. It appears he has far too much time on his hands," Cecelia said with a childish pout. "If he is married, he shall be kept quite busy with his new wife and I shall be free to do as I please. There is one lady in particular that I have high hopes for. Her name is Lady Evelyn Barker, daughter of the Earl of Elmsdale. From what I have heard she is a ravishing beauty. If all goes to plan, Uncle Jasper will be engaged to her before the soirée is over."

Frankie stared at her. "You have introduced far too many variables to control. You do not know what your uncle will say or do, or which ladies will request his favor, or which fathers will approach him."

Cecelia twirled her parasol over her head. "I cannot give away all of my ideas, Miss Turner. I like you, but I do not know if I can fully trust you yet. You must believe that I have an elaborate plan, and soon Uncle Jasper will be happily wed."

Frankie had a feeling the soirée would not turn out the way Cecelia was hoping it would, but that was not her problem. Governesses did not attend soirées, and with so many people in the house and Jasper kept constantly engaged, it would be the perfect opportunity to take a look around his study.

"In that case I wish you the best of luck."

Cecelia stopped and faced her. "Thank you," she said earnestly. "Everyone is always scolding me, so it is nice to know you support my scheme."

"Oh, no, I did not say I support—"

"You must attend as my companion, Miss Turner. I will not take no as an answer."

"No. I am afraid that would be inappropriate."

Cecelia laughed. "Oh, Miss Turner, nothing about this soirée is appropriate. You will see."

Chapter 8

The next morning Frankie was hurrying down the corridor, coins jangling in her pocket, in hopes that she might dash outdoors and buy a paper before her lessons, when Jasper stepped out of the sitting room, still scowling down at a letter.

"Miss Turner," he said as she attempted to slink past without catching his notice.

Frankie made a face at the cream-and-gold-striped wallpaper and then turned around with a pleasant smile on her lips. "Mr. Jones?"

The sunlight from the doorway to the sitting room backlit him with an angelic glow. *Rather deceiving*, she thought, considering he might be the actual devil. If he were, then he was a very nice-smelling devil. The shaving cream his valet used was infused with the most delicious scents: a hint of pine, cloves, and was that coffee? Jasper should give the man a raise.

Frankie caught herself leaning forward, the better to smell him, and straightened so quickly she was surprised her vertebrae didn't click together. When she finally met Jasper's scrutinizing eyes, she flushed against her will. She did not think anyone had such a searing, insightful gaze as Jasper Jones. It was as if he could see straight through her skull and into her secret mind. She did not like it one bit.

He leaned against the doorframe and crossed his arms. His cravat was crisply white against the strong column of his throat, and his fawn-colored trousers clung to muscled thighs. His shirtsleeves were rolled up to his elbows as if he'd been busy with ledgers and correspondence that morning and did not want to stain them with ink.

"Perdita's reply came with the morning post." He lifted the letter. "Your headmistress apologized for the mix-up, but writes that due to a bout of illness at the agency, she cannot send your replacement for a fortnight."

Frankie did her best not to react with glee. The Dove, the brilliant woman, had bought her another two weeks. Jasper waited, studying her with those dark, stomach-scrambling eyes. Frankie thought he might be waiting for a reply, but she was not sure what he expected her to say.

"Oh, er—holy Queen V! Is it the plague?"

His eyebrows lifted.

Maybe that had been too strong. "What I mean is: I am very sorry everyone is ill."

"Indeed. Against *all* of my better judgment I am going to keep you on for the intervening time. Cecelia has been happy the past few days and I do not wish to upset the routine of her life until your replacement arrives."

Frankie blinked in confusion. Once again he was considering his niece's happiness over his own desire, which was to be rid of Frankie. Could he genuinely care for the orphan who'd been thrust upon him and disrupted his rakish lifestyle?

"I accept your plea to stay," she said. She did not think it was prudent to divulge that Cecelia's happiness was due to planning a surprise soirée that he would hate, rather than her presence.

"It was not a plea. It was an order."

"Please stop begging, Mr. Jones. It does not become you."

Jasper gaped at her. "*Begging*? I assure you, Miss Turner, *I* do not beg."

Frankie took a backward step, her heel sharp on the tile. She suffered from a lack of social graces, but she was aware enough to know she was taunting him, and she could not fathom why. Perhaps it was because he seemed like a man who was so rarely taunted and very much needed to be.

Jasper advanced forward as she continued to walk backward, and she felt a bit like prey being stalked on the plains. "Need I remind you that I am tolerating you because I have little other choice? Rest assured, when your replacement arrives you will be free to torment another hapless family."

"Torment!" Frankie halted her retreat and glared at him. If anyone was being tortured it was she! Why, the man was practically an ogre. He appeared to be genuinely kind to every person in his employ except for her, whom he stared at as if she were a…a…a spy in his house.

Which, Frankie conceded grudgingly, she was. Could Jasper Jones's instincts be that good? She shivered involuntarily. The Dove had told her he was eerily insightful. What if he suspected her true purpose for being there?

Jasper must've seen the shiver because he halted his advance. In a low voice that prickled up her spine he said, "You need not fear me, Miss Turner. I am only a threat to those who scheme to hurt me or my loved ones. As that is not your intent, you have no reason to worry. If that *were* your purpose, I would be very concerned indeed."

Frankie drew herself to her fullest height, and even though that was still a good ten inches below Jasper's, she managed to look down her nose at him. If her sixteen-year-old sister could bravely dash off to help her friend, *she* could face down a man who dispensed threats as easily as he breathed.

"*Mr.* Jones," she said coldly, "I fully respect your stance on the matter, as I feel similarly. Men often underestimate women, but I assure you that if someone were to hurt a person I care for, I would make him pay dearly."

Jasper's lips parted in surprise, but she did not stay to hear what else he had to say. She turned her back on him and flew down the corridor. It was only when she reached the schoolroom that she realized her hands were shaking.

Frankie spent the rest of the day trying to entice Cecelia into the schoolroom, but when she succeeded the girl talked nonstop about flower arrangements, the terrible hunt for a harpist, and food deliveries.

"Perhaps we can calculate the cost," Frankie said desperately, hoping to incorporate even a smidgen of mathematics into the process. Cecelia airily waved her hand and declared that Uncle Jasper was footing the bill, so why bother?

The next day was similarly unproductive. The house was now under a constant flurry of activity, with servants rushing about with armfuls of flowers and trays of crystal. There were maids polishing banisters, footmen heaving boxes, and Mrs. Hollendale storming the corridors snapping out orders with every breath. In short, the house was never still long enough for Frankie to investigate Jasper's study unseen.

When at last she finally did have a chance to discreetly turn the knob to the study, she was disappointed to find that it was indeed locked. She spent that night thinking over her options and decided she needed to visit Hookham's Circulating Library for answers.

The next afternoon, after several hours of a fruitless attempt to harness Cecelia's mind in the sweltering schoolroom, Frankie gave up and dismissed her restless pupil, resigned to the fact that there would be no learning until the soirée was over.

Free for the remainder of the day, Frankie spent the afternoon perusing Hookham's shelves until at last she found the manual she sought. While returning to the Jones residence, book in hand, she fell into deep thought over a mathematics problem she had come across in *The Gentleman's Scholarly Pursuit of Mathematics and Angles*, a wordy journal title that still did not hold the record for most ridiculous name. The authors of the paper claimed their general quantic equation was unsolvable. Frankie had been thinking on it since she'd read the article, and she believed the authors were incorrect. If one applied elliptic functions, it was possible that—

She was so caught up in solving the math problem that she tripped over an apple cart, stepped in a hole left by a loose stone, and nearly ran into the rear end of a horse. Frankie had grand mathematics dreams, but for now she submitted her theorems to established journals under the name Horace P. Smith, taking every precaution to ensure her anonymity, including walking over two miles to mail the letters. It was her greatest secret. Well, now it was *one* of her greatest secrets.

Once Frankie reached her chamber—thankfully without meeting Jasper in the corridor again—she removed her dreadfully hot governess gown, extracted her hairpins, and lay on her bed in her chemise. With her blond hair gathered over one shoulder, she opened the book she'd borrowed from the library and read by the light of the lantern. When she finished, dawn was emerging beyond the window, gray and watery, and her brain was swimming with theory that she somehow needed to convert into skill.

As the first glow of sunlight touched the brick tops of the buildings across the street, Frankie drew the curtains and lay on top of the covers to sleep. Cecelia's soirée was that night, and Frankie knew there would be no wrangling her into lessons. Instead, she rested, because later, when everyone was busy with the soirée, she was going to break into Jasper Jones's study.

Chapter 9

Rockford's was having a particularly slow night. Since it had opened, it had been at full capacity most evenings, unless there was an important ball, and then it always picked up in the wee hours of the morning when the gamblers finally escaped the dance floor.

Jasper adjusted his cuffs, which were pinned with diamond cuff links, and frowned at Guy. "I know it is summer, but I do not believe we have ever had so few patrons. What do you think could be the cause?"

Guy tipped his hat to a customer and shrugged. "New moon?"

A lone lord stumbled near, deep in his cups and prepared to lose an extraordinary amount of money. Jasper owned a gaming hell to make money, not hold leading strings, but he had a limit to what he would take off a drunk man: enough to make it sting, but not enough to bankrupt him. Jasper was keenly aware that a man's fortunes supported a number of dependents, even if many of the men in his hell did not acknowledge the same.

"That ith an easy one," the lord said, stumbling to his knees. He stood again as if the fall had not happened. "They are all at your house."

Jasper stared at him. "What?"

The lord lifted his glass in the air and snickered. "Crush of the summer, that."

The man was not making any sense. Jasper did not hold functions at his house. Ever. He was not a part of the *ton*. He took their money, they looked down their noses at him, and they all coexisted in harmony because he never breached that class barrier. Jasper had no interest in fraternizing with the elite. He was aware there were titled men who would gladly sacrifice their daughters in marriage to Jasper in order to have their debts to Rockford's cleared, but the last thing Jasper wanted was an unwilling wife of noble blood. Why would he? So that she could be pitied and told she had married down her entire life? No thank you. He was much happier playing up his image as an arrogant rake while quietly bedding lonely widows eager to test out the rumors.

Or, at least he *used* to be happy doing that. Even before Cecelia had come to live with him, he had begun to find that part of his life rather tiresome. Jasper did not intend to marry, nor did he yearn for love. Why would he wish for something he'd never had, but that he'd seen ruin countless lives and marriages? Jasper did not need anyone or anything other than his gaming hell and his wits.

Why then had he begun to feel like they weren't enough anymore?

"He is drunk," Guy said. "He knows not of what he speaks."

But something was nagging at the back of Jasper's mind, some piece of information he'd misplaced. He was counting dice at the counter when the hell's butler approached him bearing a silver platter. Atop it was a single, creamy envelope with exquisitely slanted handwriting.

"Mr. Jones," the butler said stiffly, "I am terribly sorry to interrupt, and you know I would not under usual circumstances, however—"

Jasper lifted a brow. "However?"

"The housekeeper at your residence delivered this by hand several hours ago and asked that I give it to you. I told her you have very strict working conditions, but she was really quite insistent." The man blinked, as if he was still rattled by Mrs. Hollendale's fearsome bearing. "I chose to wait until you had a free moment, Mr. Jones, but I did give her my word and—"

"It is all right," Jasper said, hoping to ease some of the butler's distress at breaking protocol. He plucked the thick invitation from the silver tray, his skin humming with foreboding. He broke the wax seal and his eyes raced across the handwritten invitation. It was addressed to him personally, requesting his presence at Cecelia's soirée tonight.

His head snapped up. He'd completely forgotten that tonight was Cecelia's modest gathering with her friends.

Jasper took another sweep of his dead club, and dread skittered down his spine. "I need to go," he shouted to Guy as he sprinted out of the club, and Jasper Jones did not sprint.

Even before he reached the front door of his house a thrill of horror shot down his fingertips. Carriages choked the street so that nary a vehicle could pass. As he approached, Lord and Lady Somerville stepped down from their carriage and greeted him as if he were a part of their set.

"Splendid evening for a soirée, Jones," Lord Somerville said. His muttonchops fluttered with the gentle summer breeze. "I have to hand it to you; the urgent invitation and off-Season timing was a gamble, but you piqued the interest of the entire *ton*. Who would pass over the chance to peek into the legendary home of Mr. Jasper Jones?"

Jasper nodded and smiled and gestured them indoors, all while he thought that he was going to do it: he was going to commit murder.

He entered his home and was immediately struck by the immense size of the crowd. Every room was packed with nobility in their best evening wear and jewels, eager to break up the boredom of a long, hot summer. Music was playing from a hired quartet of strings, and a woman dressed as a Roman was plucking a scrolled golden harp. The air smelled of tobacco smoke and mingled perfumes and roasted meat. Jasper walked past the banquet room and then took two steps backward to gawk at what he saw. A dozen linen-draped tables were stacked with every type of confection, punch, and entrée one might desire: pickled oysters, deviled kidneys, delicately sliced braised beef, Angels on Horseback, Yorkshire pudding, Neapolitan cakes, crepes, soufflé, éclairs, and meringue. There were imported oranges and grapes, candy confections, and plates of olives that looked as if they'd come straight from Greece.

Jasper shook his head and kept moving. Cecelia had taken his offer to spend as much as she pleased and she'd run so far amok she wasn't even on this continent anymore. What on earth had she been thinking?

He at last found his darling niece in the formal sitting room, where tables had been set up for the ladies to play whist and for the gentlemen to play whatever card game they pleased. Even Madam Margaret was present, her gray head tipped back to enjoy the music of the young lady tinkering at the piano in the corner, or perhaps she was asleep. The atmosphere in the room was one of excitement and convivial camaraderie. Everyone was pleased to be back in London for such an unprecedented event.

Cecelia was wearing one of her new altered gowns, a sober gray that seemed to age her by a decade. Jasper frowned as he approached her. When had she grown up? Had she always been so old? He could have sworn when she'd arrived in his care she'd been at least five years younger.

She was chatting animatedly with a woman whose name he struggled to place for a moment, and then it came to him: Lady Evelyn Barker. Her father, the Earl of Elmsdale, was a member of his club, although he was of the conservative set and never gambled.

Lady Evelyn was resplendent, dressed in a pale-lavender gown that brought out the honey color of her eyes, and her chestnut tresses were artfully pinned so that several soft strands escaped and curled at her neck. She had been considered the catch of the Season for three years now, with a dowry large enough to make even the most levelheaded of men green with greed. She suffered no lack of suitors, and yet she remained unwed. A handful of men had lost bets over that. He would know; Rockford's kept the betting book.

Many people seemed to think she was holding out for one gentleman in particular, whoever he might be, but Jasper suspected her father was the true reason she remained unwed. From his observations of Elmsdale at his club, the man was demanding and would accept nothing but the best for his only daughter.

"Uncle Jasper! Here you are!" Cecelia bounded up to him and patted his arm. "Did Mrs. Hollendale and I not pull off a splendid crush?"

"Cecelia, I said you could plan a *small* gathering," he said through clenched teeth. He smiled and waved at a gentleman who'd won a fortune at Rockford's a few weeks earlier.

"Small is a relative term, is it not? This soirée is smaller than a ball, for example."

"You took advantage of my generosity."

She seemed genuinely perplexed. "But, Uncle Jasper, this gathering is for *you*."

"How do you figure that?"

"I am helping you enter society." She beamed up at him, and he was not sure if she was playacting or if she truly believed this to be something he desired. "Uncle, have you met Lady Evelyn Barker?" she asked, drawing him toward Lady Evelyn, who had watched their exchange with feline interest.

Jasper pressed his hand to his chest and inclined his head. "My lady, I am pleased you could make Miss Cecelia's soirée."

"How quaint that you allowed a child to plan your soirée," Lady Evelyn said archly.

Cecelia seemed uncertain whether Lady Evelyn was being snide or kind. Jasper was accustomed to the two-faced nature of society and smiled pleasantly even though he suspected the former. "She did a splendid job."

"I must admit, I am stunned that a midsummer party drew so many guests." *Snide.*

"The *ton* must have desired a brief visit to London."

"Perhaps, but I think it is more that the proprietor of Rockford's took the *risk* of sending an invitation to them!" *Snide again.*

Cecelia's expression turned to one of alarm, and he did his best to suppress a bubble of anger. Cecelia knew they held a different standing in society, but she did not—and how could she?— understand how forward and presumptuous it had been for him to ostensibly invite the entire *ton* to his house, during the middle of summer, and with extremely short notice. For half his life he had worked tirelessly to entertain the *ton* while remaining in his "place," and this soirée had just blurred the lines. If the lords and ladies of London's upper crust thought he supposed himself on their level, it would affect his business at Rockford's. The *ton* enjoyed nothing more than keeping everyone firmly in his or her place.

Jasper glanced around the room, noting the sprays of fresh-cut flowers, the fat cigars lined in rows on silver trays, the crystal decanters filled with liquors, and the stacks of unopened playing cards. He recalled the harpist and the quartet and the mountains of food, and he nearly groaned at the uncouth display of wealth. Luxury and opulence were all well and good when it was for the *ton*'s benefit; it was not so well received when it showcased how wealthy he'd become taking *their* money.

In short, it was a disaster, but he had no choice but to smile and greet and pretend the abomination had his blessing.

"I hope everyone enjoys themselves at this one-time gathering." Jasper nodded to Lady Evelyn and was about to depart, but Cecelia clung to his arm.

"Lady Evelyn has shared that she adores a challenging game of whist," Cecelia said hastily. "I cannot imagine anyone giving her more of a challenge than you, Uncle."

Lady Evelyn fluttered her eyelashes. "What a splendidly unrehearsed request."

Snide.

Cecelia heard the sarcasm that time, but before she could say anything Lady Evelyn added, "I would be delighted; it is difficult to find a worthy whist player, do you not agree, Mr. Jones? We shall partner with my two friends." She waved to a couple of women fluttering fans at their faces across the room. The women hurried over, and before Jasper knew it, he was seated with the three of them while one of the women expertly dealt the cards. Cecelia stood at the edge of the room and smiled brightly at him.

Lady Evelyn leaned toward him, a light floral scent clinging to her skin, and whispered, "Shall we devise a secret code?"

"That is cheating," Jasper said flatly and nodded as another card was handed to him.

Taken aback by his tone, Lady Evelyn sniffed. "And here I was led to believe you were a touch wild. I should have thought if anyone knew how to have a good time it would be a gambler."

Jasper altered his suspicions about why Lady Evelyn remained unmarried despite all the reports of suitors. Although she was objectively beautiful, there was something ugly about her personality. She may be clever and cunning, but he did not think she was particularly kind.

Jasper's blood chilled at the thought. Good lord, when had he started caring about a woman's *personality*? What was happening to him? He was a man of brief affairs—when had a woman's kindness or lack thereof ever mattered?

She laughed, mistaking the source of his horror. "Do not appear so aghast, Mr. Jones. I shall not divulge your great secret: that the powerful Mr. Jones is in fact rather docile."

Jasper gave her such a feral smile that she shrank back. These people treated him as if he were a domesticated lapdog that had forgotten how to bite. "Excellent idea, Lady Evelyn. You have your reputation to uphold and I have mine. There is no cheating at Rockford's and there will be no cheating here."

"What shall we play for?" one of her friends asked with a sly giggle.

The last thing Jasper wanted was to part someone's wife from her pin money. "No bets. Your company will lend this game all the exhilaration it needs."

Jasper had his cards discreetly fanned in his hand when movement at the door caught his attention. A woman entered the sitting room with the hesitancy of someone who was not sure if she was supposed to be there. She was shrouded in a soft pink gown that accentuated her corseted waist, the dipping neckline baring a hint of cleavage so tantalizing his skin tingled. Her silky blond hair tumbled defiantly from atop her head, and her eyes were an angelic blue behind wide, round spectacle lenses.

No, it couldn't be. Was that his *governess*?

Jasper's stomach clenched as pure, unexpected lust seared through him. After a lifetime of concealing his emotions, he was an expert in masking his appetites, but for once he found it difficult to bank the roar of undiluted desire that swept through his veins when Frankie looked his way. Her lashes dropped and she averted her eyes, but then she lifted them again to meet his stare. This time, he let the mask of indifference fall away, exposing all of his raw and primal need. Jasper gave her a slow smile, and she took a shuddering breath.

Lady Evelyn followed the direction of his gaze and her eyes sharpened. "Who is that?"

Jasper cleared his throat. "That is Miss Francis Turner, Cecelia's governess."

Lady Evelyn gave a brittle smile. "Yes, of course she is a governess. I can see it now in the quality of her gown. A *lady* would not wear so little ornamentation. And the hemline! My goodness. Did a seamstress stitch that in the dark?"

Her two companions giggled, and Jasper, who thought he would do anything to avoid burning bridges with potential clients and their families, discovered that he would not. He stood abruptly and gave a curt bow to Lady Evelyn.

"You must excuse me. I need to speak with Miss Turner about Cecelia."

Lady Evelyn frowned and her friends squealed in dismay. Jasper turned his back on them and walked toward Frankie, who was generating an unacceptable amount of interest from a few of the younger gentlemen.

The fourth son of an earl had his lips on the back of her glove when Jasper approached and growled, "That is my niece's governess."

The man quickly straightened, and the stupidly adoring expression on his face faltered when he met Jasper's stare. "Mr. Jones," he said and waved to nobody in particular before adding, "I am needed; if you will please excuse me." He hurried from the room. He owed Rockford's more than he could afford to pay, and his eldest brother would once again need to settle the bill. The earl's pockets were not Jasper's problem, but his governess attracting the attention of destitute gamblers was.

"Did you know about this?" he demanded. He did not mean to sound so surly, but he was frustrated about the gathering, and Frankie seemed the perfect person to take it out on.

"I presume you speak of the soirée? Only after the invitations were sent out."

"You did not think to apprise me?"

"No."

Jasper waited, but Frankie did not seem to see the need to expound further. "May I remind you that you are employed by me, not Cecelia?"

Frankie tilted her head. "Why would you think to remind me of that? I am not addlepated, Mr. Jones."

Jasper did not know if she was being deliberately dense or if she was really so socially awkward. If he had to guess, it was the latter. "Do you know why Cecelia felt the need to throw such a large and extraordinarily expensive soirée?"

"Oh my, I believe Cecelia is calling me over." She went to step forward but Jasper settled his hand lightly on her wrist.

"Miss Turner," he said, his mouth hovering over her rose-scented hair, "I know a bluff when I hear one."

Chapter 10

Frankie had spotted Jasper as soon as she'd entered the sitting room. He'd been seated at a card table, the very picture of languid grace and devilish charm, his legs outstretched and a set of cards fanned in hands that were entirely too nimble and clever. He'd looked so at home in the atmosphere of gambling that she had not for a moment doubted he'd been made for his life's work.

The trio of women with whom he'd sat had been eyeing him from beneath their lashes and sharing giggles with one another. The loveliest of them was a woman with a dewy complexion that only nymphs in paintings were supposed to have. Cecelia had kept sending sly glances toward the beautiful woman and Jasper, but the woman had not noticed because her focus had been entirely on Jasper, and Jasper had been staring at *Frankie* in what could only be described as disbelief. Then something else had flickered in his eyes before he'd quickly shuttered it.

Frankie did not have a lot of success discerning facial expressions, but she was trying to learn because she knew a surprising amount could be communicated without a single word. A lifted chin could mean defiance, hurt feelings, or pride. A tilted head meant sympathy or concern. A sniff was a dismissal—something she'd experienced often in her first governess placement. She had been trying to pay attention, to master this subtle language, and she'd thought she was making progress. For instance, in the short time she had known Jasper, she had discovered that he tended to narrow his eyes when he was irritated. He smiled in a cavalier way when he was concealing his emotions, and he appeared to be lackadaisical and unassuming, except his sharp and assessing eyes always gave away his intelligence.

The flicker she had seen in his eyes upon her entrance had been so brief that she hadn't been able to study it. All she'd known was that it made her feel flustered and confused, and a bit like a butterfly under the scrutiny of a scientist who had not yet classified her.

Jasper's arm had remained casually propped on the table, the cards a flash of white in a hand that sported more nicks and scars than a gentleman's would, but then she'd made eye contact with him again, and something had buzzed between them. The energy in the room had crackled, and it had taken Frankie several moments to realize he was allowing her to see what he'd instinctively concealed at first sight of her: lust.

Impossible. She must be misreading the situation. No one had ever looked at Frankie *like that*. Her mother had made it clear that men were not attracted to messy and absent women with more brains than grace.

Even knowing she was wrong, Frankie's stays had suddenly felt too tight. Jasper had given her a slow, smoldering smile that had heated the room a degree or two. If she were not entirely sure she was mistaken about his intentions, she might have faltered. Maybe even fled the room.

Fortunately, Frankie knew Jasper deeply disliked her, and she him.

"Miss Turner, I know a bluff when I hear one," he said, his lips hovering far too close to the naked skin of her neck as he halted her escape.

"Mr. Jones," she replied in her best stern governess voice, "unhand me."

"Have some propriety, young man," Madam Margaret chided, slapping him with her fan as she tottered past, drawing more than a few amused looks. It was a rare occurrence to see the fearsome Jasper Jones put in his place by an eighty-year-old maiden aunt.

Jasper instantly complied, nodding respectfully to Cecelia's aunt, but he was right: Frankie was bluffing about Cecelia calling her over. Once Madam Margaret had moved into the next room, Frankie tried to steer the topic into safer territory. "What do you think of Cecelia's new gown?"

"It makes her look too old."

"Do not be absurd; her dress is perfectly respectable for a fifteen-year-old girl. She could not continue going about in those hideous short dresses."

"Indeed, yet I did not expect her to present so differently. I will have to keep a closer eye on her now. She is only fifteen and I will not abide her drawing the attention of desperate lords with one foot in the grave hoping for an arranged match."

Frankie's breath caught in her lungs and her fingertips tingled in her gloves. "You do not believe in marriages with a large age difference in general, or only when it applies to Cecelia?"

He gave her a strange look. "I do not believe in arranged marriages at all. Should not everyone have a say in who he or she foolishly chains themselves to?"

Frankie's heart was beating so loudly she could hear the blood rushing in her ears. If he was lying about his feelings on marriage then he was doing a masterly job of it, and if he was not, then as the Dove suspected, he was innocent of the dowry thieving scheme. No man who felt as he did could coldly sentence a woman to a life of matrimonial misery against her will.

And still…she had to search his office to be sure. The Dove would not be satisfied with even a single stone unturned. When one regularly accused powerful men of the *ton* of crimes, one had to be entirely certain of their guilt. Eliminating Jasper as a suspect was an important part of narrowing down who was truly ruining the women's lives.

"Yes, every woman should have a say in who she marries."

Jasper's gaze dropped to her rose-petal gown. "Cecelia is not the only one who traded in her hideous dresses."

Frankie straightened to her full height, which did not even bring her to Jasper's chin. "That is very *rude*, Mr. Jones. I wear the governess uniform because it is considered proper for my position." Even if it *was* sinfully ugly.

"The governess uniform is an eyesore and should be banished to the back of the armoire."

"A governess gown is designed to be both modest and appropriate."

Jasper absently adjusted the handkerchief in his breast pocket. "No woman should dress in disagreeable clothes for modesty's sake."

Frankie's eyes rounded in delight. "I quite agree! What do you think of the corset? It is a torture device, is it not? Are you for the women's cause, Mr. Jones?"

"I certainly love women."

"That is not what I—"

"Mr. Jones." The walking Renaissance painting interrupted Frankie mid-sentence, her expression tight and speculative. She'd abandoned the card table, leaving her two female companions seeking another couple. "Surely whatever your governess needs could wait until the morrow? Education is all well and good, but to interrupt a social function to discuss mundane matters is quite bold, would you not say?"

Frankie turned the sweetly said statement over in her mind and concluded that the Renaissance painting had meant to cut her by implying that she was an ignorant tutor who'd risen above her station and interrupted the soirée to discuss Cecelia's education. Frankie's cheeks flamed.

"Lady Evelyn, may I introduce Miss Francis Turner, who is a *guest* this evening."

Ah-ha! So the dewy-soft woman was the lady Cecelia was hoping to make Mrs. Jones. Lady Evelyn was certainly beautiful enough, if one went for the perfect and voluptuous look. Not a honey-brown hair was out of place on her head, and her gown was flawlessly tailored and unwrinkled. Beside her, Frankie felt like the short, messy spinster she was.

Frankie curtsied and did exactly as her mother always begged her to do in social situations: She lied. "It is a pleasure to meet you."

Evelyn fluttered her fan at her chest. "Indeed."

Frankie did not know why the lady needed a fan when she was already sculpted of ice.

Cecelia hurried over, looped her hand through the crook of Jasper's arm, and beamed up at Evelyn. "My lady, you are even more beautiful than Uncle Jasper said you were."

Jasper's eyes flickered toward Cecelia, but he didn't correct her.

Frankie's stomach dipped. Of course he would find Lady Evelyn beautiful. She was exactly the sort of woman a man like Jasper would be attracted to. How could Frankie have thought for a single moment that a man as handsome and sensual as Jasper Jones would find *her* attractive, when wealthy and beautiful women like Lady Evelyn surrounded him? Had she forgotten who she was? Did she need to recall her mother's cutting words as a reminder? *My dear daughter, even if you tried very hard to act stupid so that a man would not be threatened by you, there is little I can do about your poor eyesight and unremarkable features.*

Frankie must not allow herself to forget again. It was too painful.

Evelyn continued fluttering her fan and slanted Jasper a cunning look. "What a charming child you have." To Cecelia she said, "Did your uncle say anything else?"

"Only that you remind him of a poem that once made him sob into his tea with its beauty." Cecelia smiled wickedly at Jasper, daring him to contradict her in front of Evelyn. "He said you remind him of that Greek goddess, what is her name, the gilded goddess of passion?"

"Aphrodite," Frankie murmured before she could stop herself.

"Yes, that is it. Lady Evelyn, Uncle Jasper thinks you are the embodiment of Aphrodite!"

"That is enough, Cecelia." Jasper's tone was light, but the warning in his eyes was clear.

"Oh, do not be embarrassed, Mr. Jones." Lady Evelyn shifted the fan to beat it around her face. "You are not the first to notice the resemblance between me and a Greek goddess. And here I was thinking you must find me repulsive with how you left our game of whist! Did you know last week Lord Tremfield wrote a song for me entitled 'Aphrodite's Aphrodisiac of Beauty.' You are in noble company, Mr. Jones."

Jasper swallowed.

"Miss Turner, will you accompany me to the buffet table?" Cecelia asked. Jasper opened his mouth, but Cecelia already had Frankie by the arm and was plowing through the crowd.

"That was not subtle, Cecelia."

Cecelia's cheeks were flushed with excitement. "What do you think of her? Lady Evelyn, I mean."

"She is pretty."

"She is pretty, and I am afraid not very nice, but she and Uncle Jasper will have the cutest, fattest little babes."

"Do you not think you are getting ahead of yourself? Your uncle has told me himself that he is not the marrying type. I do not see him proposing to Lady Evelyn before the night is out."

"No, he is definitely not the marrying type," Cecelia agreed. "If left to his own devices, Uncle Jasper would remain a bachelor forever with far too much time to meddle. I admit my timeline was a touch too hopeful. I shall have to orchestrate a few more meetings between them, where eventually Uncle Jasper will find himself in a compromising situation with Lady Evelyn. He is honorable, or at least I think he is, and he will play the hand dealt to him and marry her to save her reputation."

For the second time that night Frankie forgot how to breathe. "Cecelia, how could you even consider such a ploy? Does your uncle encourage that sort of duplicity?"

Cecelia scanned the obscene number of desserts on the table. "No, Uncle Jasper has strange morals. He thinks some things are all right that other people do not, but then there are socially acceptable things that he finds appalling, like forced unions. But often women are not given a choice about who they have to marry, so why should men have one?"

"That is true, but it does not make it right."

Cecelia paused in the act of lifting a cake from a tray, her brow furrowed. "You are weighting down my excitement, Miss Turner. I am off to chat with the lovely Miss Wharton, who is still unmarried but purportedly has a fine sense of humor."

Frankie watched her go with a sinking feeling in the pit of her stomach. Cecelia had only cemented her suspicion that she was wasting her time in Jasper Jones's household.

Frankie spent the next half hour wandering the soirée feeling invisible, but enjoying the scents and sights all the more for it. She did not have to make small talk—thank heavens!—and instead was able to view the party through the eyes of a fly on the wall.

The soirée was a smashing success. Who would have thought the gentry could be enticed from the country for a last-minute gathering at the home of someone other than a duke? The guests in attendance were greeting one another as if it had been years rather than months since they'd last parted. As the night wore on, the liquor levels dropped and the gambling and dancing increased. The harpist continued long after the quartet had departed to take a lengthy break, and the notes wrapped around the guests as if lulling them into a trance. Frankie had never seen such a relaxed atmosphere. Did the lords and ladies feel as if they could shake off some of the restrictions of their class because of where they were?

Eventually Frankie took a seat in the morning room where several different games were being played: poker, whist, and Vingt et Un. It was choked with pipe smoke, and men with loosened cravats and intense expressions gambled with piles of notes and trinkets like gold rings and diamond cuff links. The mood was rife with excitement and anticipation, and Frankie wondered if this was a small taste of how Rockford's felt each night.

She sat in a chair pushed against the wall to watch a game of poker. She had never played before, but it did not take her long to figure out the gist of it. In that same amount of time, she realized with dismay that a gentleman with red hair and muttonchops was cheating.

Knowing that if he were caught it would ruin the reputation of Cecelia's soirée, Frankie looked around in alarm to see if anyone else was aware. The heat of a gaze across the room drew her attention like a magnet, and her eyes clashed with Jasper's over the dozens of heads. He was leaning against the wall with his arms crossed, chatting with a portly gentleman whose waistcoat strained at the buttons. Even though he was speaking to the gentleman, Jasper's dark eyes were entirely focused on her. For a moment Frankie felt as if all the noise and bustle of the room were fading, until it was only the two of them. Then she tore her eyes from his and glanced at the redheaded man and then back. In response, Jasper slowly shook his head.

Frankie exhaled with relief, the weight of responsibility leaving her shoulders. Jasper knew the man was cheating. He dealt with this sort of thing every night; he would take care of it.

Content that all was well and Jasper was properly engaged, Frankie decided there would be no better opportunity to slip away. It was time she discovered what secrets lay hidden behind Jasper's study door.

Chapter 11

Jasper's eyes followed Frankie as she left the room, noting the far-too-interested gazes of half a dozen men. He doubted she had any idea the effect she had. Most of the women at the soirée were outfitted in feathers, flowers, jewels, and braided silks. Frankie, in her simplicity, was drawing all the more attention because of her lack of adornment. As Lady Evelyn had so snippily pointed out, Frankie's gown was plain and sleek and pink, and it made him think of other things that were sleek and pink.

A tingling sensation crawled over the back of his neck when one of the men—Lord Tarton—exited behind Frankie.

Jasper excused himself from the boring conversation he'd been suffering through, and began to follow Lord Tarton when he remembered the cheating. Halfway across the room he veered to the poker table and bent his head to say in Mr. Jonathan Parkin's ear, "Make your excuses and acquit yourself of my house immediately."

The redhead was the spare to an earldom and he curled his lip at Jasper. "Beg your pardon? Do you know to whom you speak?"

Jasper's expression remained firmly pleasant. "I suggest you leave quietly before Lord Barlow discovers you've been culling cards." Lord Barlow was staring at his hand while sweat beaded on his forehead. He was a bullfrog of a man, with wide shoulders and an ugly face. He had an ugly temper, too, and everyone knew it.

Jasper straightened and strode across the room without a backward glance. He did not need to wait and see if Mr. Jonathan Parkin had the common sense to follow Jasper's request: He knew he would. For all of his bravado, Parkin would not want to be caught cheating by the likes of Barlow. Jasper made a mental note to revoke Parkin's membership to Rockford's.

What was far more interesting than Parkin having the poor sense to risk antagonizing Barlow to begin with, was the extraordinary fact that within minutes of entering the room his governess had known Parkin was cheating. He'd seen it in the flash of alarm on her face, and then she had lifted her head and scanned the room to see if anyone else had noticed. He'd been afraid she was going to do something unwise, such as call out the cheat in front of the entire room, so he'd shaken his head to let her know that he saw and he would handle it. She'd appeared immensely relieved.

All of this begged the question—*how* did she know? There were experienced gamblers who would not have been able to tell what Parkin was doing, and yet a governess had? A governess who was also able to count cards? Something was afoot. Frankie Turner was not a typical governess, and Jasper was determined to discover exactly what she was doing in his house and for whom she worked.

But first he was going to follow Lord Tarton and make sure the man didn't do anything extremely stupid.

Jasper, always fleet of foot, followed silently behind Tarton, who weaved and rounded the corridor bend a shade too narrowly, stubbing his shoulder against the wall and propelling himself backward a few feet. Jasper shook his head in disgust. As a fishmonger's son in one of the poorest sections of England, he had seen men find the only comfort they knew in the bottom of a bottle. It was a source of heat when there was barely enough coal for the fire; it was a lick of bravery when one silently suffered beneath tyrants. Jasper knew there were demons that could be silenced, if only for a short while, by alcohol.

He also knew there were demons that could be brought forth. He'd seen men spend every ha'penny to their name for a night with the bottle while their children starved. He'd seen men provoke fights and he'd heard of them beating their wives. The effects of alcohol on the men of the *ton* were no different. Money didn't change man's basic nature; it only raised the stakes.

Jasper drank, but he never drank to excess. He had made his choice early on when he'd needed his wits about him while playing cards.

Lord Tarton was too deep in his cups to realize he was being followed. Jasper watched his bobbing back as Tarton turned down the corridor toward the sitting room. Farther ahead, Frankie's bare shoulders were visible in the shadows cast by the candelabras. She paused outside of Jasper's study door and peered over her shoulder, perhaps alerted by the sound of Tarton's unsteady footsteps.

Jasper swung his body to the wall and waited. He was in a shadow behind a bust of some war general or other that he'd inherited with the house, and he did not think she'd seen him. The tingling at the back of his neck amplified, and his fingers twitched as Lord Tarton walked toward her, swayed, and then stumbled straight past.

Jasper exhaled a breath he hadn't known he'd been holding, but then his eyes narrowed as Frankie, relieved to be alone in the corridor now, reached forward and twisted the knob to his study. The study he had made clear no one was to enter.

Curiosity mingled with irritation as he waited to see what she would do next. She knelt to the ground and peered through the keyhole before removing a slender tool from the pocket of her gown. Bloody hell, was she going to pick the lock on his study door?

Jasper silently advanced, and when he was not two feet from her, he heard her muttering, "The book says the Detector lock is foolproof, but the chances of that are not as good as Chubb and Son's may think. Now I'm supposed to move the pins, but heavens, that seems much easier said than done."

Well there went any theory of her being a master spy.

"Careful," Jasper said, "if you lift the wrong pin the lock will seize. I shall then require a regulating key and I would be most displeased."

Frankie squeaked, popped to her feet, and whirled around. Her eyes rounded with horror. "Holy Queen V! Mr. Jones, you nearly frightened me to death. I did not know you were behind me."

"That is apparent."

Frankie had the lock-picking tool hidden behind her back, and her chest was lifting and falling at a rate that gave away her anxiety. After a moment she gathered herself enough to meet him square in the eye. To his annoyance, she said nothing. She made no halfhearted excuses, did not beg his forgiveness, did not admit to any nefarious scheme. She only gazed at him, those blue eyes behind her spectacles sparkling with—frustration? Yes indeed, how dare he interrupt her prying into *his* private matters.

Jasper's need for answers edged out his patience. "Who are you, Miss Turner? You are not simply a governess."

"What do you mean?"

"For one, you count cards."

Frankie blinked owlishly, and then a soft groan escaped her lips. "Do not tell me: Cecelia?"

"Imagine my surprise when my niece challenged me to game of Vingt et Un and then proceeded to cheat right in front of me."

Frankie grimaced. "I never suspected Cecelia would use the strategies I taught her beyond the schoolroom. And here I thought myself so clever for finding an amusing way to teach her mathematics."

"Mathematics?"

Frankie nodded, and her spectacles slid dangerously far down her nose. She shoved at the frames and said, "I shall have to speak with her so that she does not fleece your guests."

Jasper experienced a jolt of alarm. "She had better not!" Even as he said it, he knew there was a good chance Cecelia was doing exactly that. "What on earth were you thinking teaching her that? No, forget that question. I do not need to tumble into the inner workings of your mind. Rather, I would like to know who taught *you* how to cheat at cards."

A line appeared between Frankie's blond brows. "No one."

"You expect me to believe that?"

She lifted a bared shoulder. "It is the truth. Cecelia taught me how to play and the strategies just"—she waved a hand in the air—"appeared." Her cheeks reddened as she took in his dark stare. "It sounds mad, I know."

Jasper studied the delicate blush of embarrassment, the wire-rimmed spectacles that were far too large for her narrow face, and the blond wisps of hair that were curling on her neck. If she was pretending, she was better at artifice than anyone he'd ever met—and he'd been rubbing shoulders with con men since he was a child.

Without considering the impulse, Jasper reached forward and brushed a strand of hair off her throat, letting his fingertips linger for a moment at the base of her neck. "And how did you know the redheaded man was cheating?"

Frankie blushed harder and pushed his arm down. "I just knew. I do not know how else to explain it."

If she was telling the truth, it would mean she was a once-in-a-lifetime mathematics genius rather than a plant from a competing gaming hell.

"I vow not to teach Cecelia any more strategies. Now if that is cleared up, you must excuse—"

Jasper gave a short bark of laughter. "We are hardly finished here, Miss Turner. You may have an unusual ability to understand cards and probabilities, but we have not yet addressed the reason you attempted to break into my study. The study I explicitly warned you not to enter."

Frankie bit her lip. "It was an accident?"

"An accident?"

"I thought it was the library? Oh goodness, is this your study? Holy Queen V, what a mistake that would have been, since you have expressly forbidden anyone from entering it. How fortunate you happened upon me and halted me from making such a grievous error."

He could smell roses on her skin, warmed by female heat, and he was surprised by the sudden urge to bury his nose in her neck. "The library door is wide-open. I can see the books from here."

"Ah. Right. But I have poor eyesight, you see."

She'd been telling the truth about how she'd learned her card counting skills, because she was, in fact, a terrible liar. Jasper mentally filed away that tidbit for future reference but could not help poking a bit more, just to see how far she would run with her ridiculous lie.

"That makes sense," he said gravely.

"It does? I mean, of course it does."

"Only I wonder why you have lock-picking tools on your person then? And why you would attempt to pick the library lock rather than fetch Mrs. Hollendale for the key?"

Frankie bit her lip again, and he could not stop his eyes from dropping to that frustratingly plush mouth. "I...I..."

He took pity on her. "Miss Turner, if you think I believe any of this, you must not know how I built Rockford's."

"How *did* you build Rockford's?" she asked, instantly curious.

"With ruthlessness and a talent for seeing through lies."

Frankie wrinkled her nose. "In that case I retract my explanation."

"That is wise. Are you ready to tell me the truth?"

The little fox actually stopped to think about it!

Jasper Jones had dealt with humanity long enough that very little surprised him, but he was utterly stunned by what she did next.

Instead of answering his question, Frankie reached up, wrapped her hand behind his neck, and dragged his mouth to hers.

Chapter 12

S he'd panicked.

The Dove had warned her that Jasper Jones was clever, but Frankie had not understood how clever he was at *reading* people. It was absolutely fascinating the way he was able to discern a truth from a lie simply by studying a person's face and the tiny reactions he or she exhibited. For someone like Frankie, who half the time could not even tell when someone was being sarcastic, such a talent was as unimaginable as being able to juggle flaming swords.

It also gave her the strangest sense of being kept on her toes. Frankie had always been book-smart, and had she not been blessed with an equally clever sister, she would have had an extraordinarily dull childhood. In Fidelia she had found someone with whom she could develop codes and equations. They had played games with elaborate rules that other children would not have comprehended, and they had pushed one another to greater conceptual understandings. Frankie had been disappointed when she'd ventured into the world and discovered that very few people were as extraordinary as her sister. The Dove was one of them; Frankie would not wager on matching her wits with *that* woman.

Jasper was another, even though they'd had entirely different childhoods. Frankie had been raised in a genteelly impoverished household that could not afford a governess, but they had always had food on the table and coal in the grate. Jasper had been raised on a wharf as a fishmonger's son, and she doubted food and heat had ever been a given. Frankie and her sister had taught themselves how to read and write and calculate using dusty tomes from the library. Schooling had likely never been an option for Jasper. Frankie had been taught—or at least her mother had attempted to teach her—how to smile and nod her head and laugh and be generally pleasant. Jasper had taken the opposite approach—ascending to his position in life through sheer ruthlessness.

And yet despite all their differences, Frankie was certain that if it came to a battle of wits, Jasper would have her on the run. In him she had found an equal, and the feeling gave her a thrilling sense of satisfaction.

Unfortunately, that meant that when he'd caught her trying to break into his study, he had not fallen for her lies, not even a little bit. And Frankie simply hadn't known what to do to extricate herself from the situation. She could not admit the truth, and every other scenario she'd quickly thought of and discarded had all led back to the same conclusion: Jasper would not allow her to leave without a satisfactory explanation for her presence at his study door.

So she'd taken the biggest gamble of her spinster life, and she'd kissed him.

When she'd tugged Jasper's mouth to hers, it had been with the full expectation that he would pull back in shock, possibly horror, thus giving her the opportunity to run away in faux tears and spinsterly humiliation.

But he didn't pull away.

He kissed her back.

None of Frankie's factual or forbidden reading had prepared her for the warm, dry pressure of Jasper's mouth on hers. How could she have ever imagined the way the rasp of his stubble would feel on her skin? Or how he would smell of aftershave and spice? Or that she'd be able to taste the liquor he'd drunk earlier on his lips as they gently moved over hers?

With aching slowness, Jasper tugged her lower lip between his teeth and sucked.

Frankie jerked her head back and touched her fingertips to her bottom lip. It was wet and plump from his attention.

Jasper arched a brow, but he did not shift away from where he'd crowded her closer to the door. His breathing was erratic and his pupils dilated, but his tone was cool when he said, "Now if you are done distract—"

Frankie lifted onto the balls of her feet and hastily pressed her mouth to his again, smothering the words. This time Jasper slid his palm around her waist, the heat of his hand searing through her corset as he pulled her forward, pinning her to the warm breadth of his body.

Although he held her closely, he hesitated for a moment, pulling back so that his lips hovered over hers. He was offering her a moment to change her mind, to slap him, to draw away in horror. She probably should. No, she *definitely* should, but she was burning and far too curious about what he would do if she stayed.

So she waited, her face tilted in invitation for him to press his lips to hers again, and was surprised when instead his hot mouth began to drift, feathering along her temple. She *shivered* when he continued his torturously light exploration, tracing his lips down her cheek and placing a soft kiss just below her jaw. "Open for me," he murmured.

There was something about the deep silk of his voice that made her anxious to do his bidding. Jasper lifted his head to stare at her wet, parted mouth, and his thumb dragged over her bottom lip. "Have you been kissed like this before?"

"No." Her voice was so thick she barely recognized it.

"Do you want to be?"

There were a hundred reasons to say no: spinsters still had reputations to uphold, she was a governess, she was spying on him... And there was only one reason to say yes: She desperately wanted to be kissed. For once, she wanted to feel desired.

"Yes."

Jasper made a noise in the back of his throat and pressed his mouth to hers, stroking his tongue inside in a hot, languid lick that had her toes curling in her slippers. His tongue continued to rub against hers, intimately, sensuously, and for one of the few times in her life, Frankie felt completely inadequate in the face of his skill. She was certain what Jasper was doing was considered wicked and immoral by polite society.

And she was certain she wanted more.

She eagerly tangled her tongue with his. In response to her boldness, he tightened his arms around her and made a growling sound. He pushed her against the door to the study, and when Frankie's shoulder blades met the cool wood it sent a shiver of excitement through her. He tilted her head back with his hand on her jaw and took full advantage of her mouth, the pace of the kiss changing from sweet and exploring to heated and ravaging, his lips moving with such unrestrained lust that she began to feel hot and confused and driven to a height of arousal that seemed to have no peak. She pulled on his shoulders, the lock-picking tools in her hand digging into his coat, encouraging him so close that he was almost crushing her against the door with his weight. If only she could get near enough, then maybe this burning need low in her belly would be sated.

A door slammed down the corridor, exploding into the moment like the crack of a whip. They sprang apart, Frankie's breaths coming out in shallow bursts and her pulse pounding in her throat. She was certain her lips and face were red from the abrasion of his stubble. If someone were to catch them like this—she felt ill at the very thought of the consequences.

Guilt, entirely too late on the draw, finally swooped in to reclaim her senses. She'd been positioned in his house to search his papers, not his mouth. What had she been *thinking*? She hadn't been, that was the problem. What had started as a solution to being caught trying to break into his study had quickly spiraled into something so much more.

It was little consolation that for the first time since she'd met him, Jasper, too, seemed off-balance, his hair mussed and his breathing uneven.

Without a word, Frankie slipped underneath his arm and escaped down the corridor. When she reached the stairs she lifted her skirts and began to run, her brain a thousand jumbled thoughts that refused to clarify into anything that made sense. She was a bundle of nerves from the kisses. She felt raw and exposed, surprised and confused to have reacted to Jasper in such a powerful way. She felt stunned that he had kissed her back in the first place. Had *continued* kissing her.

When she reached her chamber, she locked the door and ripped at her gown. Once free of her dress and corset, she slid to the floor and dropped her forehead into her hands.

Her sister was out there somewhere, and while the Dove hunted for her, Frankie had failed at her only task. Worse, she'd kissed the very man she'd been sent to investigate, even if she no longer considered him a suspect.

As a devout bachelor and infamous rake, Jasper should have passed Cecelia's needs onto a female relative or some other caretaker. Instead, he'd become actively involved in her life—to the point where Cecelia was trying to marry him off so that she might have some peace. He had refused to allow Cecelia to attend the Houndsbury house party as if he were an overprotective father rather than the king of London's underworld. To soothe Cecelia's hurt feelings, he had then permitted her to throw a soirée. When she'd run amok, he'd been angry, but Frankie knew Cecelia's punishment would be a scolding at best—and the girl knew it, too. In fact, Frankie would go so far as to say Jasper was a pushover when it came to his niece. Would the Jasper Jones she had come to know, who protected his fifteen-year-old niece like she was his own daughter, also trick other young women into marriage with cruel men?

Her gut response was a vehement *no*. Logically speaking, his care of Cecelia brought her to the same answer. And it wasn't just his care for Cecelia, but for everyone under his roof, including Cecelia's great-aunt, whom he had not been under any obligation to take in, but had anyway. On Frankie's first day Jasper had been demanding and rude and intimidating, and yet in her short time there she'd been amazed to discover that he was intensely adored by his staff. His house ran smoothly not out of fear, but loyalty. The silver was polished because the maids did not want to disappoint him. The larder was stocked because the cook wanted to please him. His clothes were laundered and finely brushed because his valet respected him. If she had to guess, she would say Rockford's operated in much the same way, which was no doubt part of the secret to its success. Could a man who inspired such fealty also conceal a darker side?

Then there was the matter of his finances. Frankie had not yet succeeded in finding his ledgers, but if the gathering below was any indication, Jasper was not lacking in funds. When a woman with the breeding and standing of Lady Evelyn was willing to overlook a man's common birth and lack of title, then he must be extraordinarily wealthy indeed. Why, then, would Jasper risk it all to pocket a little side money from orchestrating a morally filthy racket? It simply did not make sense.

Frankie lifted her head and sighed. She knew in her heart that as annoying and conceited as he could be, Jasper Jones was innocent. All she had to do now was prove it to the Dove.

Chapter 13

Jasper said his goodbyes to the last guests at 5:00 a.m. Cecelia was still awake, although she was drooping like a wilted flower. Her hair was in disarray, her gown was splattered with punch, and she couldn't string three words together without yawning. Jasper was accustomed to keeping late hours and would only require the morning to recover. Cecelia, he suspected, would sleep most of the day.

"When you awaken," Jasper warned, "we are having a talk."

Cecelia smiled sleepily at the bottom of the steps. "Was it not thrilling, Uncle? You spoke with so many beautiful, unmarried women. I could not have dreamed of a more successful soirée."

Warning bells jangled softly in the back of Jasper's mind. Why should Cecelia mention that so many of the women were unmarried?

He was about to ask that very question when she called out, "Good night!" and raced up the stairs with a burst of energy. Jasper stared after her. That made two women now who'd run from him rather than discuss Cecelia's motives for the lavish party.

Jasper scrubbed a hand over his face and loosened his cravat, his thoughts returning yet again to the kiss with Frankie. She'd kissed him, and he'd responded in a way that defied good sense. Yes, she was beautiful in an unorthodox, messy way that was mostly adorable and at times shockingly lusty. Any man would have kissed her back—except Jasper was not any man. He was her *employer* and he had a strict rule about fraternizing with his staff. He had always thought men who consorted with their servants were abusing their power, and he wanted no part of that. There were enough willing women in the world; he did not need to make some poor housemaid fear losing her job if she said no to him. He also had no interest in mixing his personal life with his professional life. When he had an affair with a woman, he took her to a separate house he kept for that purpose.

He had rules, and his reasons for them were good; and yet when Frankie had kissed him, he could not recall a single one of them. He hadn't meant to kiss her so thoroughly, but he had become so lost in her, so consumed by her, that all he'd been able to think about was tasting *more*. And when she had responded with pure enthusiasm, it had nearly sent him up in flames. He'd lost all awareness of reason, time, and place. He could only smell the roses on her skin, taste the punch on her lips, feel the straining of her body in his arms, and he'd known he would do anything and give anything to experience more of the same pleasure with her.

He supposed part of the reason he was so attracted to her was that she was uniquely complex. She worked for a governess's salary, and yet he suspected she was an utterly brilliant mathematician. Her oversized spectacles hid eyes that were so blue one could drown in them. Her high-necked, long-sleeved gowns were an insult to anyone who had eyes, but now he knew her secret: hidden beneath the drab gowns was a sweetly curved body that had clung to his with open, honest desire. *That* was the thing that had nearly undone him. Frankie was unapologetically candid, and for a man who'd lived with lies and scams and cheats as long as he had, she was as refreshing as a cool drink on a hot summer day.

It had been a long time since Jasper had had an affair—much longer than he led others to believe. He hadn't abstained because he was an angel but because he'd become *bored* with the entire pointless dance of courting a mistress only to find her as tiresome as the last. In the past, his affairs had always been a mutually beneficial and temporary arrangement with a widow. Jasper had made it clear to all his previous lovers that he was not the matrimonial type. He owned the *ton*'s most illustrious gaming hell and he dealt with the seedier side of life at night, and now he had Cecelia during the day. None of those things lent themselves to a happily married life. He had no interest in taking vows with a woman, and as his position in life did not require it, there was no reason for him to tie himself to someone who would only resent his absences each night.

All these reasons were why the kiss could not be repeated under any circumstances. Frankie was still his employee, and when her replacement arrived and she was no longer his governess, she would *still* be untouchable. She was genteelly born, and although both she and society would consider her a spinster, Jasper knew she was the type of person destined for marriage rather than an affair with a gambler who'd done such horrible things that even his own brother had not found it in his heart to love him.

Then there was the not-so-small matter of her attempted break-in. He knew she had started the kiss with the intention of distracting him, perhaps expecting him to react with shock, and he *had* been surprised, except not over the impropriety of the kiss, but by how her touch had felt like flint setting fire to all his extremities.

When it came to the combustibility between them, he thought *both* of them had been caught off guard.

It had been obvious she was new to kissing, her touch sweet and inexperienced, so it was not as if she were a seasoned courtesan spy sent by a rival hell. So what *was* she doing in his house? Who was she? Why did she want into his study so badly?

Despite all of his cool rationalizing, Jasper's blood still simmered when he thought of her mouth on his. It was clear he was going to have to keep a considerable distance from his governess while he worked on discovering why she was really in his house.

Later today he would write to Perdita's again and *demand* a replacement. The sooner Frankie Turner was out of his life, the better.

Chapter 14

Later that day, while Cecelia slept, Frankie paced her chamber and strategized about how to break into Jasper's study *without* getting caught. She only hoped she could do it sooner rather than later, especially now that his guard was up. If he brought up the reason for her attempted lock-picking again, she would simply tell him she was too curious for her own good, and hope he didn't call her bluff.

Oh, who was she jesting? Of course he would call her bluff. Which meant her only recourse was to stay as far away from him as possible. If he did not run into her, he could not ask her about his study or mention the *other* thing they'd done last night.

Unfortunately, each scheme Frankie thought of to gain entrance to Jasper's study was more outrageous than the last, and by the time she'd planned to swing from a rope knotted around the chimney and break in through the study window, she realized she'd officially lost it. She wasn't making any progress. In fact, she was going backward at that point.

That afternoon she received a package wrapped in brown paper from Perdita's. She thanked the delivery boy and raced into the sun-bleached courtyard to rip it open. With the August heat beating on the back of her neck and the scent of honeysuckle and the stench of the Thames in her nose, she read the note lying on top of the ledger inside.

Frankie,

Over the next several days there will be a number of discreet deliveries to your residence. The packages will contain the financials of the dozen grooms we have identified as Dowry Thieves. Enclosed in this package is the ledger of Lord Larchminth, the first groom. I have been through the twelve ledgers with a fine-tooth comb but I have found no commonality beyond the men's memberships to Rockford's. It is time I pass the information to the expert. I can give you a week, and then they will need to be returned to their respective owners before they are noticed missing.

I will remind you that this is sensitive information and the ledgers must be kept in a private location.

—The Dove

Frankie nearly wept with relief to have a task that might help the Dove discover who was behind the Dowry Thieves. Her failure to acquire Jasper's ledgers thus far was making her feel like a useless fool.

Her mind already on the task ahead, Frankie returned to her chamber, for once relieved that Cecelia was unavailable. She knew some of the bridegrooms had children from previous marriages, and therefore had governesses in their homes, but others did not. She did not even want to know how the Dove had come by *their* financials.

Twelve hours and three melted candles later, Frankie stared into the unlit fireplace as the clock over the mantel struck 3:00 a.m. Three more packages containing six more ledgers had been delivered that evening. Ledgers were splayed across every surface, her fingers were smudged with ink, and there were hastily scribbled notes on scraps of paper scattered about the room. There was a pattern hidden within the financials. She did not have the full scope of it yet, but she knew it was there; it danced just out of reach in her mind. Soon she would have the link that tied the men together—a link that did not involve Jasper Jones.

๛

The next morning Frankie walked into the schoolroom with shadows under her eyes. Gray light slanted through the windows, weak and watery. Cecelia was pacing in front of the bookshelf, hands interlaced behind her back, her brows drawn together. She was dressed in another hastily altered gown: this one a sedate, fudge brown that was one shade away from ugly.

When Cecelia caught sight of her she leapt forward, her cheeks rosy with excitement. "My soirée was a splendid success, Miss Turner! While I slept yesterday Uncle Jasper received a *mountain* of invitations and thank-you notes and calling cards. I knew he was occupied, so I took it upon myself as lady of the house to arrange a tea with Lady Evelyn Barker this afternoon."

Frankie blinked as she emerged from an alternate reality of numbers and selected a text from the shelf behind Cecelia. "You think to ask your uncle to join you and then discreetly disappear?"

Cecelia gasped. "I would never! That could lead to a compromising situation, since a lady must never be left alone with a bachelor. Unfortunately, Aunt Margaret has been invited to a rousing game of whist with Mrs. Hollendale at that time and will not be available to chaperone." Her eyes twinkled.

Cecelia's scheme did not sit right with Frankie, even if Lady Evelyn Barker was a far more appropriate match for Jasper than a governess in perpetual disarray. Evelyn was beautiful, well connected, and highly esteemed in the *ton*. She would be a great asset to Jasper's ambitions, while someone like Frankie would only be a liability.

And why was she even comparing herself to Lady Evelyn? Frankie had no interest in Jasper, nor he in her, even if she could not explain why a slow burn had started at her lips and traveled to her toes when he'd kissed her.

Evelyn could give her future husband all the things a man desired out of marriage: an orderly home, an heir, and entrée into society. Frankie had listened to her mother's litany of desirable qualities in a wife enough times to know she possessed none of them.

It was why, at four and twenty, she was an on-the-shelf spinster. When she was younger, bolstered by her sister's adoration and her father's amused tolerance, she had still believed she would fall in love. Had believed that, despite her mother's claims to the contrary, there was someone out there who would want a wife with intelligence and curiosity.

Then, during her first Season "out," her mother had dragged her to a small musicale put on by a third cousin. It was there that Frankie had met Mr. Broadclave, the handsomest man her sixteen-year-old eyes had ever set upon. He was two years older than her, with thick blond hair and a pretty frock coat that had made her own clothing seem outdated and worn.

She'd been bursting at the seams for an introduction, and when they finally met toward the end of the musicale, she'd known straight away she was in love.

"Do you sew?" Mr. Broadclave asked. He smiled down at her, and Frankie's heart beat wildly at the expression in his eyes.

"No," she said proudly. "I do not sew, paint, or play the piano."

Now she really had his attention. Mr. Broadclave lifted both brows. "What are you good for then?"

"I am intelligent."

He scoffed. "For a woman, perhaps."

"No, not just for a woman. I wager I am smarter than you."

He smiled indulgently. "Let us test that. Pick a subject." When she chose arithmetic, his smile widened.

There was something ugly about the smile, and it gave Frankie pause. Her mother had told her time and again that men could not tolerate a woman with intelligence, and she wondered briefly if she were making a mistake, but then Mr. Broadclave asked her to calculate a ridiculously easy equation and she could not help answering within seconds. He frowned and asked another. When she answered that one, too, enjoying the game, she asked him *a question.*

After a few moments of thinking, he leaned forward and said savagely, "You impudent little bitch. Your father barely has enough inheritance to clothe you in rags, and yet you come here acting as if you are worth even a fraction of the carpet on which you stand—and you are not."

Frankie was speechless, but that didn't stop his tirade.

"Your nasty habit of mocking men will end poorly for you, Miss Turner. You are inferior property without any skills. Your only worth lies in what is underneath your skirt, and based on your plain countenance, there is very little value even in that. It would do you well to remember your place the next time you attempt to humiliate one of your betters."

He stomped off, and Frankie stood against the wallpaper shaking with humiliation and anger.

"What did you say to him?" her mother hissed, appearing at her side. "Mr. Broadclave will one day inherit a fortune from his merchant father. It is possible he may be able to look past your small dowry."

Frankie was too shaken by the altercation to lie, and when she finished recounting their verbal volley, her mother's mouth flattened into a line. "He should not have said those things to you, but he is not wrong. It is what I have been trying to tell you since you were old enough to understand. Someone like you must be more patient and sweeter than even the most dignified lady if you wish to secure a marriage match."

"What do you mean, 'someone like me'?"

Her mother did not mince her words. "I mean someone who is plain and poor-sighted with very little grace, far too much intelligence, and a piddling dowry. No man wants to marry a woman with a superior intellect, Francis."

Frankie turned hurt eyes on her mother. "I shall never marry then!"

"I doubt you would have the choice anyway," her mother replied snippily.

Frankie groaned inwardly as she banished the memory to the vault where she kept all her secret shames. She'd thought she'd learned her lesson about men years ago, but it seemed she had forgotten it when she was kissing Jasper Jones. She was a plain, undesirable spinster, and Jasper had only returned her kiss to spare her the humiliation of rejection. No man of Jasper's wealth, reputation, and handsome visage would ever truly look twice at her. Certainly not when they could have a woman like Lady Evelyn.

Embarrassed for perhaps the hundredth time by what she'd done, Frankie vowed that from that moment forward she would act as cool as a cucumber should she run across her employer. Any and all future tingling caused by the memory of the kiss would be immediately squashed. Frankie had once heard of a method for stopping cravings: One was supposed to pinch oneself whenever one felt the craving, such as when pudding was served at dinner. The kiss was Frankie's pudding, and from now on whenever she thought of it, she would pinch herself until the memory and even the *sight* of Jasper Jones made her uncomfortable.

Pleased with her plan, Frankie's attention returned to Cecelia, who was going into lengthy detail about the types of cakes that were to be served with tea.

"I beg of you to reconsider, Cecelia. It is not right to take Mr. Jones's choice from him. Besides, plans do not always proceed as we wish."

Cecelia sniffed. "Typical governess, determined to kill all joy. Do not worry, Miss Turner. There is more to my plan than simply tea."

Frankie groaned.

Chapter 15

Lady Evelyn arrived for tea in a sweep of silk and floral powder that Frankie could smell all the way in the corridor where she stood peering around the corner. If she had to estimate, she would say Lady Evelyn's purple silk gown cost more than she would make in an entire year. Frankie glanced down at her own dark-green dress of plain cotton, the neckline so high it made her chin itch. It wasn't that she enjoyed wearing such ugly gowns, but her station required it.

"What are we looking at?" Jasper asked at her ear.

Frankie clapped a hand over her mouth before she could shriek and give away her position. She turned to find Jasper standing entirely too close and gazing at her with *entirely* too much heat.

She pinched her arm before taking a step back. She was imagining desire where none existed. "Miss Cecelia has invited Lady Evelyn to tea."

Jasper tore his gaze from her, catching sight of Lady Evelyn's skirt before she entered the sitting room. "Why?"

"Perhaps she enjoys Lady Evelyn's company."

"Does anyone?"

"You—you do not?"

"No." Those dark eyes returned to her face and roved over her cheekbones and down the front of her gown. "She is snide and conceited and dull."

"Is that all?" Frankie muttered under her breath. Unfortunately, Jasper heard her.

"No, that is not all. She also cannot count cards." Jasper lifted his hand and with one finger slid the bridge of Frankie's spectacles back up her nose.

Frankie blinked, disproportionately affected by the simple gesture. Her throat clamped and she reached over to her arm and pinched herself again. Before she could regain her senses, Cecelia howled down the hallway.

"UNCLE JAAAAAAAASPER!"

Jasper sighed and went to step past Frankie, but paused. "Why do you keep pinching yourself?"

Frankie had opened her mouth to warn him about Cecelia's plan, but at being caught pinching herself in his presence she panicked and exclaimed, "I have lessons to prepare!" She hitched up her skirts and made a beeline for the library—which indeed had its doors wide-open—and began to pace.

The library was stunning, with tall peaked windows and shelves upon shelves of books organized in the most interesting fashion, with little tabs of numbers pasted on the spines. Frankie had never seen anything like it, and yet it did not take her more than a few minutes of perusing to discover that it was an incredibly clever system.

Jasper had decorated the room for comfort and coziness rather than to function as a showpiece, and it therefore hosted a variety of overstuffed furniture perfect for curling up with a book, an unlit limestone fireplace, and a most interesting woven carpet that depicted various scenes from Greek mythology. Not, not various scenes, Frankie realized as she bent to look closer: various *gods*. Hermes, the Greek god of gambling, who could outwit almost anyone; Lakshmi, the Indian goddess of prosperity; Thoth, an Egyptian god with the head of a bird and the body of a man; Macuilxochitl, an Aztec god of excess; Fortuna, the Roman goddess of luck; Nezha, the Chinese god of fortune; and several others that she did not recognize from her patchwork studies. The rug must have been custom-made for Jasper; a literal tapestry of gods and goddesses across religions and cultures that supported luck, prosperity, and gambling.

Frankie adored it.

If Cecelia succeeded in pairing Jasper with Lady Evelyn, would the lady appreciate the rug? Or would she roll it up and have the servants store it away?

Frankie resumed pacing in front of the cold fireplace. The scents of wax and polish mingled with the fresh daisies one of the servants had placed in a vase on a round rosewood table at the center of the room, and Frankie wished she were in the library to read a delicious new tome on the study of mathematics rather than worry over Cecelia's plan. She'd lost her chance to warn Jasper in private. Should she intrude on the gathering despite the impropriety of it?

Her heels rang on the hardwood as she paced and gnawed on her lip. At last she stopped. With her mind made up, she strode to the library door.

Chapter 16

Jasper entered the sitting room, and every one of his senses tingled with foreboding. Cecelia was wearing a gown the color of mud and smiling at him with far too much innocence in her wide, brown eyes. Lady Evelyn was seated on the blue settee, her back as straight as a billiard's cue stick. An enormous plum-colored hat was pinned on her head, its brim festooned with heaps of flowers, berries, and feathers.

"Lady Evelyn," he said, inclining his head. "Cecelia, how may I assist you?"

"I was hoping you might join me and Lady Evelyn for tea."

"I am sorry, Cece, but there are matters that require my attention at present. My regrets, Lady Evelyn."

Jasper was about to take his leave when Cecelia snatched his sleeve and said, "At least let me fetch you a tea cake."

Jasper was not hungry, but it seemed important to Cecelia that he try her cake, so he nodded and waited for her to make a roundabout trip past the windows where she glanced anxiously outside, to the silver tray artfully stacked with a delectable assortment of treats.

Lady Evelyn gave him a catlike smile ripe with equal amounts of scorn and desire, and Jasper had a sudden flash of insight about how she would be in bed: she would think herself better than him and she would hate degrading herself while simultaneously loving every moment.

He could not think of a worse bed partner.

Cecelia tripped over a hatbox that had been left on the floor and went flying, landing heavily on her hands and knees. Jasper was already halfway across the room to help her up when she jumped to her feet, pointed at the floor, and screamed. A little brown mouse had chosen that moment to scamper across the carpet. It stopped not two feet from Lady Evelyn and stood on its hind legs and twitched its whiskers, no doubt smelling the sweets on the tray above.

Cecelia threw her hands in the air, screamed as if the house were burning down, and raced from the room. Her exit would have left Jasper and Lady Evelyn alone together if Lady Evelyn had not also risen with extraordinary haste, lifted the hems of her gown, and hurried after Cecelia with surprising speed.

There was a scuffle in the hallway, another shriek, and the crash of a tray on tile.

"What now?" Jasper roared as he strode to the doorway.

In the corridor was the human equivalent of a carriage crash: In her mad dash to escape, Cecelia had bumped into Frankie just outside the drawing room, who had tumbled into the maid returning with a second tray of tiny sandwiches. Lady Evelyn had tripped and stumbled over all three of them. Four women lay in various positions on the floor with sandwich dressings scattered across the tile, the silver tray still rattling in a circle as it settled to the floor.

Frankie's spectacles had gone flying and she began crawling

around on the floor feeling with her hands to try and find them, so Jasper went to her first. He plucked the lenses from the debris of triangle bread slices and cucumber coins and handed them to her. She slid them onto her face while he grasped her by the elbows and hauled her to her feet. "Are you hurt anywhere?"

"No."

He brushed a cucumber slice off her shoulder. "If you wanted tea, you could have asked."

"Oh, Mr. Jones," she whispered, stricken. "How can you even jest about this?"

"They're a few dropped sandwiches." He released her elbows when he realized he was still holding them and turned to find the maid struggling to her feet and both Cecelia and Lady Evelyn staring at them; Cecelia with a frown, Lady Evelyn with ugly anger.

Jasper extended his hand to Lady Evelyn while Cecelia vaulted to her feet and stamped her foot. "This is a disaster!"

"Are you well, Lady Evelyn?" Jasper asked once the lady was on her feet.

She brushed out her gown and straightened her hat. "I have never suffered a more undignified experience in all of my life," she snapped. "This is the consequence of consorting with stock below one's station!"

Jasper's temper reared its head, but he kept it under tight rein. He dealt with the entitled *ton* most nights. Over time he had begun feeling badly for *them* because they were trapped by ridiculous rules and customs. Lady Evelyn's comment would have rolled off his shoulders as easily as all the others if it had not been for Cecelia, whose cheeks had flushed at her words.

Frankie reached protectively for Cecelia's hand and laced their fingers together.

Jasper gestured toward the grand entryway. "We would not want to keep you from visiting those of better standing."

Lady Evelyn's lip curled. "To think I had considered you a marriage prospect. I must have lapsed into momentary madness."

Jasper knew she meant the remark to sting, as if he had lost out on a once-in-a-lifetime opportunity. "It is best we did not go down that road then," he said as gravely as he could manage.

"Indeed. You and your ill-bred niece are not worthy of me."

Cecelia's cheeks deepened to a shade of puce. "You are not worthy of *him!*" she burst out. "Uncle Jasper is good and kind and smart, and you have been nothing but cold and wicked since I met you. You might hold the title of lady, but you do not act like one."

Jasper was so stunned by Cecelia's words that he almost missed the flash of vindictiveness on Evelyn's face. Cecelia thought he was good and kind and smart? Since when? From the moment she'd come to live with him she'd behaved as if he were nothing but an insufferable pain in her neck.

Lady Evelyn stared down her nose at Cecelia. "You dear, stupid child. I hope you enjoy having a governess as a mother." With that parting comment she walked down the corridor, unhurried and as regal as if she were a queen, where the footman waited with the door open.

The three of them stood in absolute silence.

"What did she mean by that?" Cecelia asked suspiciously, looking between Jasper and Frankie. "Are you two—?"

"No!" he and Frankie said in unison.

Cecelia heaved a sigh. "You were right, Miss Turner. Plans do not always work out as we wish."

Jasper shot an accusatory glare at Frankie, who had bent to help the maid clean up the sandwiches. When she did not lift her head, he asked Cecelia, "What do you mean, 'plans do not always work out as we wish'?"

"I thought Lady Evelyn would be a lovely wife for you so I invited her here for you to...er...get to know her better."

She was telling part of the truth, but not all of it. Jasper recalled what had taken place in the sitting room. Cecelia had called him in, insisted on a tea cake, and then she'd tripped over a hatbox right before the mouse had made its appearance.

The hatbox. Why was a hatbox on the sitting room floor to begin with? How convenient was it that the mouse had appeared only moments after the hatbox had been overturned?

"Cecelia," he said, his temper shaking off its bridle, "were you planning to entrap me in marriage to Lady Evelyn by leaving us alone in the sitting room together?"

There came a knock at the front door and the footman opened it to reveal Lady Trathers, the biggest gossip in London. She waggled her fingers at the trio in the corridor.

"And you were going to have Lady Trathers interrupt us!" Jasper hissed, the entire plan surfacing with horrifying clarity.

"Do not be cross, Uncle Jasper. How was I to know Lady Evelyn was a wretched cow?"

Jasper whirled on Frankie. "You knew about this?"

Frankie and the maid had finished cleaning up the food, and the maid had left with a tray piled high with sandwich dressings. "Not exactly."

"I did not tell her about the mouse. Or Lady Trathers," Cecelia said, tapping her temple with her finger. "I did not know if I could trust her. She did tell me she thought it was wrong and warned me that plans go awry, and wouldn't you know it, that's exactly what happened."

Jasper was furious with Cecelia, but what hurt more was that Frankie had been in on the ruse. He gave Frankie a cold stare before saying to Cecelia, "Your punishment is that you must now entertain Lady Trathers for the afternoon."

Cecelia paled. "Uncle, she does not stop talking long enough to breathe."

"My sympathy is nonexistent. *You* are coming with me," he said to Frankie, crooking his finger. She followed him around the bend in the corridor while Lady Trathers left her parasol with the butler.

Frankie must have sensed the volatility of his mood because for once she did not interrupt him as he gestured her into the first room they came to: the informal parlor. It was sunny and warm in a way the formal parlor was not, and it was where Jasper wrote his correspondence when he hoped Cecelia would visit during the day.

The moment they were inside he said, "How could you let her do something like this?"

He did not understand the irrational feeling of betrayal that sliced through him. It was not as if Frankie had concocted the plan herself, but then neither had she stopped it.

"I will admit it did not sit well with me," Frankie said with infuriating calm, "even though on paper a marriage with Lady Evelyn would be advantageous to you. Cecelia seemed to like her, and as she once pointed out to me, women are sold into marriage every day; why should a man not be?" Before he could tell her exactly what he thought of that she added, "But just because it is true that women are sold into marriage every day, *forced* into marriage, *tricked* into marriage," she emphasized, looking him in the eye with each iteration, "it does not make it right to do the same to others. I was on my way to intervene when Cecelia and Lady Evelyn came running out of the room as if they were being chased by the hounds of hell and crashed into me."

Jasper flexed his hand. "You were going to intervene because you believed her plan was immoral? No other reason?"

"Ah..." She pinched her arm.

"Why are you doing that?"

"Doing what?"

"You keep pinching yourself."

Frankie's cheeks turned a delicate shade of pink. "It is an experiment that is not working, as it seems I still have an inconveniently strong desire for pudding."

Jasper had no clue what pudding had to do with anything, but he was an eternal bastion of indulgence. "Then do not deny yourself pudding."

Something flickered in her eyes, but it was gone before he could read it. Frankie straightened her shoulders and adjusted her spectacles, grimacing when her fingers came away smeared with butter. "If you will excuse me, Mr. Jones, I must freshen up."

He wanted to stop her, but he realized it was only an excuse to touch her. Frankie had done nothing wrong. Cecelia had been at fault, but even her hijinks could be forgiven as poor juvenile judgment. What he was truly angry about was how close he'd come to being forced into a lifetime of marriage to a woman he despised.

A chill slid down his spine as his eyes followed Frankie's back. Today had been a close call. If Lady Evelyn had not been afraid of the mouse and run out of the room, or if Lady Trathers had arrived before Frankie had, he would be engaged to Lady Evelyn at this very moment.

He had been lucky this time, but would his luck hold forever? Jasper avoided social situations with the *ton* as if they were the plague, and today's escapade was only one example why. Since Cecelia's soirée, there had been more invitations, more calling cards, more entreaties to join the upper class in their frivolous entertainments. Jasper had no intention of taking them up on it, but what if some other lady of the *ton*—perhaps someone whose father owed Rockford's a great deal of money—still attempted to entrap him in marriage? What if she succeeded?

Jasper paced the waxed floorboards, aggravated when he realized he'd missed the perfect opportunity to question Frankie about her interest in his study. He'd had the governess here, alone, and he'd been so consumed by the close call with Lady Evelyn that he'd entirely forgotten to get his answers.

He dragged a hand over his face. There was still time to figure out why Frankie was in his household, but he was not sure he had as much time left as a bachelor. He did not wish to marry at all, but if he did have to marry, he sure as hell wanted to be the one to select his wife. He felt a sudden sympathy for all the women who were not allowed to choose their husbands. As Frankie had said: Women were sold into marriage every day. Jasper vowed right then and there that Cecelia would never marry a man she was not completely and madly in love with.

Jasper had never loved a woman and he was sure he never would, but very few marriages were love matches, while almost all of them were about business. With a tinge of sorrow, he realized his bachelor days were coming to a close. He could wait around and hope no one else succeeded in coercing him into marriage, or he could seize control of his future and take himself off the market.

Now the question was: Who would be interested in being his bride?

Chapter 17

Frankie sat at the wooden school table and twisted her fingers together. She sighed. She tapped her foot. She had to admit to herself that she was not going to be able to enter Jasper's study without a key. There were any number of places Jasper could hide a key, and after spending the night narrowing down the probability of each potential location, Frankie had risen early, *early!* so that she might snoop around before Cecelia's lessons that morning. A fat lot of good it had done her; she had found absolutely nothing. It would be her luck if Jasper kept the key on his person. If he did, she was *never* getting into that room.

"Oh, Miss Turner!" Cecelia exclaimed, lifting her head from her poetry book, a subject about which Frankie understood very little. "You are torturing me with your silence and sighs. You might as well have worked for the Inquisition. Who would think not saying anything could be so effective?"

Startled, Frankie returned her attention to her pupil, whose chestnut ringlets lay draped over a gown that was a disturbing cross between brown and orange. "What?"

"You are angry about what happened with Lady Evelyn Barker. I promise you I did not know how completely horrid she was; I thought she was only a *little* horrid. I also did not mean to run into you and knock you into a tray of cucumber sandwiches. Uncle seemed awfully cross when he asked you to go with him. What did he say to you?"

"He was displeased that I did not warn him about your agenda."

Cecelia rubbed one of the pages between her thumb and forefinger. "Growing up is a terrible thing, is it not, Miss Turner? You think you are right about so many things, and it is humbling when it turns out that is not the case. I wish it were five years ago, when I was living at home with my father and Aunt Margaret and everything was simple and easy. It is not so easy anymore."

Frankie's heart pinched at Cecelia's words. She reached across the table and took one of her hands. "You have been dealt a terrible blow with the loss of your father, Cecelia, and no pretty words of condolences will change that. Growing up is hard, but it is also a privilege. We all make mistakes; we would not become wiser if we did not. Your uncle understands that."

Cecelia dashed a tear away with the back of her free hand. "My father loved Uncle Jasper even though they did not always get along, but he hated taking charity from him. He would be mortified if he knew I was relying on Uncle's charity now."

"Believe me when I say your father rests easy in his grave knowing your uncle is taking care of both you and Madam Margaret. As for your uncle, mayhap he saw you as a duty at first, but from what I have witnessed in the time I have been here, I believe he truly cares for you."

Cecelia sniffed in a very unladylike manner. "You are only saying that to make me feel better."

"No," Frankie said with some surprise, "it would not occur to me to do that."

Cecelia brightened. "You are right, Miss Turner. I think it truly would not. You always tell the truth. You aren't even afraid of Uncle, and everyone else treats him as if he is the king of London."

"Yes, well, perhaps I could stand to learn a little artifice."

"I like you just as you are, Miss Turner." Cecelia jumped up and gave her an impulsive hug, and Frankie, stunned and warmed by the gesture, only had her arms halfway around the girl when she pulled back and said, "I have a confession to make."

Uh-oh. Frankie did not care to be in on any more of Cecelia's schemes. "No, that is all right. Some secrets are best kept—"

"I saw you kissing Uncle Jasper."

Frankie's tongue froze.

Cecelia nodded. "At the soirée. Do not worry, no one else saw; I was alone. I was coming to ask Uncle Jasper to lend me a handful of shillings when he caught you trying to break into his study. His *forbidden* study. I hid behind the bust in the corridor to see what you would do, and you *kissed* him."

"Cecelia—"

She held up a hand. "Let me finish please, Miss Turner. I will admit that at first I was angry because you'd seemed different from all of the other simpering, scheming women out to get him, and it only made me more determined to marry him off to a woman who was sure to ship me away to boarding school. If he married *you* I knew you would never send me away and I would be stuck here, an eternal reminder of Uncle Jasper's duty.

"But after I saw Lady Evelyn's true colors yesterday, I took to my chamber and had a good hard think. I was wrong about her, and I've been wrong about Uncle Jasper all this time. He's been awfully good to me, even when I have not been on my best behavior. It made me wonder if I was wrong about you, too.

"So I said to myself, Cecelia dear, what would be best for Uncle Jasper and not *you*? First time I ever asked myself that question, it was. I've seen a lot of women throw themselves at Uncle Jasper, but he never looks at any of them the way he looks at you."

"How does he look at me?" Frankie asked. As if she were a giant thorn in his side?

Cecelia waggled her eyebrows. "Like he wants to throw you on a bed."

"Cecelia!"

"Oh, all right, I admit I do not fully understand what that means. My friend Catherine used to say it though. I am not sure why two adults would want to share a bed. Do they not usually have separate chambers? What if one of them snores? Do you know why, Miss Turner?"

Frankie opened her mouth to speak but Cecelia, thankfully, cut her off. "My friend would say it whenever a man gave a woman a dark, swoony look. She would say, 'He wants to throw her on a bed.' Then I remembered the way Uncle Jasper kissed you in the corridor. I hope someone kisses *me* like that someday, like they cannot get enough of me and they think I am the most beautiful woman in the world. And I said to myself, why the answer is right in front of you, Cecelia. Uncle Jasper would be happiest marrying your governess. So I want you to know, Miss Turner, that I shall not stand in your way. In fact, I would *very* much like to help you marry my uncle."

Frankie gaped at Cecelia. Her normally lightning-speed thoughts had slowed to the pace of molasses. Cecelia's assumptions about Frankie and Jasper were to be expected. She'd witnessed them kissing, after all, and only the very in love or the very stupid would risk kissing in a corridor outside of wedlock. Cecelia could not be expected to know that Jasper was only being polite in returning the kiss, and Frankie did not think her pride could bear explaining it to her.

She supposed she should be pleased that Cecelia was maturing enough to consider the feelings of others, but the last thing she wanted was for Cecelia to scheme to marry her to Jasper. She would die of humiliation if Jasper were forced into marrying her—the least-desired spinster in all of London—by his niece.

"I do not want to marry your uncle," Frankie said firmly.

Cecelia scowled. "Why not? You kissed him the same way he kissed you. I saw it."

"Well." Frankie struggled to keep her cheeks from flushing. "Kissing aside, I . . . I have plans for the future that do not include marriage."

"Such as what?"

"I am going to curate a women-contributed mathematics journal." It was the first time Frankie had ever spoken her ambition aloud, and she felt absurdly nervous to have shared it with this fifteen-year-old. "As long as the theorem is sound, anyone may participate, no matter their gender, race, or religion."

"That sounds boring."

Frankie sighed. "Nevertheless, I have no interest in marrying your uncle, and I assure you that despite what you saw, he has absolutely no interest in marrying *me*, so please banish the thought from your head."

"I think you are the right person for Uncle Jasper, but I promise I will not interfere. I have learned my lesson. But there's something else I'm dying to know. Why were you trying to break into Uncle's study?"

Frankie floundered. She had managed to avoid Jasper asking that very question over the past several days by dodging into various rooms every time she caught sight of him or heard his voice, and she had not expected it to come from Cecelia. Frankie could lie, but Cecelia believed her to be an honest person, and for some reason Cecelia's opinion of her deeply mattered. So, she told her the truth. "I cannot tell you."

Cecelia nodded, as if she were a sage old woman. "I thought you would say that. Is it nefarious?"

"I do not think so."

"Is it important?"

"*Incredibly* so," Frankie said earnestly. "I will share a secret with you, Cecelia. I am looking for information about someone who is doing terrible things. That information might help lead me to my sister, who has run away."

Cecelia's nose wrinkled. "Why would that information be in Uncle Jasper's study? Do you think he is the person doing the 'terrible' things?"

"I do not, but I must be sure."

Cecelia studied her with the uncanny eyes of a fifteen-year-old who saw more than she should. "It is not an accident that you are here, is it?"

"No."

"I am certain Uncle Jasper does not have your information, and I am willing to prove it. I know where he keeps the key to his study."

Frankie's heart did a slow twist in her chest. "You do?"

Cecelia nodded. "Before I tell you where it is, you must answer me this: What will you do when you realize Uncle Jasper is innocent?"

"I suppose I will leave so that I can help elsewhere." She had not thought that far ahead, but there would be no need for her to stay. The Dove might have an alternative assignment for her once she'd found Jasper's ledgers and cleared his name.

"But you and Uncle Jasper..."

"Cecelia, I am sorry you witnessed what you did in the corridor, and I understand how confusing it must be, but there is nothing between your uncle and me. He does not want a wife, and I do not want a husband. Whatever—whatever you think you saw between us, it was simply a mistake. I will miss *you* when I leave, though. I have grown quite fond of you while I've been here."

Cecelia flopped back in the chair. "Just when I thought I finally had it figured out. All right, Miss Turner. Does this count as the favor I owe you from when I lost at Vingt et Un?"

"Absolutely."

"If you are caught, please do not tell Uncle Jasper that it was I who gave you the key."

"I will not be caught. I will wait until your uncle is at Rockford's so there is no chance of him walking in on me. Tell me, how did you find the key?" Frankie was more than a little curious to learn how Cecelia had ferreted out his well-hidden secret.

"There is not much to do rattling about in this big house," Cecelia admitted, "and Uncle Jasper believes in the adage of 'hidden in plain sight.' I will meet you in the library at the strike of eight when Uncle Jasper leaves." She pointed at Frankie and in a clandestine whisper added, "Do not be late."

Chapter 18

Good for her word, Cecelia appeared in the library at the exact strike of eight and handed Frankie a brass key. "I saw Uncle Jasper leave ten minutes ago. May I come with you?"

Frankie thought about it, but then shook her head. "I do not wish to involve you any further, Cecelia."

"Fine. I did not think you would say yes anyway. Slip the key under my door when you are finished and I shall return it to its hiding place before Uncle Jasper comes home tomorrow."

Frankie closed her fingers around the cool brass key in her palm and smiled at Cecelia. "Thank you."

Frankie wasted no time hurrying down the corridor. She looked over both her shoulders, and when she was satisfied no servants were in view, she slid the key into the lock on Jasper's study door, praying it was the correct key and the lock would not seize. Jasper would know for certain that it was she who tampered with it if he needed a reset key.

Her lungs burning with held breath, Frankie turned the key, and there was a click. When she twisted the knob, the door swung inward. A rush of triumph hit her at the same time as the scents of old books, leather, and the subtle hints of Jasper's shaving cream. She quickly closed the door behind her and felt on the nearby stand for the matches. Once she had lit the lantern, she lifted it high so that its light scattered in shifting ovals across the spacious study.

Jasper's study, although luxurious, was typically appointed. There was a mammoth wooden desk positioned underneath a window, the drapes partially closed to the onset of night; a pair of stiff horsehair chairs facing the desk; and a soft leather settee across the room. An unlit marble fireplace was nothing but a shadow in the wall; beyond it, bookshelves lined the entire western wall, and in the chill and gloom of the room, Frankie felt comforted by their presence. Everything, from the dark woods and crystal decanters to the spicy scents of cologne, said that this space was entered by only one, devilishly handsome man.

Frankie was almost certain that Jasper was uninvolved with the Dowry Thieves, so why were her fingers trembling?

Jasper would be at his hell the entire night, which meant she had hours to search the study at her leisure and clear Jasper's name. Once she had, she would stay on as Cecelia's governess until she had finished analyzing the grooms' financials, or until the Dove asked her to go somewhere else.

Frankie shook off the strange melancholy that overtook her at the thought of leaving the Jones residence. She did not dare light any more lamps out of fear of alerting a passing servant, and since the single lantern would slow her search, she knew she had best begin. She lifted the flame and noted the time on the clock on Jasper's mantel. She wanted to be out of his study long before dawn approached.

Jasper's business ledger for Rockford's was easy to find: it was sitting on top of his desk. Frankie ignored it and spent the first hour searching every possible location for a second ledger. She tested all the floorboards, quietly knocked on the walls, and pulled out and replaced every book on his shelves. By the time she'd finished, she was certain that if Jasper had a second ledger for Rockford's, he did not keep it there.

Frankie set the burning lamp onto a side table and sank onto the settee with the ledger in her lap. She smoothed her palm over the embossed leather cover and slowly opened it, her heart thumping so loudly in her ears that she almost couldn't hear. Inside, she discovered columns for goods and services and the corresponding amounts. Jasper's handwriting was stark, the ink dark and bold against the page. The lack of flourishes gave away the fact that Jasper had taught himself how to write, the letters appearing almost identical to the typeset words in a book. Frankie could picture him struggling over a text, copying each letter exactly until he was fluent in reading and writing. The image of a young Jasper remaking himself through painstaking sacrifice made her chest swell. Jasper had truly defied the odds, and if anyone knew about probabilities, it was she. He never should have made it off the wharf. Yet he'd not only escaped a future of poverty, but he'd also built an empire that had forever altered the course of his life *and* his niece's life. Frankie wondered if anyone in the *ton* understood how truly remarkable such a feat was.

Frankie scanned the goods and services and mentally noted the amounts. Everything appeared to be proper and in order. There were deductions for new table linens, for beef, for candles and whale oil. Tidy rows of numbers recorded deposits from membership dues and bets. Frankie's eyes bugged when she saw the amount of money Rockford's collected each night at the gaming tables. Rockford's was raking in far more cash than she ever would have dreamed, along with a disturbing number of assets that were neatly recorded with estimated values. Jasper must've kept a small record book at Rockford's and then transcribed the details into the master ledger at home. Unless...it was possible he memorized the transactions. Frankie had heard of people who had only to see something once and then were able to recall each and every detail. She would not be surprised if Jasper was one of them.

Everything seemed to be on the up-and-up when Frankie noticed that a particular number had appeared more than once: three hundred pounds exactly. It was an enormous sum that under normal circumstances she would have noticed straight away, but Jasper's ledger was not lacking for eye-watering amounts. Frankie flipped back to the beginning of the ledger, searching for any time three hundred pounds was deducted from the accounts. The pattern quickly became obvious: on the first of every month Jasper Jones paid three hundred pounds, which was more than an army cornet made in an entire year, for "fish."

Frankie may not be well versed in the costs associated with running a business, but she knew for an absolute fact that fish, even enough fish to feed an entire gaming hell of patrons, did not cost more money than most people made in a year.

She let the ledger fall to her lap and her eyes unfocused. The description was a fake; the money was clearly going toward something else. What could Jasper Jones be buying each month for such an extraordinary sum? Could it be a case of blackmail? Could he be involved with the Dowry Thieves after all?

The flame in the lamp wavered, as if it had been disturbed by a shift in the air, and that was the only warning Frankie had before she heard Jasper's cold voice. "I see you found my key."

Chapter 19

It was a busy night at the gaming hell and Jasper had to smile and engage in pleasant conversation more than he cared to because of Cecelia's blasted soirée. It was as if the gentlemen who frequented his hell had begun to see him as more of an equal than a businessman, a shift that did not please him. Men who saw him as a friend were more likely to ask for favors, and Jasper's favors never came without a price.

A few hours after the dinner meal had begun to wind down, one of his security men approached him. "Mr. Jones, there is a young girl at the door. She says she is related to you and must speak with you straight away."

The hairs on the back of Jasper's neck stood and he crossed the gaming floor with strides that bordered on a run. It had to be Cecelia, and if she was standing outside his gaming hell a half hour to midnight, then something must be dreadfully wrong.

Jasper threw open the door and his eyes raked her over. There were no obvious injuries, and she was smiling as if she were as pleased as a pig in mud. Jasper yanked her inside and snapped at his doorkeeper, "If you ever see this young woman again, she is to be admitted immediately and not left on the street to the whims and mercies of passing men, do you understand?"

The man tipped his hat in acknowledgment and Jasper tugged Cecelia to the side. "What is the matter? Why are you here? Is the house on fire? Is Miss Turner all right?"

"Why do you ask about Miss Turner?" Cecelia asked, an odd gleam in her eye.

"She is supposed to be watching you, that is why."

"She is my governess, not my keeper."

"I can hire a keeper," Jasper growled.

Cecelia grimaced and said hurriedly, "I *am* in fact here because of Miss Turner."

Jasper's breath caught. "What is the matter? Is she ill?"

"I came here because . . ."

"Because *why* Cecelia?"

"I am pausing for dramatic effect, Uncle, but I think I will have to *show* you what is happening. Before I do, you must promise not to punish Miss Turner by terminating her employment or writing to her governess agency. If you do not make me this promise, I shall not take you to her, and believe me, you want to know what she's doing right now."

Jasper sensed a scheme, even as Cecelia's voice held conviction.

Cecelia pulled her hood over her hair. "Do you promise?"

"I promise."

He did not bother with his coat or hat; he simply followed his niece into the street, grateful that her hood concealed her identity. He did not always understand the intricacies of proper behavior for society women, but he was almost certain that being seen outside a gaming hell at midnight was cause for scandal. Cecelia was not upper class, but she had money and she had opportunities, and he would not see her waste them on foolish mistakes.

When they were almost at the house Cecelia broke her silence. "Would it make you angry if you discovered Miss Turner hosting a gentleman caller?"

Rage, hot and potent, pulsed through his veins. She had brought an unknown man into *his* house and exposed his niece to a stranger? How dare she entertain another man when she had kissed him as if she were his?

Jasper paused mid-step at the surprising and unwelcome thought. Where had that come from?

With a deceivingly calm voice he said, "Is she, Cecelia?"

Cecelia shivered. "Your voice, Uncle Jasper! You sound so cold and scary. No wonder everyone is afraid of you. My father said you once survived a three-person knife fight. Is that true?"

"Cecelia!"

"Oh, all right. I can see the answer to my question plainly enough anyway. No, she is not."

"Then why would you say such a thing?"

Her expression was hidden by the shadow of her hood when she answered, "No reason."

Jasper's relief was short-lived. Whatever Cecelia was up to, it wasn't good. He stopped abruptly outside his front door. The streetlamps had been lit hours ago and the yellow orbs of light danced along the road. The moon was struggling to shine through a persistent blanket of smog, and the heat of the day still clung to the cobblestones. The scent of their evening's supper of roasted chicken could still be smelled on the air. Everything appeared calm and typical of a late summer evening, except Jasper was convinced he was being set up.

"Is there a lady inside waiting to entrap me in marriage?"

Cecelia took his hand and tugged him up the steps. "No, I promise there is no *lady* waiting for you, Uncle Jasper. There is only Miss Turner, who I saw slip into your study after you left. I was not going to tell you, but then a brilliant thought occ—I mean, then I thought that I owed you and should let you know."

They stood inside the foyer, which was nearly tar black with lack of light. Upon hearing that Frankie was in his study, Jasper's ire returned full force. He should not have let her prior trespassing go unaddressed this long. It was time he discovered exactly why his governess was so intent on entering his study. "Go to bed, Cecelia."

"But Uncle—"

"*Go.*"

She huffed as Jasper lit a candle by the door and handed it to her. "Do not let me catch you eavesdropping."

She scowled and turned to stomp away, but he was almost certain he caught her scowl shift into a smile when she thought her back was turned.

Jasper did not have time to ponder what Cecelia was plotting. If Frankie truly was in his study, she was about to discover what happened when someone crossed Jasper Jones.

He walked down the corridor, his boots soundless on the tile. The door to his study was closed, but a small bead of light moved beneath the door. He turned the knob and entered. The room was in near darkness except for a single lamp glowing on the table by the settee, and on that settee was Frankie Turner, his ledger on her lap.

The image of her on his settee, in this personal space where he allowed no one, awakened the uncivilized part of him that he struggled to keep leashed. Cecelia's taunt about Frankie entertaining another man in his own house had riled him more than he cared for, and now, seeing the rule-breaking governess in his lair, he felt what remained of his control slipping away. "I see you found my key."

Frankie squeaked and jumped to her feet, the ledger falling to the floor and splaying face down. In the dim light her cheeks paled and she took a step back. Jasper advanced toward her, but when she fumbled beside her and snatched up the first thing she found—a discarded letter opener—and waved it in front of her, he halted and frowned.

"What the devil are you doing, Miss Turner?"

"Do not come closer!" She brandished the letter opener as if it were a knife. He could have disarmed her in an instant, but she seemed genuinely afraid. "I do not know how you are involved, but I want answers."

"As do I. What the hell are you doing with my ledger?"

"No!" She pointed the silver letter opener at him. "What are *you* doing with the Dowry Thieves?"

Jasper slowly backed up so as not to alarm her, and struck a match to ignite the lamp on his desk. Frankie relaxed slightly at the wash of light. "I do not know what you mean." He walked to the next candelabra and lit that as well, then he turned to face his fierce governess, her hair falling out of her chignon, her glasses sliding down her nose, and a letter opener clenched in her fist. "But you and I need to have a serious discussion."

Frankie's lips pressed together. "Do not think you are going to woo and disarm me with those intoxicating eyes."

Jasper lifted a brow. "*Intoxicating* eyes?"

Frankie blushed all the way to the collar of her gown, and Jasper very much wished he could see the flush move across her chest.

"You know what I mean. Do not think you will use your charms to silence me. I demand to know to whom you are paying three hundred pounds every month."

"You demand to know?" Jasper asked in disbelief. "You demand that your employer explain his business purchases after you have broken into his study and searched through his private papers?"

"When you say it like that it does not sound good, but yes. That is what I demand."

Jasper didn't know if he should laugh with incredulity or tear his hair out. "Put the letter opener down, Frankie. I am not going to hurt you."

The letter opener lowered a fraction. "Are you going to kiss me?"

Jasper leaned against the desk and crossed his arms over his chest. "Do you want me to?" Frankie's eyes fell to his lips and her blush deepened. *Bloody hell.* He knew she'd only kissed him earlier to prevent this very moment, but there was no denying they'd both felt *something* unexpected when their mouths had met. "No one is kissing anyone else until we figure out this mess."

She gave a sharp nod. "Good. But I am not putting down the letter opener until you explain yourself."

Jasper *never* revealed his hand first, but short of physically taking the weapon out of Frankie's hand, he did not know how else to deal with the situation. If she'd been a man there wouldn't have even been this much talking. "If I tell you, you will sit down afterward and explain why you are *really* in my home and why you are looking through my ledger."

She nodded. "If your response is satisfactory, then you have a deal."

Jasper suddenly felt uncomfortable, but he refused to fidget and expose his vulnerability. No one knew how he chose to spend a portion of his vast fortune, and he would have preferred to keep it that way. He had an image to uphold; an image that his business and reputation relied on. Except this nosy governess had forced herself into his business and he had no choice but to reveal his closely guarded secret.

Jasper cleared his throat and said, "It goes to the Rock Wharf School."

Behind her spectacles Frankie's eyes narrowed. "The what?"

"It's a school I founded on the wharf. It educates the children of fishmongers, fishermen, and dockworkers."

"A school," she repeated. Her hand with the letter opener fell to her side. "A school is expensive, but it would not be that expensive to run."

Jasper shrugged. "That shows how little you know of the lower classes. Do you think I opened a school and all of the parents were delighted to send their darlings off for a free education? That is not how the world I come from operates. Children are put to work as soon as they can properly help, sometimes as early as the age of four. A child in school is lost income, and there is nary a man or woman who can afford that on the wharf. A large portion of the three hundred pounds goes toward paying families to allow their children to attend. Another percentage goes toward my man who makes *sure* the children are attending and the parents aren't just pocketing the money and then making the children work anyway. The rest funds the building, heat, clothing, food, texts, ink, teachers, and other supplies."

Frankie set the letter opener on the side table. "You are educating them?"

Jasper's back stiffened. "They deserve to have a chance. I was fortunate to have been born with a quick mind for math and an even better memory." It had been his uncanny memory and penchant for ruthlessness that had been his ticket off the wharf, but they had also been the reasons others found him so difficult to befriend, much less love. Not even his own family had loved him. Unfortunately, he was sure far too many children felt the same way. "Most of the children on the wharf are not as lucky, but that does not mean they do not deserve a shot at a life with more promise than working themselves to death for food and coal. Those children are not worth any less than a lord's child, no matter what the peerage—or any governess—may believe."

To his surprise, Frankie crossed the room and took his hands in hers. She wasn't wearing gloves and neither was he, and the skin-on-skin contact was electrifying. Her hands were smooth and soft in his harder, calloused ones. "You misunderstood me, Mr. Jones. I was only trying to make sense of it. I think it is a wonderful idea. You are right; every child deserves a bright future."

Her words seared through him, branding his soul. Jasper lived on no one's approval, and yet he found that the approval in those blue eyes meant more to him than anything had in a long time.

"If your only clandestine monetary transaction is funding a school for children, why all the secrecy around your study?" Frankie asked. "In truth you only make it that much more enticing. After hearing that one must never enter your study, all one wants to do *is* enter your study. Do you not understand the contrary nature of humans? You would do better to leave it alone rather than declaring it forbidden to every person who crosses your path."

Jasper glared at her. "The contrary nature of *some* humans, my governess being the most contrary of them all. My study is forbidden because I insist on complete discretion when it comes to my clientele's financial states and gambling debts. It is why the ledger is kept here, in my personal house, under lock and key. Although it appears my security is lacking after all."

"You know, Mr. Jones," Frankie said thoughtfully, "one way toward achieving academic excellence in your school is to impart a fine understanding of mathematics. If you do not have a mathematics teacher for the children, I—"

Jasper slid one hand up her arm, and the words caught in Frankie's throat. "We can talk about that later," he murmured. "I have upheld my end of the bargain. Now it is your turn."

Chapter 20

A shiver raced up Frankie's arm, and too late she realized she was clutching Jasper's bare hand in hers and that she was so close she could smell the tobacco smoke from his club on his skin. She cautiously withdrew her hand and took a step back. She could not think when he touched her; his hands dulled the clarity of her mind, and she was left with only *feelings*, and Frankie was never quite sure what to do with those. The corner of Jasper's mouth lifted but he did not attempt to close the space between them.

Frankie's tongue felt dry, but he was right: He'd upheld his end of the bargain. Not only was he uninvolved with the Dowry Thieves, but he was actively bettering the world with his wealth. Frankie's secret heart had been right, as had been the Dove's suspicions, and Cecelia's staunch conviction. Jasper may have been feared on the streets, and he may have gambled his way to the top, but he was no devil.

She took a deep breath and said, "I am a governess. That is not a lie. I am not a very good one, however. My last charge threw his shoes into the Serpentine and had to walk stocking-footed through Mayfair."

Jasper leaned a hip on the desk and waited patiently.

She licked her lips. "I have a younger sister. Her name is Fidelia, and she is sixteen years of age. Several weeks ago she ran away to help her friend, who has become a victim of the Dowry Thieves. As soon as my mother realized Fidelia was missing, she tasked me with finding her. It is imperative that I locate and bring her home before anyone realizes she is missing and unchaperoned. If that happens, she'll be ruined. Except I wasn't making any progress, so I made a deal with someone: If I help this person expose the mastermind behind the Dowry Thieves, this person will help me find my sister."

Jasper held up his palm, and the ring he wore on his middle finger caught a yellow sliver of lamplight. "Who are the Dowry Thieves? Why did you think I was involved with them? Who made the deal with you? Start from the beginning, Miss Turner, and do not leave anything out."

So she did. She told him about the entrapment of the outspoken and troublesome women and the suspicion that a single mastermind was forcing them into compliance through threats of ruination. She explained her sister's devotion to their family friend, Lady Elizabeth Scarson, and how Lady Elizabeth had recently become a victim of the scheme. She told him that all twelve of the hastily married grooms had memberships to his gambling club. "That is why I needed to see your ledgers, to verify that you are not complicit."

While she'd talked, Jasper's expressions had morphed from interest to understanding, and then landed on cold fury. Frankie took an instinctive step back.

"Let me get something straight, *Frankie*."

She did not think it boded well for her that he'd just used her given name for the first time.

"Even though you suspected me of this disgusting scheme, you still entered my employ and broke into my study to go through my ledger?"

"That is slightly correct. I did not *really* think you were involved once I got to know you."

Her reply didn't mollify him. "What would have happened if I *were* heading the Dowry Thieves and caught you in my study? You have been naively thrusting yourself into danger with the hope of helping your sister and the person with whom you made the deal— a person you have yet to share details about, I might add—but what happens when you misstep? For a bloody brilliant mathematician, you are acting astoundingly stupid."

Frankie gasped in outrage. "I am not!"

Jasper leaned back and threw his hands into the air. "Naive? Ridiculous? Foolhardy? Which do you prefer?"

"I will have you know that I am not working—" Frankie stopped herself before she could finish the sentence: *I am not working with just anyone.* The Dove had not told Frankie to keep her identity a secret, but Frankie understood on some baser level that it was implied that the details of their arrangement would be kept confidential.

Jasper's eyes narrowed. "You are not working...?"

"I am not working under the assumption that I am invincible," she finished. She shoved at her irritating spectacles, which had insisted on sliding down her nose throughout the exchange. "However, I cannot afford to be timid. My sister is impulsive and young, and no one knows where she is. There are women being sold into lives of miserable matrimony because they dared stand up for others. Who is defending *them* now? No one. I will not sit back out of fear for my own life when I have the skills to help, even in some small way."

"Bloody hell." Jasper scrubbed his hand over his face. "I want to be angry with you, Frankie, but it seems I cannot be. Your actions have been foolhardy, but your heart is in the right place. If anyone knows about gambling with high stakes, it's me."

Silence fell between them as she contemplated the man whose presence took up more space than it should. The soft light of the lamps deepened the inky black of his hair and cast shadows over his cheekbones and square jaw. Frankie did not understand how the very sight of him could give her chills and flush her skin at the same time, but it embarrassed her that she consistently had inappropriate thoughts about him when she was certain that, other than regretting her employment, he never thought of her.

"Who is looking for your sister?" he asked, breaking the silence.

"A detective."

"The person you made the deal with—he or she is footing the bill for the detective in exchange for your sleuthing, correct?"

"Yes."

"And this person's name is…?"

"Private."

He sighed. "You know I will eventually uncover his identity."

Frankie was not so sure about that, but she had taunted him enough for one night.

"What is next?" His voice was deep and soft in the shadows.

"Now that I have cleared your name, I suppose…I suppose I shall leave soon." She did not know if the Dove would ask her to do anything more than examine the ledgers that had already been sent, or if maybe she would send Frankie to another home. Frankie hoped so; she did not want to be left with nothing to do but worry about Fidelia and worry about how she was going to help support her family now.

Jasper rounded his desk and opened one of the drawers. He withdrew a pack of playing cards and tapped it in his palm. "I do not think so."

Frankie's spine snapped straight. "Excuse me? You do not tell me what I will and will not do."

"I am your employer."

"Then I formally resign."

"Even better. Now that you are no longer under my employ, you are free to accept or decline my offer of a card game."

Despite her better sense, Frankie was intrigued. "A card game?"

Jasper broke the seal on the cards. "Poker."

"I have only seen it played once, at Cecelia's soirée."

"I have you at an advantage then, so I suggest a practice game. I suspect you will pick up on it quickly."

When he returned to stand in front of her, Frankie's breath caught. His gaze was dark with barely repressed emotion. No man had ever looked at her the way he was in that moment, as if he burned to kiss her until she was breathless and hot and needy.

No, that was her projection again, she thought bitterly.

There was no reason to play a game with him in his study so late in the evening, not when she had just foolishly resigned. And yet her curiosity was enflamed.

"What are the stakes?"

Barely civilized satisfaction flashed across his face before he said, "What do you want?"

"Are you . . . do you mean I can ask for *anything*?"

He spread his hands and gave her a wolfish smile. "Anything I am capable of giving you. Do not be afraid to think big, Frankie. I will be."

Frankie was speechless as a world of possibilities opened before her. Jasper was outrageously wealthy and well-connected. Was there a way to leverage his wallet and relationships to help find her sister? Perhaps he could help Frankie hire a second detective to track down Fidelia? Except the Dove was already working that angle, and if anyone could find Fidelia, it was the Dove, and Frankie did not dare insult her by implying she did not trust her to uphold *her* end of the bargain.

But what if there was another way Frankie could help? Now that Jasper was a dead end in the investigation, was there something else she could do to expose the Dowry Thieves? She had accomplished what she'd set out to do, but that did not mean she was ready to let this go. She wanted to help find the monster who was orchestrating the marriages. Lady Elizabeth was *her* friend, too, and nothing like this should ever be allowed to happen.

Her brain swirled in a maelstrom of thoughts and then—she sucked in a breath and clapped her hands over her mouth. *Yes!* That was it!

Jasper's eyes narrowed. "What?"

"If I win," Frankie said slowly, "you will commit to funding another charity."

"Which charity?"

"Me."

"Pardon me?"

"Did you know that at times the very wealthy fund dowries for poor girls with pristine reputations? If I win the poker game, you will stun the *ton* with your first act of public charity and bestow upon your poor, spinster governess an outrageous dowry that will allow her to have one last hope of marriage."

"*What?*"

Frankie pressed her hands together. "It is unconventional, I admit. Usually the beneficiaries of such generosity are young girls from the country. However, before I earned my spinster status, I was barely noticed during my four Seasons, so my reputation remains untouched." At the look on his face she hastily added, "It would not be real, Mr. Jones. You would not truly have to give me a dowry. But if everyone *believes* that you have been so enraptured by the goodness of your governess that you have seen fit to pad her dowry, it may be just the ruse we need to lure the leader of the Dowry Thieves into the open. When everyone believes me to have a generous dowry, especially combined with my genteel roots, I will be invited to every *ton* event. Then I shall speak my mind about the inequality of women in the mathematics field, and it will only be a matter of time before I become a target for the Dowry Thieves."

"Absolutely not!" Jasper roared.

Frankie sighed. "It would not actually cost you anything, Mr. Jones."

"It is Jasper to you," he snapped, "seeing as my tongue has been in your mouth. And the money is not my concern. Frankie, did you not see how the men looked at you at Cecelia's soiree?" At her confused expression he snorted. "Exactly. They were salivating over you as a governess. Can you imagine the attention you would receive if you suddenly had a massive dowry?"

Frankie laughed. "Mr. Jo—Jasper, you are too much. I do not have any illusions about my appearance or personality, but that is what the dowry is for. Everything can be overlooked for money."

Jasper halted mid-pace and stared at her. "You are jesting."

"No, most men can tolerate a plain spinster wife if she comes with a large-enough dowry."

A heavy pause settled between them. When Jasper spoke, his voice was silky and dangerous. "Do not tell me you believe yourself to be plain or lacking in personality?"

"Jasper, I am an on-the-shelf governess. My entire life I have been told that I am not beautiful, that I am strange, that my intelligence makes men insecure. I spent four Seasons being roundly ignored by men I would not have even acknowledged in the first place. I know what I am and what my place in the world is."

Jasper stalked toward her, fury rolling off him in waves. If she were not so entirely certain of her safety she would have melted into a frightened puddle. "Only a stupid man can be made to feel insecure by a woman's intelligence," he said, his voice low and hard. "An intelligent man would find you a delightful change of pace rather than a challenge to his masculinity."

Her eyebrows flew up, but he did not stop his advance until he was toe-to-toe with her and she had to lift her eyes to meet his. Her entire body thrummed with the thrill of being so close to him once again. She could feel his body heat, smell the tobacco smoke from his club, sense the electric current that hummed between them.

"As for your level of attractiveness, nearly every man at Cecelia's soirée was looking at you as if you were dessert."

"You do not have to—"

"But none of them matter," he interrupted, "because it was *me* who kissed you at the end of the night."

Frankie flushed further. "I have not had a chance to apologize for that. I put you in an untenable situation where you had to return my kiss or risk embarrassing me. It was very gentlemanly of you to not make me feel poorly."

Jasper gave a bark of laugher. "Do you think I would kiss a woman like I kissed you just to be *polite*?"

Frankie licked her lips. "I do not know how you typically kiss women."

Jasper's hand drifted to her waist, and at the simple brush of his fingertips, her skin erupted into chills. He lowered his head so that his mouth hovered over her ear, his breath caressing her as he murmured, "I kissed you, Francis Turner, because I could not stop myself, and I have dreamed every single night since then of doing it again. I fantasize about pulling your sweet body to mine and exploring every sensitive and exquisite dip of your mouth until you are either limp in my arms or begging for more." His lips brushed the shell of her ear and Frankie inhaled sharply. "Preferably begging for more."

She couldn't breathe. She couldn't think. Desire was pulsing through her veins and obliterating rational reason. She could barely reckon with her overwhelming attraction to him, much less grapple with the possibility that he might find *her* less-than-repulsive. Could one kiss initiated out of deceit and desperation really have affected them *both*?

Jasper lingered, and the air between them grew thick with tension. For one heady moment she thought he would introduce her to that *more* he was talking about, but then he cursed and turned away, breaking the spell.

He put distance between them by returning to the desk, where he raked his hand through his hair, his eyes hooded. "For argument's sake, let's say we make this bet, you win the game, and we go through with the ruse. What if, instead of exposing the Dowry Thieves' leader, he instead succeeds in entrapping you? You could end up engaged to a sixty-year-old man with missing teeth and hard fists."

Frankie's thoughts were still scattered, and it took her several moments before she could force them to focus on the earlier thread of conversation. Clearly, Jasper had not been as affected as she had by a mere brush of his hand on her waist.

"I..." She paused, unsure what she was going to say. She intended to be on her guard at social functions, but it was true that she could not control all the variables, as she'd once told Cecelia. She thought quickly, and a solution presented itself almost immediately. "He will not succeed in entrapping me because *you* will not let him."

Jasper's lips parted in disbelief.

Frankie nodded, satisfied with the idea. "Yes, as my new patron, you will host my stay in London under the ever-watchful eye and chaperonage of Madam Margaret, who will attend the events with us." Frankie would have to repeatedly rouse Madam Margaret from a doze, but it was the only proper way to go about the business. "With your knowledge of your hell customers' identities, and your expert ability to read body language and facial expressions, your presence will be quite handy. If someone tries to entrap me in marriage, I will demand the name of the man he paid to devise the scheme, and you will be there to make sure nothing ill comes of it."

Jasper lifted the cards in one hand and they fell in a perfect sheet into his other palm. "You want me to guard you. To act as your protective patron."

"Essentially."

"No. It is far too risky."

Frankie gave him her most charming smile. "You must not be very confident in your card skills. I have never played poker before, and you are the king of London's underworld. Surely you could not lose to a governess?"

Jasper growled. "I know what you are doing, Frankie." He thought for a moment as he idly handled the cards with his long, nicked fingers. "I am arguably the best card player in all of London. Chances are you will lose. If you do, you must adhere to the stakes."

She waved her hand impatiently. She did not care what he asked; the risk was worth it. "What do you want if you win?"

"If I win, you agree to marry me."

Chapter 21

The surprise on Frankie's face mirrored his own. He hadn't quite known what he was going to ask of her, but the moment the words were out they felt exactly right. He'd been considering marriage to protect himself from scheming nieces and mamas anyway—so why not Frankie? He did not want to marry a woman of the *ton*, so Frankie's position was not a barrier. She was rapaciously intelligent in a way that would keep him on his toes for years to come, and that appealed to him far more than he would have ever thought. Frankie as his wife, and Cecelia as his ward, would guarantee trouble and chaos and reckless schemes—and for the life of him he could not understand why the thought satisfied him to the very core.

Jasper had always thrived on challenge, and life had begun to bore him. With Frankie in it, he thought it likely he would never be bored again.

There was also the not-so-insignificant fact that he desperately wanted to strip her out of her governess gown, throw her spectacles across the room, and kiss her again—everywhere. He'd already had a taste of what passion was like with her, and it was explosive. He'd been craving more of her with every breath since. He wanted to make love to her, and the only way he could do that was to marry her. It had nearly killed him to walk away moments ago when his hand had been on her waist and she'd been looking up at him with molten eyes, her pink tongue darting out to lick her lips. But she was not a widow free to engage in a brief affair. She was unmarried. She was *Frankie*, and he would not put her in that position.

Whoever had told the woman she was plain and unmarriageable had either been blind or an ass, or perhaps both. Frankie still did not believe him when he said she was beautiful, but the truth was he had never met anyone who intrigued him on every level the way she did—intellectually *and* physically.

Jasper decided right then he would not rest until Frankie saw herself the way he did.

Tread carefully, his instincts warned. Frankie was open and honest and heartfelt, and somewhere deep inside he suspected that if he were not cautious, she would disarm him and lay open his heart.

"*Marry* you?" she howled. "Have you gone mad? Why on earth would you want to marry me?"

Jasper fanned the cards in his hands. "Why not?"

Her mouth opened and closed, then opened and closed. She fisted her hands on her hips. "I am a governess."

"I am a fishmonger's son."

"I would not lift your standing in the *ton*."

Jasper shuffled the cards with an expert flex of his hands. "That is a relief, as I have no interest in raising my standing in the *ton*. I see enough of them in my hell and I should not care to have to deal with them in my leisure time as well."

"I would not listen to you," she said plainly. She shoved at her spectacles. Jasper really needed to find her a doctor who could fit her with proper frames. "I would wish to open a mathematics journal, and if my gender were discovered it would be a scandal for the ages."

Jasper pointed with his chin toward the settee, and she followed him over. He pulled the side table in between them and grinned. "I love a good scandal."

"I am serious, Jasper. All jesting aside, this is my life and I do not wish to bet it on a game without a satisfactory reason."

Jasper laid the cards on the table and thought figuratively he might as well do the same. "Then let me be plain: I am looking for a wife. Cecelia's scheme to marry me to that viper was enough to make me reconsider my stance as an eternal bachelor. I think you and I would get along splendidly, even if you *are* bossy."

Frankie interlaced her fingers primly on her lap. "I am not bossy."

"You are very bossy, and heaven knows why I like it."

"Do you love me?" she asked curiously.

Jasper almost choked. Good lord! At least if they were married he would never have to wonder what she was thinking. "This is more of a business proposition," he said, hoping he would not wound her feelings. Jasper did not want to give her any illusions about what he was proposing. He had never been on the receiving end of love, had never *deserved* love; the things he'd done on his rise to the top were unforgivable. Neither had he ever loved anybody—the closest he'd come was what he felt for his brother and Cecelia, and that was too complicated to define. "A marriage of convenience, if you will. You would have access to my fortune and you could open ten mathematics journals if you pleased. I would have respite from my niece and the rest of the *ton*'s scheming."

"Would we have marital relations?"

"Frankie." Jasper groaned. "Would you want marital relations?"

His heart lurched at the shy smile on her lips. "Yes, I think I would."

At her admission lust roared through Jasper's veins. He leaned forward, his pulse beating heavily in his throat. "Say you'll accept the terms."

"Can I use math during the game?"

"Give it your best. But no other forms of cheating such as hiding cards up your sleeve."

"Do people do that in your hell?"

"If they try it once they do not try a second time."

She shivered. "All right, Jasper Jones. I accept your terms."

Frankie held out her hand and Jasper clasped it in his own. He tugged her forward, breathing in the scents of chalk dust from her gown and rose petals from her skin. "Then let me teach you how to play, Mrs. Jones."

Frankie inhaled sharply at the address and narrowed her eyes. "Yes, lay out the rules. It is growing late, and first thing tomorrow morning I will want you spreading word that you have generously donated a massive dowry to your poor governess."

Jasper grinned and let go of her hand slowly, so that his fingertips trailed across her palm. When she bit her bottom lip, it took all of his self-control not to throw the cards over his shoulder, press her into the settee, and soothe the bite with his tongue.

He was dealing the cards for their practice round when his conscience, which had been nagging at him since he'd proposed the game, finally got the best of him. He knew he was going to win, so was he any better than the monster heading the Dowry Thieves if he tricked her into marrying him?

Jasper had lived his entire life pressing his advantage and playing bluffs to the final moments. Revealing an edge went against every instinct he'd cultivated, and yet he found he did not want to treat Frankie the same way he did his usual opponents.

He heaved a loud sigh. "I propose an amendment to the terms."

Frankie lifted her eyes from where she'd been watching him deal the cards with practiced ease. "No. They are settled. I am not changing my terms."

"It is not your terms I wish to change."

"You do not wish to marry me?"

"That is not the issue. I do not wish to *coerce* you into marriage."

Frankie tilted her head. "You would have to win in order for that to happen."

"I will win, Frankie."

She gave him a lopsided smile and picked up her cards. "I appreciate your concern, but I am not worried."

"You will not resent marrying me?"

Frankie fanned the cards in her hand. "It does not affect me, as I intend to win. But no, Jasper. I am quite capable of taking responsibility for my own actions."

Heaven help him, he was beginning to really like this woman.

Jasper explained the rules of draw poker and carefully studied her expressions as they played the first game. She gave away nothing, even though he could practically see the wheels spinning behind her eyes. The lamps had burned down, so midway he had to light more candles, and the dozens of flickering flames cheerfully pushed aside the waving shadows. It was too warm to start a fire, yet the study still felt cozy and intimate. Jasper realized that for the first time in a long time he was having fun. He thought he had fun every night at his gaming hell, but it seemed over time the managerial role had taken over the more thrilling aspects of running a gambling club.

Jasper thought he could get used to playing Frankie in the wee hours. He could think of all sorts of delicious things to wager.

Frankie lost the practice game, and Jasper smiled indulgently and did his best to ease the sting by assuring her it happened to the best of them. Privately, he was wondering if he could secure a special license, or if they would have to suffer the banns being read.

"Are you ready to play for real?" Jasper asked.

Frankie gave a curt nod. "Yes, I believe I fully understand it now."

Jasper was impressed. Not many people could get a handle on the game after one play and then dare challenge him with such confidence.

"You deal," he said.

Frankie dealt, and while they played Jasper thought of how Cecelia would take the news about the wedding. He frowned when he remembered that Cecelia had brought him home to interrupt Frankie's search. Had she been trying to get Frankie in trouble? Or had she been plotting again?

Jasper was still deciding which motivation to attribute to Cecelia when Frankie laid out a royal flush and said innocently, "That is a good hand, is it not?"

Jasper knew his jaw had fallen, and only through sheer willpower was he able to close his mouth again. He should have been furious. He should have been embarrassed. His governess had soundly defeated him when some of the best poker players in London had not. It had been a very, very long time since someone had trounced him so quickly and thoroughly. That should have pinched his ego.

Instead, he felt a surge of pride. He swallowed back a spurt of laughter. "That is a very good hand, you little imp."

Frankie's eyes twinkled. "Are you angry?"

"Because I lost? Give me more credit than that."

"Most men would be livid to lose to their governess."

"Alas, you have forgotten that you are no longer under my employ. If anything, I am horrified that now I have to watch dozens of men falling over their own feet trying to woo you. You do realize that if you go through with this, you are not only putting yourself in jeopardy, but you are also threatening my livelihood."

"How is that?"

"The 'charitable dowry' will tarnish my image as a blackguard, but more importantly, now that you have put me in charge of your bodily safety, if any of those simpering toffs tries to put his hands on you, I'll knock all his teeth out. That will *not* be good for business."

Frankie collected the cards and tapped them neatly into a stack. "Jasper, do not be ridiculous. No one could knock out thirty-two teeth with one strike. Shall we play again?"

Jasper didn't know if he wanted to laugh or cry.

Chapter 22

Frankie did not sleep well. She tossed and turned the remainder of the night, her eagerness to begin the ruse alternating with confusing thoughts about Jasper. He pretended to be an arrogant spendthrift and rake, but that seemed to be a carefully cultivated image. In actuality, he was kind and patient, and not only with Cecelia but also with his staff and with Frankie. He had even been willing to repeal the terms of their bet because he had not wanted to press his advantage. For a man who'd risen to his current position in life through cheating, he was paradoxically honorable when it came to certain values. He did not play by society's rule book, but he had his own moral code by which he abided. That was more than she could say for the supposedly noble Dowry Thieves.

When the fingers of dawn crept beneath her shutters, she gave up on sleep and dressed in the only non-governess dress she'd packed in her valise other than the evening gown she'd worn to Cecelia's soirée. It was pale yellow with panels of sheer fabric that overlaid a stiff cotton skirt. It would not win her any envious glances from the *ton*, but it was more her style, and for the first time in Jasper's house she truly felt herself.

As she combed and pinned her hair she thought of the logistics of her plan. She would need a new wardrobe if she was going to attend balls and other *ton* events—except she did not have the funds. Frankie stabbed a pin in her hair and watched as it immediately slid several inches out of place. No wonder her hairstyles were always so dismal, she thought with resignation. Her hair had the texture of glass. She fixed the pin the best she could and studied the purple shadows under her eyes. Perhaps she could borrow money against her real, meager dowry. It was not as if she were ever going to need it.

Frankie wondered if the Dove would be pleased with her new plan, and then remembered she had yet to write that she had cleared Jasper's name. With no better time than the present, Frankie sat down at her desk and hastily penned a letter that included the details of her scheme to act as bait, with Jasper for security.

Once she finished, Frankie sealed the letter and had her hand on the doorknob when she noticed a note had been slipped under her door. Frankie unfolded the half sheet of paper and immediately recognized Cecelia's forceful scrawl.

Dear Miss Turner,

I want to apologize for telling Uncle Jasper you were in his study. That was not my plan when I gave you the key, and I do not want you to think I am a liar, but rather an opportunist who seized upon a good idea.

Good intentioned-ly yours,
Cecelia

Frankie grinned as she laid the note on the washstand. Cecelia had clearly hoped to pair her off with Jasper, and if Jasper had won the card game, she just might have been successful.

Frankie tried not to dwell on Jasper having wagered marriage. It was not as if he cared for her or had declared his love. He'd essentially proposed it as a business deal because he thought they would get along "splendidly" and it would save him from more of Cecelia's scheming. It meant nothing, and now that he had lost the game, the topic would not come up again. Jasper was going to help her expose the Dowry Thieves, and then he would find some other woman to propose the business of marriage to. She was certain that if he did not, Cecelia would see to it herself.

Frankie pushed down an unwelcome feeling of disappointment at the thought, and hurried to mail her letter. Once sent, she entered the sunny morning room to break her fast. A generous buffet was already laid out: thinly sliced cold ham and beef on a silver platter, a tray of quail eggs, a rasher of bacon, stewed tomatoes, sweet jams and pastries, and coffee and tea. Madam Margaret was already stationed by the window, her fingers trembling as she took a bite of toast.

"Good morning, Madam Margaret," Frankie said.

Madam Margaret, who was hard of hearing, did not look up from her toast.

"GOOD MORNING, MADAM MARGARET!" Frankie shouted.

Madam Margaret jolted, startled by Frankie's presence, and gave her a trembling smile. "Good morning, Miss Turner."

Frankie turned to collect a plate, but her stomach was too filled with nerves for her to enjoy the food properly that morning. She was staring contemplatively into her cup of coffee when Jasper entered. He looked at her twice, no doubt surprised that she was already awake, and veered from his course to pull out the chair across from her.

He was freshly shaved and smelled of his signature shaving cream: pine, cloves, and coffee. Frankie knew for the rest of her life she would associate those scents with the dark-eyed man across from her. His hair was styled, and his cravat was starched crisp, contrasting with a dove-gray morning jacket that fit expertly across the planes of his broad shoulders. Jasper adjusted one of his cuffs, the ring on his middle finger flashing in the morning sunlight as he did so. For the first time Frankie noticed that it was the black-engraved crest of Rockford's.

Jasper finished with his cuff and reached across the table for her teacup. "Coffee? Lovely." He took a healthy swallow. "Is Cecelia still sleeping?"

"I do not think so," she said, retrieving her cup from his hand. "Isn't the master of the house supposed to sit at the end of the table in a high-backed, kingly chair?"

Jasper crossed one booted ankle over his knee. "A king is a king no matter where he sits."

"I am astonished this room is large enough to fit all three of us *and* your ego."

His face split into a grin. "Is that any way to talk to the charitable patron donating a dowry large enough to make half the *ton* drool?"

"I am sure my charitable patron is well aware of his flaws. What are your plans for this morning, Mr. Jones?"

Jasper snitched a blackberry off her plate. "Is it 'Mr. Jones' now? I thought we discussed that."

"Jasper," Frankie hissed, her cheeks heating when she remembered why he had insisted she call him by his given name. She glanced pointedly at Madam Margaret, who was nodding off over her toast. "Have a care with what you say. And why are you so cheerful and awake? It is the crack of dawn. 'Tis offensive."

"Darling, it is nearly nine o'clock in the morning."

Frankie groaned. "Exactly."

Jasper's smile deepened, his teeth white against a tanned jaw, and Frankie's skin tingled in memory of the gentle scrape of those beautiful teeth on her bottom lip. He truly was the most sinfully handsome man she'd ever laid eyes on.

"Trouble sleeping?" The look in his eye told her he suspected she'd tossed and turned the entire night and that he thought he was the reason why.

Frankie paused with the coffee halfway to her mouth. "Slept like a babe."

"You have a wicked side to you, did you know that, Miss Turner?" Jasper reached for a slice of her bacon and Frankie slapped his hand.

"Get your own plate."

Jasper sighed and stood. A moment later he returned with a heaping plate that put hers to shame.

"I need to visit the modiste this morning," Frankie said, "but I shall need to wait until you've spread the word about my dowry so that she will be willing to see me quickly and on credit."

Jasper's teeth sank into a piece of bacon. "I'll do you one better," he said after he swallowed. "I will personally escort you to the modiste and tell her to put everything on my account. Then I shall leave you and spend the morning making calls."

"Oh, Jasper, I could not ask you to—"

He lifted a hand. "Consider the wardrobe your severance pay."

"I shall need suitable attire. It will be expensive."

"As long as I no longer have to lay eyes on those hideous governess garments, I will consider it money well spent."

Frankie lifted a slice of toast and nibbled around the edge. "We need to speak with Cecelia. She will very quickly hear of what is happening, and it is not fair that she be kept in the dark. And Madam Margaret, too."

At that moment Cecelia entered the morning room with the energy of a tornado, spotted Jasper and Frankie dining together, and broke into a wide grin. "Good morning, Uncle Jasper, Miss Turner."

Jasper waved her over. "Cecelia, we need to speak with you."

She bounded over to the table and pulled out a chair before the footman could reach it. Then she interlaced her fingers together and looked between them with slyly innocent eyes. "Yes?"

Jasper quietly dismissed the servants, and once the room was clear except for the dozing lady in the sun, he said, "I am going to share something with you, but it is imperative that it is kept an absolute secret. No one can know, and I do mean *no one*. If the secret got out it could have severe consequences for Miss Turner and someone she cares deeply for."

Cecelia's smile faded. "Do you mean her sister?"

Jasper raised an eyebrow.

"Yes, it is about my sister." Frankie said. She took a deep breath, and for the second time within twenty-four hours explained about the Dowry Thieves and her impulsive sister.

When Frankie finished, Cecelia slammed her fist on the table. "Those rats! Good for you, Miss Turner. I want you and Uncle

Jasper to make them pay for what they've done. But does this mean you will no longer be my governess?" Before Frankie could answer her eyes took on a gleam. "Can I go with you to the balls? I am nearly old enough to come out."

"No," Jasper said immediately. Before Cecelia could protest, he gentled his tone. "Cecelia, it would divide my attention to have to keep preying men away from both of you, and I must be on my guard so that Frankie does not fall victim to the Dowry Thieves."

Cecelia pouted for a moment but then gave a sharp nod. "I understand. Mum's the word." She lifted a fork and tapped the tines on the tablecloth. "Can I at least visit the modiste with you?"

Frankie smiled. "I was going to ask if you would."

Cecelia pointed her fork at Jasper. "Uncle Jasper, did you not receive an invitation to the Coswold literary reception taking place this afternoon?"

Jasper paled. "Is that one of those tedious affairs where earnest young men read terrible poetry and discuss the latest published books as if they've actually read them?"

Cecelia shrugged. "That sounds right. I am certain I saw an invitation. It stood out because it was so pretty with gold embossing and thick paper."

"I know of the Coswold literary events," Frankie said. Each summer Lady Jane Coswold returned from the countryside for two weeks to host her literary receptions, and they were always heavily attended. She fancied herself an art benefactor, and sweltering in the city was a small price to pay for doing her duty to elevate the arts, never mind that the majority of the "artists" who shared literary discussion and read poetry at her receptions were of the upper class and hardly required elevating. "If you have an invitation, that would be the perfect place to introduce me as your beneficiary."

Jasper groaned something about poorly made bets and shoved his plate aside. "I suppose we had better start spreading the news then. I would not want to miss an evening of the *ton*'s finest poetry. Come along, ladies. We have a modiste to visit."

Before he exited, he paused behind Frankie's chair and lowered his head to her ear. "When you are selecting gowns this morning, my dear beneficiary, remember how many teeth there are in the human mouth."

Chapter 23

As soon as Jasper left them at the modiste, Frankie regretted bringing Cecelia along. Frankie loved beautiful gowns as much as the next woman, especially the green shades, but she had been raised in a household that kept a strict eye on the accounts and she had been trained to spend conservatively. Cecelia had no such restraint.

"She needs three ball gowns," Cecelia informed the modiste. Under normal circumstances the modiste would have been curt with the overenthusiastic girl, but *the* Mr. Jasper Jones had visited her *in person*, so instead the modiste nodded and simpered and saw to Cecelia's every wish, all while her mouth twitched as she desperately fought the impulse to ask why Mr. Jones was buying such an expensive wardrobe for his governess.

Cecelia gave Frankie a sly look. "My uncle's newest beneficiary will need the most in-fashion cut. The lower the neckline, the better."

"No, *not* the lower the neckline the better," Frankie said.

"Beneficiary?" the modiste asked with unveiled curiosity, ignoring Frankie.

"Oh yes," Cecelia replied airily. "Many people do not know how charitable Uncle Jasper is. When he discovered Miss Turner might never wed for lack of a suitable dowry, he placed an *enormous* sum on her. We shall be like sisters now, won't we?"

Three hours later, Frankie and Cecelia exited the shop just as Lady Trathers entered. "Well, that ought to do it," Frankie whispered as the woman's keen eyes took them in and sparked with interest. Lady Trathers marched straight toward the modiste, no doubt to get all the good gossip on Mr. Jasper Jones's niece and her governess. "By the end of the day everyone will know about the dowry. Cecelia, you truly spent too much of Jasper's money."

Cecelia lifted her fan and beat the humid air around her face. "'Twas barely a dent in Uncle Jasper's fortune. Besides, if you expect to succeed with your ruse, you must look the part. It was very fortunate that the modiste had a few gowns you could purchase on the spot." Cecelia looked over her shoulder at the footman who trailed behind them carrying several flat boxes. "It must be nice to be of normal height. The gold one is sure to drive Uncle Jasp—any potential suitors absolutely mad. You must wear it tonight for your debut as the summer's wealthiest spinster."

Frankie groaned and prayed her mother did not hear about this startling turn of events, although she knew that was a prayer unlikely to be answered. Jasper's charity case would be the largest piece of gossip since the announcement of her friend Emily's betrothal to the extremely wealthy bachelor Mr. Zachariah Denholm.

Frankie really should have thought longer about the ramifications the lie would have on her family. Her mother had already been severely disappointed once when Frankie had finished four Seasons without a proposal, and when this supposedly massive dowry did not turn up a suitor, she would be devastated all over again. Frankie knew that over time the scandal of her not making a match, even when she had a veritable fortune attached to her name, would become old news, but it would never be forgotten.

Frankie did not mind—she had accepted her fate as a spinster long ago—but she did worry about Fidelia. If the Dove found Fidelia before she managed to ruin her own reputation and coming-out, she would still have to contend with Frankie's failure casting a deep shadow over her. Frankie vowed right then that she would sell every last one of the outrageous gowns Cecelia had just ordered so that she could fund a satisfactory dowry for Fidelia. Perhaps Fidelia would still have choices. Perhaps her future husband would be able to look past Fidelia's sad older sister being unable to snag a match even with the help of Mr. Jasper Jones.

When Frankie and Cecelia reached home, Frankie found a message waiting from the Dove.

Frankie—

I am relieved to hear you were able to clear Mr. Jones's name. Your letter reached me at the same time as the gossip that Mr. Jones has bestowed an innumerable sum on his governess in a shocking act of charity. Although I wish you would have shared your intentions with me before you acted, what is done is done. Someday I shall be quite interested to learn how such an arrangement came about. I believe the mastermind behind the Dowry Thieves to be extremely clever and unforgiving, so you must be vigilant when in public. I admit that your bait may be exactly what we need if you cannot find any commonality in the financial papers of the grooms.

~D~

Frankie vowed to continue looking over the financials the next morning, but now she needed to dress for the literary reception. The modiste had had two suitable gowns on hand, one of them an ethereal morning gown of white embroidered with delicate roses and greenery. The other was the gold gown Cecelia loved. The fabric was satin and so smooth that it reflected light. Tiny gold beads had been sewn across the waist and hem, making Frankie glitter with every swish and turn. The woman it had originally been designed for had had a smaller bust measurement than Frankie's, but beggars couldn't be choosers, and it really was the more appropriate gown of the two for the evening entertainment.

With a shrug, Frankie rang for Cecelia's lady's maid to help her dress, her thoughts consumed with financials and numbers.

Frankie waited for Jasper in the foyer and gulped when he appeared wearing a black coat and crisp white cravat. His dark trousers were molded to his muscled thighs, and his boots were so polished they shone. His trademark black ring flashed in the light as he tucked his tin pocket watch back into his coat and gave her a devastatingly handsome smile. Then his eyes swept over her and the smile faltered.

"Frankie, are you intent on making my job as difficult as possible?"

"What do you mean?"

"Never mind," he growled, taking her elbow. He had not yet applied his gloves, and his long, tanned fingers slid along her skin in a caress that made a flush crawl over her chest. Frankie discreetly touched her eyebrows to make sure they were not singed along with the rest of her. Despite Cecelia's claims to the contrary, Frankie was convinced Jasper had earned his devil-of-sin reputation fairly. When a man had that sort of effect on a woman with a simple elbow touch, he was sure to be dangerous indeed.

Suddenly Frankie was not sure she could stand being confined so close to him in the carriage. "Let us walk instead," she burst out. "I require air."

Jasper looked down at her with exasperation. "Have you seen the sky? It is set to pour any moment. Besides, Madam Margaret is in no condition to walk."

"Then I had best hurry if I want to avoid the rain. You may ride with Madam Margaret."

At that moment the lady in question appeared, outfitted in a dove-gray gown that had last been in fashion in 1795. Cecelia had whispered to Frankie that Jasper had tried to buy Madam Margaret new dresses, claiming it was a thank-you for her generosity in agreeing to chaperone, but that the older lady had declined, citing a preference for the more "conservative" dress style of yore.

"Madam Margaret!" Frankie gave her a genuine smile. "I think I shall walk to the reception and meet you and Mr. Jones there."

"A young lady may not walk the streets without a chaperone." Madam Margaret's voice wavered with age as she tottered toward them. Her eyes were rheumy and her gait was unsure, but she seemed more alive than Frankie had ever seen her.

Frankie sighed internally and increased the brightness of her smile. "Very well, madam."

The carriage ride to Lady Jane Coswold's took ten minutes, and Frankie was careful to fill every spare moment with incessant chatter so that she might avoid having to think about the one thing that was becoming disturbingly apparent: She was attracted to Jasper Jones. With each word she spoke, the sky grew darker and lower outside the windows until it seemed that the clouds were pregnant with rain.

She was sick of her own voice by the time they reached the Coswold town house, which stood among a row of houses not nearly as grand as Jasper's, but that possessed a dignified and wealthy air that made sure one checked the heels of one's boots for mud before entering.

They were ushered into the sitting room where the furniture had been artfully arranged to leave an open space for the literary recitals. White, fragrant flowers filled ornate vases that were so large they had to be set on the floor, and the tinkle of glasses and hum of polite conversation filled the room.

The moment the three of them entered, Frankie knew what it was to walk into a viper's den. Conversation quieted, and every set of eyes turned onto her and Jasper, and in them she read suspicion, greed, and calculation.

Jasper's arm flexed under her palm as he warmly greeted their hostess, who was thrilled beyond measure to have not only Mr.

Jasper Jones at her reception, but also Miss Francis Turner, who although genteelly bred, had never been important enough to invite before.

Frankie scanned the sitting room for familiar faces, vaguely recalling a number of the men's names from her mother's failed attempts to make her and Fidelia memorize all the peers in *Debrett's*.

It was as if she and Jasper were wearing magnets. Within minutes of Lady Jane Coswold excusing herself, men flocked to Jasper to wrangle an introduction to Frankie. Madam Margaret took up a chair nearby as Frankie's gloved hand was taken and kissed over and over.

During the next hour, Frankie was told her eyes were beautiful, her hair spun of the same gold as her gown, and that her complexion was as smooth as porcelain. Frankie smiled and nodded, and reflected that yesterday not a single one of these men would have noticed her, much less thought her eyes were "as blue as Neptune's lonely heart"—whatever that meant. It was as if her perceived wealth gave her plain looks a sudden glow. The son of an earl, a viscount, and two barons clustered around her, their breath hot with tea and their smiles disingenuous.

Meanwhile, Jasper fended off his own crowd of debutants, ambitious mamas, and lonely widows. At one point Frankie spotted him crowded by three young ladies with the exact same shade of copper-colored hair, giving them away as sisters. He met her gaze over the tops of their heads and gave her a look so smoldering that she immediately thrust her fan in front of her face and furtively glanced around to make sure no one else had noticed. She returned her attention to one of the barons, who had not ceased speaking for the past ten minutes, and she smiled woodenly, all while keenly aware of Jasper's presence sucking the air out of the room.

She did her best to keep up her end of the conversation while discreetly assessing the other men in the room. Her gaze landed on Lord Quincy, a thin man with bulging eyes and tufts of white hair climbing out of his ears. He was rumored to be in the market for a wife, as his fifth wife had recently died in childbirth. He had fourteen children, all of them girls, and bred his wives until they expired in an attempt to give him a male heir. He had great, public scorn for the female sex. Could he be behind the Dowry Thieves?

Then there was Mr. Albert Stephens, who had reportedly blown through his inheritance in six months flat. His father would only pledge him more funds if he found a wife. So far Mr. Stephens had had no luck, as he was a cruel man who'd once beat his own horse to death. If the ringleader behind the Dowry Thieves required a fee for his services, then Mr. Albert Stephens had the motive—but did he have the intelligence?

Standing beside Mr. Stephens was Lady Evelyn Barker and her father, the Earl of Elmsdale. While Elmsdale, a conservative Tory, debated Mr. Stephens, Lady Evelyn skewered Frankie with hateful looks.

"Do you enjoy poetry, Miss Turner?" A newcomer at her elbow interrupted her thoughts with a grating, nasally voice. He was tall and gangly, with sallow skin and thin hair, and wore a crushed velvet coat that had gone out of style nearly a decade ago.

"I apologize, I do not—"

"I beg your forgiveness. Of course you would not recognize me; you were but a child when I saw you last. I am a very distant cousin of your father's. The name is Mr. Lyle Farthins."

"Pleased to meet you, Mr. Farthins." She vaguely recalled the Farthins name in her family tree. "Are you enjoying the gathering?"

"I am now that I have met you."

Frankie stared blankly for a moment before realizing that was supposed to flatter her. "Oh, er—you are too kind."

"It is impossible to overcompliment a flower."

Why did everyone keep comparing her to jewels and flowers? There were far more interesting things one could compare a woman to, like a mathematics equation. Now that would be some compliment. "Are you reading a poem tonight, Mr. Farthins?"

He gave a rusty laugh. "Now it is you who flatters me."

She hadn't meant to.

"Alas, I do not have the heart of an artist, although as I stand here looking at you, I feel as if I could become one."

Frankie tried not to groan. "I do not care for poetry myself. I am much more interested in mathematics."

The somewhat handsome Lord Wilson, who stood crowded around them, laughed uproariously. When Frankie frowned, he said, "But of course you jest, Miss Turner. It is common knowledge that women are more suited to the delicate disciplines: hostessing, art, music, and the like."

Frankie pushed her spectacles up her nose. "I must respectfully disagree, Lord Wilson. Women are just as capable, if not more so, as men are in the execution of the scientific disciplines. They have much to contribute. I would go so far as to say that society is being held back from advancement by the exclusion of women in the scientific and mathematics communities."

Several more men joined the conversation, and the room began to quiet. Frankie's heart was pounding in her chest, not because she was ashamed of what she was saying, but because she was unused to such an audience.

"Surely you do not mean to imply that women have equally calculating minds as men?" Mr. Farthins gave her a patronizing smile that set her teeth on edge.

"You are right, I do not mean to imply it. I am saying it outright."

Chapter 24

There was a stir among the crowd. Frankie would have said more, but Lady Jane, ever the observant hostess, quickly clapped her hands and announced that the evening's literary entertainment was about to begin.

The crowd dispersed, and Frankie exhaled a sigh of relief. She did not know how popular debutants withstood such scrutiny event after event, Season after Season. Her relief was short-lived when her extremely distant relation, Mr. Farthins, returned to insist on escorting her to her seat, where she found herself wedged between him and Lord Wilson. Jasper was seated farther behind her with his own set of admirers. At least she had managed to make her "controversial statement" before the event began. She was almost certain tongues would be wagging at intermission.

Frankie's cheeks grew hotter and hotter over the next hour as one erstwhile man after the other stood and directed his flowery poetry in her direction, their eyes rich with romantic sentiment and their words so convoluted that Frankie did not even know what they were saying 90 percent of the time. All the while the back of her neck prickled with the heat of Jasper's stare.

When, two hours into the program, Lady Jane announced an intermission, Frankie jumped to her feet and was halfway to the door before Mr. Farthins caught up with her. She wanted to scream.

Mr. Farthins gave her an oily, understanding smile. "Might I interest you in a walk in the courtyard?"

"Yes!" Frankie cried. She was desperate for a respite. She had to *breathe*. She didn't even care if she had to suffer the company of Mr. Farthins if it meant she could leave the claustrophobia of the room.

The French doors were closed to the flowered courtyard, but beyond the glass, heat-bleached plants whipped with the wind of the oncoming storm.

"Oh drat, I forgot the storm brewing," Farthins said. "Perhaps we might investigate the library? I hear it is one of the largest libraries in town."

Frankie was already stepping into the corridor, her slippers soundless on the tile as she rushed from the sitting room without giving a thought to asking Madam Margaret to accompany her. Her golden gown, too tight to begin with, suddenly felt suffocating. She had attended plenty of society events during her four Seasons out, but the events had been smaller, and she had *always* gone unnoticed. For the first time, she questioned whether she was capable of carrying out the ruse. Never before had she been given so much attention and been under such scrutiny.

When she reached the library, Frankie instantly felt calmer. As Mr. Farthins had claimed, it was a grand room so full of volumes of text that it would have done the queen proud. It smelled of old leather and polish, and Frankie inhaled deeply just as she heard the door click shut.

She spun around in surprise. "Mr. Farthins, please open the door. You forget that it is improper for a young lady to be unchaperoned in a closed room with a gentleman."

Mr. Farthins stepped closer, the mothball scent of his velvet coat filling her nostrils. He gave her a broad, yellow-toothed smile, and the facade of flattery fell away, leaving his face harsh and twisted.

With a sinking feeling in the pit of her stomach, Frankie realized she'd made a grievous error. She'd been so eager to get away from the crowd that she had not even considered that Mr. Farthins might not be a gentleman. She had felt especially confident knowing that the leader of the Dowry Thieves would not have had time to set up an entrapment. That, she realized belatedly, had been a number of costly errors on her part.

"Alas, you are not a *lady*. You are nothing but the granddaughter of a baron, a governess putting on airs because she struck it lucky." Mr. Farthins bared more of his teeth. "As your distant cousin, I think it is only fair that I share in your good fortune."

"What do you want from me?"

Mr. Farthins blinked, reminding her of an eel she'd once observed in a sea exhibit. "Did you know that when your father and I were children, he accused me of stealing from him and then bloodied my nose? He humiliated me in front of our entire family. But that was nothing compared to what he did a decade later, when he swooped in and married the woman I loved."

Frankie gawked at him. "You—loved my mother?"

"I spotted her across the room at a country ball, and I fell for her instantly. She would have felt the same for me, too, if your father had not begun courting her. He was a half-hour gentleman and she deserved better. But he is dead now, and today I shall walk away with both his daughter *and* a fortune." He peered closely at her. "You look more like him than her, but there are enough common details that it will not be hard to pretend you *are* her."

Frankie felt ill. "I would never exchange vows with the likes of you, but I will give my mother your regards." She strode toward the door with all the regal bearing of a duchess, but before she could reach it Farthins snatched her wrist and swung her back, his grip so bruising that she cried out in pain.

"When we are married you will not leave a room before you are dismissed."

Frankie could not scream to alert anyone for help without also inadvertently compromising herself, so instead she glared at Mr. Farthins, her fear eclipsed by her fury. How dare he threaten her? "If you touch me again, another Turner shall bloody your nose."

"You little bitch. I shall take great pleasure in teaching you how to treat your better."

He shoved her against a bookshelf, his breath a sour mix of tea and quail egg refreshments. "Look at me, Miranda."

"I am not my mother!" His hands pinned Frankie's shoulders to the bookshelf, and she was pulled too tightly to his sinewy body for her legs to be effective weapons. She was powerless. Except…she had once read a text on human anatomy, and it had included a diagram of an entire skeleton (she had then hidden it beneath her floorboards, knowing she would be punished if she were caught reading something so scandalous). She recalled that the bony protuberance of a human forehead was very thick and hard. With that knowledge in hand, Frankie did the only thing she could think to do: She smashed her forehead into Mr. Farthins's nose.

Frankie saw stars and her spectacles nearly fell off her face.

Mr. Farthins howled in pain, releasing her to cup his nose. Blood spurted between his fingers and dribbled down his hands and arms, staining the fraying cuffs of his coat. Frankie didn't wait for him to recover; she sprinted to the door and was about to yank it open when Farthins snatched her from behind and threw her back against the bookcase. Droplets of blood splattered on her new golden gown and across the skin of her chest.

"You will pay for this, you—"

Air whooshed across Frankie's face as Mr. Farthins was ripped away and tossed to the ground. The scuffle that ensued was fast and dirty, and it was nearly over before it had begun. Jasper was precise and ruthless; Mr. Farthins was simply no match for his experienced fists and the fury that propelled them. Frankie could only sag against the bookcase and watch in horrified fascination as Jasper pummeled Mr. Farthins until he slumped unconscious on the floor.

Despite the beating, Jasper was barely breathing hard when he spun around to her, his cravat askew and his eyes wild and dark with rage. He had blood on his knuckles from Farthins's already-broken nose, but she didn't flinch from him when he gently cupped her cheek with his palm.

"Are you all right? Did he hurt you?"

Frankie grasped his wrist as if the touch would anchor her to reality. She licked her trembling lips and said, "My head hurts something fearsome. I smashed my forehead into his nose."

Jasper gently touched his own forehead to hers just as the first boom of thunder rattled the library windows. "There is blood on you."

"It is his," she assured him.

"What the hell were you thinking, going off alone with him? That man is vile and a petty thief. I do not know how he dared show his face here today."

Jasper lifted his head, his eyes searing into hers. His body was pressed against hers, warm and big and hard, and he was cradling her cheek as if she were the most precious thing in the world. His clean, warm scent enveloped her in a soothing cocoon, and Frankie had never felt so safe and confused in her entire life. "I was not thinking," she admitted.

Jasper growled in frustration. "Do you know how torturous the past two hours have been, watching every man in the city fawn over you?"

"It is because of the dowry."

"Mayhap that was the initial draw, but I know when a man is truly interested in a woman, and a good number of them have been charmed silly by your crooked grin and clever wit and this damned gown that shows off more curves than a governess ought to have."

Frankie took a shallow breath. "Why does that bother you?"

Lightning flashed outside the window and the skies opened, releasing a torrent of rain. Drops slashed against the windowpanes and beat on the roof overhead, all while the wind roared down the street with the howl of a freight train.

"Because it is my job to keep you safe, and you are making that difficult by wandering off with loathsome men and enchanting dozens of others. Could you at least pretend to be boring and stupid?"

"I am safe now, Jasper," she said softly. "You may let me go."

But rather than backing away, he lifted his other hand to curve around the side of her neck, his body caging hers in a way that made her feel hot and flushed, her skin overly sensitive and her stomach unstable.

"There is no way in hell I'm letting you go, Frankie." His mouth crashed down on hers.

Chapter 25

Frankie's lips were soft and giving underneath his own. She looped her arms around his neck, pulled herself even closer, and eagerly returned his kiss. Jasper's blood was still pounding from the altercation with the man lying on the floor. When he'd spotted Frankie leaving with Farthins he'd had a sick feeling in his gut, but it had been several minutes before he'd been able to extricate himself from the throng of people that kept introducing themselves and demanding his time. By the time he'd reached the corridor they were gone, but he'd known that with the impending storm it was unlikely they'd gone outside. His next bet had been the library, and he'd been right.

When Jasper had opened the door and spotted Frankie pinned against the bookshelf with blood on her dress and fear in her eyes, he'd lost his composure. It had been a long time since Jasper had felt the kind of roaring rage that had made him the man London feared, but when he'd thought Farthins had hurt Frankie, the call to violence had been overwhelming.

He didn't examine his reaction too closely beyond the fact that

Frankie was under *his* protection, and Jasper protected what was his at all costs. He'd always been territorial, but what wharf urchin wasn't?

As he kissed her, he pushed aside the fear that had sliced him deeper than the rage, telling himself it was only that he didn't care to see a woman hurt. It had nothing to do with how, in that moment when he'd seen Frankie in a situation he was meant to protect her from, he'd felt powerless. Jasper controlled everything having to do with his club, from approving the menus to recording each shilling, and he ruled his private life in a similar manner. He'd spent most of his youth a slave to chaos, having to accept his powerlessness so often that there was no room left for pride. When he'd made a success of Rockford's, he'd finally had the means and the authority he'd always craved. Then Cecelia and Frankie had entered his life. They were variables he could not control, and the fear that he could not protect them from every harm out there had his chest tightening even as he moved his lips hungrily over Frankie's.

In response to his urgency, Frankie parted her mouth and initiated stroking his tongue with hers, laying Jasper flat with the sweet openness of the gesture. She was not an experienced kisser, and yet she was so honest and generous with her affection that Jasper could not imagine being satisfied by any other type of kiss again.

He slid his hands down her back and cupped her bottom through her skirts, lifting her up and rocking her over the hardness beneath his trousers. Frankie made a little noise in response, and when he pulled his mouth away, he found her eyes glassy with pleasure. Jasper's blood was so hot he wouldn't have been surprised to find they'd fogged the library windows. He kissed her jaw, flicking her skin with his tongue and tasting her sweet floral scent before dragging his lips to her ear. He gently bit her lobe and breathed her name into her ear. She *moaned*. Her reactions to him were so raw and genuine that it awed him. Frankie Turner had none of the world-weariness of the widows he usually took up with, nor was she a cunning fraud like many of the debutants. She was something else entirely. She seemed naive in ways, and yet in other ways she was shockingly practical. He liked that she was abstract and absent and messy, just as much as he liked how clever and humorous and sweet she was.

Jasper dropped his head to her throat and tasted her pulse, even as a voice in the back of his head warned him that he was going too far. The sitting room was packed with social elites, and if someone were to walk into the library at that moment, Frankie's reputation would be destroyed.

And still his fingers traveled across her gown to brush over her breast, while his other hand continued to palm her bottom. Frankie pushed at his shoulder and looked down at his long fingers molding the shape of her. "What are you doing?"

"Touching you. Do you wish me to stop?" He wanted her to say yes for her own sake, while the devil inside of him silently begged her to say no. If she asked him in that moment to hand over his entire fortune in exchange for feeling her bare skin against his, he would be a very poor—but satisfied—man.

"I think I should like to feel it without the gown in the way."

Jasper's pulse redoubled and his mouth went dry. Before he could oblige, a particularly loud clap of thunder made a woman scream from deeper within the house. Frankie blinked, as if only then remembering where they were. She flushed and slipped out of his grasp. He let her, his sense of decency warring with his need to see her eyes haze over with desire and know that *he* was responsible for it.

Irritated with himself and his utter lack of self-control, Jasper scrubbed his hand over his face and took several deep breaths. "You need to return to the sitting room. Your absence will be noticed."

"As will yours." She looked down at her blood-spattered gown. "I cannot go back like this."

"You will have to ask a servant to fetch the lady of the house and explain to her that you had a nosebleed. Mayhap she can lend you a shawl, and it will excuse your absence."

She nodded and pointed her chin to Farthins. "Is he dead?"

"No. He should be rousing at any moment. I would appreciate it if you were gone before he does."

"What will you do?"

"I shall send him along his way." She didn't need to know that he planned to leave Farthins with a threat that would make the man wake in a cold sweat for the next month.

She lifted her eyes to his face, the blue depths no less shocking because of the thick glass of her spectacles. "Thank you."

Jasper fought the impulse to touch her again. "For knocking out Farthins, or for kissing you?" he asked in a teasing tone.

But instead of smiling, her gaze grew thoughtful. "You must stop smoldering at me from across the room, Jasper. We cannot allow anyone to believe you have designs on me. I have to remain unattached for our ruse to work."

"Smoldering at you?"

She nodded and gave him a wide-eyed, unblinking stare while she cocked her head at an awkward angle.

"What are you doing?"

"Smoldering."

"That's a lovely smolder." He cupped her elbow and steered her toward the door. "I will do my best to stop 'smoldering.' Be careful when you return, and stay close to Madam Margaret. I have heard a few grumbles about you being 'another one of those horridly progressive women.'"

Frankie halted at the doorway, excitement lighting her face. "Who said that?"

"No one who attends my club." He trailed his fingertips from her elbow to her wrist and grasped her lightly. "No more going off alone. The next time it might be a setup from the Dowry Thieves, and I do not want to see you betrothed to another man."

"You mean a dastardly, scheming man?"

"That, too."

He did not want her engaged to *any* man, although surely that did not mean *he* wanted to marry her. Yes, he thought Frankie would make an interesting companion, and he was absolutely desperate for a deeper taste of her, but neither of those things meant he loved her or that she belonged to him. He'd proposed a marriage of convenience, he'd lost the gamble, and he was fine with that. His distaste arose solely from the idea of her being married to a man who wished to flatten all of the quirks that made her unique. Frankie was one of the most special people he'd ever met. She deserved to marry someone who could see that. And when she found that person, he would be in full support of the marriage.

Relaxing, now that that he knew his resistance to her marrying wasn't due to jealousy, but rather that he simply wanted the best for her, he added, "I would not wish for anyone to dim your sparkle."

"My sparkle?"

Jasper released her wrist and nudged her into the corridor. Lowering his voice so that she could barely hear him over the pounding rain he said, "You count cards, you are disarmingly candid, and you broke a man's nose with your forehead. You sparkle, Frankie

Turner, and I cannot for the life of me figure out how to stop wanting to pull you close each time you are near and kiss you senseless."

The corners of Frankie's lips lifted. "You...*like* that I am different?"

Jasper sighed. "Apparently."

Frankie's tentative smile blossomed into a real one, revealing even white teeth and two little dimples in her right cheek. It was a stunning smile, the kind that felt like sunshine when one was the recipient, and a pit appeared in Jasper's stomach. He was on guard around debutants, widows, and other women who might angle for more affection than he was willing to grant, but with Frankie he had let his shield drop. He'd underestimated her effect on him, and she'd slowly begun to work her way beneath his defenses.

The most irritating part was that she wasn't even trying.

"However," he added gently, "you are right. I must stop smoldering at you, and what we just did cannot happen again. I do not consort with unmarried women. Unless you plan on forfeiting your win and marrying me, it would be best if we kept our distance."

"I cannot marry you!" Frankie exclaimed. "I must remain unwed for our ruse to work. Besides, you would never let me into your gaming hell, and if I were your wife I would have to insist because I would dearly love to play a few games."

"I could not allow you to play at Rockford's. You would clean me out."

"Do you mean take all of your money? Gambling must be so thrilling." Another peal of thunder reverberated through the house, and Farthins groaned on the floor. "Thank you for the brilliant insight."

Jasper needed to hurry and escort Farthins from the property, but his curiosity got the better of him. "What do you mean?"

"Do you remember my dream that I mentioned in your study? Someday, when I have saved enough money, I am going to start a mathematics journal. I have so much to contribute to the discipline and yet I am ostracized simply because I am a woman. Everyone will be able to submit to my journal, no matter their gender, race, religion, or financial status. I have thought that I would need to save my wages for a considerable amount of time, but you have inadvertently given me financial advice I would be a fool not to consider."

"What financial adv— Frankie, you cannot mean to gamble for the money!"

She looked up at him with earnest, blue eyes. "Whyever not? You did." Before he could answer she hurried down the tiled corridor in search of a servant.

Damned if he didn't admire her goal of starting her own journal. As a man who'd clawed his way out of poverty with nothing in his fists but a dream and grit, he had a soft spot for people determined to break the mold. That being said, Frankie had no idea how dangerous gambling could be, especially if one were caught counting cards.

His governess—no, his *beneficiary*—grew more perplexing and infuriating by the day.

Farthins groaned again, and Jasper's face hardened before he turned around. Time to take out the rubbish.

Chapter 26

The Dove approached the man leaning against the lamppost, hands in his pockets, light and shadows dancing over his face. He was relaxed and casual, but she knew better than to underestimate the former army colonel and half of the duo she'd hired to track down Miss Fidelia Turner. She was unsurprised when Mr. Zachariah Denholm turned, alerted to her presence far sooner than most would be, and the corner of his mouth tugged upward. He inclined his head, and she did the same.

"Why am I not surprised to see you here?" he asked, adjusting his cravat. It was an unassuming gesture, a lazy indulgence, but Zachariah Denholm was anything but lazy. He was one of the most persistent detectives she had ever known. "Have you come to check on our progress? You do know we are supposed to be on our honeymoon, but when Emily found out our first case was for her governess friend Frankie she refused to pass it up."

The Dove smiled despite herself and held her black-gloved hand out to the side, halting the catlike movements of the woman who'd been approaching her from behind, no doubt wielding a wickedly sharp dagger. "You got closer to me this time, Mrs. Denholm."

Emily Denholm—the former Miss Emily Leverton and governess—sighed noisily and stepped into the radius of lamplight. "One of these times I shall surprise the great and mysterious Dove."

The Dove sincerely hoped not. She had made a lot of enemies. If she ever lost her touch, very few would hesitate to take her down. She tilted her head toward Emily. "How did you know I was coming?"

"I was late meeting Zach when I spotted a shadow on Crescent Street and decided to follow."

That was a good five minutes ago. Perhaps she already *was* losing her touch.

Emily approached her husband, and the ice faded from his blue eyes. He wrapped his hand around her arm and tugged her indecently close, and the Dove had the distinct impression that he'd have kissed her on the public street if the Dove were not standing right there.

An ache, familiar and old, throbbed in her chest. She had once had that kind of love. She had fallen for a man who looked at her exactly as Zach looked at Emily, who'd thought the sun and stars had hung on her every word. And then he'd died, and all of the light in the cosmos had gone out.

The Dove shook away her melancholy and said, "Have you found her yet?"

Zach was too busy tracing his wife's cheekbones with a heated glance, but Emily turned her face and answered. "No, but we made progress before we had to return for Mr. Davies's engagement ball." Deputy Commissioner Wright Davies was second in command at the Metropolitan Police, and Zach's former employer. He was also the person the Dove sent most of her anonymous tips to—she did not trust the commissioner—and despite all of Mr. Davies's grumbling, he never let her information go to waste. He'd recently become engaged, and she'd gambled on Emily and Zach making an appearance at the celebration.

The Dove nodded, encouraging Emily to continue with her report.

"They are keeping it tightly under wraps, but it seems Lady Elizabeth Scarson—or Lady Pierson as she is known now—has disappeared. Lord Pierson is telling everyone they are on their honeymoon in the country, but when I posed as a maid and infiltrated his household, I discovered that the lady in question has been missing for several weeks."

The Dove inhaled. "She is with Miss Fidelia?"

Zach finally tore his gaze from his wife to contribute to the conversation. "We tracked Lady Elizabeth Scarson by following her trail of horses," he said. "'Twas an enjoyable challenge."

Emily smiled indulgently at him.

"We lost her two days' ride from her estate, but at the last stable we tracked her to, we were told she met with another woman, and they both left on the post carriage. We may have another lead, though," Zach said. He brushed a loose curl from his wife's neck.

"Is Frankie doing all right?" Emily asked with genuine concern. "I met her only a handful of times, and the last time she seemed worried about more than her sister."

The Dove did not know how Frankie was doing emotionally, but she did know that she had made a deal with the governess, and the Dove *always* upheld her end of a bargain. "I believe she is fine."

Zach reached for Emily again, his gloved hand encircling her wrist. She shivered slightly. "As soon as we are free from our obligation here, we will track down our latest lead," he said. "We will find Miss Fidelia Turner."

The Dove nodded once, her thoughts already shifting to her next task. "Of course you will. I work only with the best."

Chapter 27

The next morning, watery, after-the-storm light streamed through Frankie's window, illuminating the piles of papers scattered across her chamber. She had been awake for hours, working by candlelight and tugging on her hair as she paced back and forth. Perhaps there was no connection between the grooms other than Rockford's and she had set herself on a fool's errand.

After the library incident at the Coswolds', Frankie had awkwardly flirted and batted her eyelashes while wrapped in a shawl from her hostess to conceal her dress, and made what society would consider the most outrageous comments about women in mathematics. She had even challenged one young man to a problem-solving contest and had defeated him spectacularly, to the great embarrassment of many men in the crowd.

She had stayed close to Madam Margaret, and after another hour of poetry, had pleaded a headache, and they'd left. The entire carriage ride home, she had fought to keep from blushing as she vividly recalled her kiss with Jasper in the library, how the rasp of his chin had felt on her sensitive skin, how the wet of his tongue had drawn chills from her flesh, how his large hands had cupped and squeezed and stroked until she'd been nearly aflame.

She had held close to her heart the look of resignation on his face when he'd said he liked her as she was, even if she'd found it nearly impossible to believe. Men like Jasper, who had the world at their fingertips, did not choose women like Frankie.

Jasper had promised to keep his hands off her in the future because she was unmarried. Only a cad dallied with an unmarried maiden. In their society a woman was punished harshly for an affair, especially if she had a child out of wedlock. Jasper may have had a colorful reputation, but he was no cad.

Frankie agreed that it was important that Jasper keep his hands to himself; she did not want anything interfering with her plan to act as bait—especially not smoldering looks from her benefactor.

But there was another reason it was best they did not kiss again, and it had nothing to do with her being an unmarried woman, and everything to do with self-preservation. When the Dowry Thieves' leader was caught, Frankie's ruse would be over and she would leave, and Jasper would move on to his next widow. But would *she* be able to move on? Despite the leagues of men blinded by her financial worth, Frankie knew that without her pretend dowry she would be just Frankie again: plain, outspoken, intimidating. There would not be anyone else for her. She worried that if she continued down this beautiful, heart-racing path with Jasper, more than her pride would hurt when it all ended.

She had won the poker game against Jasper, and his intriguing offer of a marriage of convenience was off the table, especially now that he was publicly funding her dowry. Frankie was honest enough with herself to admit that a small part of her wouldn't have hated marrying him. Sure, he was exasperating and high-handed and obscenely confident, but he was also thoughtful and clever and terribly arousing.

It was for the best that they had taken this avenue instead. Jasper may find her eccentricities amusing now, but Frankie knew that over time, he would grow weary and resentful of her awkwardness. In her experience, men always thought they wanted novelty until they actually experienced it.

Frankie was lying supine on the bed with her head hanging over the edge, doubting her "expert" ability to piece together a pattern from the grooms' financials, when there came a rap at her door. Before she could jump to her feet Cecelia burst into the chamber in a whirlwind of teal taffeta and adolescent energy.

"Miss Turner, I have been *dying* to hear about the literary event and how Uncle Jas—how the men at the party reacted to your gold dress." She paused, and between one breath and another took in the papers and ledgers scattered across every surface in the chamber and exclaimed, "Whatever are you doing?"

Frankie rolled to her stomach and propped her chin on her hand. "These are the financial papers of the men who've put the 'troublemaking' women in compromising situations and forced them into marriage. They all have memberships to your uncle's club."

"That is why you are here, isn't it?" Cecelia reached for one of the papers and frowned down at it. "There must be a hundred numbers in these columns. You know Uncle Jasper has nothing to do with this. He would never stand for such a thing."

"I know that now. It is why I am looking for another commonality among them, although I am beginning to doubt there is one."

Cecelia lifted an open ledger from the small writing desk and stuck her tongue between her teeth as she squinted at it. "How did you get all these ledgers, Miss Turner? Are you some sort of spy?"

Frankie sat on the bed and nudged her spectacles into place. "I have a friend who gave them to me."

Cecelia gave a low whistle, revealing her common roots, and said, "You must have important friends."

In fact, Frankie had very few friends besides Fidelia, and she could not tell Cecelia she actually *had* been a spy employed by the woman who'd given her the financials. "The ledgers need to be returned to their owners shortly, and then I will lose all opportunity to find a deeper connection."

Cecelia ran her finger down a column of goods and numbers that belonged to Lord Nettles, a man who'd once possessed a vast fortune before he had dwindled it away at the card tables. "'Tallow, four shillings six pence; tea, thirty shillings; gold earrings, twenty pounds; fish, twenty-eight shillings; three bolts of French damask, forty-two shillings.' Heavens, this man spends a small fortune each month."

Frankie brushed a strand of hair behind her ear. "And from what I have seen, that is only a quarter of what some of the noble households spend. Before Lord Nettles lost his fortune, he—did you say gold earrings? I do not remember reading that."

Frankie slid off the bed and hurried over to Cecelia's side. Cecelia pointed at the spiky handwriting. "Perhaps it was for his wife," Cecelia suggested. "Oh wait, these are the men who later married. A mistress?"

Frankie was already deep in thought as she hopped over a pile of splayed ledgers and snatched up a stack of loose papers that were gently lifting in the breeze entering through the cracked window, the rain-washed scent only slightly tainted by the foul odor of the Thames. She flipped through to the records that belonged to Lord Sandington. "Gold-and-ruby necklace," she murmured. She had not thought anything of it; wealthy men often bought jewelry. But now...

Frankie was barely aware of Cecelia leaving the room, or of the minutes passing as she hastily made notes on a slip of paper, her handwriting so poor that only she would be able to decipher it. An hour passed, or perhaps two, and only Cecelia's return dragged her from the records back into the present.

"You look positively wild, Miss Turner," Cecelia said as she sat in a sliver of empty space on the bed. "What have you discovered?"

Frankie's eyes focused on the girl in front of her and she whispered, "Holy Queen V, Cecelia! It is the jewelry!"

"What is the jewelry?"

Frankie pressed her fingers to her temples. She was so lightheaded with excitement that she felt faint. Or perhaps she felt faint because she had forgotten to break her fast. "People have been known to hide indiscretions or illegal purchases in their ledgers by coding them as something else." Even Jasper had done it, although his was a charitable donation rather than a more insidious secret. "Every single one of these men, *every single one*, has purchased an extraordinary amount of jewelry over the past twenty-four months, bought more horses than a stable could hold, and lost innumerable sums at the gambling tables."

"I still do not understand."

"Jewelry and gambling and horses are expensive," Frankie continued. "They are easily accepted as standard purchases and losses and would not raise any flags from a property manager or anyone else who might look at the ledgers. Even I missed their importance the first time around. The purchases allow a person to claim large losses while keeping their ledger totals accurate and seemingly proper."

Cecelia's eyes flickered in understanding. "But they didn't buy jewelry and horses, or lose the money gambling, did they?"

"No." The purchases hadn't paid for the leader of the Dowry Thieves to arrange a marriage, either. They dated too far back. In fact, in each ledger the first notably large "purchase" had taken place in January two years ago. What had happened in January that had spurred all twelve grooms to begin deducting large, secretive amounts of money from their estates? What were they hiding?

The mystery was too much for Frankie to bear. "Fetch your cloak, Cecelia. We are visiting Hookham's Circulating Library for answers."

"Sorry, Miss Turner, but we cannot."

Frankie's head snapped up. "Why not?"

"You have an entire sitting room filled with suitors, and I have been sent to fetch you. Uncle Jasper is in a horrid temper."

Frankie blinked like an owl emerging from sleep. Although she'd had four Seasons, she'd never had a single gentleman caller. She had forgotten all about the possibility of morning visits from potential suitors. "Blast!"

"You cannot go downstairs like that!" Cecelia exclaimed when Frankie made her way to the door. "You have ink all over your hands, your hair is a fright, and you are wearing your ugliest governess gown." Cecelia sighed heavily as she grabbed Frankie's hand and towed her down the corridor, but there was a smile on her lips when she said, "Come along, Miss Turner. I shall see you fixed up. It is time to make a man jealous."

"I am aiming for a compromising situation, not jealousy."

"Oh, right. Yes, that is what I meant."

Chapter 28

Jasper counted twenty-seven men milling in his sitting room, each clutching flowers or sheaves of poetry, before he shook his head in disgust and gave up. Every few minutes another gentleman was announced at the door by his gleeful butler. At this rate the room would be packed as tight as a sardine tin before Frankie took it upon herself to make an appearance. He'd sent Cecelia upstairs to collect her nearly an hour ago. Where could she be?

He glanced at his tin pocket watch and was just about to stomp out and fetch Frankie himself, when she appeared in the doorway. There was audible inhalation from half the men in the room, and he was disgusted to realize he was one of them. She was dressed in a delicate, white muslin gown with embroidered flowers, the confection looking as if it had been plucked straight off the skin of a Renaissance model. Her blond locks had been curled and artfully arranged so that a few of the golden tendrils lay draped over her shoulder, the ends feathering across her skin. She smiled at the room full of suitors with such sweet openness that his stomach clenched.

The rush toward her was almost comical, and soon her arms were heaped so high with blooms that the butler had to step in and help relieve her of her burden. Jasper studied each man clamoring for her attention. He made it a point to know the financials of every man he approved for his club, and three-fourths of the men in the room were members. At least six of them were so impoverished that Jasper was planning to revoke their memberships within the month. Two of them housed mistresses, and several more had fathered bastards that they did not financially support. Not a single one was good enough for Frankie. In fact, there were only two men in the whole lot that he would ever consider letting near her: Lord Brackmore, who, although in his early forties, was steady and thoughtful if not boring; and Lord Wilson, a man with the hair of a god and the bank account of Midas, although recently Jasper had begun to hear whispers that perhaps Wilson's account was not as fat as everyone believed.

Jasper shook his head to clear the direction of his thoughts. He was standing there assessing the men as if they were truly potential suitors, which they were not—for now.

After he and Frankie discovered the identity of the Dowry Thieves' ringleader, he suspected Frankie's plan was to find a new governess placement far from London and let the furor around her quietly die. She wasn't stupid: She had to know she would be more than a spinster after this—she would be unmarriageable; any potential suitor would expect the staggering dowry. And yet she had gone through with the ruse to help save the women who'd been silenced anyway.

What Frankie did not know was that Jasper had already begun the process of transferring funds equal to the false dowry into an account run by a man he trusted implicitly. The solicitor would see to it that Frankie had access to the account whenever she wished, for whatever she wished. If she wanted to marry in the future, she could use the money to fund a dowry. If she did not, she could open her mathematics journal. It was the least he could do. What Frankie was doing was brave and selfless. For him, it was just money.

Jasper ground his molars together as he watched gentleman after gentleman kiss Frankie's fingers and make statements about her beauty that grew more ridiculous by the moment. Through it all she was gracious, but as the minutes wore on, she spoke more and more freely about the role of women in the scientific community. She was doing a splendid job of riling up a few of the men, although they did their best not show it. If he were not so adept at reading minute facial expressions, he might have missed the furious tightening of Mr. Portman's jaw, or the flash of indignation in Lord Weatherlin's pale eyes.

"Who do you think she will choose?" Cecelia asked, appearing at his side with a plate of pastries in hand.

"None," Jasper growled. "This is not real."

"It will be if one of them is successful in compromising her."

"That will not happen so long as I am breathing."

Cecelia looked at him from the corner of her eye and disappeared again, but a few minutes later he spotted her deep in conversation with Lord Wilson and Frankie. Frankie's face split into a grin at something Lord Wilson said, and Jasper's temper soured further. Surely Lord Wilson's hair was a wig? And who had allowed him to leave the house in such a shocking, peacock-colored coat? No man kept that type of lean figure without relentless exercise, which meant he was likely as vain as society claimed he was.

Frankie laughed again, a peal of true enjoyment, and Jasper's hands flexed when Lord Wilson leaned far too close and whispered something in her ear that made her blush. Before he knew what he was doing he was across the room, the other men having parted for him as if they were the Red Sea, and then he was beside Frankie and staring down at Lord Wilson with the kind of cold violence that had made more than one man think twice about his next move.

"Mr. Jones," Lord Wilson said, his demeanor unaffected except for a sly twitch of his mouth.

Jasper tried very hard to remember that Lord Wilson was still one of his best spenders. He bared his teeth. "Lord Wilson."

"I must thank you for bringing this rare jewel into our midst. I have suffered the attentions of vapid and silly women for years, but it is only today that I realize how much those women pale in comparison to Miss Turner, with her indelible wit and constitution."

"Yes, thank you so much for this delicate pearl, this rare ruby, this shining gem," a thin man piped in from the periphery. Jasper and Wilson ignored him.

"I am only doing my charitable duty," Jasper ground out.

"If there was ever a bet in the books that Mr. Jones would one day do his 'charitable duty' on such a large and public scale, the man who bet in favor of it would now be richer than Houndsbury."

Jasper sensed Frankie stiffening beside him. The dig had been couched in jest, but she had heard it as well. "What can I say? My lovely niece, Miss Cecelia, has had a profoundly benevolent influence on me."

Lord Wilson shuddered. "Do not tell me you have grown a heart, Mr. Jones. Your edge is legendary, and it is what makes Rockford's such rollicking good fun. If you go soft, I shall have to look for another gaming hell."

Voices quieted around them.

Jasper leaned forward and said in a low voice, "A wise man would have more sense than to test my 'edge.' But you are right, perhaps it would be best if you found another gaming hell."

It was a gamble speaking to Wilson in such a way. Jasper hated to lose one of his wealthiest members, but he could not afford a display of weakness. Although he catered to the *ton*, he occasionally had to remind them that when it came to Rockford's, *he* was the lord.

Lord Wilson met his eyes, and in them Jasper saw one of the *ton*'s most spoiled and entitled lords, whose first coddling had taken place the moment his penis had been identified at birth. "Now wait a moment, Mr. Jones, I was only speaking in good fun."

Tension pulsed thickly between them. Jasper let it foment for a moment before he offered a smile and said, "Of course, Lord Wilson."

Lord Wilson pressed a soft hand to his heart, his nails buffed to a shine, and turned to Frankie, who'd been watching the exchange with wide eyes. "Please accept my apologies, Miss Turner. Men should never discuss business matters in front of the delicate sex. You must allow me to make it up to you. I would be honored if you would join me for a carriage ride in Hyde Park before I return to the country."

"No," Jasper said at the same time that Frankie said, "Yes."

Lord Wilson divided a curious glance between them and arched a shaped brow.

"Yes," Frankie said again, shooting Jasper a quelling look.

"With a chaperone," Jasper added. "With *two* chaperones." God, he was being ridiculous.

Lord Wilson nodded. "Without question. A lady's reputation is all she has."

By the time the rest of the suitors had cleared out, Jasper had lost all taste for company and was so surly he knew only a solid round of pugilism would work off the edge. When the last gentleman had departed from the sitting room, Cecelia made a comment about calling on her friend before she, too, scurried from the room, leaving him and Frankie alone.

The moment Cecelia had left, Frankie whirled around and fisted her hands on her hips. "What was that?"

"What was what?" Jasper asked, decanting a whiskey and pouring a drink. He didn't give a damn about his no-early-drinks rule at the moment.

"You glowered and glared at every man who spoke to me. Half of them were practically frightened into quivering puddles!"

"A man who can be put off by a glare is hardly worth your time."

Frankie threw up her hands. "This is not *real*, Jasper! I know I have asked you to keep me safe, but you cannot keep everyone away from me or I shall never become a target."

"Good!" He slammed the glass on the table and stalked over to her. "I do not want you to become a target."

Frankie gaped at him. "Whatever has gotten into you?"

Jasper paused, fighting his instinct, his need, his *desire* to pull her close and feel her soft, sweetly curved body press into his. He closed his eyes in dread as he finally recognized the emotion that had dogged him the entire morning: *jealousy*. Jasper had spent a lifetime fighting jealousy, watching as it ate away at his family until they were bitter, angry husks. Jasper had vowed that would never be him.

Yet here he was, his blood nearly boiling with the need to strike down every man who had made Frankie laugh that morning. No jewels or riches had ever been enough to turn him green with envy, but then a governess with a brilliant brain had blown into his life like a whirlwind, and now he was left hungering to sweep her away and claim her for his own.

He needed to get away from her and clear his head.

"Do not go anywhere alone," he barked as he took a step back. "I shall be home later."

"Where are you going?"

"The club," he muttered. "I need a round in the ring."

Chapter 29

After Jasper left, Frankie dressed for her excursion to the library. She could not fathom what had put him in such a temper. If anyone had a right to be cross, it was she, who'd had to laugh and fake enjoyment for hours on end. The only person who'd been mildly entertaining was Lord Wilson, but then he'd cut Jasper, and she'd realized he was as much a ratbag as the rest. She had only agreed to the carriage ride in the hopes that it would encourage others to ask her as well, and it had. Soon afterward she had agreed to take more carriage rides and walks than her feet would ever allow. She knew some of the men were tolerating the heat and staying in Town after the Coswold event longer than ordinary in order to pursue her dowry, but others would soon be leaving, and she could only be grateful for their departure.

Jasper had told her not to go anywhere alone, but she assumed he meant on carriage rides or walks with gentlemen. She did not think Hookham's counted, so after tea, she set off twirling a gray parasol that matched the gray silk dress Cecelia had lent her. She wished Cecelia could have come, but she was meeting an old friend for tea, and Frankie could not wait. She was determined to find the connection between the grooms, even if it meant her eyes went crossed.

And her eyes nearly did cross before she found something of interest. She was seated at a varnished table in the back of the library, peering through her spectacles at her tenth newspaper from January 1836, when a headline leapt out at her: SCOTT SILVER MINING EXPEDITION A FRAUD. It had been buried in the financial section, and the accompanying article was no longer than three lines.

Frankie remembered reading about the Scott Silver Mining Expedition a number of years ago. At the time there had been big, splashy headlines about Mr. Jonathan Scott, an American who owned a Prussian silver mine that was disgorging thousands of pounds of silver each day. Men had rushed to invest in what was to be a sure thing. As a result, investment prices had shot up and become so exclusive that fights had broken out over them.

When the furor died down, the public forgot about the mines, while those who'd been lucky enough to invest had waited to reap the rewards. That had never happened. For such a massively successful con, the scandal had earned very little print space when the fraud came to light. There was no question that someone had paid the newspapers off in order to ease the humiliation of the investors. If Frankie were not obsessed with the papers, she would have missed it like the rest of the *ton*.

Frankie left the paper splayed open while she went and hunted down copies of the newspapers that had been circulating during the Scott Silver investment rush. To her disappointment, the papers had not printed the names of the investors, but the gossip rags had had no such restraint. They had speculated wildly about who'd been lucky enough to sink their money into the venture.

Frankie's heart did a slow turn in her chest when she read through the names. Twelve of the twenty purported investors were now married to the troublemakers with healthy dowries.

That was about ten too many for a coincidence.

She bit her lip. The men who'd invested in the Scott Silver Mining Expedition had lost their fortunes, plain and simple. Yet someone had paid to keep the news very quiet. Over the following months, the investors had then supposedly overspent on luxury items, and it had appeared to society that they'd "lost their fortunes" at gaming tables rather than in the mine.

She thought of the jewels and horses the men had listed in their ledgers. Someone had advised them to record their investment losses in smaller increments, and to spread them out over several years as a way to preserve their dignity. It was one thing to lose a fortune to Lady Luck, it was another thing entirely to lose it investing in an elaborate con. A gambling loss could be tossed up to bad luck, but the latter could only be due to stupidity.

It was all coming together, like an equation that seemed unsolvable until a key segment fell into place. Someone powerful had watched the gentlemen lose their fortunes and had seen it as an opportunity. He'd saved the investors from public humiliation, advised them on how to cover their tracks, and then promised them a way to recoup their losses by finding them wealthy brides.

"What do you get out of it?" Frankie whispered, as if she were talking to the head of the operation himself. Could he have devised his plan in order to silence the "troublemaking" women? It seemed unlikely—they had no real power. So then *why*? Who was he? A businessman? A politician?

On a scrap of paper, Frankie jotted the names of the eight men who'd invested in Scott Silver and still remained unmarried. She looked them over, her pulse kicking. On the list were two earls, three viscounts, a baron, and two marquesses. If she wanted one of the remaining investors to rise to her dowry bait and lead her to the ringleader, she had to attend the same events they did. The problem was that most of the *ton* was in the country for the summer, and she doubted that nobility of their rank were planning to attend events like the Coswold literary reception.

But there *was* someplace where all eight men were certain to be. Every year the Duke of Houndsbury hosted a house party widely considered the greatest crush of the summer. It was such a monumental social event that even the genteelly impoverished like Frankie were aware of it, and it was considered quite a coup to secure an invitation. The Houndsbury house party always drew a large attendance because of its outlandish hunts, extravagant spreads, and the glamorous ball that concluded the weeklong festivities. It was the very event Cecelia had been dying to attend ever since Frankie had arrived at the Jones household.

Frankie's face blossomed into a smile. If Jasper was irritated about the suitors that morning, he was going to be *really* mad when she insisted on attending the Houndsbury house party.

When the shadows had stretched over the streets and it was nearly teatime, Frankie finished the letter she'd penned to the Dove at the library detailing all she'd found and asking about her sister, and mailed it on her way home.

When she walked through the door to the town house, she exhaled with contentment, but scant moments later Jasper came thundering into the foyer.

"Where have you been? I asked you not to leave the house alone."

"Surely I can walk to Hookham's without a chaperone." She

pulled the list of eight names from her reticule and handed it to him.

Jasper shoved the list into his pocket without looking at it. "Frankie," he said, moving forward so that she had to take a step back. He continued his advance until she was pressed against the gold-papered wall where any passing servant could see them. He caged her in, one hand flat against the wall over her head and the other lightly grasping her chin. "You are all the *ton* is talking about. Did you read the headlines today? You were in every single newspaper as the wealthiest maiden in London. That makes you a target, and not only for the Dowry Thieves. You are a target for weasels like Farthins, for rakes like Wilson, and for any other common thief or monster who takes it into his head to kidnap you for ransom, or worse. When I told you not to go out alone, it was not only the Dowry Thieves I was worried about."

Frankie chewed on her bottom lip. She hadn't considered the pitfalls of pretend wealth. No wonder women with money could not venture out alone.

Jasper's heated eyes fell to her mouth. With the pad of his thumb, he traced her lower lip, smoothing over the place she'd bitten. His eyes were scorching, but his calloused touch was gentle. Acting on instinct, she took his thumb between her teeth and flicked her tongue across the tip.

Jasper's eyes widened, and something wild and raw raged inside. He lowered his head until his mouth brushed her temple, his hand sliding from her chin to wrap around the side of her neck. This man was feared by all of London. She'd watched him beat someone unconscious with these very hands, and yet she'd never felt safer than she did when she was caged in by his body, his palm curved around her neck.

"Please tell me you will take this seriously." His lips continued their feathery light exploration, drifting over her cheek until his teeth caught her earlobe in a gentle nip.

"I will," she breathed, as his free hand fell from the wall to cradle the back of her skull. He tilted her head, arching her throat, and kissed an exquisitely sensitive spot on her neck.

Every inch of Frankie's skin felt overly sensitized. She clutched his coat and pulled him closer, wishing she had more experience so she would know what to do next.

"Promise," he growled.

"I promise."

In reward, Jasper trailed wet, open-mouthed kisses down her throat, and Frankie delved her fingers into his hair. The strands of black hair were short and silky, his shaved jaw rough as it moved over her skin, marking her with a red flush that he soothed with his eager mouth. Frankie no longer knew where she was—or cared. All she knew was that if Jasper didn't help ease this unbearable ache, she'd—

"Uncle Jasper!" Cecelia exclaimed.

Frankie gasped in mortification and buried her face in his chest.

Jasper instinctively shielded her with his body as he partially turned. "Yes?"

Frankie heard Cecelia's impatient toe tap on the floor. "You and Miss Turner told me you were not going to marry."

"That is correct," Frankie mumbled. Taking a deep breath, she gathered the courage to look Cecelia in the eye and stepped away from Jasper, hoping to heaven her skin wasn't as red from his ministrations as she suspected it was. "When I arrived home your uncle was worried for my safety."

"He does not kiss anyone else when he is worried."

Frankie had nothing to say to that, and apparently neither did Jasper because an awkward silence fell over the foyer.

"I must pack," Frankie practically shouted, her voice ringing off the tile.

Jasper frowned. "Pack for what?"

But Frankie was already running for the stairs and did not answer. The sooner they unveiled the mastermind behind the Dowry Thieves, the sooner she could take a nice governess situation on the coast far, far away from the temptation of Jasper Jones.

Chapter 30

A letter from the Dove arrived with the morning post. Frankie snatched it from the messenger and ripped it open in the corridor.

Frankie—

You brilliant, brilliant woman! I am at this very moment going through the Scott Silver investment scam with a fine-tooth comb. Your suggestion that the mastermind may be a politician sounds remarkably plausible. I am all too familiar with that breed of human and what they are capable of. The Chartist movement is gaining traction—the working classes want the vote, and it is making the House of Lords nervous. It is very possible someone has taken it upon himself to quell the "troublemaking women" in order to ease the tension. I am cross-referencing the information I already have against men in the Lords. In the meantime, I must alert you that several of my governesses have reported grumblings in their houses about that "upstart Turner woman." You must be vigilant at the Houndsbury house party; marriage is not the only way to silence a woman.

As for your sister, the detectives I hired are following a new lead. I have recently learned that Lady Elizabeth Scarson ran away from her new husband. The detectives have yet to find your sister—but I suspect when they do, they shall also find Lady Elizabeth.

I will send a messenger along presently to collect the ledgers.

Stay safe, and do not take unnecessary risks.

—The Dove

Frankie took a deep breath and pressed the missive to her chest. The news that Lady Elizabeth had run away from her husband filled her with joy, because the Dove was right: It had Fidelia written all over it.

Frankie found Jasper in the grand entryway, having just returned from his morning errands. He smelled of horses and summer heat, and his hair was windswept and the heels of his Hessians were dusty. Frankie walked straight up to him and said, "I need to speak with you."

Jasper nodded solemnly. "Does this have to do with what happened in the foyer yesterday?"

Frankie blinked. "What are you talking about?"

A muscle twitched in his jaw. "I compromised you. Mayhap not in public, but it was done anyway. If you wish me to marry you, I will honor my duty."

"As romantic as that is, I need to discuss something else."

Jasper arched a brow. "You do not care that Cecelia caught me kissing your throat?"

Frankie flushed and wrinkled her nose. "It is not the first time she has seen us kissing. Do you *want* me to care?"

Jasper made a noise of disgust. The butler appeared at his side balancing a silver tray stacked with mail, and Jasper nodded his thanks as he took the correspondence and followed Frankie into the library. He was sorting through the letters when he said, "So what is the matter you wish to discuss?"

"Do you still have the invitation to the Houndsbury house party?"

"I believe it is somewhere, although I ought to have thrown it straight in the rubbish. House party indeed! I would rather eat a live frog."

"We need to go."

Now she had his attention. Jasper set the stack of mail on a side table and crossed his arms over his chest. "We do not *need* to attend a *ton* party that will host the biggest names and purses in the kingdom. Believe me, that way lies trouble. You are stirring up enough trouble right here."

"All eight of the remaining Scott Silver investors that I told you about yesterday will be in attendance."

"Even more reason to avoid it."

"Jasper!" She huffed in exasperation.

Jasper withdrew the list of eight names she'd given him from his pocket. "Tell me more about this."

Frankie launched into her discovery from the day before, and when she finished, Jasper studied her with a gleam of pride in his eye. "You clever fox. If it were socially acceptable to have a woman of good standing in my hell, I would woo you until you accepted a job at Rockford's."

Frankie brightened. "I can dress like a man." Before he could tell her no, she shook her head. "No, never mind. I think I shall look forward to a nice, calm governess placement on the coast when this is over." Far, far away from the scrutiny of the *ton*. Far enough that maybe without the constant reminder of her unworthiness, her sister would have a fair chance at finding a suitor.

Jasper crossed his arms over his chest and studied her with an expression she could not read.

Frankie cleared her throat and returned to the topic at hand. "My best shot at drawing out one of the Eight is at the Houndsbury party."

"There are a thousand ways to compromise a woman at a house party. They become unruly at best. Madam Margaret or I would have to be with you every moment, and even then—what if I looked away at the wrong time and something happened to you? Something worse than being caught with one of those cads?"

His worry echoed the Dove's, and it gave Frankie an uneasy feeling of foreboding. "I have no choice." Not if she wanted to help stop them from ruining the lives of more women.

"There is always a choice."

She could see that it was on the tip of his tongue to refuse to take her, when through the opened library door she spotted Cecelia drifting down the corridor, as bored as any fifteen-year-old girl could be. "THE HOUNDSBURY HOUSE PARTY WILL

BE THE MOST EXTRAORDINARY EVENT OF THE SUMMER!"

"Why are you shouting, Frankie?"

Frankie leaned closer to the door. "THERE WILL BE A BALL AT THE END OF IT!"

Cecelia dashed into the room, her hands clasped over her chest and her eyes shining. "Oh, Uncle Jasper! Please reconsider letting us attend! I promise I will not scheme while I am there and I won't do anything illegal if only you will let me go. I am terribly tired of rattling about this old house and it would do wonders for my image to be seen at the largest party of the summer. I have heard talk of it all over Town and I have been in a state of despair knowing that you will not allow me to attend. But with Miss Turner and Aunt Margaret with me, *surely* it would be appropriate."

Jasper glared at Frankie. "That was low."

She smiled innocently at him.

Jasper sighed and relented, as she knew he would. He did not have the heart to say no to both of them. "I will write to Lady Houndsbury expressly."

Cecelia screamed and ran from the room, excitedly babbling about the new gowns that had been delivered the night before. Before Frankie could follow behind, Jasper laid a hand on her arm and said darkly, "If she causes trouble, I shall hold you responsible. Trust me, Frankie, you do not want to be indebted to me."

Frankie shivered at the hot promise in his eyes, and thought that maybe she wouldn't mind so terribly much.

Chapter 31

The open carriage was stifling, and it wasn't because of the late summer heat. Cecelia had not stopped talking from the moment they'd ascended the steps to the barouche to travel to the Houndsbury estate, and her incessant and inescapable chatter was giving Frankie a headache. Jasper had taken the seat in the sun, as was proper of a gentleman, while Frankie and Madam Margaret were shaded by the folding hood. Frankie had offered to sit in the sun, but Cecelia had insisted on squeezing in next to her uncle with an exuberance reserved for youth. Even the whip of wind and clatter of horses' hooves could not drown out Cecelia's rambling.

Frankie understood that Cecelia was excited, but her concentration had limitations. It didn't help her already scattered thoughts that every time she glanced at Jasper he seemed to be staring at her as if he were thinking of all the different ways he'd like to undress her. Lounging in the seat with his arm across the back, he looked every bit the Luciferian rake he was purported to be.

Frankie fidgeted under his gaze until at last, while Cecelia was digging through her bag to find and reexamine her new set of gloves, all the while narrating each and every gown she would wear them with, Frankie hissed, "Do stop staring at me as if I were a piece of gooseberry pie."

Jasper's fingers flexed on his thigh. "Now that is a delicious proposition."

Frankie was not sure what he meant, but she was confident it was scandalous. She cursed how little she knew about relations beyond what she had learned in bits and pieces from books. She glanced quickly at Madam Margaret, who was nodding off in the shade, and said in a low voice, "How do you mean? How might one go about *eating* a woman?"

"Are you deliberately trying to torture me?" At her look of confusion, he groaned. "Then you are unaware you are a temptress."

A temptress! It was a term Frankie *never* thought she would hear associated with her person. She smiled brilliantly at Jasper—the smile she reserved for moments when she felt the greatest gratitude, whether it was for a splashy sunrise, a solved equation, or a sharply intelligent remark. Her mother had once told her it was the only beautiful thing about her because she had such lovely teeth. Frankie had never forgotten that.

Jasper sank back in his seat, his arm falling to his lap, and stared at her with slightly parted lips.

"You could show me," Frankie said, trying her hand at the seductress role.

In a flash his eyes heated in a way that made her stomach dip. Perhaps one did not taunt a man like Jasper Jones.

"…and I shall save the dusky-rose pelisse for the morning walk in the garden…" Cecelia continued, unaware or uncaring that they were having a side conversation.

For one wild moment, Frankie imagined throwing herself at the man whose knees nearly touched hers as the carriage jostled down the rutted, dusty road. Terrified she might actually do it, Frankie forced her attention to Cecelia, and even though she felt Jasper's gaze on her, she refused to look at him again.

"Are you pleased with your ball gown?" Frankie asked Cecelia, attempting to regain her breath. It felt as if her corset had shrunk two sizes.

"I *love* it!" Cecelia shrieked. Before she could elaborate on the gown's number of delightful qualities, Jasper called out to the driver, who slowed the horses to a stop.

"If you will pardon me, ladies, I am going to ride the rest of the way." Jasper nimbly leapt to the ground, and they waited while he untied his mount from the back. Once he was in the saddle, the barouche began rolling again. Frankie made the mistake of looking past Cecelia only to have a perfect, eye-level view of Jasper's muscular thighs moving rhythmically with his horse.

Frankie swallowed and wiped the perspiration from her brow with a mostly useless lace handkerchief. Pushing at strands of hair that had slipped from her chignon, Frankie wasn't sure if her new traveling gown was too hot or if she was still reacting to Jasper.

"Why will you not marry Uncle Jasper?" Cecelia asked, jerking Frankie out of her lustful trance. "I know he offered after I saw you two"—she darted a glance at Madam Margaret—"*talking* in the foyer. Is it because of me? Do you not wish to be saddled with an orphan?" Her defiant stare didn't fully hide the vulnerability in her eyes.

"I must remain an available target until we have revealed the man behind the Dowry Thieves, Cecelia." Frankie did not bother detailing the other numerous reasons she could not marry Jasper.

How would she tell a fifteen-year-old that she was too odd and unlovable? That Jasper could have any *normal* woman he wished? That she cherished her independence? She could not, so instead she added, "If ever there was a compelling reason *to* marry Jasper, it would be you."

Cecelia eyed her suspiciously. "Do you mean it?"

"I do. You are a rousing, clever, kind young woman, and I am proud to have had you as a pupil, no matter how briefly."

"You are only saying that to spare my feelings."

Frankie frowned. "No, that would not occur to me."

Cecelia choked on a sob. "Oh, Miss Turner, I sometimes forget how brutally honest you are."

"Then you may trust me when I say that is the case."

Cecelia surprised Frankie by throwing herself into her arms. Frankie held her while Cecelia inelegantly snorted back tears. At last she let go of Frankie and sighed. "I cannot wait to see what happens at the house party."

Jasper rode beside the carriage with the August sun pounding relentlessly on his back. He had started the trip determined to keep his hands off Frankie. Cecelia had caught them kissing twice already, and if she were anyone but his niece, he and Frankie would already be married. He was putting Frankie in far too many risky situations and it was making him a cad. He would not touch her again; his honor demanded that he treat her better.

He thought he'd been doing a fine job hiding the thousands of ways he was thinking of undressing her, when she'd made the comment about gooseberry pie. He'd been unable to temper his street-filthy thoughts, but instead of being offended, she'd been curious. It had nearly done him in.

What *had* done him in was her smile. She had curved her lips at him, and it had felt as if his entire world had tilted on its axis. She had flattened his pathetic attempt at restraint with a single, genuine flash of teeth. Jasper could handle any con, any trick, any long game; he'd seen it all and done it all before. But the unadulterated pleasure in that smile? That was uncharted territory. And he found that he was greedy for more. More of Frankie's smiles. More of Frankie's happiness. How would she look when she was entirely uninhibited and being introduced to the pleasures of the flesh?

Jasper shifted uncomfortably in the saddle and cursed his wayward thoughts. It was a long-enough ride without having the added discomfort of too-tight trousers because he could not stop thinking about the brainy beauty traveling in the carriage beside him.

The midday sun continued its assault, and by the time they arrived at the Houndsbury estate, Jasper was perspiring like a fountain. As the barouche trundled up the long drive, he reviewed his mental file on the Duke of Houndsbury. Houndsbury had inherited fourteen properties at the tender age of twelve, and when he'd matured, had shrewdly multiplied his wealth. Jasper had not dealt with the duke himself, as the duke was well-known to steer clear of the card tables. He'd been quoted as saying "gambling is the fool's surest way to lose money." Houndsbury's son, the Marquess of Dalkeshire, was that fool. Dalkeshire was a devoted patron of Rockford's and an inveterate loser.

The sculptured hedges gradually gave way to a breathtaking view of Houndsbury House, a colossal neoclassical manor nestled in two hundred acres of rolling green grasses. A pond, complete with a dribbling fountain of Venus, was situated at the front of the manor so that the circular carriageway wound around it to deposit passengers. Clearly the duke's business acumen had not been exaggerated.

The barouche rolled to a stop at the front entrance, where orange-liveried servants scrambled to open the door and set out the step. Madam Margaret, Cecelia, and Frankie descended onto the crushed sandstone drive and lifted their faces to the staggering sight.

Constructed of ivory Derbyshire limestone and marble, Houndsbury House was one of the finest country homes in all of England. Jasper knew this because he had asked Guy to pull as much information on the estate as he could before Jasper left the city. Jasper didn't go into any situation without being thoroughly prepared. One never knew when one might need the upper hand.

Through Guy's research, he'd learned that Houndsbury House boasted 126 private rooms, a Baroque suite of state apartments, two ballrooms, and a long hall displaying some of Europe's most culturally relevant paintings and sculptures for the perusal and promenading of guests. The eighty-horse stable block and carriage house were nearly as magnificent, with Doric columns and a cupola atop a clock tower.

That was a lot of space in which Frankie could become ensnared in the ruination game.

Jasper had known on paper how wealthy Houndsbury was, but seeing it in person was another matter entirely. When he returned to Rockford's he was going to increase Dalkeshire's line of credit.

The women were escorted into the black-and-white-marbled great hall, and Jasper followed behind.

"The duke and duchess are enjoying a game of croquet on the south lawn with a number of guests," the butler informed them.

"There is also a game of cards in the blue drawing room. You are welcome to join if you should like."

Jasper nodded as their luggage was carried in.

"Although perhaps the ladies would prefer to rest after the dusty ride," the butler continued, turning to Cecelia and Frankie, who appeared dazzled by the white marble busts lining the great hall. Madam Margaret did not seem as impressed. The butler gave a slight nod to the footmen, who started up the grand staircase with their luggage.

Jasper's accommodations were on the second floor in the east wing, while Frankie and Cecelia were given connecting chambers on the third floor next to Madam Margaret. His chamber was tastefully done in dark woods and rich green fabrics, and it smelled pleasantly of lemon and heather. He had to admit, it was refreshing to breathe air devoid of smog and stench.

After Jasper had washed and donned a fresh shirt and coat, he found his way to the gold receiving room to wait for Frankie and Cecelia, who'd blithely told him resting was for dead people. He suspected they would be a while, as both women had to change out of their traveling gowns and into afternoon dresses and then wait for Madam Margaret.

The moment he entered the receiving room the oddest sensation crawled over his skin. He had not felt such dread since the time his former partner and cronies had ambushed him and nearly gutted him.

Jasper quickly assessed his surroundings; this was not a slum or an alley heaped with garbage; it was a grandly appointed room in one of the wealthiest estates in England. The ceilings were domed and painted with Renaissance frescos; the fireplace was solid ivory marble, and the walls were papered with pale green and cream. The room was as long as it was wide, with rows of windows that stretched to the ceiling and allowed an undisturbed view of the manicured lawns and gardens that extended to the tree line on the distant horizon. Every detail dripped with old money: the brocade settees, the gleaming lid of the piano, the six-foot golden harp in the corner. Bunches of fresh-cut flowers were displayed on every available surface, and their floral perfume mingled with an array of bottled scents. Several young ladies were writing correspondence in the corner, and another was playing the piano—badly. A half dozen gentlemen were discussing the next day's hunt by the opened French windows. There was no reason for the sense of alarm that lifted the hairs at the nape of his neck.

Jasper stepped farther into the room and the piano stopped. It seemed as if one long whisper swept through the space, and he could have sworn he heard, *Is that Jasper Jones?*

He tried not to groan. Gossip was reason number twenty-seven he never attended house parties.

Jasper thought to pass the time by reading the day's news, but before he had reached the ironed paper, there came a mocking laugh from behind his shoulder. It sent chills straight up his spine.

"I did not think I would see the day a fishmonger's son dared attend a duke's house party, and with an uncouth orphan and a charity case governess in tow."

Jasper schooled his expression before turning to face Lady Evelyn Barker. Evelyn was wearing a gown the same shade of honey as her rich and glossy hair. She would have been beautiful if it were not for the vengeful twist of her mouth. Clearly, she had neither forgotten, nor forgiven, the mouse escapade. He had not considered that she would be present, but he should have. Evelyn, along with every other eligible young woman from London, would be here.

The summer house party was, in essence, an extension of the Season. Reason number ninety-seven he avoided them like the plague.

Before Jasper could consider how he wished to respond, Frankie walked hesitantly through the receiving room doors next to Cecelia and Madam Margaret, obviously feeling as out of place as Jasper did. Neither he nor Frankie belonged in the *ton*, and they were not as at ease as Cecelia, who did not have a firm understanding of class barriers.

Frankie was wearing a striking silver gown that revealed an ample amount of cleavage. A row of soft pink blossoms was pinned around her waist, and strands of escaped blond hair framed her enormous spectacles. The ensemble gave her a delicate, fairylike quality that made Jasper's inner protector want to destroy anyone who dared hurt her.

Some of his possessiveness must've shown in his eyes, because Lady Evelyn tittered cruelly and said so that only he could hear, "No one can understand why Mr. Jasper Jones, who has never had a thought for anyone but himself, should suddenly find the call of charity and donate an enormous dowry to his governess. But *I* know that despite the dowry and outward appearance of duty, you wish to claim the odd little spinster for yourself."

Fury bubbled close to the surface, and when Jasper turned his gaze on Lady Evelyn, she took a hasty step back. He was not the usual docile gentleman she enjoyed bullying and berating: He was a violent gambler from the wharf—as she took repeated pleasure in reminding him—and he let her see exactly what that meant. "You will not speak of Miss Turner in such a way again," he said, his voice a steel blade. "She may not have your respect, but she will have your silence, or there will be consequences of which you cannot yet dream."

Lady Evelyn flattened a gloved hand to her mouth. Cecelia wormed her way through a gap between two women and approached them. His niece was dressed in a fashionable maroon gown, and not for the first time Jasper wondered when she had grown so tall.

"Uncle, you must—oh, greetings, Lady Evelyn." She spoke to Evelyn with such cultivated and cool disdain that Jasper thought she must've learned at the knee of the woman herself. "You must excuse me, I have need of my uncle."

To Jasper's enormous relief, she dragged him toward the side of the room where Frankie lingered uncertainly. Madam Margaret had seated herself beside the piano to enjoy the music, seemingly deaf to the discordant notes. "I do not know what you said to Lady Evelyn, but I thought she was going to faint."

"She made a disparaging remark about Miss Turner. She will not again."

Cecelia nodded in approval. "Sometimes it is good that you are so big and scary." She patted him on the shoulder, and under her hand Jasper did not feel big and scary at all.

Chapter 32

W hat do you think of the party?" Frankie asked Jasper when he and Cecelia approached. Lady Evelyn was staring at his back from across the room, her expression one of undisguised jealousy.

"I think it is terribly dull."

"Oh, Uncle Jasper." Cecelia shook her head. "I am afraid you do not understand the meaning of a good time. Miss Turner, will you join me for a walk in the gardens? It is becoming rather crowded in here." She gave a significant look in Lady Evelyn's direction.

More carriages had arrived, disgorging guests by the dozens. The receiving room was filling with lords and ladies and bachelors and maidens who all greeted one another, exclaimed over the travel and the weather, and quietly assessed the social lay of the land. Frankie's eyes narrowed when Lord Wilson walked through the door. She had felt "ill" when it was time for their carriage ride, and so she had not seen him since he'd cut Jasper the morning he'd come to call on her.

"Mr. Jones!" a man cried, wending his way through the crowd.

He was trailed by two impeccably turned-out women and three men with pomaded hair and lace cuffs. "What a surprise to see you here." The man clapped Jasper on the back. He was unarguably handsome, with thick black hair, brown eyes, and an aristocratic nose. He was dressed grandly, but lacked the fussiness of his peers. "The trip was awful, was it not? Have you heard about Lord Wexler? Quite the scandal." The man spotted Cecelia, who was watching him with open curiosity. "Although that story is for another time when we are in less delicate company. Who is this ravishing young woman?"

It took Frankie several full seconds to realize the man was talking about *her*. Ravishing? Since when? Since she had a fortune in a dowry, she thought bitterly.

Jasper's jaw was unusually stiff. "Lord Devon, allow me to present Miss Francis Turner."

Frankie's ears perked at the sound of his name, and her fingertips tingled. Lord Devon, Marquess of Devon, was one of the eight names on her list. She was fully aware of the impoverished state of his inheritance and was stunned by how fashionably he still dressed. He must have bought the finest available clothing on credit to appear wealthier than he was, perhaps so that he could fool an unsuspecting woman into marriage, or an unwise man into a loan. Frankie had always known the *ton* to be deceitful, but never before had she been privy to inside knowledge about their finances, and with that knowledge, the lies took on new intent. She wondered if this was how Jasper always viewed nobility. They were not gods shrouded in tradition and wealth to him; they were mere mortals with debts that he owned and secrets he knew. If knowledge was power, then Jasper Jones was indeed a very powerful man.

A slow, catlike smile unfurled across Lord Devon's lips. He

reached for Frankie's hand and pressed a wet kiss to her glove. "It is a pleasure to make your acquaintance, Miss Turner."

Frankie's heart sped up. This was what she had come here for. She could not bungle her role. "Pleased to meet you, Lord Devon."

Cecelia smiled widely at the marquess. "Lord Devon, we were about to take a walk in the gardens. Would you care to join us?"

"I am sure Lord Devon has better things to do," Jasper said.

Lord Devon laughed. "If only that were true. Let me introduce my acquaintances. This is Miss Mary Harlan, Lady Charlotte, Mr. Tupper, Lord Foxwith, and Mr. Foster."

"It is a pleasure to make your acquaintance," Lady Charlotte purred, deftly maneuvering herself between Frankie and Jasper and batting her eyelashes in tandem with her fan. Frankie instantly disliked the woman and her disgustingly perfect coordination. "I would *adore* a stroll in the gardens. We have only been here a few hours and I am already bored to tears. Mr. Jones, you shall have to regale us with all of your wicked tales."

"I fear my reputation has been exaggerated," Jasper said, politely holding out his arm. "I am but a modest proprietor."

Lady Charlotte took Jasper's proffered arm, and Frankie had the strangest urge to bat the woman's hand away.

"Your modesty is misplaced, Mr. Jones. I fear I am an entirely wicked woman and I simply *adore* a wicked story."

Frankie ground her teeth together and thought she would *adore* kicking Lady Charlotte in the shins.

Frankie invited Madam Margaret to join them, but as they were a large group and did not need a chaperone, the older lady declined. Just as the group was about to exit through the French doors with Cecelia in the lead, Frankie heard a familiar voice call out to her. Shocked, she turned, and with a confusing mixture of surprise, pleasure, and dread, watched as her mother bore down on her.

Mrs. Turner, although a few inches shorter than Frankie, swooped in and brushed her lips across Frankie's cheek. As she did, she whispered, "Darling, this color does not become you."

Frankie flushed, suddenly feeling self-conscious in the silver gown, and all too aware that Jasper was watching every minute reaction flit across her face. She schooled her expression and turned to the curious group. "I would like to introduce my mother, Mrs. Turner."

Her mother smoothly exchanged niceties with the small party, and not for the first time in her life Frankie felt the insurmountable distance between them. Her mother was a beautiful woman, her rich hair threaded with only a few silver strands to give away her age. With a button nose, rosy cheeks, and a plump and curved body, her mother had never failed to make it known how disappointed she was that Frankie and Fidelia had inherited their father's lighter coloring and straight figures.

Although Frankie had spent her youth wishing she could have been born with even an ounce of her mother's beauty, it was really her mother's ease in society that made her despair. Mrs. Turner slipped among the nobility as if she were born and bred to be one of them, and not for the first time Frankie wondered if her mother had wished to marry a man who would one day hold a title.

"What are you doing here?" Frankie asked when the others lapsed into conversation.

Her mother arched a brow. "I came to chaperone my daughter, who *apparently* is in possession of the largest dowry in London. Upon learning of our relationship, the duchess was kind enough to extend me an invitation." Her mother laid a gloved hand on Frankie's arm and nudged her to the side. "What happened, Francis? You told me you were taking a governess position that would help you track down your sister, and the next thing I hear, your employer has bestowed upon you an outrageous dowry. I was unaware that your governess position was with *the* Mr. Jasper Jones," she hissed. "Had I known, I never would have allowed it! Did you keep it from me on purpose? That man is an upstart and beneath our dignity. Your grandfather was a *baron*, Francis. Do you know how poorly it reflects on our family to accept charity from a man like Jones?"

Her mother straightened and smoothed a hand down her skirt. "Nevertheless, what is done is done, and it seems our fortunes may finally be turning. With such a sizable dowry, it is possible even *you* will make a match and save our family. I no longer know if we can rely on Fidelia to do it, especially as you have been unable to locate her."

Frankie was struck by the arrogance in her mother's words. Her family was barely scraping by, and yet simply because of the circumstances of his birth, her mother dared look down on a man whose wealth rivaled the duke's?

There were a number of things Frankie could have said in that moment. She could have told her mother she was being a horrid hypocrite to act as if they were worth more than the very man who'd given her daughter an outrageous dowry. She could have said it was unfair that her mother had put the onus of finding Fidelia on Frankie, while *she* continued to flit about society pretending they were not courting destitution. As the beauty of the family, her mother had spent a lifetime expecting everyone else to cater to her and clear the way so that she might continue doing the one thing she loved above all else: socializing.

Frankie could have told her mother how guilty she felt for failing to secure a marriage match. Marriage wasn't only about prestige, it was also about financial security, and Frankie's oddities and inability to find a husband had thrust them toward devastation and heaped too much responsibility on Fidelia's shoulders. Frankie's guilt was why she'd taken on the governess positions, and why she had agreed to shoulder the burden of tracking down Fidelia.

She could have said all of that, but instead what came out of her mouth was, "You are mistaken about Mr. Jones. He is both kind and honorable, and more than worthy of our respect."

"Oh, Francis." Her mother gave a world-weary sigh. "You know nothing about men." She peered over Frankie's shoulder at Jasper, her eyes narrowing as if he were a bug she wished to squash. "I cannot fathom why he chose you unless...he has not taken liberties with you, has he?"

"No."

"No, I did not think so. I have heard that Lady Evelyn Barker has set her sights on him, and *she* is both graceful and beautiful."

While Frankie was not. Her mother did not have to say the words for Frankie to hear her message. Frankie twisted her fingers together, feeling the familiar guilt that she was not, and could not be, more of the daughter her mother wished for.

"Now that I think on it more, it makes sense that he chose to sponsor you. If anyone needs help securing a marriage match, it is you. Well, I suppose if his money is good enough for Lady Evelyn, then it is good enough for my daughter. As long as you do your best to distance yourself from him, I think you will have options. I heard Lord Benton is looking for a wife."

"Mother, he is in his eighth decade!"

Her mother gave her an impatient look. "Darling, you may have a generous dowry attached to your name now, but I have *also* heard you've been causing quite the stir with your insistence that women are equal to men, especially in mathematics. Do not say I have not warned you how men react to a woman with your intellect. You would be lucky if Lord Benton agreed to marry you. Thank goodness I have arrived. I can take over as your chaperone and help you secure a proper match."

"That will not be necessary," Frankie said with a tinge of panic. "Madam Margaret is chaperoning both me and Cecelia." With her luck, her mother would put her in a compromising situation before the Dowry Thieves could. Her stomach twisted at the thought of spending the next few days flinching under her mother's digs about all the ways she was inferior to every other woman there. Frankie thought her mother loved her, or at least she hoped she did, but that hope rarely soothed the stings of her mother's barbs.

"Madam Margaret?" When Frankie pointed out the woman half-asleep beside the piano, her mother scoffed. "That simply will not do, Francis."

Before Frankie could protest, Jasper approached and sketched a half bow to her mother.

"Mrs. Turner, it is a pleasure to meet you. I can see from whom Miss Turner inherited her beauty."

Frankie's mother sniffed at his address and extended her hand as if she were the queen. Frankie wanted to sink into the ground with humiliation, but Jasper only flashed Frankie an amused look before he brushed his lips across her mother's glove. Involuntarily, Frankie imagined those lips on *her*, and she flushed harder.

"Mr. Jones," her mother said coolly, "I must extend my gratitude for your charity toward my daughter. As a spinster, she would not make a marriage match without your generosity."

Jasper let go of her mother's hand and his gaze cut to Frankie. "Oh, I doubt that. Miss Turner's unique attributes are quite enchanting. Even without the dowry, she could have her pick of bachelors."

That was patently untrue, and her mother seemed taken aback by the lie. "Er—how very kind of you."

"Uncle Jasper, can we please go? Oh, Miss Turner, is this your mother?" Cecelia swept into a dramatic curtsy. "Miss Turner is— was—my governess, and she was the best one I ever had."

Again, Frankie's mother seemed speechless. Frankie could understand. Both Jasper's and Cecelia's statements had been outrageous. Not a man in the room would have looked twice at Frankie without her dowry—as her four Seasons had already proven—and she was not even a passably good governess.

Lord Devon chose that moment to interlope, and he proceeded to do what neither Jasper nor Cecelia had managed to do: sweep her mother off her feet. By the time he was done with his flowery compliments and useless niceties, her mother was as rosy-cheeked as a girl. Knowing what Frankie did about Jasper's character compared to Lord Devon's, she was disgusted with her mother's shallowness.

"We were about to take a walk in the gardens," Lord Devon said, smoothing his hand over his perfectly coiffed hair. "I would be disconsolate if you did not allow me to walk with your delightful daughter."

Her mother tittered and nodded, and Lord Devon shot Frankie a smile that was more calculating than charming. "After you, Miss Turner."

Left with no choice, Frankie stepped forward. She snuck a quick look at Jasper, but his expression was flat and unreadable. For some reason, it made her stomach clench.

Chapter 33

The party walked down a vibrant, sloping lawn to an expertly curated flower garden that was more along the size of a field. A crushed white seashell path wound through the blooms, offering stone benches every fifteen yards for the ladies to stop and rest their feet. Water fountains and birdbaths glittered with sunlight, and the constant sound of running water was as soothing as the soft hum of lazy bees floating from one blossom to the next.

The group naturally separated, with Cecelia steaming ahead to explore, and Lord Devon falling into step beside Frankie. Behind Frankie, Jasper walked with Miss Mary Harlan and Lady Charlotte, and behind them trailed her mother and the three dandies swinging their canes.

Lord Devon stood half a head taller than Frankie, and he walked in that lazy, unhurried way only men of leisure could. As they traversed the first pathway, he insisted on helping her over a flower stalk that had fallen across the seashells, which was so absurd that in her disbelief she allowed it. Once he had her hand in the crook of his elbow, he did not release it.

"How did you find your travels?" he asked, jumping forward to bat an offending bloom out of the way so that it would not touch her. Did he think her fashioned of brittle glass?

"It was not wholly pleasant," she answered, "although I believe a woman could design a carriage with shade for more than two people."

A secret knowing touched his eyes. "I have heard of your clever mind, Miss Turner. I admit I am far more familiar with poetry, music, and art, but I would be eternally in your debt if you would enlighten me on the subject of mathematics."

Frankie hesitated. "Truly?"

"Truly. I fear I am a disgrace to the Devon name, as I can hardly multiply two numbers together. There will be parlor games tonight. Perhaps while the others make fools of themselves, you and I could retreat to a quiet corner and you could school me."

Her heart was pounding out of proportion to the light exertion. There was very little Lord Devon could do while they were in the sitting room in full view of the others. Would he try to coax her out of the room in some way? Would this be her opportunity to get some answers?

Before she could formulate a response, there was an earsplitting shriek, followed by another scream. The women with Jasper were jumping about as if their feet were on fire. Lady Charlotte went pale and swooned, and Jasper barely caught her before her head hit the ground.

The other men dashed forward to help while Cecelia doubled back to see what all the fuss was about.

"Likely a toad or a snake," Lord Devon said before Frankie could respond to his proposal.

"Do you really suppose so?" she asked, wrinkling her nose. "That seems an awfully silly thing to faint over."

He laughed, and she was struck by how donkey-like he sounded. He wore a beige frock coat over tight gray breeches, and his fashionable muttonchops and mustache were shiny with perspiration. "You are a refreshing addition to society, Miss Turner. The women are so often silly, especially when a handsome and wealthy bachelor is in residence."

Frankie frowned at the thought of Jasper being the wealthy and handsome bachelor he referenced. Devon took advantage of her distraction by picking a purple violet from the ground and tucking it behind her ear. She was astonished by the liberty he'd taken. "Has anyone ever told you how similar your eyes are to sunstruck sapphires? Leave it to Mr. Jones to have mined a gem in the rough."

Frankie was thoroughly exhausted of being compared to geological deposits. Why was everyone insisting on calling her a gem, a jewel, a ruby? She cared even less for the inelegant snort her mother barely concealed with a cough as she approached them. Frankie knew her mother thought her a lump of coal.

She was fighting the two-pronged discomfort of being caught between Devon and her mother, when she felt the smooth glide of a leather glove over her bare skin, and a hand curved around her upper arm. Frankie did not have to look over her shoulder to know the hand belonged to Jasper; she recognized him by the telltale scent of his shaving cream and by the tension and heat he emanated. Her unease evaporated. With Jasper she always felt safe.

Jasper plucked the flower from her hair and twirled it in long, clever fingers. "Lord Devon is mistaken if he believes there is any chance of me parting with this *gem*." He met Lord Devon's gaze head-on. "She is *mine*."

Chapter 34

While walking in the garden, Jasper had been reminded with every step why he despised the house parties of the upper crust. The women he escorted were flirtatious and foolish and boring. What he wouldn't give to hear Frankie matter-of-factly estimate the exact acreage of the gardens and how many blooms were in it.

He had not expected the arrival of Frankie's mother, and by Frankie's reaction, neither had she. He'd been struck by how different Mrs. Turner looked from her daughter, with her darker hair and delicate features. She was not ugly by any means, but she had none of the special light that made Frankie sparkle. Frankie hid her soft curves, brilliant eyes, and adorable dimples well, but once a man had seen them, he would never forget they were there.

When Frankie's mother had pulled her aside, Jasper had carefully observed the emotions flitting over Frankie's unguarded face, and a knot had begun to tighten in his stomach. She'd appeared defeated, resigned, and once he'd even caught a flash of disgust. Jasper began to suspect Mrs. Turner was the reason Frankie thought herself plain and undesirable.

Unable to stay away when she was so distressed, he'd walked over to introduce himself and had caught the embarrassment on Frankie's cheeks when Mrs. Turner had treated him as if he were something she'd rather wipe her feet on than speak with. Jasper was familiar with the type—he dealt with people like Mrs. Turner nightly—and he no longer allowed it to affect him. What had bothered him was how it had hurt Frankie.

He knew Frankie was probably anxious about her mother interfering with her plans to ensnare one of the Eight, but Jasper was grateful there was another pair of eyes on her, keeping her safe. He wanted the Dowry Thieves stopped, but not at Frankie's expense.

Still, he would keep careful watch over Mrs. Turner. If he thought she was making Frankie feel worthless, he would step in. Family was important, but no one was allowed to make Frankie feel bad.

Jasper was still lost in thought when one of the women shrieked as if she'd taken shrapnel, and in the ensuing melee Jasper glimpsed Frankie speaking privately with Lord Devon, who was showing *far* too much interest in her. That Devon was one of the names on Frankie's list made Jasper's insides raw. Devon was handsome and titled and destitute, and that made for a dangerous combination.

When Lord Devon had taken the extraordinary liberty of tucking a violet into Frankie's golden-spun hair, a surge of possession had risen in Jasper's chest, and before he'd thought it through, he'd plunked Lady Charlotte on her feet and was charging toward Frankie and Devon.

"Jasper!" Frankie's tone was more relieved than censorious, which his nearly caveman-like statement about her belonging to him warranted. "I believe you mean I am your charity project and therefore under your protection."

Jasper tucked the violet back into her hair, letting the strands slip across his gloves like satin, cursing the barrier.

Lord Devon watched them with confusion, her mother with tight-lipped suspicion. Jasper gave Devon a wolfish smile, and in response Devon unconsciously puffed his chest. He was not as tall as Jasper and he was built more leanly, but years of leisurely ennui had left him soft and weak. Having been born to privilege, Devon could rely on his name, his perceived wealth, and his connections to get by. Jasper had to rely on his wits first, his reputation second, and his fists third. They were from two entirely different worlds. Devon was a gentleman who'd probably never thrown the first punch. Jasper had no reservations about being the first to get his knuckles wet.

Devon bowed out of the silent standoff by taking an unconscious step back, but his pride would not accept defeat so easily. "I see Mr. Jones requires a moment of your time, Miss Turner, so I will acquit myself of your company. I look forward to our tête-à-tête this evening."

Before Jasper could tell the man to piss off, Frankie batted her eyelashes and said, "I eagerly await the moment."

"Tête-à-tête?" Frankie's mother interrupted, halting the man's exit. She fluttered her fan in front of her face. "My lord, I do hope you mean in the presence of others."

Lord Devon gave Mrs. Turner an oily smile edged with frustration, and Jasper barely held back his grin. "You may be assured of it, Mrs. Turner."

Cecelia raced back to them at an unladylike trot. "Lady Charlotte says she was bit by a snake, but I don't see any marks on her ankle."

Lord Devon's eyebrows flew to his hairline and Mrs. Turner

looked at Jasper's niece as if she were an uncouth urchin from the street. Cecelia had obviously said something unacceptable, but damned if Jasper knew what.

Frankie apparently did. She put a protective hand on Cecelia's arm and smiled conspiratorially at Lord Devon. "I know it is considered scandalous for a woman to mention any of her body parts, but a fine horseman such as yourself must already have an excellent understanding of anatomy."

Lord Devon heard the innuendo as clearly as Jasper, except Jasper knew Frankie had no idea she was making one. Lord Devon smiled at Frankie as if he wanted to take a bite out of her.

Jasper grasped Cecelia with one hand and Frankie with the other. "You'll have to excuse us," he snapped, "the dinner gong rang." Lord Devon sketched a bow and moved past them to comfort the abandoned Lady Charlotte. Jasper felt Mrs. Turner's eyes on his back as he practically dragged Frankie and Cecelia back up the garden slope toward the house.

"That Lord Devon." Cecelia sighed as soon as they were out of earshot. "He is *g-o-r-g-e-o-u-s*."

"He is not that good-looking," Jasper said.

"Speak for yourself," Cecelia retorted. "If he asked me to marry him, I'd jump into his carriage in a jiffy."

"*Cecelia!*" Jasper and Frankie cried in unison.

"What? What's so wrong with climbing in a carriage?"

Frankie groaned. "Cecelia, Devon is one of the Eight."

Cecelia seemed stunned for a moment and then her face darkened. She pointed her chin over her shoulder to get a better look at Devon. "That rat. I ought to go back there and—"

"You will stay far, far away from Devon and every other man here." Jasper's jaw was so tight he was afraid he might crack a tooth.

He had been unforgivably stupid to allow Cecelia to come. It was bad enough that Frankie was flaunting herself as bait. If something happened to Cecelia, he would never forgive himself. He'd begun spreading the word that Cecelia's dowry would not come into effect until her coming-out next year, but desperate men made desperate choices. "You are fifteen, and there are a number of men here who would happily ruin you for your future fortune no matter your age. I should have left you at home."

"No, no, I promise I will behave," Cecelia said, instantly contrite. "I will always stay in sight and I will not cheat anyone at cards."

Jasper stopped in his tracks. "Was cheating at cards even on the table?" he nearly shouted. If men had attacks of the vapors, he was well on his way.

"Jasper, let go," Frankie said, pulling her arm. "You do not need to haul us about as if we are naughty children."

"Yes, Uncle Jasper, let us go. I did not even hear the dinner gong. You have awfully good hearing."

Jasper released both of them and took a deep breath. He was legendary for keeping a cool and level head in heated moments. It was how he had faced some truly dangerous situations with steady hands. And yet here, at the Houndsbury house party, he felt more out of control than he had in years. He was on someone else's territory playing by someone else's rules. He could not control all the variables, and a single misstep could be the ruination of one of the women at his side.

Chapter 35

Dinner was an elaborate and lengthy affair. Frankie sampled a parade of courses: soup, broiled salmon, braised beef and tongue, roast, Yorkshire pudding, cherries, and glazed cake, and began to understand why the Houndsbury house party was considered the grandest event of the summer. Everything from the fine linen tablecloths to the gleaming silver candlesticks, the servants that acted with swift and prompt attention, and the outrageously expensive wine, reminded Frankie of how far from home she was. How lonely Jasper must have been on his ascent to the top! Frankie was intimidated, and *she'd* been raised by the son of a baron. She could not imagine the amount of fortitude it must have taken Jasper to breach the barrier the upper class so diligently fortified with their silly customs, rules, and lavish displays of fortune.

The women were outfitted in bright silks and feathers and scents, while the men cut dashing figures in crisp cravats and tailored coats—although none were so fine and imposing as Jasper. When Lady Charlotte rested her fingertips on his forearm and gave a charming, tinkling laugh at something he'd said, Frankie had to turn away and smile blindly at the man beside her. She had no idea what her dining partner was talking about. All she could think about was Lady Charlotte, who appeared to be a genuinely sweet and *adoring* woman, and the way Jasper was listening to her every word as if his very life hinged on it.

"You are staring," Frankie's mother said through tight lips. She lifted her wineglass and took a dainty sip.

"What?"

"You are staring at Mr. Jones."

Frankie was indeed staring again. She tore her eyes away and lifted her own glass. "This has a been a lovely dinner, has it not? Have you heard the gossip about Lord Wexler?" She'd hoped to distract her mother, but she should have known better. When her mother had determined to say her piece, she said it.

"Francis, I saw how that man looked at you today when he returned the flower to your hair. Worse, I saw how you reacted to him."

"How—how did I react?"

"You leaned into him as if he were your safe harbor."

Frankie's heart fluttered in her breast. "You are mistaken. Mr. Jones and I—" *Have only kissed. Are only here to uncover a nasty plot. Will never be together.* "—are here to find me a husband."

"Francis," her mother said gently, setting her glass on the tablecloth. "I know you think I am hard on you, but it is only because I do not want to see you hurt. Mr. Jones is a known rake, which means if he expresses interest, there is only one thing he could want from you. You must not allow him to ruin your reputation when you finally have a chance to secure a good marriage match."

Frankie stared into her wine, her mother's words hitting their intended mark, but for a different reason. Frankie knew Jasper's reputation as a rake was carefully cultivated and mostly untrue, but if her mother thought there was something between them, it was possible others might, too. She could not allow that, not when she had a chance to make headway with Lord Devon. Not when she was so close to getting answers.

For the rest of the dinner she did not look at Jasper once, even though she could have sworn she felt his eyes on her.

When the guests reconvened in the parlor for after-dinner games, Frankie was more than ready to get away from Jasper, her mother, and the effervescent Lady Charlotte. She did not have long to wait before Lord Devon appeared at her side.

And so the ruse began.

Jasper was in a foul mood by the time the party guests reassembled in the sitting room. During dinner, Frankie had been sending him secretive little glances until her mother had spoken to her in a voice so low Jasper could not catch what was said, but Frankie's shoulders had stiffened and her cheeks had whitened. He'd throttled the impulse to jump across the table and grasp her by the chin and shout that whatever her mother had said, it wasn't true. But then she would not even look at him afterward; instead, she had allowed Lord Tharlowe to entertain her for the rest of the meal. Jasper would occasionally catch snatches of their conversation, all of it tantalizingly fresh and interesting, while he was bored stiff by the very dull Lady Charlotte on his left, and the so-icy-it-hurt Lady Evelyn on his right.

Drinks with the men afterward had been just as tiresome. Jasper did not hold a title, but he was still easily one of the most powerful men in the room because he had something the others did not: information. He was the keeper of London's darkest secrets and debts, bets and failings, wins and losses. He knew more about the *ton* than the most adept gossip rag—but his knowledge was not for discussion or sale. He would not have become king of London's hells with loose lips.

That did not stop others from trying to pry, however. He'd spent the ensuing hour dodging invasive questions and giving outright refusals when necessary. This, he thought bitterly, was reason number thirty-two he avoided house parties like the pox. Only when Frankie and Cecelia went up to bed later that night, Frankie's cheeky wink at the bottom of the stairs easing some of the strain he felt, did he finally relax. One day over, six left to suffer through.

If Jasper had thought the house party would improve over the course of the week, he would have been sorely mistaken. The following days were filled with more mundane conversations and sly prying than he'd had to endure in quite some time. At least when the night ended at his hell, he went home to the quiet of his house. Here, there was a never-ceasing stream of entertainment and socializing that ground on his waning tolerance.

It did not help that Frankie's mother was doing the best she could to pack Frankie's days with outings and excursions with every bachelor in residence. Frankie was promised to take strolls, play games, and listen to music with dozens of suitors, although she spent most of her evenings in the sitting room charming Lord Devon and giving Jasper rage-induced fantasies about ruining the already impoverished man.

As the days stretched interminably, Jasper's patience began to thin. Although Frankie and Cecelia seemed to be having a splendid time, he could not wait until he could sweep them into the carriage and take them home again. The constant vigilance was tiring, but what was getting even older was seeing *his* Frankie enchant and laugh and share her sparkling wit with men who thought they had a chance in hell with her. None of them were good enough for her.

After another elaborate dinner on the sixth day, Jasper entered the sitting room to rejoin the women after cigars with the gentlemen, and immediately sought out Cecelia and Frankie with his eyes. Frankie was promenading the room with Lord Devon, while Cecelia and Madam Margaret tried to convince Lady Charlotte to play the piano. Mrs. Turner was sitting on the settee, her eagle-like gaze assessing Lord Devon along with other potential suitors in the room. When she saw him, her lips pursed.

Over the past week, Mrs. Turner had made her dislike of him clear even though he had given her daughter a dowry. He was low-class, an upstart, and he had an unsavory reputation. It did not help matters that he could not seem to stop undressing Frankie with his eyes. For that grievance he could not fault her mother—if a man looked at Cecelia the way he was looking at Frankie, he'd bloody the fool's nose.

Frankie gave a fake laugh at something Lord Devon said. Jasper knew it was fake, because when Frankie truly laughed everything about her sparkled and her spectacles slid so far down her nose they nearly reached the tip.

"Shall we play a game?" Lady Houndsbury asked the mingled guests, clapping her hands together cheerfully.

Lord help him. Jasper lifted a snifter of brandy from a tray and tossed it down his throat. Reason number fifty-two he hated house parties: parlor games.

"How about blindman's bluff?" someone called out.

"Played that two days ago. Why not charades?"

"Forfeit!"

"Sardines!"

"Sardines it is," Lady Houndsbury said. "We all know the rules, do we not? One person will hide and the rest of us will go look for him. When you find the hidden player, you must then join him. The last person to find the group must pay a forfeit."

Several sly glances zipped across the room. Everyone loved a Victorian house party that allowed for sanctioned sneaking off.

"Who volunteers to hide?" Lady Houndsbury asked.

Cecelia, the blessed thing, volunteered immediately.

Lady Houndsbury smiled. "You have one minute to hide, dear. And lest we end up searching all night, I must confine you to the first two floors."

Cecelia squealed and raced out of the room.

Jasper groaned inwardly when the irksome Lord Tharlowe chose him as a partner, and frowned when he saw that Lady Evelyn had chosen Frankie. He could not fathom her motives, especially after her rude comments earlier that week. Did she intend to harangue Frankie as they searched the vacant corridors?

Frankie shot him an equally confused look as Lady Houndsbury officially declared the game begun, and Lady Evelyn took Frankie's arm and towed her from the room. The back of Jasper's neck prickled. He was about to follow after them when Lady Houndsbury and Mrs. Turner halted him. He could not simply disregard his hostess and Frankie's mother, so he suffered several minutes of the duchess's pleasant commentary, all while his instincts screamed that he needed to find Frankie.

At last Lady Houndsbury gasped and said, "Oh my, I hope I have not put you gentlemen at a disadvantage in the game. Go, go, carry on, you two." She ushered them out the door. "I wish you the best of luck!"

Jasper was about to take off when Mrs. Turner halted him again. Grinding his teeth, he turned and waited for her to say her piece while Tharlowe meandered out of earshot.

"Mr. Jones, I hope you know how delighted I am that you have given my daughter a new lease on life. She was certain to have died a poor spinster, and for her dowry you will forever have my gratitude. However, do not mistake gratitude for ineptitude. I do not know what your intentions are with my daughter, but I will not allow her to become entangled with a rake."

Jasper was too impatient to find Frankie to carefully meter his words; his instincts were buzzing so loudly that his palms were sweating. The house party had remained sedate the past several days, and Lord Devon and the other seven Scott Silver investors had been unfailingly proper. It all made Jasper itchy. In his experience, this much calm meant a buildup to something explosive. "Mrs. Turner," he said, taking a step to the side, "I know your concern comes from a place of love, but let me make *myself* clear: You underestimate your daughter. She is clever, sweet, and one of a kind. She is also perfectly capable of making her own decisions."

Her mouth fell open in shock, but he did not linger to smooth over the rough edges of what he never should have said. Instead, he took off down the corridor, with Tharlowe trotting to catch up to his long strides and commenting about Jasper's enthusiasm for the game. Tharlowe was an easygoing man with thin red hair and a cache of jokes that he'd taken pleasure in reciting the entire night. He began telling one as they raced down the corridor, but Jasper was not listening. Frankie and Evelyn were gone. Frankie should be safe with Evelyn, apart from the other woman's sharp tongue, and Jasper tried to convince himself that he was acting irrationally, yet he could not shake the feeling that something was afoot.

Dismissing the bottom floor, which was filled with giggling sets of seekers, he took to the grand staircase, with Tharlowe on his heels.

"She is your niece," Tharlowe puffed behind him. "Where do you think she is hiding? She is a young woman, so I imagine nowhere too dusty."

"It is clear you do not know Cecelia," he muttered. If anything, Cecelia would find it great fun to force everyone to crowd into the dustiest, dirtiest place in the house. He grunted when he realized Tharlowe was yards behind him. The man was slowing him down. "Let us split up. You take that corridor and I shall search this one."

Before Tharlowe could agree or disagree, Jasper jogged down the corridor to the left. He was passing by a linen closet when he heard a noise from within. He wrenched it open and was startled when Lady Eloise and Lady Serena sprang apart. Lady Serena, a fresh-faced debutant from the previous Season and one of Lady Evelyn's devoted followers, had swollen lips and the neckline of her gown was pulled dangerously low.

"I did not see anything," Jasper said, and gently closed the door.

He began opening doors along the corridor, his blood rushing in his ears and his mouth turning dry. He thought about calling out for Frankie, and her name was on the tip of his tongue, when he rounded a bend and spotted a partially opened door. In the distance he heard a noisy group of sardines seekers, laughing and rustling, their voices nearing with every step.

Jasper dashed forward and shoved the door wide, just in time to catch Lord Devon springing away from Frankie with a calculated expression of guilt on his face. Frankie's eyes were flashing with fury and her fists were clenched at her side.

"Did you touch her?" Jasper asked, his voice so filled with menace that it should have warned Lord Devon his life hung in the balance.

Lord Devon smirked. "Oh heavens, we have been caught, Miss Turner. I suppose the only honorable thing to do is marry."

Chapter 36

The last person Frankie had wanted to pair with was Lady Evelyn, but the other woman had snatched her arm before anyone else, all while giving Frankie her customary glare.

"Despite what happened at Miss Cecelia's tea, you know her best," Evelyn explained as she swept Frankie out of the room, "and there is nothing I enjoy more than winning. I fear I have a bit of a competitive streak."

Now *that* Frankie believed. Lady Evelyn seemed entirely too accustomed to getting whatever she desired.

Evelyn released Frankie's elbow almost immediately, as if she was repulsed by Frankie's touch, and suggested they search the second floor. The pink silk of her skirts swished against Frankie's own, and her cloying floral scent wrapped around them like a cloud. "I suppose I must ask you to forgive my horrid temper the last time we saw each another at Mr. Jones's house," she said stiffly. "I was angry, and I said terrible things. My father is forever telling me that I am opening my mouth when it ought to stay closed."

"Thank you for apologizing." Frankie did not forgive her, but she respected that Lady Evelyn was attempting to right her wrong. Mayhap she was not the worst person Frankie had ever met.

"I have been playing parlor games in this house for years, and had I to guess, I would say she went this way." Lady Evelyn pointed down the long corridor. "There is a grand suite around the bend that is so large it would fit all of us perfectly. The Duke of Marlboro stays there when he visits."

Frankie thought it more likely that Cecelia would choose a spot that was terribly *inconvenient* for everyone to fit into, but she did not want to make Evelyn feel bad when she was trying so hard to be civil, so she mumbled an agreement and followed behind.

"In here." Evelyn twisted the knob to the grand guest suite and pushed the door inward. She sailed into the first chamber and called out, "Cecelia, are you here?"

Frankie followed, her jaw going slack as she scanned the massive room. Evelyn had not been exaggerating when she'd called it a *grand* guest suite. The main bedroom could easily fit three of Frankie's already opulent guest room inside. Its high ceiling was painted with chubby angel babies in an elaborate heaven scene. The arched windows were twice as tall as Frankie, and the wallpaper was textured and velvety. A towering gilt-framed bed with sheer white curtains was the centerpiece of the room.

"Wow," Frankie breathed. She bent to examine the crisp designs on the molding framing the window. The chamber had been decorated for someone very important indeed. No wonder the Houndsburys always reserved it for the Duke of Marlboro. "This is beautiful."

"Drat." Lady Evelyn scowled. "I do not see her. There is an

adjoining room. I shall take a quick look. Would you take a peek in the wardrobe?"

Frankie dutifully drew open the heavy double doors of the wardrobe, but it was empty save for a stack of clean linens. She'd just closed them when she heard Lady Evelyn's footsteps behind her. "She's not here," Frankie said.

"No, but I am."

Frankie gasped and whirled around, horrified to find Lord Devon standing between her and the partially ajar door. He smiled softly, but his eyes danced with greed and maliciousness. In an instant Frankie realized she'd been skillfully trapped. Had he been following them, waiting for the opportunity to catch her alone?

Frankie's throat seized. She knew that at any moment some-one would walk through the door and catch them—the only way the setup worked was if prying eyes found them alone together. Before that happened and her life was destroyed, she *would* have answers.

Frankie stood to her fullest height and shoved her spectacles up her nose. "Where is Lady Evelyn?"

"I have locked her in the adjoining room."

On the heels of his words, Frankie heard a furious pounding from the door across the room accompanied by a string of muffled threats. Frankie's heart was beating so hard in her chest she thought Devon might be able to see the imprint of it on her skin. "Who is behind this?"

Lord Devon's satisfied smile slipped a fraction. "What do you mean?"

"Who saved you and the other Scott Silver investors from social humiliation? What was his price?"

The smile dissolved and his lips flattened. He took a menacing step toward her. "What do you know, you little bitch?"

"I know enough," she said. "And I am not the only one. You will not get away with this."

Devon's fist flexed, his knuckles bulging white, and then his palm fell open. "I do not care who knows. I have already procured a special license, and we will be married before any scandal breaks." He shook a lock of hair off his forehead and adjusted his cravat with an assured twist of his wrist. "You should know, Miss Turner, that this will be the last threat you ever make toward me. When you are my wife I will have your silence, or you will have nothing but misery."

Frankie balled her own fists and was thinking about punching him in the nose when the door burst open. Her heart sank, and then exploded a split second later when the silhouette of a darkly handsome and furious man filled the doorframe.

"Did you touch her?" Jasper's voice was silky with the promise of death.

Devon sprang away from her. "Oh heavens, we have been caught, Miss Turner. I suppose the only honorable thing to do is marry."

Frankie was so angry she wanted to scream.

Jasper closed the door behind him, locked it with the key that had been left in the knob, and pocketed it. His voice was deadly calm when he said, "No one is leaving until this situation is resolved."

Devon was a fool if he was not quivering in his boots.

"There is nothing to resolve, Jones. You do not need to call a duel. I will respect Miss Turner's honor and marry her."

Jasper ignored him, instead looking her over from crown to foot. "Are you all right, love?"

She nodded, but she was so enraged that she was trembling. She had been foolish to think she was different from the other compromised women simply because she'd been expecting the trap. She had been prepared, and still she had been caught off guard. What chance had they ever had?

Jasper walked languidly to the desk by the window and took a seat as if he had all the time in the world. "I have a proposition for you, Devon."

Devon folded his arms across his chest and said with such false earnestness that Frankie wanted to choke him, "There is no proposition that could sway me from following through with my gentlemanly duty. I am no cad, Mr. Jones."

Jasper propped his elbow on the desk and lazily twirled his finger. "Rockford's."

Frankie gasped, and despite himself, Devon cocked his head with interest. "I am listening."

"When the party of onlookers you arranged to walk into this room arrive, they will find the door locked. It will take them time to chase down the master key. No one is compromised until that happens."

Devon shifted uneasily. "If you think you will intimidate me into walking out of this room without a fiancée, then you are sorely mistaken. Even if you throw me out, I will spread gossip far and wide that Miss Turner and I were kissing."

Jasper's face was so cold and expressionless that Devon might have just told him his favorite food was duck. Frankie, on the other hand, was so livid that she was fisting her hands over and over again.

"One game of piquet," Jasper said. "If I win, Miss Turner is mine. When those people walk through the door you will say you caught *me* kissing her."

Frankie's blood thundered at the possession in his voice.

"And if I win?"

"If you win, I will transfer ownership of Rockford's to you."

"No!" Frankie cried.

Devon considered and then said dismissively, "Rockford's would be too much effort."

Jasper shrugged. "That is why I have a manager. I barely do anything but drink and socialize. And believe me, the annual profits from Rockford's make Miss Turner's dowry look like street change."

Now he really had Devon's interest. The lord studied Frankie speculatively. "What happens with *her* if I win?"

"If you win Rockford's, I take Miss Turner. No negotiation on that point."

"So either way you get the woman. If I win the game, I take Rockford's, but if I lose, I am left with nothing. That is quite the gamble, Jones."

Jasper nodded and Frankie's throat squeezed. She could not let this happen. "I wish to marry Lord Devon!"

Devon scowled at her. "Quiet, woman. You have no say in the matter. I need to think. There are others who may be affected by my choice. But if Rockford's is as profitable as you say it is . . ."

Jasper pulled a pack of cards from his pocket just as the knob turned forcefully on the door. They heard voices outside and someone knocked. The three of them stood silently as the knob twisted a few more times and then stopped.

"You have thirty seconds to make your choice."

Devon paced back and forth in front of the bed as he raked his hand through his hair. Finally, he said more to himself than to Jasper, "The dowry is a sure thing, but winning Rockford's is not."

Jasper smiled, and there was something a bit feral in it. "I can promise you that when Miss Turner is making your life miserable, and I guarantee she will, because *no one* silences her, you will rue the day you tossed aside the opportunity to be the richest man in London."

Whoever the Dowry Thieves ringleader was, Devon did not want to make him angry, but his greed was mightier than his fear because his eyes glistened with undisguised avarice. "If she is so wretched, why are you willing to gamble your club for her?"

"Because she is dear to my niece, and I find I will do anything for Miss Cecelia."

Frankie would cry herself to sleep for the next five decades if she had to marry Lord Devon, but she could not allow Jasper to gamble away his life's work because she had thought herself too clever to be caught by the Dowry Thieves. She had dragged him into this, and it was not fair that he had to pay the price. He had scraped and saved and sacrificed for Rockford's. He loved it as dearly as one might love a family member, and she would not let him gamble it away on her.

She batted her eyelashes at Devon. "I am an angel. I would never make your life difficult."

"She broke Mr. Farthins's nose," Jasper said.

"He deserved it!"

"She stole the key to my study and went through all of my personal papers."

"That was *one* time, Mr. Jones. I sincerely hope I do not have to hear about it for the rest of my life."

"She taught my young and impressionable niece how to gamble."

"That was a misunderstanding."

Devon was eyeing her with something akin to horror. "I have heard that these types of women are difficult, but this is beyond the pale! I accept the wager."

Jasper broke open the package of cards and gave him such a cut-throat smile that it sent chills down Frankie's back. "Let us begin."

Chapter 37

Frankie watched with sick horror as Devon quickly racked up points. Devon's lips curved under his drooping mustache as he neared the hundred-point threshold while Jasper trailed behind. The blood rushing in Frankie's ears dulled the sounds of footsteps and accusations of misdeeds that were being shouted from the other side of the door. She was saved no matter what—Jasper had ensured that. Her heart fluttered at the thought that at the end of this, she would be his wife. No matter what happened, this shrewd, ruthless, and secretly-soft gambler was going to marry *her*. Yet she had no business lingering over the strange sensation that stirred in her chest, not when he still stood to lose everything.

She would not hate marrying Jasper, but she hated that she was being gambled for like a piece of property. Hated that being caught in the same room with a man unchaperoned had tainted her *value*.

Frankie trembled with the injustice of it, and all the while Jasper played as coolly as if he were not a matter of points away from losing his life's work.

Jasper dealt the last hand just as a heavy fist thudded on the door.

"Who is in there?" a man shouted.

"Tell them you need a moment," Jasper said to Frankie without taking his eyes off the cards. "Sound breathless."

Frankie's cheeks flushed but she called out, "I need a moment."

Jasper's concentration never wavered as he and Devon played the final hand.

Frankie thought she was going to be sick all over the floor when Jasper finally set down his cards. He lifted his eyes, and they bored into Devon as he announced his score.

Devon was sitting across from Jasper at the mahogany desk, and when he heard the score the blood ran out of his cheeks. "No," he whispered.

Jasper leaned forward and said something to Devon that Frankie could not hear. Devon's already bloodless face paled further, and he jerkily pushed his chair out, as if to get as far away from Jasper as possible.

Jasper turned eyes on her that were still dark with murder, and she lost some color herself. "Open the door...darling."

Frankie twisted the key as the pounding increased, and the door swung open. In rushed a small gathering of people; the originally scheduled onlookers had attracted the attention of several other seekers, her mother and the duchess among them.

Lady Evelyn raced across the carpet to Frankie and looked as if she were going clutch Frankie's hands before remembering herself. "Are you all right? Someone locked me in the adjoining room and I was only just now rescued. Who could have played such a nasty prank on us?" She turned to glare at Lord Devon. "Was it you?"

Devon appeared too shocked to answer.

Lady Houndsbury stood behind Evelyn, quivering with all the proper rage of a hostess whose party had been made tawdry.

Flanking her were two busybody lords who loved nothing more than to fan the flames of gossip, along with Lord Wilson. Her mother's face was flushed with humiliation. Lady Trathers, the queen of gossip herself, was also among the party. Her eyes darted gleefully over the scene, keenly taking in the scattered cards on the table and Lord Devon's trembling form.

It had been a carefully cultivated crew, and it left no doubt in Frankie's mind that every part of this setup had been meticulously planned.

Jasper swept the cards into his hand and tucked them into his jacket pocket as he stood from the desk.

"What is the meaning of this, Lord Devon and Mr. Jones?" Lady Houndsbury demanded.

Jasper looked pointedly at Lord Devon, who cleared his throat and said weakly, "I was searching upstairs and thought to check the duke's suite. When I entered..." He faltered. Jasper gave him a steely glare. "I...discovered Mr. Jones and Miss Turner in a compromising situation."

There were gasps from the busybodies inside the doorway, and Lord Wilson's eyebrows flew upward. Frankie could practically see the calculation in everyone's eyes as they wondered how they could be the first to spread the news.

She could not bear to look at her mother, so she focused on the duchess instead.

Lady Houndsbury drew herself to her fullest height and stared down Jasper with all the power and might afforded by her position. "Do you intend to do right by this woman, Mr. Jones?"

Jasper met the duchess's eyes with calm assurance. "Yes, my lady. Miss Turner and I will marry as soon as I obtain a license."

Lady Houndsbury studied the three of them as if they were

naughty children caught with their hands in the biscuit jar. Everyone waited with bated breath. Lady Houndsbury was an important matriarch in society, and as this was her house and her legendary party, everyone would take their cue from her on how to react.

"Well then," she said with a sniff, "never let it be known that a Houndsbury house party is dull. This is, after all, the place where the infamous bachelor, Mr. Jasper Jones, became betrothed to his future wife."

Frankie was amazed. Lady Houndsbury had taken a potentially delicate situation and turned it into an enviable coup for herself.

There were rounds of congratulations, all while Lord Devon stood in the corner breathing as if he had just run after his horse. He looked more frightened than angry. Was it Jasper he was so afraid of, or the Dowry Thieves ringleader?

Jasper cupped her elbow, and they filed out of the room behind the rest of the party. "I must speak with you," Frankie whispered.

"Tonight."

摶♦黎

They returned to the drawing room, and after the others arrived from the sardines game, were roped into playing a number of other parlor games amid sly offers of congratulations. Throughout, Jasper's heart did not slow. Each moment that had taken place in the grand guest suite was permanently imprinted on his brain. He had never felt such all-consuming fear as he had when he'd run into the room and realized what was happening. Only years of practice had allowed him to pretend indifference, when inside his organs had been wringing and squeezing until he'd been afraid he'd be sick.

When he'd thought Devon was going to turn down the wager,

he had not known what he was going to do, but whatever it was, it would have destroyed the world he'd built. There was no way he was going to let Frankie marry the man: whether he admitted the dowry was a scam and suffered the hit to his gambling hell, or he grabbed Frankie and Cecelia and ran abroad.

Fortunately, Devon's greed had outweighed his good sense, and he'd taken the odds. Those odds had not been in his favor. Jasper had cut his teeth on piquet.

As for the fact that he was now betrothed to Frankie...he could not even begin to wrap his head around it. All he knew was that she was finally safe from the Dowry Thieves.

While the guests transitioned into charades, Frankie pulled Cecelia to the side. Jasper watched from across the room as emotions flashed over Cecelia's face: anger, worry, relief, and finally happiness.

Frankie's mother was a different story.

As soon as Frankie turned from Cecelia, her mother was waiting. They exchanged low, furious whispers. Frankie's agitation was written all over her: in the way she bunched the fabric of her skirt in her hand, how she worried her bottom lip, and the subtle hunching of her shoulders. Jasper knew her mother was worried about what sort of man he was, but there was something else going on between Frankie and Mrs. Turner—a dynamic that had crystallized within the first few days of her mother's arrival.

For the rest of the night Cecelia was the star of the crowd. Still possessing the charm of a child, she thrilled the group with both her exuberance and innocence, and got away with the most outrageous comments as a result. At one point she asked Lady Houndsbury how much the marble mantel cost. Jasper hadn't been raised in good company, but even *he* knew that was tactless.

Lady Houndsbury chuckled at Cecelia's forthrightness, but Jasper pulled her aside and begged her to keep her questions about finances private.

"Why?" she wanted to know. "You talk about money with me."

"I am not part of the peerage. These people will think you are common and coarse if you ask questions about money."

Cecelia looked at him from beneath her lashes. "Perhaps I *am* common and coarse."

"Indeed you are."

Cecelia stamped her foot. "How dare you!"

Jasper snatched her wrist before she could flounce off. "You and I are cut from the same cloth, Cecelia. We have the same blood running through our veins. We cannot change our lineage, and we will suffer a fool's failure if we try. We can live only by our own code of conduct, our own sets of values. You may be coarse and common, but you are also bighearted, curious, and humorous. I would take you over any one of these women, who are none of those things but happen to possess a *lady* before their name."

Because she was an adolescent—and an angry, grieving one at that—Jasper expected his words to float in one ear and out the other. So he was stunned when she threw her arms around him and kissed him smack on the cheek.

"You are not so bad yourself, Uncle Jasper. I know you think you are, but it's not true. My father used to say that you wouldn't let him love you because you didn't think you deserved it, but he did love you. He told me so. And I do, too." Then she whirled away in cloud of lilac perfume and the dust she'd collected while hiding in the boot closet.

Chapter 38

Jasper stared after Cecelia, some unknown part of him stinging as it thawed. His brother had loved him? Loved him enough to tell his *daughter*? And what had she meant that he would not let his brother love him? All his life he had cared only for the approval of one person, and that had been his older brother. When his brother had died, so had the part of Jasper that hoped one day he would earn the love of the only person who'd stood by his side through it all—and the shell inside his chest had turned to ice. Now, to hear that his brother had always loved him, that Cecelia loved him ... Jasper was so stunned he could not move, he could only feel the painful throbbing in his chest.

Was what Cecelia claimed true? Did he think he was a bad person unworthy of love? When Jasper was born, he'd been so large he'd torn his mother apart, and she'd never physically recovered. She'd died when he was four, and he had the distinct memory of seeing accusation in her eyes every time she looked at him. His father had resented his children, and Jasper and his brother had been put to work too young. His brother had started thieving, but

Jasper had excelled at gambling and conning. He'd been charming and charismatic, and his memory had been uncanny. Over time, when he gambled he had learned how to read the other children, and then the adults. He knew whom to goad, who would respond to boasting, and which player would lose his temper if Jasper said rude things about his mother. Wherever Jasper went, people lost money. He had no friends, but he had plenty of enemies.

He made even more on his rise to the top.

Did he deserve love? Jasper honestly didn't know, but if someone with as good a heart as Cecelia was willing to give him a chance, he would do his damnedest to try and be worthy.

For the rest of the night Jasper closely watched Devon. The man did not speak to anyone out of the ordinary. He did not slip off for a clandestine meeting with the ringleader. He did not act as if anything were out of sorts at all. If it were not for the rigidity of his posture and the incessant tapping of his finger on his thigh, Jasper would have thought he was completely unaffected by the earlier wager. But as the hour grew later, Jasper did not miss the way Devon flinched every time there was a loud noise, or how he perspired more than usual. His eyes kept flickering to the doorway, as if he wished to escape. It was clear Devon was afraid of someone— perhaps someone in this very room.

Jasper kept close tabs on the man well after the women had excused themselves for the night, and only when several of the gentlemen decided to retire—Devon among them—did he allow him out of his sight.

Once in his chamber, Jasper was debating whether or not to slip a note under Frankie's door, when he heard a light rap. His coat was off, his shirtsleeves were pulled out of his breeches, and his cravat was dangling untied on either side of his neck, but he did not consider his state of undress when he quickly opened the door. He knew who would be standing outside.

He looked both ways, grabbed Frankie by the arm, and hauled her inside. "Are you mad? What if someone had seen you?"

She was still dressed in her evening gown, although her hair was in greater disarray than usual. "We are already betrothed." When he would have commented how, in good society, that did not give them license to slip into one another's rooms, she held up her hand to silence him. "I want to know what you were thinking."

Jasper arched a brow, crossed his arms over his chest, and leaned back against the door. "Excuse me?"

Frankie whirled on him, fisting her hands on her hips. "You gambled Rockford's. Rockford's! Are *you* mad? Have you lost all good sense? Devon is so lazy and stupid that he would have run all your hard work into the ground within months. And what would you have done without the income?"

"I have more than enough money saved to live in the highest luxury for the rest of my lifetime and the rest of Cecelia's. Rockford's is extraneous now; it is no longer necessary. It is no longer the most important thing in my life."

"Do not lie to me."

"I am not lying. Cecelia is my life now. *You* are my life now."

"You could have lost everything."

"All I cared about was losing you."

Frankie's lips parted with surprise.

Jasper's gaze traced over her cheekbones to her mouth. "Are you disappointed that you have to marry me? I was not left with a lot of choices, but I will always respect your wishes, Frankie. If you want a way out, I will do my best to give it to you, although it will most certainly require relocation."

"Is that what you want? A way out?"

"No." Jasper felt as if he were drowning in the blue depths of her eyes. "Marry me, Frankie."

Frankie pressed her palm to her stomach. "You do not have to ask. We are already betrothed."

"Yes, but I want you to *choose* me." At the soft plea escaping his mouth, Jasper realized he was so far gone that he didn't even recognize himself anymore. He'd lived a lifetime of rejection, but for the first time it truly mattered to him that someone wanted him. Not his money, not his reputation, but *him*—flaws and all. "Because I choose *you*, although you would be forgiven for questioning that, considering the circumstances. From the moment you walked into my life you have frustrated me, irritated me, and pulled me into one harebrained scheme after another. And yet I find myself waking each morning with a smile on my face, anxious to hear what you will say next. I walk past the schoolroom when I have no business being there, only to catch a glimpse of your disheveled hair and hear the exasperation in your voice when Cecelia does not love the numbers as much as you think she should. You are bold, and you are so beautiful you make my heart ache. It was why I gambled for your hand back in my study—because at the time I was just beginning to realize how nice it would be to have you in my life permanently. But tonight I discovered it was not just *nice,* it was *essential* that I did not lose you."

Frankie's eyes were luminous behind her lenses. "I do," she said softly. "I do choose you."

She did not say more, but he did not need to hear more—at least for now. He pulled her toward him and buried his face into her neck and breathed deeply.

Frankie tugged on the hair at his nape, and he lifted his head. "Just so we are clear, when we are married, I want exclusivity."

The devil inside him curled its toes in delight. Her possessiveness said more than any words she'd spoken.

"No widows?" he asked, reaching behind him to turn the key in the lock.

"No widows, no mistresses. Only me."

Jasper wrapped an arm around her waist and slowly backed her toward the bed. "You are all I need. Will you abide by the same vow?"

The backs of her knees hit the edge of the bed. "Yes, unless we mutually decide otherwise."

She was ever the pragmatist, Jasper thought as he trailed a finger down her chest and hooked it in the front of her gown. The flickering light from the candelabra spread a warm glow over her face. "That will never happen."

Frankie smiled up at him, that slow-blossoming smile that could have been responsible for the Trojan War had she been born three thousand years earlier, and Jasper found himself as thoroughly enchanted by her as Menelaus had been by Helen.

She took off her spectacles and set them on the bed behind her.

"Can you see well enough without them?"

She sighed. "No, I have the sight of a mole. My mother says it is from all the close reading and studying of sums."

Jasper brushed a lock of hair from her cheek. "Then why did you remove them?"

"They are hideous."

He leaned past her, picked up the spectacles, and slid them back onto her face. "You are beautiful with and without them. I have a particular fondness for women in spectacles."

"You do?"

Not until he'd met her, but now he could not imagine finding a woman without them attractive. He stroked his palm down the front of her throat and her head tilted back on a sigh. Jasper cursed at the offering and took a step back. "You should go back to your chamber. I will see you in the morning, and we can begin to figure out the logistics of the wedding."

She pressed her fingertips to her throat, as if to memorize where his touch had just been, and frowned. "We are betrothed."

"Yes," he said, although he did not think it had been a question.

"We are to marry as soon as possible."

"Yes."

Slowly, she began to withdraw pins from her hair, letting her locks tumble free. Her hair was as straight and fine as a sheet of gold, and Jasper's rib cage could barely contain his pounding heart as he stood entranced by her. He cleared his throat. "What are you doing, Frankie?"

"You have already kissed me, you have called me a temptress, and you are going to be my husband. In the near future, we will engage in the marital act, will we not? I do not see the need to wait."

Jasper swallowed hard. She was so damned frank, so damned clinical. In that moment, he wanted nothing more than to destroy the factual image of consummation that she'd built up in her mind. He wanted to shatter her with pleasure, so that she could never speak about joining again without going soft in her center and blushing.

"We should wait until you are ready."

In response Frankie spun around and lifted her hair off her back. She looked over her shoulder and said, "In the future, do not presume to tell me what I am or am not ready to do. Unless *you* need more time?"

"No, I do not. But I have done this before, Frankie, and you have not. Are you certain you know what you are asking for?"

"Jasper, until tonight, I thought I was going to die a spinster and never experience what so many others allude to. I have waited a long time, and I am afraid . . . I am afraid this engagement still feels so ephemeral. I want this one real thing, tonight. Give me this one, tangible thing."

"This betrothal is very much real, Frankie. The Duchess of Houndsbury has given us her blessing. There is nothing ephemeral about it. You *will* be my wife."

"Then there is no reason not to undress me."

She had him there, and Jasper did not know why he was fighting her so hard. There was nothing he wanted more than her first sighs, her first gasps, her first sweet clenching. And she was right. What was the difference between now and two weeks from now?

He slowly began to unbutton the hundred tiny clasps at the back of her gown. "I hate women's gowns."

"I suppose you could lift my skirts instead?"

"Not for our first time, love." He pressed a hot kiss to the back of her neck, and she shivered. "If you want to stop at any time, tell me."

"I do not want to stop."

He pressed another kiss lower on her spine. "You will tell me if you change your mind. I want to hear you say it."

"I will tell you."

Her gown fell in a pool at her ankles, and when her corset gaped open, she took a deep breath of pleasure before it joined her dress. She stepped out of both of them, and without waiting for him, shimmied out of her chemise and drawers and turned around so that she stood before him wearing nothing but garters, stockings, and slippers.

Jasper's mind went blank. He had imagined Frankie in the nude, but the reality was far better than even in his wildest fantasies. Her breasts were the perfect size for his hands, with one slightly larger than the other. They were topped with pale pink nipples that were already puckered in the cool air. Her rib cage was so narrow that he thought he might be able to span it with one hand; and her stomach was soft and decorated with several moles that he was itching to explore with his tongue. At the apex of her thighs was a thatch of slightly darker golden curls that made primal possession roar through his veins.

Jasper had seen a fair number of women in the nude, and yet with Frankie standing before him he could not recall a single one. He wanted to tell her that she was beautiful, but the words were stuck behind the lump in his throat.

"I like that," she said, nodding in satisfaction. "You look dumbstruck."

"I am. I am honored to be the first and last man to have the privilege of seeing your glorious body in the nude."

The dimples in her cheek deepened as she grinned up at him. "Unless, when the thrill wears off, we opt for marriage in name only. Now take off your clothes."

Chapter 39

Frankie was deliberately provoking him. Jasper was possessive and protective, and she knew—had always somehow known—that if they ever joined together, he would claim her as much as any vow could. The growl he made in the back of his throat and the darkening of his eyes sent a thrill straight down her spine.

"The *last*."

"We shall see."

Jasper began to undress, never once taking his gaze off her, and she followed his motions in fascination as his body was revealed little by little. When he dropped his cravat on the floor, her eyes traced over the thick column of his throat. When he unbuttoned his shirtsleeves, she raked her gaze over the wide expanse of male chest dusted with dark hair. His stomach was taut, and the hair on it tapered into a line that disappeared beneath the waist of his trousers.

"You are eating me alive with those looks."

She waved her hand. "Do not stop."

Jasper gave a low laugh and shucked his boots and trousers. Frankie had seen the male member in a number of artworks, but she did not recall it ever looking quite like *that*. Fully aroused, Jasper's anatomy was proportional to the size of the man.

Frankie stepped forward and lifted her hand, but before she touched him, she hesitated.

"Touch me wherever you want, however you want, love."

With his permission, she boldly smoothed her palms over his bare chest, reveling in the feel of the crisp, wiry hair and the smooth, warm skin of the man beneath. She pressed her palm over his heart and felt the beat in her hand. When she looked up, she found him watching her through heavy eyelids.

"I would like to make you mine, now," she said.

The words were like a blade to the taut string of his control: and with that one sentence, it snapped. Jasper lifted her to him and kissed her, forcing her mouth open with the pressure of his thumb on her jaw so that he could shamelessly plunder. She allowed him entrance, opening to him with a low hum in the back of her throat.

After a drugging kiss he released her and dragged his hands down her back, the calluses of his fingertips rough on her skin, and cupped her bottom in his palms. With ease born of well-used muscles, he lifted her so that she could wrap her legs around his waist. Frankie gave a little shriek and then laughed before she linked her arms around his neck and fell back into the glory that was kissing Jasper. The man was sinfully talented when it came to using his tongue, and she could not seem to get enough of his taste.

She was still exploring his mouth when he flexed his arms and she felt the velvet length of him rubbing through her wetness. The contact was so shocking that she broke the kiss and pulled her head away. She was breathing heavily and she felt achy in all those secret places no one ever talked about.

Jasper's jaw was tight when he said, "Do you want to stop?"

"No-o, not exactly."

"What does that mean?"

"It means that I do not know how to do this. I won't know if I do something wrong." Frankie was used to easily excelling at whatever intellectual task she undertook, but this was so far out of her area of expertise that she did not even know where to begin.

Jasper rubbed against her again and her eyelids fluttered. "First, you cannot possibly do anything wrong. Second, the best way to go about making love is to talk." As he spoke he pumped his arms, his muscles bunching with the effort of holding all her weight, and slid her back down for another long, sensuous rub that forced a groan from her throat.

"Talking?" she gasped.

His eyes were so penetrating, so focused on her, that Frankie felt as if she were the only person that existed in the world. "Yes, talking." He lowered his eyelashes and said quietly, "For example, do you know that I have been dreaming of feeling you clench around me, sweet and hot and wet?"

Frankie was not sure what he meant, but his tone was so worshipful that she knew it was filthy and delightful all at once. There was nothing mild about what she felt for Jasper Jones. She yearned for his touch, ached for him with such longing that it had become an almost constant need. Everywhere he brushed her skin she burned. Every time his eyes stroked over her, she melted. The pleasure he'd brought to her with only a few kisses was soul-shattering. She was almost afraid of what the marital act would do to her.

Frankie tunneled her fingers into his hair and leaned in to kiss his ear, copying his earlier technique and nibbling on his earlobe before blowing hot air.

"*Frankie.*"

He dropped her onto the bed and landed on top of her, once again catching her mouth in a wet, branding kiss that had her toes curling. He moved down her neck to her breasts and took a nipple into his mouth. Frankie gasped, coming up off the pillow as he gently suckled and tugged before turning his attention to the other breast, all while continuing to pleasure the first with his fingers. The double assault sent a lightning strike of desire directly to her center. She squeezed her legs around his hips and threw her head back, pleasure building in her so rapidly that she was panting.

Jasper read her body as easily as she read math patterns. He slid one hand down her belly and delved his fingers into her curls. He'd barely brushed her when she violently crested.

Shapes burst behind Frankie's eyelids as her entire body tightened and pulsed. Her nails dug into Jasper's upper arms and she pressed her mouth to his skin to muffle her cries, and then she melted into the mattress, a woman transformed into a boneless puddle. She was sated and satisfied and simultaneously greedy, because she still wanted more. More of him. More of them coming together, combining flesh and chasing pleasure.

Jasper gazed down at her with a mixture of stunned discovery and primal satisfaction. "Your breasts are so sensitive."

"Is that bad?"

Jasper nuzzled into her cleavage, rubbing her soft skin with the dark scruff of his day-old beard. "Oh no, sweetheart. That is very, *very* good."

Frankie's shy smile quickly turned into a moan when he returned to mouthing her breasts. While he lavished one with attention from his tongue, he used his clever fingers on the other, slowly working her into frustrated tension once again.

Feeling that he had had more than enough control, Frankie reached down and grasped his member in her palm. Jasper stilled, and the look in his eyes turned feral. He hissed between his teeth as she slowly explored him, moving her hand up and down and rocking her palm across the soft, velvety tip.

"Stop," he ground out. He caught her wrist and pinned it, along with the other, over her head. "I will finish in your hand otherwise."

Frankie's heart pounded in her chest. This big, powerful man holding her hands over her head while his nude body was pressed into hers was one of the most erotic sensations of her life. Her skin was damp with perspiration and she felt enveloped by the male scent of him, pine and leather mixed with the lemon furniture polish used to clean the room. She feared she would forever become aroused by the scent of lemon polish from therein out.

Jasper's breaths were ragged as he slowly nudged against her opening. Frankie thought perhaps he was hesitant, so she wiggled her hips so that he would enter her an inch or two. She was so wet that the tip easily slid in.

"*Fuck*." Jasper pushed into her farther, and Frankie's rocking hips became less about trying to entice him to enter her and more about attempting to find space for him. He eased into her slowly, inch by inch, allowing her body to grow accustomed to him, until at last he was fully seated. Frankie breathed in through her nose and exhaled through her mouth.

"Are you in pain?"

"No, it is more that I am uncomfort—oh!"

Jasper had taken her nipple into his mouth again and simultaneously pulled out a fraction and then reentered her, causing a sunburst of sensation to radiate from between her legs. Her lower belly felt heavy and tight as he repeated the action. Each time he pulled out a little bit farther and returned with a little more speed. Just as Frankie thought she had reached the height of pleasure from their union, he widened her legs and bent her knee, driving deeper and grinding against a spot that made her gasp.

"Do *not* stop that, Jasper!"

He grinned down at her, his teeth a slash of white in his tanned skin as he continued to roll his hips in a way that made her entire body tingle and tighten. His eyes were focused on her face, on her mouth, on her most minute expressions, as if he were learning her body like he would a new card game, reading her level of pleasure and committing it to memory.

Then his pace shifted, slowed, and he began to move in her so tenderly that her eyes welled with tears. He cradled her head in his palms and kept his gaze locked on hers as she began to rock with him, their bodies blending together. Their mouths clung and she dug her nails into his back, desperate for release again.

Jasper broke the lingering kiss and withdrew completely, to her dismay and confusion. "What are you doing?" she moaned.

"You have a tendency toward bossiness—"

"You are hardly one to talk."

"—which has me thinking you might like to be in control for a bit." He rolled onto his back, his chest rising and falling, and pulled her on top so that she straddled him. He clasped her hips in his hands and helped her lower down. Her cheeks turned red at the obscene sight of his thick member impaling her, the sensation sending goose bumps straight up her arms.

"You are in control now," he rasped.

She tentatively rocked on him and readjusted her spectacles. "Oh, I like this."

"I thought you might."

"You are gritting your teeth, Jasper. Does it hurt?"

He braced her hips with his hands. "No, it does not hurt."

Frankie sighed as she took her turn experimenting, moving degree by degree, then faster and slower until she found the perfect rhythm. The action of him entering her combined with her most sensitive bundle of nerves rubbing against his pelvis was almost too much to bear. Then he brought his hands up to palm her breasts and she shattered again, the intensity such that she nearly burst into tears. Jasper lifted her off him just before he pulsed, splashing a white substance onto his belly.

Sperm, she thought vaguely, having once read the word in reference to horse breeding.

She collapsed beside him, and he quickly wiped himself off before pulling her to his chest, both of them breathing laboriously, their bodies slick with perspiration. He traced lazy circles on her shoulder until she finally lifted her head. "That was different from what I expected."

"How so?"

"It was…incredible. How do newlyweds ever leave the bedroom?"

He gave her such a smug look that she could not help laughing. "Of course it could have been a fluke. We may need to try it again tomorrow to be sure."

She may have been forced into marriage with Jasper Jones, but she was beginning to think the perks would be well worth it.

His response was a kiss that made her heart squeeze.

Chapter 40

Frankie was curled contentedly in his arms. Jasper nuzzled into her rose-scented hair and thought he could stay in that exact position for the rest of his life. His hand was wrapped around her rib cage just below her breast, and he felt her heart slowly settle into a steady beat.

She'd surprised him. When she'd reached her crisis from mostly breast play, he'd realized he'd stumbled upon the perfect partner: She was as intensely aroused by his touch as he was by touching her. She'd raced toward her release with the determination of someone who was going to become insatiable. Fortunately, he was more than happy to take care of those needs, and as often as she wished.

Their joining had been carnal and satisfying, until something had shifted, and he'd found himself moving with her as if in a dream. While gazing into her expressive blue eyes, he'd realized he'd crossed that unspeakable line.

Despite decades dedicated to bachelorhood and emotionally detached affairs, he'd fallen entirely, stupidly, and undisputedly in love with his future wife. The first day he'd met her, he'd warned her not to fall in love with *him*. It would have been an amusing anecdote if it were not so exasperating. Perhaps he was mistaken about his feelings. Perhaps this was only a case of infatuation.

Yes, infatuation. That was what he felt for her.

Frankie lifted her head, and over her shoulder she gave him a slow, hair-curling kiss.

No. It was definitely love. *Bloody hell.*

Jasper's hand flexed around her waist, and she snuggled her bottom into his groin. In response he licked a spot on her neck and she sighed. It was fine, he told himself. Surely plenty of men actually loved their wives?

Perhaps it would be best if for now he kept it to himself. Frankie had already been coerced into marriage with him; the last thing she needed was for him to start spouting off about love like one of the dandy poets at the Coswold literary reception.

The last thing *he* needed was to hear that, despite what his darling niece thought, she was incapable of loving him back.

Frankie rubbed the arch of her foot over his. Jasper had not known until that moment how sensitive and erotic feet could be.

"Do you think the mastermind behind the Dowry Thieves is here?"

"It is possible."

She shifted to rubbing her foot over his calf, and there was that damned feeling in his belly again. "Who among us could be so cruel?"

Jasper nuzzled her neck. "I do not know. But I suspect whoever is behind it has had a difficult life. Mayhap he has wealth, but he is clearly lacking in morals and values."

"You have not had an easy life either, but you have not let it turn you into a monster."

"That depends on who you ask."

"No, Jasper." She turned around to face him, her eyes solemn and fierce. "You are not a monster."

"I threatened to disembowel Devon."

Instead of shirking away, she laughed. "No wonder he looked so pale after you spoke to him."

"I had to ensure he honored the terms of the bet."

"Thank you," she said quietly, the candle flames reflecting off her lenses as her eyes searched his. "I will forever be in your debt."

"Husbands and wives do not keep score."

She gave him a dimpled smile. "Do you know, Jasper, that if you keep saying things like that, we may never get out of bed?"

Jasper's groin stirred. "Do you have any idea how enticing you are?"

It was the wrong thing to say, because she stiffened beside him. "Do not lie to me." She went to climb out of the bed but he tugged her back until she lay beneath him. "No, Jasper. You have said I am beautiful and all sorts of lovely things that I know are not true. But now that we have lain together, I do not want any more false flattery between us."

Anger stirred beneath the surface of his skin. "Let us put an end to this right now, then. You are perfect, Francis Turner." She started to speak but he placed his palm over her mouth. "No, you can have your turn to talk in a moment. Let me say my piece. I know you have been told your entire life that you are too plain and too smart, too loud and too uncultured, and too *everything*—and I strongly suspect it is your mother who has been implanting those falsehoods in your head, so I want to be very, very clear when I say this." He stared into her wary eyes. "You are everything that is perfect. Your little dimples, your gorgeous smile, your messy hair and your big spectacles, your tendency toward being so candid it stings, your wit and intelligence, the way you make love—everything about you is exactly perfect *for me*. It is as if you were *made* for me. I have spent years avoiding marriage because I could not imagine my life with any woman, and then you walked into my house and now I cannot imagine living without you. So the next time you think that you are not enough, know that you don't have to be enough for anyone or anything else, because you are *everything* to me."

Bloody hell. He had just finished telling himself he would not spill his heart to her yet, and here he might as well have ripped it out and lain it at her feet. He removed his hand from her mouth but she didn't speak, she only continued to stare up at him. "Say something."

"I—I do not know what to say. I was told no man could ever like those qualities about me."

"Do I look like your typical high society gentleman?"

She slowly shook her head. "No. You are a better man than every single one of them."

"No, I am not. We are all monsters in our own way; my way just happens to be more visible than theirs. But I *am* better at seeing you."

"How can you say those beautiful things to me and then call yourself a monster?" She furrowed her brow. "I will work on believing you when you say you like my oddities—and rest assured I will remind you of your claims when you are exasperated with me—if you will work on believing that you are a good man."

Jasper brushed his lips against hers and said softly, "I would do anything for you, Frankie."

Her dimples appeared. "Not a monster, but mayhap a devil. *My devil.*"

They kissed again, and it was tender and lingering and full of heart. Finally she sighed and rolled out from underneath him and stood to dress.

"Where are you going?"

"I must return to my chamber before Cecelia awakens." She gave him that war-inciting smile over her shoulder, and her blond hair swept across her smooth back like a wave of gold. "We are not married yet."

She bent over, her delectable derriere in the air, and Jasper reached forward to fondle her bottom. She purred. Purred! To hell with reputations. He was sliding his hand around to her lower belly when she pulled away, chiding him with a look. "I need your help with my gown."

Jasper clenched his jaw. "This marriage cannot happen soon enough."

He pulled his trousers over his hips and then helped tighten her corset and buttoned the hundred buttons on her gown, which was ninety-nine too many in his opinion. "What did your mother say to you in the sitting room?"

"Oh. That she was disappointed that I had thrown away my chance to marry some sort of peer, she thought my spoiled actions were typical, since I never think about the family or my reputation, she hoped I did not regret tying myself to a rake, she warned me that because I am so plain you will likely take many mistresses and I will have to look the other way, and on and on."

"I do not like her making you feel bad."

Frankie turned and cupped his cheek. "I do not think she intends to be cruel, Jasper. I like to think she loves me and wants the best for me, even though I am an eternal disappointment to her."

"Frankie, you are not a disappointment to her," he said, astonished that she could not see what was behind her mother's insults, when it had taken him only a matter of days to figure it out. "She is *jealous* of you."

Frankie laughed, but Jasper did not. Her merriment faded. "You are serious? How could she be jealous of *me*?"

"How could she not? You have walked your own path your entire life. You are gorgeous, intelligent, and feisty. You have managed to retain your whole self, body and soul, while I suspect—"

Frankie's eyes narrowed. "You suspect what? Do not dare to lie to me, Mr. Jones. I shall have none of that."

"I suspect she wishes she had done things differently."

"You mean not marry my father?"

He lifted a shoulder.

Frankie thought about that. "You may be right. There have been times where I have sensed that she is not a happy person, and that perhaps she wishes she had married higher in society. But if she *is* jealous, and I still find that hard to believe, I do not think she knows it."

"That I agree with."

After re-pinning her uncooperative hair, Frankie was presentable enough to return to her chamber.

"I am disappointed that I did not solve the mystery of the Dowry Thieves," she admitted at the door. "I was so close to saving other women from Lady Elizabeth's fate."

"We will figure something out—together. We are a team now, Frankie."

She brightened. "You are absolutely right, Jasper. Just because this ploy did not work, it does not mean another won't."

"Now wait just a min—"

She gave him a dimpled smile and slid out the door, leaving him staring at the wood-carved panel in what was becoming an all-too-familiar feeling of exasperation.

Chapter 41

The Dove slipped into the temporary chambers of Parliament as if she were a shadow. After the great fire had destroyed the Palace of Westminster in 1834, Parliament had been moved to temporary accommodations while the palace was rebuilt. Security was embarrassingly lax, and she had had no trouble finding her way into the chambers and committee rooms. Her source had given her a map with a location for the records closet. Tonight, she was going to pull on the loose threads the Scott Silver scam had exposed.

Her feet were soundless on the corridor floor. When she reached the room where the records were being stored, she used several small tools to quickly and effortlessly disengage the lock. She would never assign one of her governesses a mission like this—but the Dove had a specific skill set. Breaking into Parliament was child's play.

Although she did not train her governesses in the art of lock-picking, she did train them in espionage. She had handpicked each of the women at Perdita's. Their reasons for accepting varied: some wanted revenge against the *ton* or felt a sense of duty to right the wrongs of the world, while others needed a second chance. She had built her organization with an eye toward creating the single largest network of informants within the homes of the *ton*, where transgressions almost always went unpunished. She had done so by paying her governesses well, training them well, and keeping them as safe as she could. That meant she never sent them on missions that could ruin their reputations, like this one tonight.

And yet somewhere along the line, she had failed.

Frankie Turner was a brilliant mathematician the likes of which the Dove had never seen—and in her previous life the Dove had worked with some of the kingdom's finest. Frankie was piercingly smart, and her motivations for working for the Dove were pure. She had also made apparent a glaring hole in the Dove's curriculum.

The Dove had eyes and ears everywhere, and she'd recently heard of a curious scene that taken place behind the Coswold town house. An eyewitness had seen Jasper Jones drag out a bloodied Mr. Farthins and sit him among the waste. According to her informant, Jones had then leaned down and said something into the man's broken and swollen face that had made Farthins turn to the side and retch. Only a stupid man would have tangled with Jasper Jones, but no one had ever accused Farthins of possessing an abundance of intelligence.

The Dove found Jones to be a fascinating enigma. His reputation was fearsome, and he operated within his own gray boundaries of the law, but then so did she. He seemed to have taken his unexpected role of protecting Frankie to heart, and she wondered how her governess had managed to engage the fealty of a man like Jones, who did not align himself with anyone or anything that was not to his benefit.

The Dove did not doubt that the violent altercation with Farthins had involved her governess, and that gnawed at her conscience. Frankie had not graduated from Perdita's, but still, the failure was the Dove's. She had sent Frankie in unprepared. She had given Frankie's bait scheme her blessing, and it seemed the governess had already required Jones's intervention.

The Dove quietly pushed open the door to the records room and returned the tools to her pocket. Her former governess, Emily Leverton—now Emily Denholm—had come face-to-face with a deranged killer, but Emily had grown up on the streets, and she'd known how to defend herself. Could all of her governesses do the same?

The answer had been a spear through her chest. Most of the women she recruited were genteelly bred and from families that teetered on destitution. They had been taught needlework and how to play the piano and how to paint—all skills that were necessary for educating their young *ton* pupils. At Perdita's they learned additional skills: how to listen, how to question, and how to report. Most importantly, they were taught how to make a quick exit. The Dove had strict rules for her governesses: *Never* accuse. *Only* report. *Do not* interfere.

But it was not enough. In fact, it was downright naive. No matter how often she hammered those rules into her girls' heads, she could not control chance, and chances were that some of them would become embroiled in situations that could not easily be escaped. If she did not teach them how to defend themselves, then she was doing them a severe disservice.

She had recently learned of a governess named Miss Ivy Bennett, who was teaching secret self-defense classes over a modiste shop in the country. Apparently, the Dove's secretary's sister was a devoted attendee. The Dove had asked her secretary to discover the location and time of the next class, as she was very keen to meet Miss Ivy Bennett and see what the other woman was made of. The Dove's governesses were lacking in basic self-protection skills that she did not have the time to teach them. Perhaps Miss Bennett was her answer.

The Dove was supposed to be at Miss Bennett's class that very moment, but the opportunity to search Parliament had presented itself when she'd been alerted that several of the guards had contracted cholera, and exposing the Dowry Thieves took precedence over her desire to hire Miss Bennett, or her interest in learning more about a disturbing pattern emerging that involved Miss Bennett's employer, Viscount Brackley.

The Dove lit a candle and pulled out a wooden drawer filled with papers, pushing her concerns about self-defense to the back of her mind. She got a whiff of ink, tobacco, and the horridly pungent musk of the records keeper. The public and private bills had been organized by year and included the vote tally of each.

The Dove glanced at her pocket watch and lifted out a stack of bills from 1836, the year Scott Silver had been revealed to be a scam. She had only four hours until daylight, and she had mountains of paperwork to sort through. She had a hunch that Frankie's suggestion that the ringleader might be a politician was right. The Dove had also begun to question if the fee she'd assumed the ringleader charged for his services was in fact a cash transaction, or something more insidious.

Her fingers were black with ink by the time she finished going through the records, but she had her confirmation: The Dowry Thieves' ringleader wasn't after money. He was after votes.

There had been a number of private and extraordinarily conservative bills submitted over the past two years that had been too radical for most of the Lords, made obvious by the fact that only twenty-one men had voted for each bill. Her eyes had bugged out at the insanity of the bills; it was as if the bill author had wanted to repeal all social progress made over the past century. As she'd thumbed through each proposal, she'd counted twenty-one tallies for each one. Always twenty-one. The twenty Scott Silver investors, and the ringleader.

She'd cursed that the Lords did not keep track of who cast what vote, but she'd narrowed down her suspect pool considerably. The ringleader was male, titled, and an active participant in the House of Lords. He would have conservative values, although that was not entirely helpful, since the House of Lords was notoriously conservative as a group. The ringleader would have to be active in society, and he would have to regularly attend social functions in order to know which women were being vocal, and how to best trap them. He might even have an accomplice.

The Dove blew out the candle and exited the room, locking the door behind her. It was time she visited a few old friends who sat in the House of Lords. Some of them had terribly sharp memories and might recall who had voted for the extreme bills. And she was *certain* they would remember that they owed her.

Chapter 42

The next morning, the Houndsbury estate was in a brilliant whirl of activity. While gentlemen prepared for the grand foxhunt, servants prepared for the evening's ball. The ladies, meanwhile, were entertaining themselves with walks and other genteel games. Cecelia and Frankie had chosen croquet and were playing on the south lawn under a midmorning sky of white and steel when Jasper arrived.

Frankie had never played croquet before and she had discovered, much to her delight, that she was exceptionally good at it. All it took was a few quick calculations of angles in her head, and it seemed she was able to put the balls exactly where she wished.

Cecelia was outfitted in a white-and-lilac-sprigged morning gown that made her appear her age for once, and she boisterously ran back and forth, alternately cheering on the more sedate ladies and nudging Madam Margaret awake.

Frankie whacked a ball and was unsurprised when it sailed through the wire arch, her skills seemingly unaffected by her lack of sleep. She'd lain awake a good portion of the night recalling every last touch she and Jasper had shared, and feeling squirmy and pink with the memories. From there she had spiraled into worry about her sister, worry about the troublemakers, and worry that she would not find any evidence of the identity of the ringleader.

The result of all her worrying was that Frankie had not solved any of her problems, but she *had* lost a good deal of sleep.

"There you are." Jasper's voice sounded from behind her shoulder, deep and sensuous. Her body reacted instantly, tingling and tensing with pleasant anticipation. "I heard complaints in the drawing room that croquet was no fun because an upstart kept winning, and I immediately knew where to find you."

Frankie pushed at the bridge of her spectacles. "Truly? They are upset?"

"People do not like to consistently lose. They enjoy the illusion of chance. Mayhap toss a game or two, and you will find that your opponents will come back for more."

"Is that how you run Rockford's?"

"I take it into consideration."

"I really must visit."

Jasper rubbed the back of his neck. "You are aware that honorable society women are generally discouraged from frequenting gaming hells?"

Frankie used the end of her croquet mallet to smack a fly. "Thank heavens I am not an honorable society woman."

Jasper gave her a devilish grin. "Cecelia appears quite engaged in the game, and I have need of your assistance inside."

Frankie nodded and excused herself. Did she imagine the sighs of relief from the other women? Cecelia waved to her and Jasper as they headed across the green, springy lawn toward the main house. "You are not hunting?"

"No."

"Why not?"

"It is not a fair fight. They let loose a fox, and then on horseback and with their hounds sniffing, they stampede after it like ham-fisted oafs. 'Tis a cruel sport."

Frankie wondered how on earth he had managed to maintain his reputation as a heartless cad. He was fiercely protective, and she had witnessed him beat down Farthins, but anyone who knew him must've also known that beneath the roguish exterior was a man whose sentiments were made up of gold and jam and everything gooey and sweet.

"Are you feeling all right?" he asked as he led her up the staircase. "With everything that happened yesterday?"

"I am disappointed that I fell so easily into their trap, but I am more determined than ever to out the monster who designed it."

Jasper gave her an inscrutable look. "I meant everything that happened between *us*. The betrothal and what we did after."

"Oh, that."

"Yes, that."

She considered. "I quite enjoyed it."

Jasper smiled.

They had reached the door to his chamber and Frankie narrowed her eyes. "What exactly is it that you need my help with?"

"It is a math question," he said, twisting the knob.

Once inside, he locked the door and pulled her to him. His mouth descended on hers with such hunger that if she had not known any better, she would have thought it had been ages since he'd been with a woman instead of twelve hours. Frankie wound her arms around his neck and breathed in the scent of him. The window was opened and the smells of summer wove between them: freshly cut grass, wildflowers, and dried clay.

His tongue tangled with hers and his hands slid into her hair. Her pins needed only the smallest excuse to slip out of her locks, and they did so then, clattering to the floor. With her hair falling in a sheet between her shoulder blades and Jasper's hands roving down her back, Frankie pulled away and said, "Jasper!"

"Right, yes, the math problem. Lie on the bed."

Frankie happily did as he bid. Sinking into the center of the bed with her knees bent and her elbows propping her up, she waited while Jasper untied his cravat and dragged it slowly off his neck. He pulled it taut between both hands and approached her with the prowl of a large cat.

He sat on the edge of the bed and laid the strip of silk across her eyes. "It occurred to me last night that there are certain things I did not have a chance to do with you, and I knew I must rectify the situation immediately. Turn your head, darling."

Frankie could have said no and she knew he would have respected her boundaries, but the idea of being blindfolded and reliant entirely on her other senses was far too intriguing. She turned her head, and he settled the cravat over her eyes and tied the knot on the side so that it would not be uncomfortable. His consideration had not yet ceased to amaze her.

The room instantly went dark, and Frankie felt the mattress shift as he stood. The lemon polish smelled stronger, the brocade blanket beneath her fingertips rougher, the rush of blood in her ears louder. "What math problem do you need help with?" she rasped.

Cool air brushed her thighs as he flipped her skirt above her knees. His warm hands cupped her ankles over her stockings and smoothed upward. "Angles," he said, his voice rough. He'd reached the tops of her knees, his fingers brushing across the smooth skin above her stockings, but to her surprise he didn't stop there; instead he trailed his fingertips higher to her drawers. Slowly he tugged on the string until the knot released, then he hooked his thumbs inside the waistband and dragged them down her legs, leaving her completely bare and open to him. Frankie was almost grateful for the blindfold so that she did not have to blush at the sight she must've made.

His palms were back, this time scorching the insides of her thighs as he pushed them apart. She felt hot breath on the skin above her knee, then a smooth lap of his tongue. Frankie flexed her fingers in the fabric of the coverlet. His lips drifted, light as a butterfly's wings, higher up her leg.

"Angles?" she gasped dumbly.

"Angles." He kissed her on her inner thigh where the skin was thinner. He sucked and licked and then blew a stream of air on the wet flesh. "I am going to place my tongue on you, and you are going to tell me if I have the angle right."

"That is not really a—*Jasper*!"

He'd moved his mouth while she spoke, kissing her directly between her legs. Frankie was stunned. Such a thing had to be unorthodox and taboo and improper, and yet in that moment she was extraordinarily grateful that Jasper Jones was *not* a proper gentleman who would only do proper gentlemanly things to her.

He was sinfully wicked, and he did sinfully wicked things to her.

Jasper's hands held her thighs apart as he licked and sucked and stroked her with his tongue and lips. Then he inserted his finger and Frankie saw stars. The pleasure was intense, but he was avoiding the one place that had made her peak the night before.

"You are missing an angle."

Jasper murmured into her and she shivered. "This one?" He flicked his tongue across the nub of nerves and Frankie cried out.

"Yes!"

"Not yet."

Frankie squirmed, but Jasper held down her thighs and she loved that, too. After a few more minutes of beautiful torture, he tucked his arms under her legs and pulled at the neckline of her gown. Realizing what he wanted, Frankie helped until her breasts were bare. Her nipples instantly puckered, practically begging for his touch. Jasper strummed his fingertips across them, tweaking and plucking and gently rolling. At the same time, he at last paid attention to that special spot, and with the flat of his tongue on her center and his hands on her breasts, Frankie screamed as she exploded.

Jasper was on her in a moment, swallowing her cries with his mouth as her body continued to convulse, until at last she fell as limp as a dish rag. She breathed heavily for a moment and then pushed the cravat onto her forehead. Jasper was lying next to her, his eyes hot and needy. "Did I hit the right angle?"

"You know you did. Why are your trousers still on?"

"I thought you'd never ask." He shucked them in record time and entered her already liquid center, her inner muscles still tremoring with pleasure. She tightened around him and crossed her ankles behind his back. As soon as he started moving the pressure began to build again. A bird chirped outside their window and the horn signaled the start of the hunt, but Frankie only vaguely registered the background noises as he entered her at an angle that gave her chills.

Her skirt was bunched and cumbersome at her waist, and Jasper growled as he batted it away. "Let me undress you."

"No, it is too annoying to re-dress. Let me on top again instead."

He rolled onto his back, taking her with him, and she rocked back and forth on him while he cupped her breasts, and it was not long before they both reached a blinding peak.

Frankie tumbled inelegantly off him and lay face down on the bed. Jasper took the opportunity to gently smack her bottom and nip her ear. "Thank you for your mathematical expertise."

She made an unintelligible noise into the cover.

"When we marry, I want you to wear my ring."

She shifted onto her side and reached for his hand. She ran her tongue around his middle finger, just above the silver-and-black crest of Rockford's. "This ring?"

Jasper's eyes darkened. "I meant a wedding ring, but perhaps you have the right of it after all." He slid the ring off his finger and tried it on the fourth finger of her left hand. It was far too big. It was even too big for her thumb. Jasper clamped the ring between his teeth and reached around her neck to unclasp the silver chain she was wearing. Frankie watched, oddly aroused, as he used his teeth to slide the ring onto the chain and then re-clasped it around her neck.

"Now everyone knows you are mine."

Frankie touched the silver band, which was still warm with his body heat, and her heart tripped. "How will everyone know you are mine?"

Jasper gave her a mysterious smile. "I have an idea, but you shall have to wait until we are properly married to learn what it is." He leaned forward and pressed a kiss to the ring, which rested over her heart. "This is where it belongs."

Frankie laughed. "As a necklace?"

But Jasper was not laughing. He stood abruptly, his sudden

absence leaving an impression in the mattress and cool air where his body heat had been. He pulled his trousers on and raked a hand through his hair. Frankie sat up and smoothed her skirts over her knees. "What is the matter? Did I say something wrong?"

Jasper had abandoned his efforts to dress and was pacing at the foot of the bed in only his trousers. His feet and chest were bare, and a magnificent chest it was. Dark hair curled over the supple heft of muscle, and her eyes devoured the trail of hair that ran across his ridged belly. "No, you did not say anything wrong. The problem is with me. I am having a difficult time keeping my true feelings to myself."

Frankie's pulse stopped. "You do not want to marry."

"What? *No.*" Jasper dropped to his knees by the bed. "The problem is that I *want* to marry you, and I would have eventually begged you to consider accepting me, even if a card game had not forced us into it. I love you, Francis Turner. I'm bloody well in love with you."

Frankie's heart squeezed and released, squeezed and released. Her breath deserted her and she could only stare at Jasper's earnest face before hers. Did he truly love her, or did he only fancy himself in love with her? She knew she vexed him half the time, and the other half of the time he was vexing her. She was not beautiful, like Lady Evelyn, or rich, or cultured, or any of the things he could have if he wanted. No matter what he'd said the night before, she knew she was not remarkable in any way other than her affinity for numbers.

Frankie enjoyed Jasper's company and she was thrilled with what they'd done in bed. That was more than most arranged marriages had. Very few married couples actually loved one another. Frankie was terrified that if she allowed herself to believe he loved her, she would be giving him the power to destroy her.

"Er, thank you," she said.

Jasper sighed and pressed his forehead to hers. "You do not have to say it back. Yet. I can be a patient man."

"No, you cannot."

"Well, I would prefer you realized you loved me sooner rather than later," he admitted. "Perhaps this will help. I want it all, Frankie. Love, children, family. Noisy holidays, laughter at the dinner table, making love on the sofa when the children are finally asleep. My whole life I have thought all I needed was money, success, and petty enjoyments. Then Cecelia came along and everything began to change, but it was not until you showed up, standing in my sitting room with your forthright candor, that I realized I was missing out. I didn't have love growing up, or a tight-knit family. I had my brother, and even he was resentful of me. I do not want to spend the rest of my life consorting with widows and throwing money around. I want a family. I want love and laughter and mathematics facts. I want *you*."

Frankie could only stare at him, her lips parted. Jasper Jones, infamous rake and gambler, was telling her he wanted a *real* marriage, the kind with all the strings and obligations. The kind where, if the person betrayed you, it slayed you.

Jasper continued, "I do not know what doubts are swirling about in your mind, but I am sure they have nice, rational reasons behind them."

"They do!"

He lightly gripped her chin and stared into her eyes. "Not everything is logical, Frankie. Some things are just plain magical."

Before she could reply, they heard a shout of alarm from outside, and then a woman screamed long and loud.

"Cecelia!" they both gasped.

Jasper yanked on his boots and quickly tied his cravat while Frankie hastily fixed her hair, and they both ran down the stairs to the croquet lawn. Several of the hunting party had already returned from the hunt, their faces grim. Two women were screaming with hysterics and were being led inside to recover with smelling salts.

Frankie's heart was in her throat until she spotted Cecelia in the thick of it, watching the adults speak in low tones with avid interest.

Jasper reached Cecelia before Frankie did, and pulled her into an embrace. "Thank God you are all right, Cece. What is happening?"

"A murder," Cecelia said in awe. "The hunters found a body in the woods."

"Who is it?" Jasper asked.

Frankie's skin prickled hot and then cold. She already knew the name before Cecelia answered. "Lord Devon."

Chapter 43

Lord Houndsbury stood among the throng of distraught guests. The men's mouths were grim lines, their hunting rifles held at their sides; the women, including Frankie's mother, waited with pale faces and watchful eyes. Houndsbury was not a large man, in fact Jasper probably had a foot of height on him, but he had the indomitable presence of someone who was used to making decisions and having them followed. Jasper had heard that Houndsbury was a no-nonsense sort of man, but that he was also fair, and had a weakness when it came to his wife and spendthrift son.

Houndsbury turned to one of the younger men and said with a voice as steely and unruffled as his hair, "Send to London for a police inspector. Deliver our request personally."

The man bobbed his head and dashed off to the stables.

"Perhaps we are being hasty," one of the lords said, his voice high and his hands shaking. "He was shot. The men were out hunting. It could have been an accident."

Houndsbury straightened his shoulders. "Then we must examine the body."

A few of the men shifted on their feet at the word *we*.

"I should also like to see the body," Frankie piped in.

Jasper did not let his surprise show on his face. It was a skill he'd honed with years of practice, and in that moment he was grateful he had, because never had he been so stunned as when his future wife declared she wanted to examine a dead body in front of the Duke of Houndsbury. Heavens, Devon had nearly lost his mind when Cecelia had said the word *ankle*, and now his betrothed wanted to see a body?

Frankie's mother, who'd wedged her way to Frankie's side, hissed something at Frankie, but she shook her head.

Before any of the shocked men could reply, and before Cecelia could shout that she, too, wanted to go—which Jasper was sure she did—Frankie added, "I may able to tell if it was an accident or intentional."

The high-voiced lord snorted. *"You?* How?"

"Mathematics."

Houndsbury studied Frankie for a moment before lifting a brow at Jasper.

"Miss Turner is her own woman," Jasper said in response to the duke's obvious request for permission. "However, anyone who doubts that she is a brilliant mathematician will reveal himself to be a fool."

Mrs. Turner's mouth parted in surprise, and a keen look entered Houndsbury's eye. "Very well then. Mr. Jones, Miss Turner, and Lord Pemberwith, come with me. Lord Trawley, lead us to the body."

Jasper turned to Lady Houndsbury and Frankie's mother. "Your Grace, Mrs. Turner, I would ask that you escort Miss Cecelia and Madam Margaret back to the house, and please do not let Cecelia out of your sight. If there is a murderer on the loose, no young girl should be left unattended."

Cecelia opened her mouth to protest, but Lady Houndsbury had drawn herself to her full height and hooked her arm through Cecelia's. "Quite right, Mr. Jones. Rest assured that Miss Cecelia will not leave my line of vision until you return." She gave a brisk nod to Cecelia. "We women must stick together in times of trouble."

All of Cecelia's protests died on her lips as the Duchess of Houndsbury held her arm and spoke to her as if she were an equal. Cecelia's eyes filled with admiration, and she glanced up at the older woman as if she were an idol that she wished one day to become.

Jasper's estimation of the Houndsburys increased. There were very, very few people in their position who were still able to show compassion. Even Mrs. Turner appeared struck dumb by the duchess's ready acceptance of his niece.

Lord Trawley was one of the men who'd found the body, and his face paled as he reluctantly led the small party back into the shadowy growth of the forest.

Jasper and Frankie brought up the rear of the group. She had to keep lifting her skirts to step over moss-carpeted logs, but she did so without complaint. The heat was oppressive beneath the cloud-blanketed sky, and not even the canopy of leaves offered relief.

Normally Jasper would have enjoyed the rare excursion into a green-dappled forest, the scents of late summer in the air and the lazy drone of flies looping through branches overhead. In the distance he heard the tinkling of a stream, and even just the sounds of rushing water managed to cool him a bit. Yet today he could not shake the feeling that Devon had indeed been murdered, and that he and Frankie were, in some way, involved.

"Do you think the ringleader murdered him because we foiled

his plan?" Frankie asked in a low voice, her thoughts obviously running along similar lines. She lifted a strand of hair from her sticky neck and Jasper's thoughts detoured as he imagined licking the perspiration off her skin.

He pulled a handkerchief from his pocket and handed to her before extracting another and wiping his brow. "It has crossed my mind."

"Why not simply find Devon another wife?"

That very question had been nagging at him from the moment he'd heard Devon was the deceased. "I do not know."

"Was it a punishment for failing? A warning to others not to do the same? Or was it for some other reason entirely?"

A suspicion was forming in Jasper's mind, but he did not wish to worry her, so he remained silent.

"Well, out with it."

Jasper turned to her in surprise. "What do you mean?"

"You have a thought you are not sharing with me. You told me we are a team now, did you not?"

Jasper was simultaneously impressed that she'd been able to read him when so few could, and worried that such an ability would not bode well for him in their marriage. "I do not want to worry you unnecessarily."

She narrowed her eyes.

"I am wondering if Devon was killed because he failed to silence you specifically. As you said, the ringleader could have chosen an alternate wife for him. It is possible the person in charge knows you are onto him, especially if Devon had the opportunity to speak with him before he was murdered. That would make you a threat to the Dowry Thieves' entire operation, and the leader's reputation in particular."

Frankie worried her lip and shoved aside a prickly bramble branch. "Then why kill Devon, and not also me and you?" At Jasper's silence she sucked in air. "You do not think we are in danger, do you?"

"I do not know. It is possible a stray hunting bullet killed Devon, as the others have postulated. However, I have not lived this long by ignoring my instincts, and my instincts are screaming that when we get back to the house, we need to pack our bags and leave."

His blood fizzed with the creeping sensation that danger lurked near, and every one of his finely honed instincts whispered *warning*. Those instincts had allowed him to walk out of ambushes twice in his life, and he would be damned if he disregarded them now when the lives of the most important people in the world were on the line. No one would hurt Frankie or Cecelia while he still breathed.

To his surprise, she did not argue. "Then we leave."

"One thing is for sure," Jasper said quietly as the sounds of rushing water grew closer. Ahead, Lord Houndsbury's bright-red hunting coat stood out like a splash of blood against the shades of green and brown. Devon would have been wearing a bright coat as well, which made an accident even more unlikely.

"What is that?"

"If Lord Devon was murdered, the ringleader is here among us."

Chapter 44

Frankie had seen dead bodies before; everyone had. She'd viewed her great-aunt Salome after she had passed—along with a number of other loved ones over the years—and thusly inherited her great-aunt's spectacles. But the bodies that had been washed and laid out in Sunday finery for final mourning had not prepared her for the gruesome scene before her.

Lord Devon, who had been sneering at her only the day before, lay flat on his back, his eyes staring unseeing into the steel sky as if they were still shocked by some final image. His face was gray and stiff, the upper half of his body sprawled on the ground while his feet lay in the water. The stream gurgled and rushed over his bobbing boots. But it was the dark, raw wound in his chest that made Frankie pause and take several deep breaths through her nose. It appeared as if something small had tunneled through his ribs, exposing the gory, meaty bits within.

Jasper's hand closed around the back of her sweaty nape and he tugged her close enough to whisper, "Are you all right?"

She blinked, breathed, and nodded. It comforted her that Lord

Houndsbury, for all his stature, and Lord Trawley did not look any less affected than she.

"Well, he was certainly shot," Lord Houndsbury said in a strained voice.

Frankie edged closer to the body and peered down at the chest wound. She noted the black smudges on Devon's shirtsleeves and the fact that he was wearing the same evening frock coat he'd had on the night before rather than hunting attire. She circled the upper body, focusing on visual measurements. "May I see your rifle, Your Grace?"

Lord Houndsbury seemed startled by the request, but he held it out for her inspection. She studied it for several moments, turning it this and that way, focusing particularly on the barrel, and handed it back. "I believe he was murdered."

"Preposterous!" Lord Trawley snapped. "What gives you the right to make such a wild accusation? It is every bit as possible, in fact more probable, that he was killed by accident."

Jasper stiffened beside her. "Let the lady speak."

"*She* is no lady."

"Say that again," Jasper warned, "and I'll show you a hunting accident."

"Enough!" Lord Houndsbury roared. "Miss Turner, explain yourself."

Frankie felt a warm glow from Jasper's defense of her. Her mother had never found it prudent to defend her oddities. It was a unique feeling to know that she had someone at her side.

"First, he is wearing his evening frock coat rather than his hunting coat. That leads me to believe someone murdered him late last night, rather than his death being a result of a hunting accident this afternoon. If that is not enough to convince you, look at the powder burns around the wound." All of their eyes fell to the ragged hole in Devon's shirtsleeves. Jasper inhaled sharply. "When one hunts, one typically fires far enough away that there is no residue of gunpowder from the explosion on the target, am I correct?"

Lord Houndsbury nodded, but Lord Trawley's eyes flashed with anger. "Why does that matter? Perhaps Devon took a late walk and a nearby poacher fired on him by accident."

"If that were the case, Lord Trawley, the poacher would've had to have been so close that it would have been impossible for him *not* to know he was firing on a man rather than an animal."

Lord Trawley did not have anything to say to that.

"There is more," she continued. "Do you see the size of the bullet wound? What kind of hunting rifle makes that small and that clean of a wound? If the circumference of the barrel Lord Houndsbury is carrying is indicative of the average hunting rifle, then a hunter could not have inflicted Devon's wound. Rather, it was likely the result of a much smaller weapon, such as a derringer."

Lord Houndsbury lifted his eyes from Devon's chest, and in them she read acceptance of the facts and approval of her methods. "Miss Turner, not only have you displayed more fortitude than half the men here today, but you have also displayed twice as much brains. If you are ever in need of employment, I could use someone with your intelligence and constitution."

Frankie was astounded, and so was Lord Trawley, because his mouth rounded in disbelief. Never in her wildest dreams had Frankie imagined that one day the Duke of Houndsbury would not only address her directly, but also call her intelligent and strong.

She glanced up at Jasper, and he was smiling down at her with pride written all over his face. But the pride was quickly overtaken with worry. He lifted his head and said to Houndsbury, "Lord

Devon was murdered, which would suggest the killer is a guest on premises. It would be too conspicuous for the murderer to leave directly after, unless he happened to be the man you sent for the inspector."

Houndsbury's face was solemn, and his shoulders sloped, as if he carried the weight of the world on them. His rifle rested in the crook of his arm, and he was still wearing the leather hunting gloves he'd put on before his property had become the scene of a murder. Those leather-clad fingers tapped on his thigh as he contemplated a decision. After a moment he said, "No one leaves."

"Excuse me?" Lord Trawley cried. For once Frankie agreed with the irritating lord.

"Until the inspector arrives, no one leaves," Houndsbury repeated. His gaze was iron when it settled on each of them. "Whoever killed Devon is still here, and here he shall remain."

Frankie sensed Jasper thinking quickly at her side, but he did not say anything.

"I will send someone out to collect Lord Devon." Houndsbury turned to face the direction of the house. "You are all witness to the position of the body should the inspector ask."

Trawley trotted after Houndsbury, who, for all his silver age, moved with the purpose of a much younger man. Frankie and Jasper fell in step behind.

Once enough distance separated them from Houndsbury, Jasper pulled up short, grabbed her by the upper arms, and tugged her in for a quick and crushing kiss. "I know that was unpleasant, but you were brilliant."

Frankie rested her cheek on his chest and steadied herself with the beat of his heart and the rhythm of his breath. "Whoever murdered Devon did it in cold blood, Jasper. He looked Devon in the eye and shot him through the heart. Who could do something like that?"

"There are a lot of bad people in the world. At times, I am one of them." He traced his finger along the chain that held his ring, snug between her cleavage. "Lucky ring," he muttered.

Frankie swatted at his hand and repositioned the necklace. "You may have done bad things in the past, Jasper, but you have never been a bad man."

He tilted his head to the side, the pale light from between the leaves sliding over his dark hair. "It seems I have been successful in fooling you."

"You aren't fooling anyone." She looked ahead to the disappearing back of Houndsbury. "What will we do now that the duke is insisting everyone stay?" She scooped a stick off the forest floor and began walking again, thwacking leaves with it as she went.

Jasper's jaw was tight. "Unfortunately, we cannot leave now without arousing suspicion, so we stay, and we stay together. No one goes off alone."

"That extends to you as well."

His lips were starting to curve when he froze. The pure instinct that had him tensing made the hairs on the back of her neck stand straight.

"Jas—"

Without warning he shoved her. Frankie landed hard on her hands and knees, her palms stinging as twigs jabbed through her gloves and into her skin. Before she could react, she heard a loud *crack*, and splinters of bark rained over her head.

Everything that followed was a kaleidoscope of images, scents, and sounds: shouts from ahead, the acrid bite of gun smoke in the air; another rifle firing, dogs barking, a flash of Jasper's dark-blue coat as he plunged into the forest, and then someone was hauling her to her feet. She straightened her spectacles and realized she'd been unable to see because they'd been askew. Grasping her arms was Lord Houndsbury. He was out of breath, as if he'd just sprinted back to her. "Are you injured, Miss Turner?"

"I am fine," she said through numb lips. "Where is Mr. Jones?"

"He ran after the shooter."

"The shooter?"

Houndsbury's gray eyes shifted over her shoulder, and she spun to see what he was looking at. The tree behind her was missing a chunk of bark, the wound deep enough to reveal the tender pulp beneath.

"Holy Queen V. Someone just tried to kill me!"

Chapter 45

When Jasper returned to the main house, he found Frankie pacing on the lawn. Several men stood with her, and he assumed Houndsbury had assigned them as protection. The moment she saw him she pushed through two broad pairs of shoulders and ran toward him. She almost threw her arms around him before apparently remembering where they were, and instead stopped toe-to-toe and said, "What happened?"

Jasper wanted to squeeze her tight and reassure himself that she was all right. If he hadn't felt the telltale burning of eyes on the back of his neck in the forest, she might be dead this very moment. He would have tugged her closer regardless of decorum, if she were not impatiently waiting for answers along with everyone else. So instead of throwing her over his shoulder and carrying her to his room, where he could lock her up safe forever, he pulled his handkerchief from his pocket and wiped the back of his neck. "Bloody dogs."

Frankie blinked. "Pardon me?"

"Some of the hunters were heading back, and their dogs were

chasing a rabbit. In a twist of misfortune, I got caught in the melee. By the time I made it through the pack, the shooter was gone."

"Did you see any footprints?"

Houndsbury appeared in the doorway at that moment, spotted Jasper, and hurried over. "Well?" he barked.

"The shooter eluded me, Your Grace."

"No footprints?" he asked, unknowingly echoing Frankie.

"The ground is too dry, although there were broken plants where he stood."

"Blast! He got away with murdering one man on my property and nearly another. I want him found!"

"He left something behind."

Frankie and Houndsbury stilled. Jasper shifted so that his back was to the steps and only Frankie and Houndsbury could see what he held in his fist. He opened his fingers, and lying crumpled on his palm was a scrap of sapphire-blue silk. "This was caught on the bark of the tree where he stood."

Houndsbury stared at the sapphire silk, his mouth tight with fury. He knew as well as Jasper that shades of blue were currently in fashion for men. "From a vest? A piece of his handkerchief? I'll have every closet turned inside out."

"That is, of course, at your discretion, Your Grace, but I wonder if it would tip him off? He would dispose of the clothing before we ever got to his chamber, whereas if we wait, we may catch him inadvertently wearing this less-popular sapphire color."

Houndsbury's jaw worked, but he nodded in agreement. "Perhaps it would be wiser to have my servants quietly search the guest chambers during the ball. Have you shown anyone else?"

"Only you and Miss Turner."

"Keep it that way. I have ordered the stables and carriage house closed. No one is to leave the property until the inspector arrives from London."

"How are the guests reacting?"

"Women are fainting with the vapors left and right, and the men are either angry or uneasy."

"One of them is playacting."

Houndsbury adjusted the cuffs on the red hunting coat he still wore. "Yes. Among us walks a murderer."

"Miss Turner is in danger," Jasper said flatly. "I request that she be allowed to leave." And by *request*, he meant *demand*. She would be leaving whether Houndsbury liked it or not. He had been willing to stay before the direct attempt on her life, but there was no way he was allowing her to brush shoulders with the person who'd shot at her.

"You are not a man someone says no to, not even a duke, so I will ask you to consider what I am about to say." Houndsbury met his gaze with more quiet assurance than half the men who frequented his club. "If you leave now, when the party disbands, Miss Turner will once again be in danger, except then she will be on the London streets where the perpetrator could disappear in a heartbeat. If you remain here, you narrow down the suspects and the avenues of escape. You have a small window of opportunity to eliminate the threat to your betrothed. I suggest you take it."

Jasper's pulse beat in his throat.

"Does the betrothed have any say?" Frankie asked.

"No," Jasper said automatically, but at her scathing look he paused, took a deep breath, and amended his statement. "Yes, of course you do."

Houndsbury chuckled. "Marriage will suit you just fine, Mr. Jones."

"I am staying," Frankie said plainly. "I will not be run off, especially now that I know how much my presence upsets the murderer."

"You are an extraordinary woman." Lord Houndsbury studied her as if she fascinated him. "But I must caution you against going off alone. Do not allow yourself to be singled out by anyone, not even those you may consider friends. You will be safest among the other guests."

Frankie nodded. "That is sound advice I intend to follow."

Houndsbury glanced toward the steps where several guests hovered, speaking in hushed whispers. "Her Grace wishes to proceed with the ball tonight, and perhaps she is right to do so. It may calm everyone's nerves to return to normality."

It was late afternoon, which meant preparations for the ball were already well underway. It seemed absurd to host a ball after what had transpired that day, but Lady Houndsbury had a keen understanding of the delicate sensitivities of her own class, and Jasper suspected she was right to march onward with the festivities. The only thing worse than a frightened aristocrat was a bored aristocrat.

Houndsbury was called indoors to attend to an urgent matter, and Jasper led Frankie to her chamber. Once they were safely locked inside, he pulled her into his arms and held her tightly, breathing in her delicate scent of roses and resting his chin atop her silky blond head. "I almost lost you."

He released her, and she adjusted her spectacles. "But you did not. You saved my life, Jasper."

"As long as I am breathing I will do anything to keep you safe, Frankie. I do not need marriage vows to make that promise."

"And I will keep *you* safe."

Jasper traced his thumb down the side of her face. "I am starting to think you have already saved me."

"From a lifetime of scheming mamas and torrid affairs?"

Jasper didn't laugh. "From a lifetime of loneliness."

Frankie reached up and pulled his mouth to hers. Her kiss was soft and so sweet that he nearly wept.

At last she pulled away and said, "I need to dress for the ball."

He hated that he could not simply lock her and Cecelia up safe like his greatest treasures, but he knew Frankie would never stand for it. Besides, Houndsbury was right: It was paradoxically safer for them to be among the other guests.

He left her with a final quick kiss, needing to dress as well. His attire would conceal a few lethal surprises, because tonight he would be on the hunt for a killer.

Chapter 46

"Uncle Jasper, you must stop staring at Miss Turner like that." Cecelia's sausage curls dangled like fringe from a lampshade, and when he gave her an extra swing they fanned out from her scalp.

"How am I staring at her?"

"Like you want to throw her on the back of your horse and gallop away."

It wasn't that far off the mark. Ever since Frankie had nearly taken a bullet, he'd thought of nothing other than how to keep her safe so that he could spend the rest of her *long* life telling her every day how much she meant to him.

He was not sorry he'd told her he loved her earlier that afternoon. It would have come out eventually, and as Jasper had already come to realize, he had little desire to keep secrets from Frankie. But maybe he hadn't needed to spring everything on her at once: love, children, and lets-grow-old-together all in one bundle was a lot for anyone to take in. Hell, it had even been a shock to *him* to discover he felt that way. He should have known when he told her he loved her that she would not say it back.

That didn't mean it didn't sting. In life Jasper always went for it all. He had not wanted a gaming hell; he had wanted *the* most successful gaming hell. He had not striven to live comfortably; he'd wanted to buy crystal chandeliers and outrageously expensive Scotch. Jasper never did anything half-measure, but with Frankie he had shown his cards and she had said *thank you*. For the first time in his life, he was willing to take what he could get, because he could not imagine a life without her, even if she was never able to love him the way he loved her.

"I am staring at her because Lord Falmouth is behaving boorishly." He glared across the floor at the earl, who was grinning with far too many teeth as he danced with Frankie.

Cecelia stepped out of sync with the music, but what she lacked in skill she made up for in enthusiasm, and each one of her steps was executed with confidence and gusto. Jasper was a strong-enough dance partner to keep her contained, but he feared for the man who was not and risked being spun into a column.

The ballroom dance floor was packed with guests. Most of the men were wound tight from the earlier hunt and news of the murder, and were imbibing more than they typically might. The remaining seven Scott Silver investors were tight-lipped and pale. If Devon's murder had been a message to them, they'd received it loud and clear. The women, having experienced the boredom of a long morning of croquet followed by the stunning violence of the afternoon, were bright-eyed and eager to talk. The result was a crackling energy that was not unlike the mood in Rockford's on a full moon.

The Houndsburys had spared no expense for the crowning

event of their house party, and unlike Cecelia's soirée at his house, the *ton* would not make digs about the mountains of food in the anteroom or the excessive amount of liquor and champagne being freely poured. It was rather the opposite: because Houndsbury was a duke, they expected nothing less.

Lady Houndsbury had engaged a double quartet, and the musicians must have been affected by the energy in the room because the music was loud and lively. Six glass-bead chandeliers dripped from the barrel-vaulted ceiling and reflected prisms across the waxed wooden floor. The ballroom was stuffy despite the opened doors, and the resulting perspiration enhanced the floral perfumes and licorice-scented colognes so that the dance floor was a dizzying sensory assault. Jasper had always moved easily within crowds, and he found tonight's atmosphere as intoxicating as another man might find liquor to be. Cecelia clearly felt the same, because her cheeks were red and her eyes were sparkling.

And yet beneath the buzz of energy, darker currents swirled: fear, danger, and imminent violence. Jasper had, on occasion, felt it in his own club, and it was always a race to identify the brewing conflict and neutralize it before it came to a head.

Tonight was much the same, except this time Frankie's life might be on the line. He'd wanted to keep her close to his side, but in typical fashion she had calmly stated her low chances of being murdered in a ballroom full of people, and swished away.

"Lord Falmouth is not being boorish, Uncle Jasper. He is dancing with a stiff back and stiff arms, and that seems appropriate to me."

"It is not how he is holding her, it is how he is looking at her." Jasper clenched his teeth together. Lord Falmouth was gazing at Frankie with such calculating lust that it was taking everything

Jasper had not to walk over there and smack the thought right out of the man's head.

Cecelia released his hand, did a tight little spin, and then jumped back into his arms. "Miss Turner can take care of herself. You know what I think? I think she agreed to marry you to save her reputation, but *you* agreed to marry her because you love her."

The remark was, once again, all too astute. "You are correct."

"Now before you deny it, I saw how—wait, *what?*"

"You are correct. I love Miss Turner and I told her so today."

Cecelia sighed dreamily. "Someday I hope I make a man look as sick as you do right now, Uncle Jasper."

When the music ended Jasper kissed Cecelia on the cheek and took her hand. "Let's go steal Frankie."

"Uncle Jasper, I cannot dance with both of you."

"I am not leaving you alone tonight."

Cecelia tugged on her hand. "I will stay in the ballroom, I promise. Please, Uncle Jasper. This is my first time at a crush like this, and I could not bear it if all anyone talked about after was how Mr. Jones towed around his niece like she was still in leading strings."

"I assure you that is not what people will be talking about." Still, she made a fair argument. It was the same one Frankie had made an hour earlier when she'd blithely left his side. Jasper ground his teeth together. "Fine. I am trusting you to stay in the crowd, Cecelia. If you feel even a prickle of unease you come straight to me. And for the love of God, do *not* dance with one of the seven remaining Scott Silver investors."

Cecelia stuck her nose in the air. "I would not go near them with a ten-foot pole."

"I will be watching you."

"When aren't you?" she retorted, and spun on her heel.

Adolescents!

Jasper made his way through the crowd of people who were searching for their next dance partners. Frankie was still talking with Lord Falmouth, and beside them stood Lady Evelyn and her father, Lord Elmsdale. Evelyn looked as comfortable in the ballroom as a Scot looked on horseback, and her cheeks were flushed prettily with the heat. She had inherited her poise from her father, the Earl of Elmsdale. Elmsdale was impeccably turned out in black evening wear accented by diamond cuff links and a silk cravat the color of pure snow. Gray patches at his temples and lines at his eyes were the only indications that he was thirty years older than his daughter. Although Elmsdale was a member at Jasper's club, Jasper rarely spoke with the man. The lord never gambled, seeming content with the fine meals and brandy-led discussions in smoke-filled rooms. Jasper had not seen Elmsdale before tonight, which meant he must have arrived that evening. The duke was allowing guests to enter, but not leave. Jasper mentally crossed the earl off his list of suspects; a man who was traveling from London could not have pulled the trigger on Devon late last night.

Frankie finally took her leave of Lord Falmouth, and Jasper stepped beside her. Leaning close to her ear he said, "This gown would look better lying on my chamber floor."

Frankie burst out laughing.

"That was not the reaction I was hoping for."

She pressed her fist to her chest where the thin, silver chain disappeared between her breasts. He knew his ring was on the end of it, and it gave him an odd, savage sense of satisfaction that she still wore it.

"Sor—sorry," she gasped in between peals of laughter. Her merriment was drawing more than a few gazes, including that of Lady

Evelyn. He knew some of the guests would admire Frankie's resilience after her near-death experience that afternoon, while others would whisper that only a woman with an addled brain could laugh that hard mere hours after someone had attempted to kill her. "How many women have you said that to, Jasper?"

He started to say none, and then realized that might not exactly be true. Chagrined, he said, "I shall spend the rest of my life coming up with original ways to ask you to disrobe."

She wiped her eyes underneath her glasses. "I shall enjoy that."

"Dance with me."

"Jasper, we have already danced once, and it is inappropriate for—

"*Dance with me.*"

"Fine. *One* more dance."

Jasper pulled her close for the waltz, curving one palm around her waist and interlacing the fingers of his other hand with her own.

"That is not how you are supposed to hold my hand."

Jasper stepped forward as the musicians struck the first chord. He gave her a wolfish, barely civilized smile as his fingers stroked her lower back, picturing her as she had been earlier that day: blindfolded and open to him, her body writhing and shuddering beneath his touch.

"Stop looking at me like that," she whispered.

"Like what?"

"Like you are thinking of me in the nude."

"But I am."

Frankie bit her lip and leaned forward. "What a coincidence, because I am thinking of you in the nude as well."

Jasper fought the urge to sweep her into his arms and carry her up to his chamber. Since that was not an option with a murderer among them and Cecelia to care for, he nudged her closer, and she relaxed into his arms like softened wax. They fit together perfectly, the silky top of her blond head just below his chin, her rose-scented warmth enveloping his senses, the curves of her body sinking into the hard planes and angles of his. He had thought he was a man fitted to a lifetime of bachelorhood, but it turned out he had only been waiting for Frankie.

"What are you thinking about?" Frankie asked, peering up at him. The lenses of her spectacles reflected the chandeliers overhead, refracting the candlelight into showers of golden dots.

Jasper spun her in a tight circle. "I am thinking I have not seen a single scrap of sapphire-blue silk tonight."

"Neither have I. While I dressed this evening, I made a list of all the guests who are also members of Parliament."

"How many?"

She screwed up her nose. "More than thirty. But, Jasper, I cannot shake the feeling that I am missing something right in front of me."

That made two of them.

The music ended and Jasper reluctantly released her. "Do not leave the ballroom."

"I will not." Frankie shuddered. "I would not care for another attempt on my life."

The third son of a marquess immediately claimed Frankie for the next dance. As Jasper watched them meld into the crowd, a woman said at his shoulder, "It would be proper for a gentleman to ask his future mother-in-law to dance."

He turned and bowed to Mrs. Turner, knowing the time had come for him to face her disapproval. Her ball gown was modestly cut and a rich chocolate color, her gray-threaded hair expertly styled, and her throat accented with a single ruby pendant dangling on a velvet ribbon. Again, he was struck by the differences between mother and daughter. Although both were beautiful in their own ways, he never would have guessed they shared blood if it were not for a few shared features.

The music started, and he stepped forward while Mrs. Turner did the same, exchanging positions in smooth adherence to the steps of the dance. Mrs. Turner's expression was unreadable, her mouth set, and Jasper steeled himself for the sharp edge of her tongue.

But it seemed she had the same ability as her daughter to surprise him, because when she spoke, the words were not what he'd expected. "You defended my daughter in front of the Duke of Houndsbury today."

Jasper's dark brows lifted.

"Why?"

"Because Frankie is incredible, and everyone should know it."

"She is not like other women."

"No, she is not. Thank heavens."

Mrs. Turner twisted, her skirt wrapping around her body before falling back into place, and she lifted her gloved hand to press it against his. "Someone shot at my daughter today and you saved her life. I do not often have occasion to admit that I am wrong, but I am beginning to think that you are not all your reputation makes you out to be."

Jasper considered how to respond and decided only the bare truth would suffice. "I am not perfect, Mrs. Turner. I have committed my share of misdeeds, but I love your daughter, and for the rest of my life I will work to ensure her every happiness."

Frankie's mother gave a crisp nod. "She loves you, too, I think."

"I am not sure she does. I am not even sure she believes *she* is lovable."

"Perhaps some of that is my fault. I can see by the look in your eyes you agree. I have done what I thought was best for Francis but...mayhap I did not handle her the way she needed. She and her sister are so odd, so very much like their great-aunt Salome, that I simply did not know what to do with them. I do love them, though."

Jasper was aware of Frankie dancing a distance away, and knew she was probably dying to hear what he and her mother were discussing.

Mrs. Turner sighed. "I fear you will have to undo some of the damage I have inflicted. Francis could use someone on her side. I have not always been that person."

The music ended but Jasper said, "I will always be on her side."

"Make sure of that, Mr. Jones. I am entrusting her life in your hands." She nodded once, and some of the pressure in Jasper's chest eased. He doubted he and Mrs. Turner would ever have an overly friendly relationship, but they had forged a tentative alliance for Frankie. Frankie's family was important to her, especially her sister, and Jasper would do all he could to help her strengthen those relationships.

He scanned the ballroom for Cecelia and spotted her dancing enthusiastically with a young baron whose cheeks were flushed with the exertion of keeping up with her. Jasper was about to head toward Frankie again—drawn like a moth to a flame, he thought with an exasperated shake of his head—when a soft voice spoke behind him. "I require an audience with you, Mr. Jones."

He turned around. "I have nothing to say to you, Lady Evelyn."

"Please," she pleaded. "I wish to make amends. I left Miss

Turner alone while we were playing sardines, and I never should have. It is my fault you are betrothed to her now."

"Your apology is not necessary. You were a victim as well, my lady."

Lady Evelyn laid a gloved hand on his arm and looked beseechingly upward. "I will not rest easy until I have cleared my conscience. Do not be so cruel as to deny me."

Jasper sighed internally. "Very well. Say what you wish."

"Not in here," she implored, "on the balcony."

Jasper checked again to make sure Cecelia and Frankie were both safely engaged among the crowd before he followed Evelyn through the crush of perspiring, jostling bodies, and onto the balcony. The clouds had swept out, leaving the velvet night sky studded with stars. They were not the only ones seeking respite from the heat of the ballroom; in fact, there were so many couples on the balcony that it was nearly as crowded as the dance floor.

"Come," Lady Evelyn said, heading toward the stairs. They led into the gardens, but Jasper would be damned if he followed her into the jungle of blooms. He came to a hard halt at the foot of the steps when she would have started toward the garden path.

"This is far enough," he said flatly.

Lady Evelyn's ball gown was a sedate navy, but the moonlight washed it into a pale gray. She sighed and walked back to him. "Very well, Mr. Jones. I have asked you out here so that I can apologize away from prying eyes. The things I have said about Miss Turner in the past were cruel and careless, and I never should have left her alone during the game of sardines." The apology sounded fluid and sincere, but her expression was far from contrite. In the pale moonlight, her eyes were as cunning as ever. Unease niggled in the back of Jasper's mind.

"Again, your apology is not necessary, but if it makes you feel better, I will accept it."

"Mr. Jones, I have brought you out here for more than the opportunity to make amends. I must ask, and please do not mistake my motivations because I ask only for your benefit, what do you *really* know about your betrothed? I understand you offered marriage out of honor, but you must be aware there are ways out of a betrothal. You could do better than an awkward and troublesome governess."

Jasper's instincts were buzzing louder by the moment and would not be ignored. The word *troublesome* tumbled over in his mind. "What makes you think she is troublesome?"

"Surely you can see how she riles the men with her uncouth mathematics displays and talk of equality. It is a woman's duty to provide a beautiful home, robust heirs, and polite conversation. Many doctors warn that a woman risks becoming barren if she engages with the sciences. I would not be surprised to learn that Miss Turner is already unable to have children, and I would not wish that for you. I would never forgive myself if I did not warn you about who you have taken as your betrothed." She tapped her folded fan to his breastbone and slowly dragged it down his chest. "There are other women more suited to the position of Mrs. Jones. Other women like me."

Jasper caught Evelyn's wrist in a firm grasp. "Not in this lifetime, my lady."

Lady Evelyn's eyes shifted as something over his shoulder drew her attention, and then they widened in horror.

Jasper felt the brush of air at his back a split second before pain exploded in his skull, and the stars in the night sky faded.

Chapter 47

Frankie knew she was in the arms of a slender gentleman who smelled of sugared punch, but everything else about him escaped her notice. She had watched with curiosity as Jasper and her mother had danced and spoken with quiet urgency, and then again with a flare of anger when Jasper had left the ballroom with Lady Evelyn. The three of them had agreed they would not go off alone with anyone, but it appeared Jasper thought that rule only applied to her and Cecelia. Admittedly, the likelihood of Lady Evelyn posing any harm to Jasper was slim, but he would be furious if Frankie did the same.

She was relieved when a few minutes later Lady Evelyn returned to the ballroom. Jasper must have made his excuses and remained outdoors for fresh air. Whatever Lady Evelyn had needed from him, she'd apparently not received it, because the usually cruel tilt of her lips had been replaced with flat fury. Her rage was so palpable that Frankie nearly stopped in place, and it was only the momentum of her partner that kept her moving forward.

Her dance partner spun her around, but Frankie kept her eyes on Lady Evelyn until a head popped in front of her face. "Miss Turner, I must speak with you at once," Cecelia said, shadowing the back of Frankie's dance partner so that she might remain face-to-face with Frankie. Frankie thought their odd little dance sandwich would cause more of a stir than if she simply excused herself. The moment she did, Cecelia grabbed her hand and hauled her to the side of the dance floor.

"What is so urgent, Cecelia?"

Cecelia's cheeks were flushed and her brown curls were sticking to her temples and neck with perspiration. "You will not believe what I overheard."

Frankie took Cecelia's trembling hands in hers. "Take a breath, Cecelia."

Cecelia sucked in a dramatic breath and exhaled noisily. "No one pays much attention to me, even though I have a massive dowry, because Uncle Jasper has put a flea in everyone's ear that the dowry is invalid until I am sixteen *and* that he will evict any man from Rockford's if he so much as looks sideways at me. I heard *that* one from a couple of old biddies on the croquet court. No one is as quiet as they think they are."

"Well, you *are* too young, Cecelia. You are only fifteen."

Cecelia waved her hand. "I would have cared a fortnight ago, but since I have been here, I have seen all the dull and distasteful things the debutants have to suffer through, and I have changed my mind and vowed I shall not formally come out to society this Season."

"What was the urgent matter, Cecelia?"

"Oh! See, no one pays much attention to me so I hear the most interesting things. For instance, the day before yesterday I heard

Mr. Wharton say he wanted to bury his face in Lady Evelyn's quim whiskers. What are quim whiskers, Miss Turner?"

Frankie's mouth fell open. "Do not say that so loudly! They are... lady parts."

"Oh." Cecelia's cheeks flushed. "Ohhhh. How did you know that, Miss Turner?"

Frankie was not about to tell her about her stash of forbidden books. "Cecelia, focus."

"Right. So I was wandering along the wall and I overhead one of those rotten Seven say he was frightened, and another of the Seven hissed at him to shut his mouth lest *HE* overhear." Cecelia bounced on her toes. "The ringleader is in this very room, Miss Turner!"

Frankie's heart turned over in her chest. She'd known it was likely he was here, but to have it confirmed... She lifted her head and scanned the room as if she could sight him, now that she knew he was in residence. As she did, she spotted Lady Evelyn making her way along the outer edge of the ballroom, laughing and nodding as she went. Her head was twisting left and right as she greeted those who called out to her, but she never slowed her walk toward the exit. Perspiration beaded on her brow, and Frankie could not blame her; it was unbearably hot in the ballroom. Lady Evelyn nodded to Lady Charlotte as she pulled her handkerchief from her reticule and blotted her brow.

Frankie's blood turned to slush.

The handkerchief was a perfect sapphire blue.

Suddenly it was as if each point on the Dowry Thieves' timeline was a symbol, and in front of Frankie's eyelids the symbols rearranged into a formula that finally, *finally* made sense. Both she and

Jasper had made an assumption that had blinded them to the true nature of the Dowry Thieves' ringleader.

She needed to find Jasper straight away so that...sudden panic stole her breath. Jasper had left with Lady Evelyn, but only Evelyn had returned.

"We need to find Jasper *immediately*."

Cecelia must have heard the urgency in her voice. "What is the matter?" she demanded as Frankie set off at a trot for the balcony doors. Cecelia stuck closely to her side and did not ask again when Frankie didn't answer. Frankie scanned the balcony but did not see Jasper.

Her scalp tingling with dread, she lifted her skirts and raced down the steps to the garden, praying that he had found himself lost in the maze, or had rolled his ankle in the darkness or some other such foolery.

Frankie was about to dash into the maze when the moonlight glinted off a shiny metal circle in the grass. Cecelia noticed it as well and picked it up, turning it over in her hand. Her face was anxious when she showed it to Frankie. "This is Uncle Jasper's tin pocket watch," she said. "He fusses with it all the time, and I once heard him say it was the only possession he had of his father. He would not leave it out here."

Frankie's breaths came short and hard. "Something is terribly wrong, Cecelia. I do not know what has happened to Jasper, but I fear he is in grave danger. I last saw him with Lady Evelyn. She brought him out here and only she returned. Worse still, I have reason to believe it was she who shot at me today."

Cecelia cried out in alarm.

Grabbing Cecelia by the wrist, Frankie dragged her back up the balcony steps. "I must find Lady Evelyn."

"I am coming with you."

"No, I need you to stay and keep an eye on the Seven." Frankie gestured at one of the seven remaining investors engaged in dance. "I do not have time to fully explain what I suspect, but I need to be sure they do not become a further threat. You must not approach them under any circumstances. Do you understand?"

Cecelia's eyes narrowed fiercely. "They will not leave my sight."

Frankie impulsively kissed her on the forehead and hurried out the ballroom door. She pushed through guests in the entry and did not care when they huffed or made exaggerated comments about governesses who did not know their place. She scanned the foyer for Lady Evelyn but did not see her.

Desperate now, she exited through the front of the manor and circled around to the stable block and carriage house. Cecelia had said Jasper would never leave his watch behind, and Frankie knew Jasper would never leave her and Cecelia behind.

Lady Evelyn had already killed once. She would not hesitate to do it again.

Frankie slipped along the shadows and pressed herself to the side of the carriage house. A moment later a carriage rumbled past, the clatter of horse hooves and the turn of wheels lifting a plume of dust. Through the carriage window Frankie caught sight of Lady Evelyn's profile. She must have paid the groom a handsome bribe in order to leave against strict orders from Lord Houndsbury.

Foolish groom, Frankie thought with rage. *She* would not want to tangle with Houndsbury.

The moment the carriage was out of sight Frankie burst into the stables and demanded the groom saddle a mare for her.

The groom reacted to her haste and tone of authority and began to bridle a mare before he remembered his orders.

"Sorry, milady," he said, tugging on his cap. "No guests are allowed to leave."

"And yet I just witnessed Lady Evelyn's carriage exit," Frankie said. She straightened to her fullest height. "If you do not bridle a horse for me, I shall find Houndsbury this *very moment* and tell him exactly what you've done."

"Please do not, madam," he begged.

"Finish bridling the horse *now* and you shall have my silence."

The man hesitated, probably cursing his bad luck, and then did as she asked. Frankie did not wait for him to put the saddle on before she threw her leg over the horse's back, baring her ankle and scandalizing the entire barn, and took off at a canter.

Wherever Lady Evelyn was headed, Frankie would be her shadow. Within minutes Frankie caught sight of the carriage and slowed her horse, riding far enough back that Lady Evelyn would not spot her. She prayed with every cell in her body that Jasper was alive and well.

"I am coming for you, Jasper," she whispered. "Hang on."

Chapter 48

Jasper returned to consciousness, his head throbbing and his wits scrambled. His hands were trussed tightly behind his back, and he was jostling about as if a hammer were being taken to his bones. It took him another minute to realize he was on the floor of a carriage that was traveling over extremely rutted roads.

He had not made a sound, but the boots by his chin shifted, and before he could make any further sense of his location, a white cloth soaked in sweet liquid was pressed to his nose and mouth, and once again he slipped into darkness.

When Jasper resurfaced he was no longer knocking around like a bearing in a rattle. His brain screeched as if he'd overindulged in drink, and the back of his skull pulsed with a dull ache. He flexed his hands and found his wrists still bound. He dozed for a moment and then snapped fully awake when he remembered what had happened. He'd been speaking with Lady Evelyn at the ball when someone had struck him from behind. Where were Frankie and Cecelia? Were they all right?

He was sitting on a hard chair, his arms pulled behind him and roped together, and his legs were also tied to the chair, effectively immobilizing him. The room was cool and musty, as if it had been closed up for quite some time. White sheets were draped over the furniture, creating eerie lumps in the shadows. Several lamps were lit, and in their weak glow he spotted two figures huddled together by the cold fireplace. He blinked, clearing the last of the fog, and heard one of them say, "He is awake."

The figures moved closer until they were clearly visible, and even two decades of gambling could not keep Jasper's astonishment from showing. Standing before him were Lady Evelyn and her father, the Earl of Elmsdale. Lady Evelyn was still resplendent in her navy ball gown, while her father was as stiff-lipped as if he were conducting a vote in Parliament.

Other than Evelyn and her father, Jasper appeared to be alone in the room, and he prayed with all his might that Frankie and Cecelia were safely back in the Houndsbury ballroom, drinking punch and dancing among the hundreds of guests.

"You are an imbecile," Lord Elmsdale said in a flat, harsh tone. It took a moment for Jasper to realize the earl was speaking not to him, but to Evelyn. "This is why women are not fit to lead. You should not have acted without my consent."

Lady Evelyn's eyes were pleading when she spoke to her father. "Lord Devon disrespected you and our mission. You saved him from social ruin, and how did he repay you? Instead of seizing the opportunity to marry that loudmouthed governess, he announced to everyone that *Mr. Jones* had compromised her! When I spoke to him later that evening, he told me he'd gambled the woman away, and that Jones likely knew everything. How stupid does a man have to be to gamble against the devil of London's underworld? Besides, I knew Devon had been giving you trouble about the vote, Father. I did what I had to in order to keep the mission pure."

"You are fortunate I arrived in time to clean up your mess."

Evelyn wrung her hands together. "I was going to take care of Jones and the governess myself. I did not need you to follow us outside the ballroom and knock him out."

"How were you going to take care of him, Evelyn?" Lord Elmsdale's lip curled with loathing. "By luring him into the hedge maze and shooting him as well? Houndsbury has locked down the estate, and it cost me a small fortune to bribe the stable groom into allowing us to leave tonight. Do you truly think Houndsbury would allow multiple murders to take place on his property and tarnish his reputation without investing every resource at his disposal into discovering who the culprit was?"

Evelyn's lip quivered, but Elmsdale did not spare her another glance. It was as if she had faded into the smudged and tattered wallpaper of the abandoned home and had not spoken at all. Instead he addressed Jasper. "You shall never have a daughter because your life ends here, far away from the pride and reputation of Lord Houndsbury." The look he sent Evelyn was sharp with disapproval. "Daughters are tireless burdens. They come squalling into life and do not stop squalling until they are married and become someone else's problem."

Evelyn's face turned ashen. "Father," she whispered.

Jasper's blood ran ice-cold. If they succeeded in murdering him, Frankie would be next, and he could not, he *would* not allow that to happen. "I have a niece," he said, his voice thick in his throat. "She needs me."

"Ah yes, the uncouth Miss Cecelia. From what I have heard she is as brash and loud as her former governess. It would be best for the world if she disappeared quietly." At Jasper's look of terror Elmsdale sighed. "I do not mean murder, Jones. I still have several men in need of a wife, no matter how young, and your niece has a generous dowry that will be available to her next year. Murder is despicable and I would never stoop so low if I did not have to fix Evelyn's errors. Again."

Jasper was used to Evelyn's cruel and cutting tongue, but in front of her father she became a shadow of herself, silent and pale, her eyes begging for approval from a man who cut her down at every turn. No wonder she was so unpleasant, Jasper thought. She had spent her entire life trying to measure up to a bully who would always find her lacking simply because of her sex.

"You mean to marry Cecelia to one of the seven remaining Scott Silver investors," Jasper rasped.

Elmsdale's eyes hardened. "How did you figure it out?"

Jasper wanted to say he had not and that a woman had, just to see the surprise on Elmsdale's face, but he did not want to endanger Frankie further. "I noticed a pattern in the type of women who were marrying," he said vaguely, "but I have kept the knowledge to myself. Miss Turner knows nothing about it."

"He lies!" Evelyn shrieked, jumping forward. "I heard her through the door when Devon compromised her. I heard *her* say Scott Silver."

"You are mistaken," Jasper said coolly. "The door was thick. Miss Turner knows nothing. And when I spoke with Devon, I made him aware I knew about Scott Silver in such a way that kept Miss Turner in the dark."

Elmsdale shifted his white cravat a millimeter to the side. "You must have misheard, Evelyn. Why would Mr. Jones share important information with a *governess*? Use the limited sense God gave you."

Evelyn quivered with rage, and despite himself Jasper felt a pinch of sympathy for her. Elmsdale's refusal to see a woman's value was a weakness, and it was one Jasper fully intended to exploit. He needed to survive the night so he could return to Frankie and Cecelia.

"I did not mean to cause trouble with Lord Devon," Jasper continued. "I thwarted his scheme because I wanted to marry Miss Turner myself and recoup the fortune I rashly bestowed upon her."

Elmsdale studied him as if he were a pupil that had deeply disappointed him. "Do you think I am a fool, Mr. Jones? Do you think I am unaware that you do nothing to curb the nonsense your governess and niece spew to all and sundry?"

Jasper shrugged, and although his ribs screamed, he kept his face placid. "Your mission is not mine, my lord. That does not mean I do not support it."

Elmsdale crossed his arms over his chest. "The world is changing, and not for the better. Common men, *landless* men, are clamoring for voting rights as if they have the intelligence to make educated decisions. Women are asking for the vote as well. Women! Simpering, silly creatures who have no grasp on the realities of life and therefore should have no say in how it operates. These *females* are growing louder, demanding more and more for the poor, the children, the birds. It does not end! There used to be a time when manners and decorum were a requirement, not a mere suggestion. With every progressive act passed we dilute the natural order of society and slip deeper into the gutter.

"Two years ago, twenty peers with upright morals were scammed out of their money, and I knew I could not allow them to become laughingstocks of the papers and society. The peerage must work together if we are to rein in this wild mare called progress. I paid the papers for their silence, and I taught the men how to hide their losses. I saw an opportunity in their misfortune, a way to help us return the world to how it should be."

Every word out of Elmsdale's mouth sent streaks of rage through Jasper's veins. The "weak" women who bore children and raised them, who held families together and worked harder than half the men he knew, were the backs high society rode on. They worked silently, thanklessly, *tirelessly*, so that others might succeed. He thought of Frankie and her utter mathematical brilliance. How many inventions, solved math problems, stunning novels, moving symphonies, and comedic plays had never come to fruition simply because the creator was a woman? Society suffered this staggering loss because it was a man's world, and the men in power were so very terrified of losing their white-knuckled grip on control.

"You found the investors women with rich dowries so they could recoup their losses," Jasper said.

Elmsdale nodded. "Not just wealthy women, as you noticed, but the women who were openly contributing to society's degradation. The men gained a fortune, and the world gained the women's silence. It was beneficial to all involved."

All but the women, Jasper thought, tightening his jaw.

"Evelyn helped me devise ways to entrap the women so that they had no choice. It was the perfect plan. *Was*," he said, glaring at Evelyn.

Jasper's eyes flickered to Evelyn. If she felt remorse about selling out her own sex, she did not show it. Behind his back he subtly shifted his hands. There was zero slack in the ropes.

"You did all of that without expecting anything in return?" he asked, hoping to keep the earl talking.

Elmsdale's mouth turned down. "If that is your crass, wharf way of asking if I was paid, the answer is no. My service was for the country."

Jasper thought about what Evelyn had said when she'd been defending Devon's murder. *I knew Devon had been giving you trouble about the vote, Father.* He sucked in a quiet breath. "Your payment was their vote in Parliament."

"Votes for the greater, conservative good," Elmsdale snapped. "Although we often failed, we did manage to pass several laws thanks to our combined efforts, and effectively blocked some of society's more disgusting equalization. I apologize for what comes next, Mr. Jones, but surely you understand how imperative it is that we continue our good work."

Elmsdale held out his hand, and Evelyn sulkily placed her silver-plated derringer in it. The weak lamplight caught on the metal of the barrel that had killed Devon and shot at Frankie. Jasper and Frankie had made a grievous error assuming the shooter and the ringleader were one and the same, and now they would pay the price.

"That is unnecessary," Jasper said. "I do not intend to share what I have learned here tonight."

"I appreciate your discretion, Mr. Jones, but I simply cannot take the risk. You know Evelyn murdered Devon, and you know I have been influencing the Parliament vote. On the rare chance Miss Turner is also aware of those facts, she, too, will have to be silenced." He took a moment to stare down Evelyn, his eyes steely with distaste. "I do not take pleasure in having to clean up my daughter's messes, and I certainly do not take pleasure in murder.

That is why, assuming Miss Cecelia has remained ignorant, we shall arrange her marriage instead."

Jasper's heart throbbed with one wrenching beat before it hardened into stone. He had not fought and bit and scraped to survive on the streets only to be done in by a tiny silver gun. He willed himself to survive the bullet. It was a small caliber, and if it did not hit any vital organs, it was possible he could stanch the bleeding—if he had his hands free. He tugged on the ropes again as Elmsdale pointed the derringer at his chest.

"Remember who you have taken up arms against," Jasper said, his voice so deadly and cold that Elmsdale faltered. "My wealth and reach are unprecedented, and I always have contingencies in place. If anything happens to Miss Turner or Miss Cecelia, it will trigger an automatic investigation and put a bounty on the perpetrator's head. You and your daughter will be dead within days." He leaned forward as far as he could, allowing all the violence in his soul to touch his eyes. "You should know that the sort of men I retain will not rest until they find the perpetrator and bring his—or her—head to my solicitor."

Evelyn gave a strangled cry, and Elmsdale's breathing turned shallow. For several moments he took in Jasper's measure before he nodded gravely and lifted the derringer again. "I understand, but this is a cause I am willing to die for."

Jasper opened his mouth, but Elmsdale shook his head. "There is nothing else you can say, Mr. Jones. All I require from those beneath me is silence."

Before he could pull the trigger, Lady Evelyn screamed and pointed behind him. Elmsdale whirled around. An insidious curl of white smoke had slid beneath the door.

Elmsdale lowered the gun and strode to the door. When he wrenched it open, smoke billowed into the room, thick and acrid.

"One of the lamps must have caught fire!" Evelyn cried. She coughed and looked over his shoulder. "Shoot him so we can leave!"

"Shut your mouth!" Elmsdale roared. "This is why you should not speak! You cannot see opportunities right in front of your face, you stupid woman. We will let the fire finish him. There will be no bullet to discover when the ashes cool, and we will have one less murder on our hands."

Evelyn tossed Jasper a hateful glance, and he knew if the gun were in her hand she'd shoot him with glee. She lifted the crook of her elbow to her nose and Elmsdale pulled his cravat over his mouth, and they disappeared into the white plume, leaving Jasper to burn.

Chapter 49

As Frankie followed Lady Evelyn's rattling carriage, her fear manifested into a single prayer: *Please let Jasper be all right. Please let Jasper be all right. Please let Jasper be all right.*

She did not know if Lady Evelyn would take her to Jasper; all she knew was that Evelyn had been the last person to see him, and with the revelation that Evelyn was Devon's murderer, Frankie was terrified that Jasper would be next.

The night air was scented with a bouquet of the day's lingering odors: the sweet smell of newly cut hay, the floral of honeysuckle and jasmine, and the heat-ripened richness of wild blackberries. Grasshoppers competed for attention with the rattle of carriage wheels and the heavy fall of hooves. Even though it had been a warm day, Frankie shivered from the chill of the night—or perhaps it was from fear.

If something should happen to Jasper she would *never* recover. In a short time he had become everything to her: confidant, partnering detective, lover, and friend. If that generous, dangerous, and loving soul were wiped from existence—

Frankie could not even bear to finish the thought. She had not told him any of those things when she'd had the chance. She had been too afraid to be vulnerable, too scared to open her heart and give someone the power to hurt her. Too self-absorbed to believe that someone could truly love her for who she was.

Jasper had had a hard life devoid of even basic human comforts, and still he'd been willing to take a gamble and tell her what was in his heart even when she did not have the courage to hear it. And what had she done to return his love? She'd said *thank you*.

Frankie grimaced at the memory.

A vise squeezed her heart as she shadowed Lady Evelyn's carriage to an intersecting road. She had to be in love with Jasper, because if she was not, then what was this crushing, all-consuming feeling seeping into every fiber of her soul? This feeling that if Jasper were taken away from her before she had the chance to tell him how much he meant to her, she might as well curl into a ball and cease to function? This feeling that she wanted only the best for him, forever, and that she would do anything to be by his side during his hardships and sickness, during his happiness and celebrations?

Shame prickled hotly beneath her skin. When she found Jasper, she was going to bare her soul to him and tell him the truest thing she knew: She loved him. She loved him with everything she had.

Lady Evelyn's carriage trundled up the drive to a dark estate with an abandoned feel to it. Frankie guided her mount to the side of the drive where the hedges grew thick, and dismounted. She tied the reins to a branch before creeping silently across the grass to one of the darkened windows.

Frankie's palms were damp in her gloves and her pulse was in her mouth when she cautiously peeked through the glass. The room was empty.

Frustrated, she snuck around the side of the house and peered into one dark window after the other. The furniture in the rooms was draped with white sheets, and the only movement came from the occasionally startled mouse. The house appeared to be abandoned, so why had Lady Evelyn come here?

After a full circuit she made her way to the carriage house where Lady Evelyn had parked her carriage, not bothering to unhitch the horses. Did that mean she did not intend to stay long?

Frankie crept up to the carriage and looked inside. It was empty. No Jasper.

With a surge of desperation, she turned back to the house and noted a soft glow coming from one of the windows now. She hurried toward it and cautiously peered in. At first she saw nothing, but when she craned her neck her breath snagged in her lungs. He was there, her future husband, trussed to a chair with his head hanging down. Was he dead? Did he still breathe? What had Evelyn done to him? In the shadows of the room she spotted two figures speaking to one another, but she could not make out either of them, although she knew one had to be Lady Evelyn.

Frankie had no weapon with her. She had not even thought to sneak a knife from the kitchens. She closed her eyes in despair. She'd been in such a rush she had not thought what she would do if there was an altercation.

Her eyes snapped open and she pressed her lips together in determination, her brain leaping into action, considering and discarding a dozen different ways to free him. Lady Evelyn was a bitch, but Frankie was fighting for the man she loved. If it came to it, she could best Evelyn.

The variable was the other person in the room. Who was he, and how was he involved with the Dowry Thieves?

She was backing away from the window to return to the stables to search for a weapon of some sort, when a hand closed over her mouth and a voice whispered in her ear, "Do not scream."

The hand muffled Frankie's involuntary shriek, and then it dropped away and Frankie spun around and threw herself into the woman's arms.

Fidelia was sturdier than she'd ever been, and she smelled of expensive soap and perfume. Frankie held tightly to her sister and tried hard not to cry. "You are all right! You are here!" She pulled back so that she could study what little of her sister's face she could see in the moonlight. "You look healthy, Fidelia. You look… happy."

It was only then that she saw her sister was not alone. Beside her stood another young woman, this one only two years older than Fidelia. In the moonlight she, too, was radiant, although dressed in a simpler manner than Frankie was used to seeing. "Lady Elizabeth Scarson, is that really you?"

Lady Elizabeth grinned, and Fidelia pushed at her spectacles, which had been inherited from their great-cousin Lucy. "Elizabeth has taken her jewels and run away from her horrid husband, and we have decided to live together on the Scottish coast. I shall be her companion." A soft smile passed between them. "I meant to write home but…I was not sure how accepting mother would be of my decision not to come out to society. It was not until Elizabeth and I began to hear about other intelligent young ladies marrying absolute boors that we began to suspect something was afoot. In the beginning we had simply thought Elizabeth's 'compromising situation' was a terrible misfortune, but later we began to wonder if the same thing was happening to the other women. The only problem was that we did not know where to start looking for answers."

"Then we met someone," Elizabeth interjected softly. "Well, then we met *them*."

Fidelia nodded. "A man with ice-blue eyes and a woman with dark curls approached us outside the rooms we had temporarily rented. We had slowly been making our way to the Scottish shore, so I do not know how they found us with our constant movement, but they did. What were their names, Elizabeth?"

"Mr. and Mrs. Denholm."

"Right. They said they'd been hired to find us because you were worried about me, Frankie."

The Dove had come through after all, Frankie thought with some amazement. Frankie had thought her governess friend, Emily, was on her honeymoon, but it seemed the Dove had taken her end of the bargain seriously and engaged only the best detectives in England to find Fidelia, even though it had meant asking them to postpone the celebration of their wedding.

"I knew I had to swallow my worries about mother's reaction and write home, but then I heard of the charitable dowry your employer had bestowed upon you, Frankie, and I was so frightened that you would end up in the same position as Elizabeth. I needed to warn you immediately."

"We certainly could not sit around sipping tea while you became a target," Elizabeth added. She pushed at her hair and gave Frankie the round-cheeked and dimpled smile she remembered from when they were children. "We had thought that as the *ton*'s newest catch you might attend the Houndsbury ball, and so we have been traveling nonstop to reach you in time and warn you. We only just arrived when we spotted you leaving the stables. We tried to flag you down, but you were going so fast and wearing a ballgown while bareback, so we knew something must be amiss. That's why we followed."

Frankie shook her head with chagrin. Some spy she made. She had not even known she was being followed. "You were right to suspect there is more behind the marriages. Lady Evelyn has been arranging the compromising situations, although I do not have all the facts yet. I do know that she has killed a man already, and she is aware Jasper and I have discovered her scheme."

Fidelia's eyes widened at the mention of murder. "Who is Jasper?"

"Mr. Jasper Jones is the employer who gave me the charitable dowry, and he's the man I am going to marry. He's the man...I love."

Elizabeth and Fidelia exchanged a look of surprise. Frankie could not blame them. It had sounded strange even to her, and yet simultaneously freeing.

Frankie continued. "Evelyn somehow spirited him from the ball, and I followed them here. When I looked inside, I saw Jasper bound to a chair. There is someone else with the lady, although I did not see who. I fear she has brought Jasper here to kill him."

"Are you certain that is her intention?"

"I am positive. If Jasper is left alive, he will deliver retribution with a steady hand and he will not rest until she has paid for her crimes. If she has any sense at all she will murder him while she still has the chance."

Fidelia gave a soft cry of dismay. "I do not know who this man is, but if you love him, then he is my brother. I should think the three of us could stop her."

"Not if she has a pistol, and I have reason to believe she does. The person with her is another unknown variable."

"We need a pistol, too," Elizabeth declared. "We will have no chance otherwise. All we have is this." She snapped open a wickedly sharp pocketknife.

"I was about to head to the stables to look for a weapon when..." Frankie inhaled sharply and clutched Fidelia's arm as a brilliant idea took hold.

"You have a plan," Fidelia said. It was not a question; she knew it for fact. She and Frankie had been best friends their entire lives.

"The stable is run-down, and whoever abandoned it left behind scattered supplies. There were buckets of moldy grain and a rotted box of what looked like sugar cubes for the horses."

Something sparked in Fidelia's eyes as she immediately caught on. "Perhaps there is saltpeter in there as well."

"Am I missing something?" Elizabeth asked, her eyes darting between them. She sighed. "Of course I am."

Frankie took her brave, and not-so-foolish, sister by the shoulders and they began to plan.

Chapter 50

Jasper fought the bonds of the ropes, and when they did not budge, he used his weight to rock the chair back and forth, scooting it across the floor. Although smoke was billowing into the room, he did not yet hear the crackle of fire. He hoped it was still far enough away that he could make it to the window.

His heart pounded against his ribs as he inched across the floor, praying he would not topple himself over. He had to get to Frankie and Cecelia. He had to protect them from Evelyn and her father.

He blinked as a figure appeared in the smoke, a black silhouette walking through it as if in a dream. The female shape grew larger, and Jasper wondered if Evelyn had convinced her father to let her turn back and finish him after all. Then the woman emerged through the white cloud, and Jasper saw with both elation and horror that it was Frankie.

Coughing, he shouted, "Fire! Get out, Frankie!"

Instead she ran to him, dropped to her knees, and threw her arms around his waist. "Oh, Jasper, are you all right? I was so frightened. Did they hurt you?" She rubbed her palm over the stubble of his chin, having discarded her gloves at some point since the ball. Her hands smelled both sweet and salty and singed by flame. Satisfied that he was uninjured, she leaned forward and pressed a soft kiss to his mouth.

"As much as I love this, Frankie, there is a fire in the corridor."

"Oh that?" She waved her hand. He noticed for the first time that she was carrying a sharp folding knife. "That is a controlled chemical fire made to produce a lot of smoke." She began sawing through the ropes around his ankles. "Fidelia found saltpeter in the shed."

"Fidelia?" he asked as the ropes frayed. "Your sister? She is here?" The last strands snapped. Frankie quickly moved around the chair to his wrists, and when his hands popped free, Jasper did not waste any time rubbing them; he grabbed Frankie's hand and they ran outside.

"They're gone," Fidelia exclaimed, appearing around the corner of the house with another woman at her side. "The carriage took off like a bat out of hell." She scanned Jasper from boot to brow, and her lips formed a little O shape. "I am Fidelia, Frankie's sister. *You* are my future brother-in-law? Holy King E, Frankie. I suppose we are both full of surprises, are we not?"

One might be forgiven for thinking Frankie's sister was her identical twin, but Jasper immediately spotted a number of differences: Although each woman wore a pair of spectacles far too large for her face, Frankie was slightly taller, her hair straighter, and her eyes a deeper blue. Fidelia's smile, although beautiful, did not compare to Frankie's slow-blossoming sunshine smile.

"I have a feeling I have missed something important," he muttered as he and Frankie jogged to her horse.

"Sorry!" Frankie shouted over her shoulder to her sister. "We need to ride back to the Houndsburys as fast as possible! Jasper's niece may be in danger!"

Jasper vaulted onto the horse and pulled Frankie up behind him, and with her arms tight around his waist they set off for the Houndsbury estate.

"How did you find me?" he shouted back to her.

"Cecelia discovered your pocket watch on the ground, and Lady Evelyn was the last person to be seen with you. I followed her here and that's where I met Fidelia. How could we have been so stupid, Jasper? She is the ringleader!"

"No," Jasper said, "her father is."

Frankie squeezed his waist, and Jasper urged the horse to go faster. They had a lot they needed to say to each other, but there would be time for that later. Now they needed to reach Cecelia before Evelyn or her father did. Lord Elmsdale had promised he would not hurt Cecelia, but Jasper did not trust him, nor did he trust that Lady Evelyn would not take matters into her own hands once again.

When they reached the Houndsbury estate they slid off the horse and hurried toward the ballroom. Jasper squeezed between lords smoking outdoors, all while holding tight to Frankie's hand and not caring when more than a few rude comments were muttered in their wake. Music and muted chatter drifted on the evening air, but knowing that a monster hid within the innocent ambiance only pushed him to move faster.

They were running by the time they burst through the ballroom doors. Jasper anxiously scanned the crush of flush-faced gentlemen and laughing ladies. "Come on, Cece, where are you?"

He spotted Madam Margaret, sitting in a chair against the wall, eyes glazed as she enjoyed the double quartets. Theoretically, that meant Cecelia shouldn't be too far—

"I see her!" Frankie exclaimed, and she plunged into the crowd. Jasper dashed after her. Cecelia was half-hiding behind a potted palm like a storybook spy, but the moment she spotted him the tension in her face dissolved, and when he reached her, she threw her arms around him and squeezed him tightly.

"Uncle Jasper! You are all right!"

Jasper thought he had aged ten years in the past two hours.

Cecelia's voice was muffled in the fabric of his coat. "I was so worried." She peered across his chest at Frankie and said, "I knew I could count on you to rescue him."

Frankie wrapped one arm around Cecelia and one arm around Jasper, and they stood there holding one another, a trio of misfits. *His* family of misfits.

Several moments later his instincts whispered that he was being watched, and when he turned, he found Lady Evelyn and Lord Elmsdale burning holes into his back. The lady's eyes were black with fury, but it was her father's flat, emotionless countenance that made Jasper's skin crawl.

Lady Evelyn touched her father's sleeve, and her eyes darted toward the terrace doors.

"Oh no they do not," Frankie hissed, having followed the direction of his gaze.

"No," Jasper agreed. "It ends tonight." He released Frankie and Cecelia and strode forward to do the one thing he'd always tried to avoid: draw attention to himself in a room full of nobility. Standing in the center of the ballroom, an immovable pillar around which the dancers eddied, he roared, "PARDON ME!"

The dancers closest to him stopped and stared at him in shock. Again, he hollered, "PARDON ME!"

Lord Houndsbury frowned, and with a sharp gesture from him the strings fell silent. The guests murmured as they glanced at one another and then at Jasper, who had become the center of their scrutiny in the middle of the ballroom. From the corner of his eye, he spotted Lady Evelyn and Lord Elmsdale begin to edge toward the open doorway.

"If you will please halt Lord Elmsdale and Lady Evelyn's exit," he said. A wave of chatter went up from the crowd, and it only grew louder when, after a brief hesitation, the duke nodded toward the male guests closest to Elmsdale. The men exchanged awkward looks, but encircled the earl to escort him and his daughter forward.

Jasper felt the itchiness of hundreds of eyes on his face. His cravat was too tight, and the room was insufferably hot. Then, a blond head appeared by his side, and he found Frankie standing resolutely next to him. His heart rate slowed. She did not care about this display of ill-bred behavior that would no doubt become the most gossiped-about moment in the history of the *ton*. She did not care about the fallout to her reputation for associating with him. She cared only about him. She was there for him.

He did not need to hear her say she loved him. Her actions said it. She had saved his life, and she would stand by him.

"What is the meaning of this?" Lord Elmsdale asked as he and his daughter were marched forward. His authoritative voice was the picture of genteel indignation.

Jasper opened his mouth, but at Frankie's light touch, he paused. "Let me."

He did not want her to make the accusation. He did not want her bearing the brunt of society's disbelief and displeasure when she denounced an earl for wrongdoing. He would do anything but stand by and watch as they dragged her name through the mud. He and Frankie had no proof that linked Lord Elmsdale to the scheme—casting suspicion was the only weapon they had, and he was determined to be the one to wield it and suffer the consequences of doing so.

Except it seemed there *was* one thing that could make him step back, and that was his respect for the woman at his side. He had a chance to prove to her that he would never hold her back no matter the circumstances. That he would support and respect her decisions, and that he would be there for her through it all. He gave her a terse nod.

Frankie smiled up at him, that brilliant, devasting tilt of her lips, and turned to address the crowd. With a clear, loud voice she said, "Two years ago, twenty peers invested in the Scott Silver Mining Expedition and lost their fortunes."

There were murmurs, as the gossip from two years prior returned to the forefront of the *ton*'s memory.

"They would have been ruined, but one man in this room saw an opportunity. Lord Elmsdale paid off the papers to keep them from speculating about the lost fortunes, and then promised to help each man find a wealthy wife to replenish his loss. In order to accomplish that, Elmsdale entrapped innocent young women in compromising situations."

There were shouts of disbelief, and Lord Elmsdale shook his head with grave sadness. "I am an upstanding member of the peerage, and my family has served England for generations. How dare you make such horrid, unfounded accusations, madam?"

"It is true!" Lady Elizabeth Scarson broke into the cleared circle around them, breathing hard from the horse ride there. There were gasps as the peerage recognized one of their own. Mrs. Turner clapped her hands over her mouth as she spotted her daughter, Fidelia, hovering behind Lady Elizabeth. "I was maneuvered into a compromising situation with Lord Pierson. I was a victim of this man's scheming."

Lord Elmsdale's facade did not so much as flicker. "I have far more important matters to deal with, such as running this country. I have neither the time nor the interest for meddling in women's affairs."

"That is because you did not meddle in their affairs." Jasper turned to the woman standing beside Elmsdale. "Your daughter, Lady Evelyn, arranged the compromising situations. And when one of those compromising situations did not work out—such as it did not with Lord Devon and Miss Turner—she killed him."

A wave of voices swept through the room. One woman screamed, another fainted. But the most common expressions were anger and disbelief.

"You are a rotter, Jones!" one man shouted. "Accusing a lady of murder! I shall pull my membership from Rockford's expressly."

"Please do," Jasper said in a flat voice.

"Why would Elmsdale go to such trouble?" Lord Houndsbury asked thoughtfully, his eyes traveling over the father and daughter in question. "What was the motive for Elmsdale saving the investors' reputations? Why would he bother securing them wives with large dowries?"

"Because," Jasper replied, lifting his voice so that even those in the back could hear, "they repay Elmsdale in the form of votes in the House of Lords."

If he'd thought the reaction before had been loud, this one was nearly a roar. Jasper spotted one of the seven Scott Silver investors, and smiled at Lord Collins, whose face was waxy and shining with perspiration. "Tell them, Lord Collins," Jasper taunted. "Tell them who has been forcing your vote."

Houndsbury whipped around to stare at Lord Collins. The thin man's eyes darted between Houndsbury and Elmsdale, his jaw visibly quaking. It would be fair to say he was caught between a rock and a hard place. Lord Houndsbury was a massively wealthy, massively powerful duke. Lord Elmsdale was an earl and an influential figure in the House of Lords, and he was glaring at Collins now as if he could spear him with his eyes.

Collins pulled a handkerchief from inside his coat and mopped at his forehead. Before he could answer, a man with padded shoulders and a monocle slapped a heavy hand on his shoulder. Jasper had watched the man with the monocle work his way toward them through the crowd over the past minute. Behind him stood a number of men wearing the uniform of the Metropolitan Police.

"Buck up, Collins," the man with the monocle said cheerfully. "Today is your lucky day. You shall not be required to grow a spine." He turned toward the Duke of Houndsbury and inclined his head in greeting. "Your Grace."

"Mr. Wright Davies, deputy commissioner of the Metropolitan Police," Lord Houndsbury returned dryly. "I am so pleased you could join in the madness. I know my man delivering news of the murder could not have made his way to London yet, so to what do I owe the pleasure of your company?"

Mr. Davies gestured to the men behind him, who quickly surrounded Lord Elmsdale and Lady Evelyn. A constable clicked iron handcuffs around Lord Elmsdale's wrists. "Lord Elmsdale, you are under arrest for blackmailing members of Parliament and for swaying the vote. We have a dossier of evidence from an anonymous source, as well as a written statement from Lord Pierson, who has recently seen the need to confess to his misdeeds."

Lady Elizabeth Scarson looked surprised at that news about her husband. Elmsdale, however, received it with all the stoic grace of his generation. He did not bluster nor shout, but allowed the constable to lead him toward the ballroom door, all while maintaining a dignified lift of his chin.

"As for you, Lady Evelyn," Mr. Davies said solemnly, "you have been accused of murder."

"You cannot prove that," she snapped.

"Check her reticule for a derringer," Jasper said. "I saw her stash it there when she and her father threatened to shoot me earlier tonight."

"And a sapphire-blue handkerchief," Frankie added. "It will be an exact match for the one Jasper found at the scene of my attempted murder yesterday."

Houndsbury's eyes sharpened at that, and Frankie's fingers gripped Jasper's forearm as a constable took Lady Evelyn's reticule from her. First, he withdrew a sapphire-blue handkerchief, and Jasper watched as Houndsbury's lips flattened. Then, with two fingers, he lifted out a shining, silver-plated derringer.

The faces of the *ton* in that moment would have been comical if it were not all so tragic, Jasper thought, as Lady Evelyn was also led, red-faced, toward the exit.

When she neared Frankie she halted and with cruel delight said, "I locked myself in that room the day we played sardines. My only regret is that Lord Devon didn't get the chance to teach you your place."

Frankie was unmoved. She simply adjusted her spectacles and said, "Lady Evelyn, I think you should be more concerned about the place *you're* going."

Chapter 51

A few days later Frankie received a letter from the Dove and learned that it was she who had sent the police to the Houndsbury estate, not that Frankie had doubted for a moment that it was the Dove's "dossier" of evidence that had spurred the police into action, or that it was the Dove who had "convinced" Lord Pierson to confess.

Although Lord Elmsdale was being charged with manipulating the vote, the police could not prosecute him for arranging the compromising situations. The Dove assured Frankie she was dedicated to making sure every news outlet on this side of the Atlantic had the full story of what Elmsdale had done. Although Elmsdale had admitted to manipulating the vote, there was always the possibility that with his political power and sway he would be let off with a slap on the wrist. The Dove would ensure that if that happened, his reputation would be so tattered he would never be welcomed into a decent home again.

Ruining his reputation was only justice.

As for the Scott Silver investors who'd already tricked their way into marriage through the grotesque scheme—the press was tearing them apart with unmitigated glee. They were being called Fallow Fellows, Grim Grooms, and Silver Shag-bags, and they would live out the rest of their days shunned from good society. Frankie felt sympathy for the brides, but she knew that in secret some women were rallying in the brides' support.

In the last line of the letter, the Dove said she looked forward to reading Frankie's first published mathematics paper as Mrs. Jones, and if Frankie ever found herself looking for a challenge, she need only contact her.

As for Fidelia, after the constables had escorted Elmsdale and his daughter from the ballroom, their mother had hurried over to her, and to everyone's surprise, had thrown her arms around her daughter. Then, as if feeling she had exhibited too much emotion, she had proceeded to roundly scold Fidelia for her "thoughtless disappearance" and "thank goodness" her older sister was going to marry well (which drew raised brows from Jasper), and "by a pinch of grace they'd managed to keep her escapades quiet and her reputation intact so that she could return home."

Before their mother could drag Fidelia back to London by her ear, Fidelia had planted her feet and firmly told her she was going to be Lady Elizabeth's companion.

Upon hearing that Lord Pierson, Lady Elizabeth's husband, had confessed to his part in the scheme, Lady Elizabeth was not sure where her marriage stood or whether she might be granted an annulment, but it did not matter. Her family had an estate in southern Scotland, and she would live there regardless with Fidelia.

"But what about finding a husband?" their mother had gasped.

"I do not want or need one."

"And when Lady Elizabeth tires of your company? What will you do then?"

Elizabeth and Fidelia had shared a look that Frankie's mother missed. "I will not tire of her," Lady Elizabeth had vowed, and Frankie's heart had squeezed at the pure tenderness in her words.

"Besides, Mother," Frankie had added with a hint of relish, "I made a brilliant match, as you said not five minutes ago. I shall be able to support Fidelia in the future should she need it."

In the end, their mother had relented only because Fidelia had threatened to share her whereabouts for the past few weeks if she did not. Their mother would rather have a daughter who was a companion to a wealthy lady, than have a daughter with a tarnished reputation.

Cecelia, who had watched the exchange with wide eyes, had fallen immediately for Fidelia and Lady Elizabeth, who were of similar age to her, and had begged Jasper to let her plan a trip to Scotland for the holidays. He was still considering.

Frankie had just folded the Dove's letter when Jasper entered the morning room, poured a cup of coffee, and sat down across from her. He frowned at the missive. "Is that from Perdita's?" When Frankie nodded, he said, "Frankie, love, I think you correspond with your governess agency more than two lovers write one another."

Frankie pushed the letter toward him. "Read it."

As Jasper read his eyes grew wider and wider, until at last he lowered the letter and whistled. "This woman, the Dove, runs an underground network of governess spies," he said, "and you were working for her. She was the person you made your deal with."

Frankie nodded. "This was my first assignment. She knew I wanted to find Fidelia and I needed her help to do it."

"She must be an extraordinary woman with an extraordinary amount of power and information. I should dearly love to employ her."

Frankie laughed. "I do not think she is looking for employment."

"That is a shame."

Frankie stood and wandered around the morning room, trailing her fingers across the sleekly polished surfaces. "I have been thinking we should have another card game."

Jasper's eyes gleamed. "Poker?"

She nodded. "This time I set the terms. If I win, you allow me into Rockford's. If you win, we ride to Gretna Green."

"Done." Jasper rose, strode to the rosewood chest of drawers at the side of the room, and returned with a pack of cards. As he dealt them, he said, "Thank you for saving my life."

"I suppose we are even on that score." Frankie fanned her cards so that it looked as if she were concentrating on them, when in reality she was studying Jasper from beneath her lashes. He was as handsome as always, in a crisp cravat and deep-gray morning coat, his dark hair waving and his brows drawn together in focus. There was a band of lighter skin on his middle finger where his ring had lain for so long.

They played in deep silence, and when Jasper laid down his winning hand she smiled and said, "We head to Scotland at dawn."

He did not return the smile. "I want you to have the wedding of your dreams, Frankie. If you want a grand affair with all of society invited, then that is what you shall have, the card game be damned."

"Jasper, neither of wants the *ton* at our wedding, gossiping and judging. All we need are a few close friends and family." She collected the cards and tapped them into a perfect pile. His eyes immediately zeroed in on his too-large ring, which she had slipped onto her fourth finger at the end of the game. When his gaze met hers, it was dark and suspicious. "Did you lose on purpose?"

Frankie blinked innocently.

Jasper stood and walked around the table, never breaking eye contact. He knelt down in front of her chair and placed his palms on either side of her. "You are wearing my ring on your hand."

She nodded, breathing in the scent of him, reveling in his nearness. She traced her fingertip over his cheek. "It is a symbol."

"A symbol of what?"

She cupped his jaw and looked him deep in the eyes. "A symbol of my love."

Because she was watching him so closely, she did not miss the slight hitch in his breathing. "You love me?"

"Jasper Jones, despite your warning the first day we met that I should not fall for you, I have gone and done just that. I am deeply, indisputably in love with you." She gestured to the pile of cards. "I am sorry, but you gambled your heart knowing the terms. There is no backing out. You are mine now, and as soon as we reach Gretna Green, you are mine forever."

"I thought you'd never claim me," he said, a smile spreading across his face. "I am relieved we are marrying sooner rather than later, as your wedding present is already in the works."

Frankie clapped her hands together. "What is it?"

"I'd tell you, but perhaps it would be better if you visited Rockford & Turner's and saw the name change for yourself."

Frankie gasped. "Truly? You renamed your hell? For *me*? And I can go inside?"

Jasper laughed and kissed her, long and deep. "Would it be any fun if you were not scandalizing the *ton*? What is mine is yours, love. *I* am yours. My life has been an unsolved equation, and you, Frankie, are the final sum."

Frankie gave him a brilliant smile. "See? Math always makes sense, even in love."

Epilogue

Miss Ivy Bennett had been reading, along with the entirety of London, about the Dowry Thieves scandal in the newspapers all week. She folded the newspaper, the latest headline having finally pieced together what was turning out to be a stunningly audacious operation meant to silence strong women and sway the vote.

This, Ivy thought, was *exactly* why she'd begun her secret women's self-defense classes. She firmly believed that every woman should know how to defend herself in a variety of situations. It was a shame that so few were taught the basic skills, and so Ivy had decided to fill in the gap.

"No one has seen him since he was at Harrow," a maid whispered to another servant as she loaded a tray with tea. Ivy had decided to break her fast in the kitchen instead of the sitting room because it was where she heard the best gossip. Ivy had a shameless love for whisper networks and regularly read gossip rags and *The Tatler.* "I hear he's grown into an awfully surly fellow. Made a fortune abroad, he did, and now he's been called back and he innit happy about it."

Ivy had arrived at the crumbling Brackley country estate a month ago as the newest in a string of governesses, and had been presented with eight lively girls who stumbled through poetry and made clumsy stitches, but could not throw a decent punch. They had just lost their father, although as far as Ivy could tell they'd barely noticed. Their half brother, born to the deceased viscount's first wife, had been called back from the Continent to take up his father's mantle. He was expected to arrive any day now, and the house was in an uproar as the servants scrubbed and polished and prepared with an eye toward pleasing the new master of the house.

"Do ye think he'll still be handsome? Cook says he used to be a cunning lad, with chestnut hair and eyes as green as a cat's." Another maid, Roberta, sighed dreamily.

Cook turned from the stove and growled at them. "Best to work your hands instead of your mouths."

The maids scurried from the kitchen, and Ivy, confident that she had heard all the juiciest bits of gossip for the morning, rolled up the newspaper, stuck it under her arm, and strolled out of the kitchen. Once in the corridor she unrolled the paper again, remembering an article she had seen on weather patterns that she thought would make an interesting lesson, when she smacked into something solid and warm. Ivy's knees buckled, and she would have sunk to the ground had that something solid and warm—a man—not caught her inelegantly under the armpits and hauled her to her feet.

"Thank you," Ivy said breathlessly.

"Perhaps you might extricate your head from the newspaper and watch where you are walking in the future."

"Watch where *I* am walking?" she repeated in surprise, looking up at the man from whom the surly reprimand had come. He was glaring at her, his eyes an unusual emerald shade and bloodshot from either too much drink or exhaustion. His hair was richly brown and a touch too long, and his strong jawline had not been shaved in at least a week. Despite his rumpled appearance, he smelled not unpleasantly of horses and leather. "It is you who ran into me. I suggest *you* pay more attention. Clearly you are new here, so I will tell you that the viscount is expected tomorrow, and from what I hear he will not tolerate clumsy servants."

The new footman, or perhaps a valet hired to wait on the viscount, arched a brow and crossed his arms over his chest. "Is that so? Are you acquainted with this viscount?"

"No, he has only recently inherited the title." Ivy tucked a strand of curly hair behind her ear and smiled up at the servant, knowing it would bring out her dimples. He may have been rude at first brush, but everyone deserved a second chance. "Do not fret; I am sure you will excel at your duties."

"And what, pray, are *your* duties around here?"

"I am the governess."

"Ah," the man said softly. He leaned against the corridor wall as if he intended to speak with her for a while. "The eight girls. How are they?"

"This is my first month," she said, hedging the question. Why should a valet or footman care about the educations of eight young girls?

"A month, and yet you know that a viscount you have never met does not tolerate clumsy servants?"

Ivy lifted a shoulder. "I cannot help hearing gossip."

"What other gossip have you heard?"

Ivy was about to say more but thought better of it. She did not know this man well, and gossip, although integral to a servant's daily life, was still frowned upon. "You shall have to listen for yourself. All I will say is that he has a reputation for being quite the grump, so take care you do not antagonize him."

The new servant glowered down at her, a line appearing between his brows.

"Oh, I am sure he looks just like that! You must have a gift for the theater."

At that moment the butler approached from the end of the corridor, halted in his tracks with an expression of horror, and bent into a formal bow. "Lord Brackley," he stammered, "we were not expecting you until tomorrow."

"I rode ahead."

Ivy's lips parted. _Lord Brackley?_ She squeezed her eyes shut and wished with all her might that she were anywhere else in the world but standing beneath the half-amused and half-disgusted gaze of the new Viscount Brackley, whom she had just told was a grump to his face. When she opened them again she was, unfortunately, still standing in the corridor.

"Please see to my luggage, Evans," Lord Brackley said.

The butler nodded and slid past. When he was behind Lord Brackley's back he motioned with his head, a not-so-subtle message that Ivy should move along. He did not have to tell her twice.

"Excuse me, Lord Brackley," she squeaked and began to edge by him. "I am late to my duties."

"What is your name?"

"Ivy. I mean, Miss Ivy Bennett." Was this the part where he dismissed her after only a month in her new position? Ivy had taken the position rather than marry the monster her father had chosen for her to wed. It would not do for her to be dismissed after two fortnights.

"Miss Bennett, perhaps you had better focus on the education of my sisters rather than idle gossip about my demeanor."

"Yes, my lord." Ivy snapped her heels together, saluted smartly—as she had seen her military brother do dozens of times—and turned her back on the viscount's stunned visage before he could see the smile spreading across her face. The viscount was indeed grumpy, but Ivy had always had enough cheer to go around. The most important thing was that she lay low enough that he did not get wind of what she was teaching his sisters.

Ivy turned the corner and started to whistle a spritely tune. In truth, she was not terribly worried about the grouchy viscount halting her lessons—she had always been excellent at keeping secrets.

Don't miss Lindsay's next book in The Secret
Society of Governess Spies Series

NEVER TEASE
A VISCOUNT

Coming in 2026

Author's Note

Dear Reader,

Did you know there was a real fishmonger-turned-gambling-hell owner in 1828? His name was William Crockford, and he was a fishmonger who ended up the wealthiest self-made man in London due to his "unmatched skill for gambling." In a *Smithsonian Magazine* article titled: "Crockford's Club: How a Fishmonger Built a Gambling Hall and Bankrupted the British Aristocracy," we are told William Crockford was born into poverty and received very little education. However, when he was a teenager, Crockford "discovered he had a talent for numbers and a near-genius for the rapid calculation of odds—skills that quickly freed him from a lifetime of gutting, scaling and selling fish." Crockford would go on to build one of the most luxurious gambling hells of his time on the fashionable St. James's Street, and he would speedily relieve the *ton* of their family fortunes.

Inspiration for Jasper came from Crockford, although he is not meant to *be* Crockford. I was fascinated by the story of a man who found a way to cross class barriers, and I wanted to write that story in *Never Gamble Your Heart.* Jasper has a happy ending—as does Rockford's—but the same cannot be said for William Crockford, who eventually lost his fortune. If you want to learn more, I highly suggest reading the *Smithsonian* article mentioned above.

When it came to Frankie's charitable dowry, I took a number of fictional liberties. There have been several recorded instances of dowries given to women through charitable means in history: Archconfraternity of the Annunciation was a Roman charity that provided dowries (*New World Encyclopedia*), and *Monte delle doti* was a public fund in Florence created to provide dowries (*New World Encyclopedia*). According to the article "Comparative Study on Dowry System" in the *International Journal of Social Sciences and Humanities Invention*, in Europe, "Providing dowries for poor women was regarded as a form of charity by wealthy parishioners."

That being said, I did not come across research that suggested this was a common occurrence in early Victorian England, although that does not mean the research does not exist. In *Never Gamble Your Heart*, I built upon the idea of a charitable dowry by combining it with the well-documented concept of Victorian philanthropy.

Last but not least, the Dowry Thieves were entirely founded in my imagination, but I cannot help but wonder if there were men in the Regency and Victorian eras who purposely compromised women so that they might have access to their dowries. We may never know, but in *Never Gamble Your Heart*, the Dove knows, and she wants justice for those women. Perhaps this is my way of delivering justice for any woman it might have happened to in real life.

Acknowledgments

This book wouldn't have been possible without the expertise and guidance of a number of people that I'd like to thank here. A thousand thanks to:

Emily Sylvan Kim, my agent and unfailing supporter. Thank you for being the first person to read this book and tell me it was one of your favorites. I couldn't do any of this without you.

Junessa Viloria, my wonderful editor. Your gentle comments and insights are always exactly what my books need. Thank you for believing in The Secret Society of Governess Spies, and for pushing to make these the best books they can be. I'll forever be grateful that you gave this series a chance.

The Forever team that has worked so hard behind the scenes on this book: Jordyn Penner, Editorial Assistant; Dana Cuadrado, Associate Marketing and Publicity Manager; Shelly Perron, Copyeditor; Stacey Reid, Production Editor; Xian Lee, Production Coordinator; Daniela Medina, Cover Designer (thank you for two BEAUTIFUL covers so far); Taylor Navis, Interior Designer; and Rebecca Holland, Managing Editor.

Acknowledgments

. of the booksellers and librarians who have stocked my book, ad it, talked about it, and hosted me for events. Your hard work is what gets books into readers' hands. I am so grateful for your support!

The book clubs who have hosted me—thank you! There is nothing I love more than talking about books. (And Carlie's book club—thank you for making "noodle" dishes.)

Readers and reviewers—thank you, thank you, thank you! You all are *amazing*! I appreciate your support more than you'll ever know. Putting a book into the world is a vulnerable process, and for those of you who told me you loved Emily's story and couldn't wait for Frankie's—that meant everything. I hope you enjoyed reading this one as much as I enjoyed writing it.

Those of you who answered my mathematics questions (I am, unfortunately, a thousand leagues away from being as brilliant in mathematics as Frankie), especially my engineer brother, Matt, and my engineer friend, Jason.

The historical romance authors and 2024 debuts who have become friends and colleagues along the way. I *love* the historical romance and book community, and I feel refreshed and grateful every time I get to meet another author.

My family and friends, who came out in a BIG way to support *Never Blow a Kiss* and who kept me encouraged while I wrote *Never Gamble Your Heart.* Your support has meant everything. I especially want to thank my mom and dad, Heather and Josh (who might have all of Aroostook County reading my books), and Matt and Carla. Thank you so much to my aunts, uncles, and cousins who have bought my books and talked about them, and thank you to my incredible friends who have done the same. (Victoria, you have been very good for my ego.)

My children, who refer to my books so far as: the orange book, the purple book, and the green book. I hope I'm modeling the hard work it takes to go after your dream. I will forever cherish your cards and celebrations for my books. I love you.

My husband, who works a staggering amount of overtime and yet still finds ways to give me alone time to write. Thank you for supporting this dream and for never once wavering in your belief in me. Thank you for building me a shelf for my books, and for teaching our children how to cheer me on. I'm forever grateful that I gambled my heart on you.

About the Author

Lindsay Lovise writes historical and contemporary romances with brave heroines and a dash of mystery. Although she earned degrees in English and teaching, she always knew she wanted to write stories about love. When she's not writing, Lindsay is reading (probably romance), drinking coffee, and avoiding laundry. She currently lives in New York, but she was born and raised in Maine, where the winters make for perfect reading weather.

You can learn more at:
LindsayLovise.com
Instagram @LindsayLovise
Facebook.com/LindsayLoviseAuthor